BEWITCHING PASSION

"Where are we? May I uncover my eyes now?"

"Not just yet," Selena answered in a saucy voice, stepping closer to him and beginning to unbutton his waistcoat.

"Are you disrobing me?" He was filled with mixed emotions at the prospect.

She bent towards him and began kissing his chest, as she bared it beneath his shirt—each kiss followed by a wet stroke of her tongue. "You're a clever lot, you English."

"But what if someone happens upon us?"

"This is *my* place. A secret place only I know of."

"I don't think I like this," he said with renewed trepidation, as her hands moved downward and began undoing the front flap of his breeches.

"Oh, but you will," she assured, her voice now sounding like an unearthly mix of feline purr and siren's song.

If any part of Stafford doubted his hearing in this, what he experienced next told him he shouldn't. "Dear God," was all he could seem to choke out, a nearly climactic shudder running through him. *"How* are you doing that?"

She withdrew her mouth from him just long enough to answer. "It's magic," she said in what seemed a jesting tone. "And ye must never question magic, love, lest ye scare it away for good and all . . ."

Advance praise for SWEET SORCERY:

"5 STARS! Fabulous . . . poignant and droll, a combination that only the great authors can achieve. [SWEET SORCERY] is priceless, and will be recognized as one of the top five romances of the year."

—*Romantic Times*

"Pure ambrosia . . . Fantastic!"

—*Rendezvous*

ROMANCE FROM JO BEVERLY

SWEET SORCERY

Ashland Price

Zebra Books
Kensington Publishing Corp.
http://www.zebrabooks.com

ZEBRA BOOKS are published by

Kensington Publishing Corp.
850 Third Avenue
New York, NY 10022

First Printing: March, 1997
10 9 8 7 6 5 4 3 2 1

Printed in the United States of America

To Debbie Fumanti
and The Amazing Adventure Company—
Thank you, dear friend, for sharing so much
positive magic with the world!

One

Let this truth be known of Celtic magic: that it should neither be used to harm *nor to permit harm to be done.*

Wexford, Ireland—1809

He was watching Selena again! She could *feel* it. He was spying on her from his palatial manor, through that fancy telescope of his!

"Come away from the window, Nola," Selena hissed to her black cat. "Don't be givin' him the satisfaction of knowin' that *we* know that he knows."

Her familiar was perfectly aware of what she meant by this, of course; but, true to her often heedless feline character, she lingered beside the cream-colored lace curtains for a moment longer before complying with her master's wishes and jumping from the sill.

With a single prolonged "meow," the creature not only registered her protest at being ordered to the floor, but the warning she'd been issuing for the past several days. *He'll be down here again and again to look for us. You cannot stave him off forever!*

"Oh, I can't, can I?" the witch retorted. "Great swaggerin' English bully! Thinkin' he can force us from our ancestral home, when he himself has scarce been here a fortnight!" Narrowing her eyes at the sheerly draped window, Selena thrust her right forefinger in the direction of the manor, and her pet couldn't help flinching at what she imagined had just happened on the recipient's end. "Then let him come searchin' for us half-blind. That's what I say!"

Lord Stafford Pearce gave forth a yelp and jerked away from the lens of his telescope. "Bloody Hell!"

The efficient steward of the manor, seeming always within earshot of his new employer, came darting into the parlour at Stafford's exclamation.

"What is it, sir?"

By this time, Lord Pearce was well away from the offending instrument, his left hand pressed to his profusely moist right eyelid. "This deuced thing has poked me in the eye, Mr. Flaherty! Dead in it, I tell you! Where on earth did you purchase it?"

The tubby servant rushed over to him, obviously seeking to study the telescope. "Why, from Talbot's dry goods shoppe in town. 'Tis the only place in the whole of the county that proffers this sort of thing. But they guarantee their merchandise. I have never heard a complaint about it, save for yours just now, sir," he concluded, running one of his stubby thumbs purposefully over the glass's gold-rimmed eyepiece.

Stafford fixed him with as much of a glare as his good eye could manage. "Am I to understand that you don't believe me?"

The steward's sanguine cheeks went suddenly pale at the indignation in his new master's voice. "Oh, Heavens, nay, my lord. If you say the glass poked ya in the eye, then I am sure it must have."

Still shaken by the inexplicable assault, Stafford felt down to his waistcoat pocket and withdrew a silken handkerchief from it. Then, somehow finding the nerve to try reopening his injured orb, he stood blotting the tears it spilled forth in response. "Christ's Church, I can hardly see out of it," he muttered.

"I'll have one of the stable boys ride to town and fetch ya the doctor then," Flaherty offered, seeming eager to flee his wrath, even if just for a moment or two.

Stafford reached out with his free hand and caught him by the shoulder. "You shall do no such thing! Have you no notion how daft I'll be made to seem if word gets 'round that a spy-glass tried to blind me?"

The steward turned back to face him with a chary expression. "Aye, well, but that *is* what you are claimin' happened, is it not, sir?"

"Yes. But only between you and me, Mr. Flaherty." The Englishman, having been forced to regress in his recovery to almost full closure of his eye, again attempted to open it now. His lashes fluttered like the teetery movements of a newly hatched chick. Then, giving up once more, his upper and lower lids closed over it and he reapplied the kerchief with a grimace. "Let us speak of this to no one else, mind you."

"Very well, my lord. I'll not tell a soul . . . You were—were lookin' down at that cottage again when this befell ya, were you not?" he added gingerly.

"I was, as it happens. So, what of it?"

The Irishman cleared his throat uneasily. "Oh, nothin', sir. Nothin' a'tall. I was simply wonderin'."

Stafford narrowed his good eye at him quizzically. "No, really, Mr. Flaherty. I insist that you elaborate. What would the direction in which I had the glass pointed have to do with the damnable thing attacking me?"

"Why, nothin', sir. Nothin' a'tall," he repeated with emphasis.

"There *is* someone living down there, isn't there," Stafford shot back knowingly. "I thought I saw smoke coming from the place's chimney earlier. Then there was a dark figure at its nearest window. And this sheepish inquiry from you now. I demand to know what it is you're not telling me!"

Flaherty gave his head a vigorous shake, his jowls flapping a bit with his vehemence. "Mercy, there's nothin' to tell, sir. That thatch has been vacant for years, as I've said."

A shrewd laugh issued from low in Stafford's throat and he again put a hand on the servant's shoulder. " 'Tis some kith or kin of yours, isn't it, my good man. Someone to whom you owe a favor, no doubt. So you permitted them to take up residence here at Brenna Manor, before I arrived to assume my uncle's place as lord."

"Nay. That is not it—"

"Well, good enough," the Englishman interrupted with a dismissive shrug. "You will find me amply forgiving about such matters. I simply ask that you go down there and tell whomever it is that, now that this estate is mine, I shall require a sufficient rent to be paid me by anyone occupying its thatches."

To Stafford's amazement, his steward's jaw dropped at this request, as though he'd just been asked to march into the very bowels of Hell.

"Nay, nay, I tell ye, my lord! 'Tis no friend or family of mine lives down there! 'Tis no soul a'tall, from what I know of it!"

"Good Heavens, man, calm yourself," Stafford said with a mollifying air—Flaherty seeming, after all, just about the only ally he'd inherited since coming to this markedly unwelcoming country. "If you've nothing to do with the matter, you've nothing to do with it. I'm content to believe you. I'll simply go back down there myself now and have another look round."

Though it was clear the servant tried to hide it, Stafford couldn't help noticing how he winced slightly at this declaration. "But we're very soon to sup, sir. Are you sure you want to stray so far at this hour?"

The Englishman knit his brows in befuddlement. "How can supper possibly be served without me? I'm the only one your staff waits upon, for Heaven's sake."

The steward donned a shaky smile. "Oh, aye. How true. I suppose we'll simply have to delay it, in that case, my lord . . . That is, if you're *certain* you want to walk all the way down there," he concluded cautiously.

Feeling finally able to uncover his impaired eye, Stafford

slowly drew the kerchief away from it. He stood squaring his jaw, as the room came into fuller, if blurrier focus for him. "I am," he replied resolutely.

"Very well, then, sir. But I—"

"You what?" the Englishman pressed at his servant's continued tongue-biting.

"I think it best that you take one or two of the hounds down with you. It bein' so close to sunset."

"Are you intimating that some of the local upstarts would actually attempt to harm me on my own land?"

The Irishman gave him a solemn nod. "That they might."

Fighting back a nervous gulp, Stafford straightened his posture and gave his burgundy waistcoat an authoritative tug downward with both hands. "So be it, then. I am never one to retreat from a fight, especially over what is rightfully mine. I shall take a *pistol* as well!"

Selena's cat suddenly tensed, where she lay near the cottage door. The witch, in turn, walked over to the thatch's manor-side window to surreptitiously confirm what they both suspected. Brenna's new owner was headed down to search their humble home once more.

Let's away, the pet exclaimed, scrambling to her paws.

"Nay, Nola, dearest. We are stayin' this time," Selena replied with a defiant smirk. "I want a better look at him."

He's different than his uncle, the feline warned in a growl. *Not under your spell yet!*

Continuing to appear almost amused, the witch strode over to the hearth with her accustomed gracefulness. Then, with a mere wave of her right hand, she extinguished its fire. "Yes. I know. And I've been thinkin' that I shan't seek to make him fall in love with me, as I did his predecessor."

But why not? How else can you control him?

Selena turned back to face her cat with a contemplative expression. "I am not sure. But I do want to try somethin' more challengin' this time around, you understand. Till the old man died, I never realized just how bored I was with our arrangement. So, if this be a livelier one takin' his place, why not have some fun with him for a while? What harm could there be in it, really? All of Ireland knows 'tis far past time the English were given a lesson or two regardin' stealin' our land!"

But he could destroy us; if you let him get too close.

The sorceress laughed under her breath, "How?"

There are ways. There always have been. Please don't become too full of yourself!

Selena continued to look only slightly swayed by her familiar's admonitions. "Ah, Caesar's right-hand man, are ya now? Warnin' me to remember that I am mortal. Yet ye mustn't forget, that I am anythin' but!" With that, she threw her arms high over her head, whispered a few words of a spell, and she, her cat, and their cottage's furnishings were made invisible. At no risk to themselves, they'd be able to stay and watch, as Lord Stafford Pearce again invaded their long-held abode.

Stafford called his English foxhound back towards him as they both neared the seaside thatch. Then he drew his gun and made his deliberate approach of the whitewashed dwelling.

Though the Irish Sea's tide could be heard slapping the rocky shoreline with a lulling regularity, Stafford would not allow himself to again be tricked into believing that there was anything regular or normal about this place.

Why, only minutes before, he'd distinctly seen grayish smoke trailing from its chimney; yet now there was no sign of it. And the play of light and shadow within, the movement, which his telescope had helped him detect against the reddish round of the setting sun, had completely disappeared, too. It was as though not even a breeze from a cracked window was present to account for the earlier stirring of the cottage's curtains.

He, therefore, drew up to the thatch's entrance with trepidation. Certainly considerably more than he'd been willing to reveal to his steward. As his dog lowered its snout and sniffed eagerly along the bottom edge of the dwelling's only door, Stafford held his breath and pressed down upon its thumb-latch handle with a dampish palm.

At one slight push from him, the door was flung wide open, and his companion bounded inside with its raised nose smelling in all directions.

Stafford's entry was, of course, a great deal more tentative. Clutching his pistol with both hands, he peered into the relative darkness within, his weapon moving slowly from side to side, even as his eyes did.

Empty. The place was just as vacant as it had appeared on the last couple of occasions when he'd been down to inspect it.

But this time was different, he told himself. This time he was suddenly aware of the inconsistencies that had escaped his notice. Though supposedly uninhabited, the thatch bore no trace of cobwebs or mustiness. What was more, he'd finally succeeded in catching its elusive occupant in the act of trying to warm it with a fire.

Without further hesitation, he made his way to the hearth and extended a palm towards the ash-coated logs within it.

"Still hot, Radolf," he said triumphantly to his hound. "Whoever was here could extinguish the flame, but not its heat. That is to say, not in the time allotted. Well," he continued, rising and turning away from the fireplace, "this is all the proof I need to convince me. It makes no matter what that dullard Flaherty contends. I shall return to him at once and see a guard posted down here henceforward. We'll soon catch our trespasser in the very act!"

At this, to Stafford's surprise, the cottage door suddenly slammed shut, and he and his dog were left standing in even deeper darkness.

"Dear God, how did that happen?" he asked with a gasp,

his pistol now aimed at the entryway. "I don't remember noticing any wind as we walked down."

The hound, as though sensing the heightened state of alarm in his master, stopped his sniffing about and froze. His upturned tail relinquished its accustomed wagging and stood stone-still as well.

"Mother Mary, he's a beauty, isn't he?" Selena whispered to her familiar, as the two of them hovered, still invisible, near the ceiling of the cottage.

" 'Tis all right," the witch began again, when her pet failed to reply. "You can answer me. He'll not hear you. Neither of them will."

But he knows somethin's afoot, the cat murmured back. *The heat from the logs was enough, Selena, but now you slammin' and lockin' the door. He'll realize we're here! Don't ya see?*

"Oh, how you do fret, Nola darlin'," the sorceress said with a laugh. Then, pushing away from one of the ceiling beams, she floated down to hover, in prone position, just at the level of the new lord's head. She would almost have looked the part of a guardian angel, if not for her flowing raven hair and Gypsy-like features.

"Fie. I wish there was more light in here," Selena grumbled, reaching out and running two fingers over the right side of the Englishman's face. "I can see that he's rather swarthy and his cheekbones manly sharp and high beneath this evenin' stubble, but I would so like a better look at the color of those fine large eyes!"

He'll feel *you,* her familiar hissed down to her.

Selena laughed again and, continuing to brush her fingers lightly over the side of the intruder's face, dared to blow a stream of hot breath into his right ear. "Nay. He seems as unaware of my touch as he is my image."

Let him go, please, *Selena! Unlatch the door and let him be on his way. He has a gun, mind ye!*

"Silly cat! Why would he shoot at somethin' he cannot even see? What point would there be in it?"

Just come away from him now, Nola insisted. *Before one of us is hurt!*

The sorceress gave forth another mischievous laugh. "You've simply no darin'. That has always been your failin', my dear. I've not seen an ounce of play in ya since you were a kitten." To underscore this criticism, she brought her face even closer to Stafford's. Then, taking hold of his shoulders with both hands, she pulled him to her and planted a wet love bite upon the side of his neck, just below his right ear.

"Oooh, salty," she declared, withdrawing her lips from his flesh with an appreciative smack. "Nearly as salty as a strappin' laborer diggin' rocks from a field all the livelong day. One could almost believe he's earnin' his keep here, from the taste of him."

Lord, there now, the cat exclaimed in return. *See how he's put his hand up to where you kissed him! He felt you, Selena! I told ya he would. Now enough of this game, before it's too late!*

A delighted grin spread across the witch's face. "Aye. It almost looks as though he knows what I just did to him, doesn't it? . . . I wonder, then, *what else* he might be made to feel," she added, her tone suddenly more prankish. In that same instant, she dipped downward and clapped her right palm to the crotch of the Englishman's tight-fitting riding trousers.

Selena, Nola yowled. *I cannot believe you would stoop to such an act!*

At this the witch jerked her hand away, biting her lower lip in an effort to stifle the bawdy laughter that was welling up in her. "Simply tryin' to determine if I've amply frightened him, is all. Gents do that, ya understand. They grow aroused when they're threatened. 'A hanged man's hardening,' my sweet grandma Elvira used to call it, since so many mortal males face their executions in that tumescent state . . . And what a *fine* state it is in this one," she praised, her voice suddenly reflecting an odd mix of vengefulness and desire.

Enough now, the cat declared in her most menacing snarl.

Get ye back up here, lest I decide to leave ya forever at your own devices. I'll give a count of three. Then, I swear, you'll be without a familiar for good and all!

Having come to know all too well through the centuries just how difficult it was to find and train such a facilitating spirit, Selena gave the lord's privates a soft parting squeeze. Then, groaning like a disgruntled child, she caused herself to float back up to the ceiling.

But perhaps her partner in magic was right. Maybe a neck bite and a bit of a grope really were more than enough to claim on this, her first encounter with Brenna Manor's new owner. There would, after all, likely be many days and *nights* ahead for them both: this broad-shouldered, barber-cologne-scented, would-be evictor and her.

Feeling suddenly freed from some sort of invisible, mesmeric hold, Stafford wasted no time in getting to the door and throwing it open to the comforting sunlight without. Not remaining even long enough to close the place after him and his hound, he hurried back to the great house at an almost embarrassingly quick pace. A pragmatic man, he'd never before even entertained the thought that such things as ghosts and hauntings could be real . . . Not until now, in any case.

Two

Just as Stafford reached the manor's front door minutes later, the ever-vigilant steward swung it open with a broad smile of greeting.

"Oh," Lord Pearce said with a start. Then he stepped back and clapped a hand to his chest.

"Did I take you by surprise, sir? I'm frightfully sorry! 'Tis just that I spied ya walkin' back up and, well . . . 'tis, in truth, such a relief to see you've returned. Ya know how I worry about those rabble-rousers with the 'cause' gettin' hold of ya."

Stafford exhaled a long breath and gestured impatiently for the portly servant to get out of his way as he entered. "A brandy, Flaherty. I could use a drink before supper, if you please," he announced, as he made his way briskly through the huge front hall and into the adjacent parlor.

The steward hurried after him, entering the adjoining room an instant later with an expression of deep concern. "Of course, my lord. But might I ask what's happened to ya? You suddenly look so deathly pale."

Fearing that his eyes might betray some part of the mortifying experience he'd just been through, Stafford let his gaze fall to the polished toes of his knee-length boots, as he sank down upon the nearest settee. " 'Tis nothing, my good man. Now, do go and fetch that drink for me."

To Stafford's amazement, this otherwise accommodating fellow not only failed to leave the room, but he actually turned and shut its doors behind him, as though seeking privacy for them both.

Pearce offered him a glare, as their eyes met once more. Looking unfazed by it, however, the steward began speaking again in a greatly lowered voice.

" 'Tis all right, you know, sir. You can tell me what happened. 'Twill not leave this room. I swear it."

"Are you deaf? I have just told you 'nothing.' And, by God, *nothing* is all I have to say! Now, bring me a glass of brandy, before I'm forced to go in search of it myself!"

Flaherty gave forth a nervous laugh. "Ah, that certainly won't be necessary. I'll get it for ya forthwith, my lord, I simply thought . . . well, what with you bleedin', ya might have run into a bit of difficulty down there."

"Bleeding?" Stafford echoed. He was just about to press a couple fingers to the right side of his neck, when he stopped himself. As inexplicable as his experience was minutes before in the thatch, it had clearly also been of a sexual nature, and he didn't wish to further embarrass himself with this servant by letting on that he was the slightest bit aware of this fact.

"Aye, sir," the steward replied, lowering his head like a ravenous goose as he drew closer. "Just below your right ear. It appears as though you've been bitten or somethin'."

Pearce reflexively clamped a hand to the spot in question. He realized in that instant, however, that he simply hadn't done so fast enough. Indeed, the expression his companion now donned was almost as unnerving as the act that had inspired it.

"Jesus, Mary, and Joseph, it looks to be a *love suck,* my lord," he whispered incredulously.

"Oh, rubbish," Stafford shot back, springing to his feet and rushing over to a nearby wall-mounted mirror to get a look for himself. In truth, however, he didn't need one. Now in his mid-thirties, he'd certainly had enough experience with women to know when such a blemish was likely to develop.

He stood studying it in the glass, nonetheless; feigning ignorance still seeming to be his best course. "Good God! I can't imagine how that got there."

Unfortunately, his servant didn't seem to believe this claim. Biting his lower lip against an obvious onrush of amusement, his reflection in the glass told Stafford that nothing he could say would change the fact that this bright red mark was what it was.

"I'm terribly sorry," Flaherty managed to choke out. "It truly was not my intent to pry."

Stafford turned back to face him with as much umbrage as he could summon under the circumstances. *"Pry?"* he repeated in a raised voice. " 'S'death, 'pry,' you say? I've only just come to this country, man! And you and the rest of the staff have kept me busy every bloody moment since, showing me the lay of the land. So *when* on earth would I have found the time to flush out any dalliance?" he demanded.

Despite a commendable attempt at sobering himself, the steward continued to look tortured with his urge to chuckle. "Oh, right ya are, sir. When would ya have, indeed?"

Finally losing all patience with the situation, Pearce pulled his high collar upward, concealing the hickey as best he could. He then cut to the heart of the matter. "Damn it, Flaherty! I want a watch posted at the door of that cottage night and day, starting at once. Something is very much amiss here, and do not think for a moment that 'tis my intention to simply ignore it!"

Selena had fed her cat and had just begun to partake of a late supper, when she again sensed that someone was headed for her thatch. She rose from her plate of roast pork, boiled cabbage, and buttered bread and crossed to her eastern window. Stealing another look out of it, she scanned the huge expanse of lawn that lay between her modest dwelling and the manor house.

"That's odd, isn't it, Nola? I can hear someone out there, yet there's no one in sight."

Her familiar stopped her after-dinner grooming and set both of her forepaws back down on the floor where she sat. Then her velvety black ears moved about in obvious search of the subtle sounds her master claimed to be perceiving.

Yes. I hear somethin', too, she said with a meow after a moment. *But 'tis not footsteps. 'Tis, rather, someone breathin'.*

Selena narrowed her eyes and slowly turned her head from right to left, searching the seeming silence for such a rhythmic sound. After a second or two; she padded to the door and pulled it open just enough to peer outside.

"Eddie?" she asked, her tone half-surprised and half-relieved, as she caught sight of a short blond male who was sitting just to the left of the entrance. She opened the door more fully, and the youth looked up at her with a startled gasp.

"Faith, Edward O'Malley, what are you doin' out here?"

The eight-year-old, having been leaning back against the facade of the thatch, instantly straightened and pushed up to his feet. "Oh, nothin', Mistress Selena," he said blushingly. "The steward just sent me down to guard the place is all."

Though the witch's earlier encounter with Brenna's new owner had made her pretty well aware of how this order had come to be issued, she pretended ignorance. "Guard it, ya say? From what, might I ask?"

Wiping dirt from his flaxen-clad behind with both hands, Edward the stable boy began shifting his weight from foot to foot. "Mr. Flaherty didn't say. From trespassers, I guess."

Selena bit her lower lip against a whisper of a laugh. "Trespassers, is it? How ridiculous! Get yourself in here, lad, before ya catch cold in this damp evenin' air."

He shook his head, his thick mop of hair bouncing slightly. "Nay. I shouldn't, really. The steward is sure to be cross with me, if he peers down here and sees I'm not where he said to be."

"But just look at yourself! Dressed in nothin', save a thin shirt and those threadbare trousers of yours. Sure, 'tis a safe enough wager you'll take sick sittin' out here in the sea's chill, and that would certainly be a far worse fate than any thrashin' fat Flaherty could give ya."

Eddie laughed, of course. In spite of himself. He always laughed when she called his employer by that less-than-flattering epithet. And seeing him giggle, with the disarming spontaneity of a toddler, always made Selena laugh as well.

"Come have some supper with me, and I'll put out one of my curse dolls to sit in your stead for a while."

His eyes grew wide with enthusiasm. "Would ya, mistress?"

"Of course, ya silly thing. Shiverin' out here for God alone knows how long. You had only to knock and ask me, ya realize. Haven't I always been willin' to come to your aid?"

"That ya have," he confirmed, his smile broadening.

She stepped away from the door and motioned for him to enter. As he did so, he made a beeline for the fire which she again had crackling in the hearth.

"Now which curse doll should we use, I wonder?" she asked, lingering in the doorway.

" 'Twould have to be the blond one," Edward declared, turning back to face her with his palms extended behind him in obvious craving of the fire's warmth.

"But, of course, boy. How clever of ya! 'Twould have to be the blond one, indeed," she replied with a playful wink. She hurried over to an ornately painted folding room partition in the rear of the cottage and disappeared behind it. When she emerged seconds later, she was holding a life-sized cloth doll which had a shaggy head full of yellow yarn.

Tucking it under her right arm, she carried it outside, its limp, trouser-clad legs and bare stubby feet dragging behind her. After arranging it into a sitting pose, much like the one Eddie had struck while guarding the place, she came back inside and shut the cottage door behind her with a shiver.

"Begorra," she muttered, pulling her long black shawl more tightly around her, "you're takin' some woollens from me when ya leave here. I won't have ya runnin' about Brenna so scantily clothed! Though it saddens me to have to say it, you're practically an orphan with that father of yours off racin' horses as much as he does. I just might have to put a stay-at-home spell upon him," she concluded, giving her head a disapproving shake. "Come and eat."

"Can you do that?" Eddie asked, his voice rising with wonder, as he crossed obediently to where she now stood at her dining table, dishing up his food.

Pulling out a chair for him, she gave the question a few seconds of thought. "I fancy so. That is to say, I haven't yet tried such an incantation, but I should think the gods would see fit to bless it. 'Twould be for a good enough cause, after all."

The stable boy sat down and, taking hold of the table's edge, drew his chair up under it until his chin was centered squarely over his steaming plate of supper. "Should I say grace?" he asked before diving into the meal with his usual rapaciousness.

The witch took her place across from him. "Only if ya want to, lad. Ya know where I stand on such things. 'Tis never one's words that matter, so much as one's deeds in this life."

"Well, then," he replied with an impish smirk. "I think I'll forgo the prayin'. Just for tonight, anyway."

"Good enough," Selena replied, reaching out to give one of his wrists a pat before returning to her own dining.

"Father says he's a bit afraid you'll not get on with the new lord," Eddie announced several seconds later, his mouth bulging with several heavily buttered bites of bread.

A smile tugged at one corner of the sorceress's lips. "Is he, now?"

"Aye. He says he fears ya might get angry at this one, the way ya did when the last lord was new to Brenna, and give us all a week of the craps again."

Selena's amused expression suddenly sank "I'll do nothin' of the sort! Why, I didn't mean for it to happen in the first place." Her right hand began to close into an angry fist about her serviette. " 'Twas just that—that the codger made me so furious, ya understand. The English are all the same, the way they come here and start orderin' us about! . . . But I never, never meant for that curse to spill over onto all of County Wexford, my dear boy. You must believe me," she added, her voice cracking with remorse.

He turned, his mouth again stuffed with food, and offered her a wide-eyed nod. "Oh, I do. Faith, I was just in diapers when it happened, so what did I care? 'Twas my mother who saw the worst of it, of course."

"And a very good mother she was, too, Edward. Don't ya ever forget it. 'Tis such a terrible shame I was not able to save her when your little sister was born. I'm not one for losin' patients ordinarily, as ye know."

He shook his head, slowing his eating slightly, as though out of respect for the emotion-charged topic they'd stumbled onto. "Ah, don't be blamin' yourself again for that. Father says ya did a lot more to ease her sufferin' towards the end than that fancy doctor in town. And, Lord knows, ya never ask for nearly as much pay neither."

Selena smiled at this last remark, knowing it had to have come, like most of Eddie's comments, from his father. The stable boy wasn't, after all, old enough to gauge how much compensation was reasonable for such services. Nevertheless, she thanked him for the praise.

"So you've met the new lord of the manor, have ya?" she began again after a moment.

He nodded, rushing to chew, so he could swallow and answer her. Before doing so, however, he took a swig of the apple ale she'd poured for him. "Aye. On the day he first came here," he replied, raising his right wrist to his lips and wiping them on his shirt cuff.

"And how did ya find him?"

"You mean the pair of ya haven't yet met, mistress? Not in a whole fortnight?"

"Nay. We haven't. And, mind, don't go tellin' him about me either, lad, lest we risk my not gettin' on with him as your father said. That is, 'tis my intention to make his acquaintance in my own way, ya understand."

Edward nodded.

"So, anyway, how did ya find him? Do you like him thus far?"

The boy shook his head. "Nay. He's even more gruff than his uncle was. But he looks to be much younger. That's good, isn't it?"

"Not necessarily. It likely means he'll live a great deal longer than the last lord, and, if it happens that he truly is a bad-tempered fella, he could make our lives troublesome for a good many years to come."

Her guest took another long drink of his beverage, then set his pewter mug back down with a stifled burp. "Well, you'd just have to do away with him then. Aye?" he asked, his tone shockingly insouciant.

"Good gracious, child," she exclaimed in a hushed voice. "Do ya not hear yourself? 'Tis *murder* you're speakin' of, and not even sorceresses are permitted to take a life!"

His cheeks reddened at her suddenly scolding tone. "Nay, mistress. I suppose not. I'm sorry."

"Aye, well, I know ya are," she assured, wanting to return to their former, affable mood. "In any case, the answer is nay. I fear my only recourse, should he turn churlish on us, will be to make his life at Brenna so miserable as to persuade him to leave here of his own accord."

Eddie seemed satisfied with this response "Oh, aye. That would be good, wouldn't it. But maybe it would be best to simply make him fall in love with you, as ya did his uncle. That is to say, old Prescott did all he could to please ya. So could ya not just cause that to happen again? Ya know, take the strain off the rest of us."

Selena shrugged. "Well, I could, I suppose. But men can make such pests of themselves when they're in love. I'm not sure I've the energy for another betrothed so soon after the last lord's death. Even we witches must rest from time to time, ya see. Then, too, what if this new fella has given his heart to someone else? I'm not altogether certain I can win him over, if he's already smitten."

"Already has a ladylove, ya mean?"

"Aye."

The boy shook his head and leaned forward to one of the serving dishes to help himself to more of the pork. "Nay. None of us have seen him with any visitors. And father says he seems a gent unto himself. Which means, I guess, that he isn't very friendly, to men *or* ladies. He's rather gruff, as I said. And I've found he angers very quickly, especially when it comes to findin' horse droppin's in the stables. He even threatened to cane me over it Tuesday last! But, luckily, Father was here to defend me!"

"That *beast,*" Selena blurted. "Now you listen to me, Eddie O'Malley, if he ever dares threaten ya again, I insist that ya come straight to me with it! And we'll soon see who ends with a red bottom," she concluded in a growl. To her dismay, she looked down and saw that her right hand had again tightened to a white-knuckled state about her cloth dinner napkin. "Ah, God help me," she said under her breath. "I mustn't let my bad temper overcome me with this new lord as well!"

Stafford Pearce gave forth a pained gasp, his legs tensing where he sat reading in his spacious bed. Though he couldn't imagine what could possibly have been the cause of it, his buttocks suddenly stung as though they'd just suffered a savage lash with a cane!

Grimacing, he dropped his open book to the bed's coverlet. Then, placing his palms at his sides, he lifted one throbbing cheek from the mattress and then the other. Managing to sidle, on his hands, over to the right edge of his bed, he got gingerly to his feet.

He shook his head in bewilderment and reached back with a finger to touch his inflamed flesh through the velvety fabric of his bed robe. Just as he'd feared, even the lightest pressure caused his posterior to burn all the more.

He made his way over to his suite's door and closed it. Then, taking up the oil lamp from his left bedside table, he proceeded to his room's full-length oval mirror in an effort to catch a glimpse of what might have developed.

Once he reached the looking glass, he turned around and, extending the lamp behind him with one hand, he pulled up his robe and night chemise with the other.

There it was! Clear as day. A lash mark as red and long as any the headmaster at the boy's school he'd attended had ever inflicted upon him!

He let the hems of his clothing fall back to his ankles and entertained the idea of requesting that Mr. Flaherty bring him up some ice from the larder. There was, after all, nothing like it for dulling the pain of such a wound.

He stopped himself, however. The eye-poking episode that afternoon, followed by the mysterious love bite which had formed on his neck before supper, had made him seem crazed enough, without his adding *this* to the steward's list of doubts about him.

The manor was, indeed, haunted. As daft a conclusion as this was, it was the only one Stafford could seem to reach, as he made his way back to the left side of his bed and returned the lamp to the adjacent nightstand.

Not wanting to cause his posterior any further discomfort, he elected to climb back onto the down mattress on all fours and carefully lower himself to a prone position upon it. Then, with a groan, he let his face fall into one of the bed's plush pillows.

He'd known, from the first day he'd come to Brenna, that he was not altogether welcomed. That much had been apparent in its servants' monosyllabic exchanges with him and the sudden silences that always fell over them whenever he entered a room in which they were conversing.

Nevertheless, the possibility that he could be actively cursed somehow by the manor or its occupants had simply not occurred to him. In point of fact, his Uncle Prescott, the estate's former lord, had never complained—either in writing or during Stafford's many visits with him—of feeling in anyway menaced by the place. On the contrary, the old man had seemed positively jubilant most of the time and always in a hurry to return to Ireland after his brief trips back to London. Both of which only seemed to confirm their gossipy relatives' claims that the dyed-in-the-wool bachelor had been won over by some dark-haired Irish temptress who'd provided him with every possible pleasure of a conjugal relationship, while somehow sparing him any of its burdens.

Unfortunately, Stafford hadn't considered it appropriate to ask Prescott about this remarkable young lady. Potential heirs did well, after all, not to pose too many embarrassing questions to their future benefactors. So Stafford had never even managed to learn her name; and, probably out of respect for his uncle's reputation, Brenna's staff had apparently disposed of any trace of her after his death. As if to evidence this, Stafford's discreet searches through several of the drawers and cabinets in the manor had not yet turned up so much as a single written reference to the woman or a piece of her clothing.

It was as though she'd never existed. But indeed she must have, for what other reason would a wealthy Englishman have for so cheerfully remaining year after year in such an inhospitable place?

Stafford would simply have to send for an investigator, he decided. He'd met a man in London, several months back, who'd claimed to possess second sight when it came to finding missing persons. Half sleuth and half metaphysician apparently, this gent now struck Lord Pearce as perfectly suited for discovering the answers to Brenna's secrets.

Though Stafford had had all he could do to keep from laughing at the man's outlandish claims, when they'd met at a mutual friend's dinner party, he had, out of sheer force of habit, retained the fellow's business card. And how very glad he was of it now!

Three

After supper and a dessert of berry pie topped with sweetened cream, Selena and her young guest went and sat before the fire.

"Why is it ya never married Lord Prescott?" Eddie asked, wriggling to a comfortable position in one of her Carver chairs and planting his elbows upon its polished wooden arms.

Having grown accustomed to the lad's candor, she answered him with a good-natured smile. "Because witches rarely wed, child, and even more rarely do they choose mortals for such purposes."

"So you *can't* marry one?"

"I didn't say I couldn't. I simply said 'tis not done. 'Tis well . . . akin to weddin' below one's station, ya see."

"But father says that marryin' the lord of Brenna, either this one or the last, would give ya claim to the manor. So, why live in this little thatch and dress as the rest of us do, when you could have the Pearces' wealth all about ya?"

She laughed and waved him off. "Ah, I don't give one whit about their riches and those dear-bought party gowns I used to have to corset myself into for old Prescott. Don't ya understand? 'Tis not some man's holdin's I want all about me, but Nature. And, ya must admit, I'm far closer to Her here by the sea, than I could ever be in that enormous man-made home up there. Just you mark my words now. See that ya do," she went on, with a reverent solemnity to her voice. "When that grand manse finally crumbles in the wind and rain, or is ravaged by fire and its ruins overrun by plants and vines, 'tis Nature that will know final supremacy. Sure, she's the one force you can rely upon in this world, lad, and no other."

"That's right, isn't it," he said, his expression suddenly knowing. "Air, fire, water, and earth. They're how you work your magic, aren't they?"

"Well, they are the wattle and daub of it, true enough. But, lest ye forget, it also requires a good deal of heed and strength of will, to say nothin' of aid from the gods, to do what I do . . . Of course, air, fire water, and earth don't simply belong to sorcerers, Eddie Their power belongs to everyone. That is why the Church and the English have always been so bent upon snuffin' out my kind. 'Tis far easier to control the masses, once you have taken their native magic from them so they can't fight back. And I'm sure you will notice as well that mortal *men* hate us practitioners of the earth's spellcraft even more than mortal women do. That bein', of course, because we females are plainly so much better at it," she explained with a slightly biting laugh. "So that is why I've been so decided upon stayin' at Brenna through the years. The place has always needed a witch about to countervail the might of the outlander bullies who keep comin' here to claim it."

"And that's also why the local folk have always allowed ya to stay, aye? Because ya look after their interests. At least that's what father says."

"And how very right he is, boy. Do ya think for one moment that the likes of fat Flaherty and the town's constable would permit me to dwell here without payin' rent, if I were not servin' to keep the true rule of the place in Irish hands?"

"Nay. I guess not."

"Of course not. While I shall grant ya that they're fairly afraid of my wrath, 'tis, rather, the good that I bring to pass here that keeps me from bein' burnt at the stake or hung, as has happened to so many of my less fortunate ancestors."

"So then you'll stay at Brenna till the end of time?"

"Mercy, no. I shall die one day, even as you will, and the

Heavens will have to send another sorceress to serve here in my stead. Why, even now, I am beginnin' to feel that I haven't as much vigor for my craft as I once did. 'Tis Nature startin' to call me back to Her, ya see. Callin' me back to her soil to rot with her leaves, just as she does with you humans. The only difference bein' that she gives my kind two centuries or more before we begin to even hear the call. But faintly, on the wind, it comes to us as well. In the autumn especially, when the earth has its day of reckonin' with the realm of the dead . . . Ya can't know what I mean at your young age, of course. Not when every one of the world's scents is so keen to your nostrils and every change of season a fresh new beginnin' to be embraced with great anticipation. But you'll know whereof I speak one day, when your senses begin to grow dull, and winter, spring, summer, and fall start to come 'round so fast that ya can barely find time to enjoy them before they've passed."

His eyes widened with obvious apprehension and he shook his head slightly. "Oh, nay, mistress. I hope that never happens to me! It doesn't sound in the least bit pleasant."

She laughed under her breath. "But you don't just lose ground with age, Eddie. I'm happy to tell that ya gain some, too."

"Aye? And how is that?"

"Well, first of all, ya come to understand that time isn't as real as it seems. Oh, I know how you humans pride yourselves on the newfangled instruments ya fashion to measure it. But the truth of the matter is that time is not so much a thing to be gauged, as it is Nature's way of simply keepin' everythin' from happenin' at once. Just think of the awful state this world would get into, if events weren't spaced out the way they are. If not for time, for instance, you and I and everyone else at Brenna Manor would be exactly the same age! And All Hallow Eve and May Day wouldn't be their proper six months apart. Why, I would venture to say, if such were the case, we'd have to celebrate them both on the same date! Faith, lad, 'twould be a frightful mash, wouldn't it."

"Oh, aye," he wholeheartedly agreed. "But if time is so needed, how can ya say 'tis not as real as it seems?"

"In *time* you'll know, lad, since all knowin' comes with time. But, perhaps 'real' is not as precise a word as I could have used," she added thoughtfully. "Maybe 'twould be better to say that time is not so rigid a thing as we might think it. That is, you will likely find, as I have, that time will become more like different colored beads on a necklace to ya with each passin' year. Your thoughts will carry you backward on the string to memories so vivid 'tis as if you're livin' them all over again. And time shall also lead ya forward, until you're returned to where ya began. Whence you arose. From the earth and its water and soil."

While the stable boy appeared to be trying to consider this explanation with due seriousness, it was clear that he was not nearly as at peace with the prospect of his remains mingling with decaying leaves as his hostess seemed. "Could ya take me flyin' tonight, do ya think?" he asked, obviously much more enthused about this new subject.

Selena shook her head. "Oh, I don't know. Do ya not remember what happened the last time? How cross your father was with the pair of us, when ya broke free from me, *while foolin' about,*" she put in pointedly, "and ya fell into those bramble bushes?"

"But I wasn't hurt," he blurted defensively.

"That's not the point, is it? The crux of it is, you might have been! And what if I had found myself unable to mend ya? That happens sometimes, I hope ya realize. I'm skilled at healin', but not infallible, mind. No sorceress is."

"But father is not even here right now. He's off in Galway for a steeplechase."

"What will it matter where he is, if he comes home to find his only son wearin' splints from head to toe?"

Her guest couldn't seem to help laughing at the ridiculous image this retort apparently brought to his mind.

" 'Tisn't in the slightest bit funny, Eddie! Lettin' go of a witch, when she's been good enough to take ya on a flight with her, is a thoughtless and spiteful thing to do!"

Looking amply chided, the stable boy dropped his gaze to his lap. "Aye. It is, isn't it." He waited a penitent second or two before raising his large blue eyes to her once more. "And that is why I'm swearin' to ya now, mistress, that I will never *ever* do so again."

She squinted at him in an effort to plumb his soul for his sincerity in the matter. "Oh, all right then," she finally agreed. "You harpy from Hell in the guise of a lad," she snarled. "But 'twill only be a short trip, mind. I'm tired from havin' made Nola and myself invisible against the new lord's visits to this thatch. And I've a full-moon ritual to perform tomorrow night, so I shall be needin' the rest of the evenin' to grind my herbs for it."

Eddie, seeming more than pleased with these terms, wasted no time in springing to his feet and crossing to offer a hand to help her out of her chair.

"Will ya be joinin' us, Nola?" Selena asked her familiar as they moved towards the door.

The black cat lifted her head, where she now lay near the dining table. Then she gave forth a plaintive meow which said she neither planned to go along, nor did she approve of the boy doing so.

" 'Tis all right," Selena assured her. "He understands that we shall land at once, if he so much as removes one of his hands from around my waist. Don't ya, Edward?" she added sternly.

"Aye, mistress."

Still seeming to object to the decision, Selena's cat set her head back down between her forepaws and shut her eyes, as though choosing to simply ignore them as they took their leave.

"Put this on," the witch called after the lad, pulling one of her black capes from the wall peg beside the door, as Eddie exited the cottage.

He turned back to her just in time to catch it as she tossed it to him. Then, before stepping outside herself and shutting the thatch's door behind her, Selena grabbed the broom, which she always left standing to the right of her threshold.

"All right then," she said, as Eddie stood fastening the cape's jeweled clasp at his throat, "round this way as usual, so we aren't in view of the manor."

Selena headed to the back of the cottage with her half-pint guest on her heels. Having brought forward the long cape's trailing hem, the child now had it draped over his right arm.

When they reached their point of departure, he came to a stop beside her and stood perfectly still, previous flights having taught him, apparently, just how touch-and-go the takeoff phase could be.

Gripping the broom's long stick with upturned hands, Selena thrust it out horizontally before her, her arms locking at the elbows. Then she shut her eyes and began to whisper one of the Gaelic spells which enabled such objects to take to the sky.

Lighter and lighter the implement grew in her hold, until, after a breathless moment or two, she thought it safe to test its air-worthiness. Letting her fingers slowly uncurl from the handle, she opened her eyes to see that the broom was gradually ascending in the moonlit darkness of that summer night.

"Well, we had best mount it before it flies off on its own," she said teasingly.

Edward laughed, continuing to look on in wonder as the besom hovered before them. The length of it moved back and forth slightly, as though it were a newly saddled stallion champing at the bit to race away.

It was always this way with little Eddie, Selena acknowledged with a satisfied smile. Though he'd seen this phenomenon at least half a dozen times, he always appeared utterly awed at the sight of such an object floating in midair. And that, Selena realized now, was why she found herself willing to take him on flights. There could simply never be a more appreciative audience for her craft.

Though she had only three feet to fall if this yet proved a

false start, Selena very carefully took hold of the wooden handle and lowered her posterior onto it. Then, once she'd swung her left leg around the tip of the stick and was comfortably seated astride it, she reached back and gestured for Eddie to get on as well.

He did so, his youthful diminutiveness making him even more agile at it than she. As his full weight came to bear, however, the broom took an abrupt dip—the tips of its long conically bound bristles being driven into the ground by the motion.

"Lord, boy," she exclaimed, never before having felt this happen with him. "You must have gained an entire stone this summer!"

"Aye. I guess so. Father says I'm definitely taller, anyway."

"Well then, lean yourself forward a bit, for mercy's sake. 'Tis never good, after all, to be too weighed down in the tail."

He instantly obeyed, his arms coming up to wrap about Selena's slender waist.

"Aye. That's better," she confirmed. "Land's, child, I suppose you best gather your flights while you're able, since there's danger ya might simply grow too heavy for 'em soon."

As his arms closed all the more tightly about her, it was clear that he fully intended to take this advice.

Without another word, Selena raised one hand and, like a dandelion seed carried on a slow hot wind, she and her passenger drifted upward. Up past the whitewashed back of the cottage, to the level of the newly thatched roof, and higher still, until their eyes were flush with the topmost branches of the towering oaks which stood several feet to the left of them.

" 'Tis a lovely night for this, isn't it," the eight-year-old observed in a reverent hush. "What with the stars twinklin' through the treetops this way."

"That it is," she replied, with a whisper of a smile in her voice. "That it is, indeed. Now just ya see to it you keep that cape closed about ya, lest the wind gain the advantage with us both up here."

Eddie shifted a bit, as though to rearrange the garment slightly.

"Are ya ready, then?" Selena inquired.

"I am."

Finally feeling certain of this, she issued another Gaelic command to the broom and, sloping its bristles down once more, it shot upward like a hawk taking wing.

Though the wind force, which its sudden acceleration created, deadened Selena's hearing, she was aware of the gleeful sounds her passenger was making in response to this precipitous climb. He loved it, of course. What boy wouldn't have? But his steady, strong hold upon her said that she needn't fear his taking his enthusiasm too far, as he'd done on their previous flight.

Once they were well above the trees, Selena ordered the besom to slow down and level itself out, and, with this done, she and her companion began sailing leisurely through the night sky over Brenna's sprawling grounds.

Pushing on the tip of the broom's handle, she steered them towards the great house. With its scores of windows already darkened at the accustomed early retirement of its staff, this shortcut to the rest of the estate's cleared land seemed safe enough to her.

Of neoclassical design, the manor's flat gray roof shone brightly in the glow of that evening's three-quarter moon. Over the south colonnade and ballroom, the library and formal western dining chamber they flew. Then they traveled past the front hall and the huge flower garden beyond—its statuary and center fountain looking, from their greatly heightened perspectives, like toy furnishings outside an elaborate doll's house.

"The new lord is sleepin'," Selena called back to her passenger. "His dreams are softenin' his heart towards us, even as we speak."

"But how can ya know that?"

"Witches just can, Eddie," she answered with a confident smile.

Four

As the light of the next day began streaming into his bedroom windows, Lord Stafford Pearce awoke with a groan from the most interminable and embarrassingly erotic dream he'd ever had. In it, he'd found himself starved for the amorous attentions of a woman. And not just any woman, but a black-haired Irish *peasant,* of all people. One who insisted upon completely ignoring him every time he came near her!

He gave forth a soft laugh in memory of it, his eyes traveling up to focus upon the dark wooden beams of his bedchamber's ceiling. There was nothing in the slightest bit prophetic about the dream, he assured himself now, by the consoling light of day. He had never courted a female of such obviously low birth and he was quite certain he never would. Indeed, as he thought back upon this crofter's shoddy clothing and soiled bare feet, he couldn't begin to imagine why his sleeping self had pursued her with such shameless fervor.

It had been as though he'd stopped thinking altogether. As if the only portion of him commanding any blood flow was that part he usually kept so judiciously under wraps in his trousers! And off the unruly devil had led him amidst his reverie, racing across Brenna's grounds like a beagle on the scent of a hare!

Though Stafford had never, in his waking life, indulged in such depravity, he'd actually found himself *begging* this beautiful brunette to let him claim her just once. In exchange for— and this was, by far, the most perverse part of the dream—full ownership and rule of the manor. Likely, he realized now, the highest price ever paid by a man for a single swive!

But how absurd it all was, he assured himself again. English lords didn't go about bargaining to sleep with Irish peasants, and most assuredly not with dark-haired ones. Any man worth his salt knew that blondes alone were worth dickering over, and only then if they showed absolutely no signs of becoming too dependent.

With a disgusted humph, he slowly raised himself to a sitting position and leaned back against his bed's broad headboard. The discomfort he experienced in doing so, however, instantly reminded him of an occurrence which he wished had simply proven part of a dream as well.

Someone or something had caused a long welt to form on his backside roughly nine hours earlier, and, feeling the lingering pain of it now brought his first order of business for the day rushing back to mind. After relieving himself in his chamber pot, he would have to find the card that English metaphysical investigator had given him. Then he would pen the fellow a missive which said that his services were badly needed and would be handsomely remunerated, if he would only be good enough to travel to Brenna forthwith.

Roughly half an hour later, Stafford was seated for breakfast in the manor's east dining room, just as he had been at eight o'clock each and every morning since his arrival in Ireland.

"Stay here and eat with me," he said to his steward, as Flaherty bustled past the room's long cherry-wood table en route to the kitchen.

The Irishman stopped in his tracks and, as usually happened whenever Stafford made such unexpected requests, Flaherty turned and offered him a thoroughly flustered look. "Oh, I shouldn't, sir. My place is with the rest of the servants in kitchen."

"Rubbish," Pearce replied, using his foot to push out the

chair to the right of where he sat at the table's head. "I am master of this household now and I say 'tis perfectly acceptable to partake of your meals with me, when you're asked. Besides, I've a couple of matters which I wish to discuss with you."

Continuing to appear terribly ill at ease with this invitation, the steward handed the dust cloth he'd been carrying to a passing maid and hesitantly walked over to his new employer.

Allayed by Flaherty's compliance, Stafford smiled at him once more. Then he leaned back in his Queen Anne chair and exhaled a contented breath. "Ah, mornings are lovely here at Brenna, are they not?" he said, squinting slightly against the orange glare of early sunlight which streamed in through the room's many eastern windows.

"Indeed, my lord," the steward answered with far less appreciation than Pearce was displaying.

"Do relax," Stafford urged, as he again looked over to see that, far from enjoying this respite from his usual morning duties, the hefty Irishman was perching upon the edge of his assigned seat as though poised to dash from a burning building. "I'm merely seeking some top of the morning small talk from you. You needn't be on your guard in my presence at *all* times, mind."

Flaherty, in response, donned a clumsy little smile of his own and did his best to ease more of his girth onto his chair.

Before Stafford could begin addressing the issues on his mind, however, their breakfast emerged from beyond the swinging door of the adjacent kitchen on three steaming platters. The first, carried by a frizzy-haired redheaded lass, who appeared to be not much older than fourteen, contained the usual pile of slightly overfried eggs. Balanced upon her other upraised palm was a plate of thickly sliced bacon. The third of the dishes was a mound of stewed tomatoes which, as with all of the cook's offerings, was far too generous in quantity for Stafford and Flaherty—to say nothing of the lord alone. This was poised on the capable right hand of a pale-complexioned lass, whose sleek black hair, Stafford had observed, was always tied back by a satiny length of light-blue ribbon. Resting on her other palm was a mercifully smaller platter of scones.

As was his habit, Mr. Flaherty began at once to tell the girls where each dish should be set upon the table, his eyes flashing warnings here and there, as a parent giving silent, yet stern direction to his children amidst church services.

They were all rather charming together, Pearce thought, continuing to lean back in his chair as the servants executed their daily breakfast choreography with as little noise and confusion as they could seem to manage.

What a serious business it was to them all, he marveled. This presentation of meals three times a day, during which the slightest splatter of tomato juice or the smallest smudge of butter often ended in a surprisingly severe scolding from the fat steward. This was, to Stafford's further surprise, usually followed by wrenching wails from whichever hapless maid had committed said blunder.

Able to recall very few of such disturbances among the seasoned servantry at his parents' estate in London, Pearce couldn't help fighting a laugh now. His gaze wandered down to the white linen tablecloth before him, then up again to the young maids' equally prim white pinafores, where they were affixed, high upon the bodices of their puffy-sleeved black frocks.

With all of them looking so starched and crisp and smelling of laundry soap from head to toe—Stafford was finally beginning to understand how this less-than-polished staff had ultimately come to grow upon his Uncle Prescott.

They were, without intending to be, a very entertaining lot. Their occasional disorganization was strangely disarming, their frequent incompetence inexplicably endearing.

With the morning's four key dishes safely arranged upon the huge table now, the last of the cook's preparations quickly followed. Into the dining room it was brought, steaming even more profusely than its predecessors. It was a breakfast porridge in a large tureen. A runny concoction which had been offered to

Pearce every single morning, without fail, since his arrival and which he had, equally unflaggingly, refused to even sample.

"I was thinking, Mr. Flaherty," Stafford began again, reaching out to help himself to some of the bacon, "that, should it prove too troublesome for us to continue posting a guard outside that seaside thatch, we might do best to simply burn it down. What say you to that idea?"

Pearce's attention was fixed upon his steward just long enough to hear him gulp in response. Then, from out of the corner of his eye, he saw all hell breaking loose at the opposite end of the table. The china tureen, containing the porridge, suddenly fell from the third maid's hands somehow, the resulting explosion of hot cereal evoking horrified gasps all around.

The poor girl might just as well have sheared the tip off a volcanic Mount Vesuvius for all of the commotion that ensued. Before she could even drop to her knees to begin trying to clean up the mess, her two peers were on the spot with the linen serving towels they had hanging from their right forearms and the steward was getting to his feet with a thunderous push backward on his chair.

"No," Stafford snapped, reaching out and grasping one of Flaherty's fleshy wrists. "I insist that you remain seated and finish your meal!" He paused to narrow his eyes at him quizzically. "Much as I know how you love finding reasons to flee me whenever that damnable cottage is spoken of, you are going to stay here now and discuss it."

Still looking quite disturbed by the mishap, the Irishman drew in a resigned breath at this order and pulled his chair back up to the table.

"Now what is it, man? *What on earth* is it about that place that causes you and your subordinates to come so unhinged at the very bloody mention of it?" Stafford demanded in an undertone.

"Why, nothin'. Nothin' a'tall, sir. The silly wench is just clumsy," he went on, casting another searing look in her direction. "Sure, 'tis the *third* dish she has dropped this week alone, my lord, so ye must not gauge the sentiments of the rest of us by her actions."

Though he made this declaration with an almost-convincing finality to his tone, Stafford continued to wear a skeptical scowl. "Are you saying then that you think destroying it might be in my best interests?"

"Nay. Not for the world, sir! Why, that thatch has been standin' for nigh onto a century. It was, if I might say so, one of your uncle's very favorite dwellin's on these grounds, so filled with the history of the place is it. Thus burnin' it seems to me a very bad idea indeed . . . That is, if you will pardon me for sayin' as much," he added, as if suddenly mindful once more of his lower station.

"Even on the chance that the party or parties whom I have seen trespassing down there might be rebels attempting to gain a stronghold in the cottage, you believe it should be left intact?"

Flaherty issued a nervous laugh. "Ah, faith, my lord, we've no reason to believe those with the cause would hazard establishin' a camp so near the manor. By the saints, the constable would lock 'em away for good and all, if they were caught doin' anythin' of the sort! So, aye, sir. I truly think 'twould be a shame to take a torch to it," the Irishman fervently concluded.

"Very well then," Stafford replied with a pensive nod. "For the time being, in any case, it shall continue to stand. So, what of the guard I asked you to post at it last evening? What has he to say, now that he's passed a night alone down there?"

Though Flaherty appeared a bit more composed now, Pearce could tell that this question had caught him off guard as well.

"What? Ed—Edward, sir?" he stammered. "Why he's not said a word to me this mornin' of anythin' unusual occurrin'."

"Edward? Edward who?"

The steward swallowed the mouthful of scone he'd been chewing with another gulp. "Edward O'Malley, of course, my lord."

"Edward O'Malley? What? You mean Eddie the *stable boy?*" Stafford asked in disbelief.

The Irishman's cheeks reddened with obvious chagrin. "Well, aye, sir. He was the only one I could spare for the task."

"Good God, man! He cannot be a day over seven!"

"Oh, but he is, my lord. Ye mustn't let appearances deceive ya. He's fully eight this summer."

"So I'm to understand that you sent a little boy down there for the night?"

The steward grew more sheepish. "Well, aye. He was the only hand I could carry on without, as I've said. And, in truth, sir, he knows the place better than the rest of us. He was born in that thatch, ya see. And he plays down there from time to time, when his work is through."

Pearce couldn't help letting his mouth continue to hang open with astoundment. After the chilling experience he'd had in the cottage just the day before, he couldn't imagine a mere lad weathering an entire night beside it. "But what if there had been trouble? Were you not concerned that the child might be—overpowered by whomever is squatting therein?"

"Ah, nay, sir. Eddie is Irish through and through. There's no one hereabouts who holds anythin' against him, you can be sure. What is more, he has a good strong voice, so we'd have heard him cry out, if he'd been in need of help."

Stafford shook his head in continuing disbelief. "Mr. Flaherty, I find myself speechless. I had honestly come to think you a more sensible sort than this!"

"But I *am* sensible, my lord," he said defensively. "I really thought Edward capable of guardin' the thatch. What's more, I still do."

Pearce pursed his lips at this insolent response. "Very well then. You shall see that the boy is brought to me after breakfast, so I can question him about anything he might have learned of the place thus far."

The Irishman paled at this request. "What?"

Stafford took a sip of his hot tea before answering. "You heard me, Mr. Flaherty. I wish to speak to the lad when we are done eating. Please arrange it."

"Aye, sir," the steward hesitantly agreed.

The two men finished out their meal in uncomfortable silence, and the maids exchanged apprehensive looks before retreating to the kitchen with their porridge-soaked towels.

Half an hour later, little Eddie O'Malley was ushered into Stafford's study by Flaherty.

"Well, well," Pearce greeted, rising from his desk with as welcoming a smile as he could seem to produce. Though he was painfully aware that he had once been a youngster, he'd never much cared for them, and he knew he would find it difficult to succeed at putting this one at ease. "Do sit down," he invited, pointing to one of the hooped-back chairs that were positioned a few feet in front of his desk.

"Go on," the steward bent to encourage in a hushed voice. In that same instant, he let go of Eddie's arm and gave him a pat on the bottom as if to fire him in the desired direction. With that, Flaherty stepped back and lingered in the doorway.

"Yes, yes, sit down, Edward," Stafford said again. "By all means, do make yourself comfortable."

Though slowing his pace markedly as he made his way across the room, the stable boy proved obedient in this. Within just a few seconds, he was seated far back in one of the large chairs, his forearms draped over each of its spindle-supported armrests and his feet not quite reaching the floor.

Stafford took his eyes from the child just long enough to let them travel back to where his steward still stood. "That will be all, Mr. Flaherty. Thank you. And please be so good as to close the door behind you."

The servant's wavering smile sank. Then, issuing a nervous cough, he backed out of the room, obligingly shutting the door as he went.

"Well, now, Eddie," Pearce began again, sitting back down at his desk, so that he might come closer to eye level with the lad, "My steward tells me you spent the night guarding the seaside thatch for me. Is that true?"

"Aye, sir."

"Then, I wonder, can you tell me what you saw down there in all that time?"

"Why, nothin', Lord Pearce."

"You mean to say no one came sneaking about the place. You saw no one stirring?"

"What? As a prowler, ya mean?"

"Just so, boy," Stafford praised. "That is precisely what I meant."

Eddie shook his head. "Nay, sir. There was no one down there who shouldn't have been."

"No travellers or tinkers, perchance, happening by in search of shelter for the night?"

His blond mop of hair flapped back and forth once more in another negative answer. "Nay. No one of the kind. I swear it."

Pearce leaned forward and looked him more squarely in the eye, his tone gentler as he spoke again. "And no odd goings-on either, lad? For, if such were the case, you have my assurance that I would not think you daft for saying so."

Edward looked suddenly befuddled. "Pray, pardon me, my lord, but could ya tell me what ya mean by 'odd goin's-on' exactly? I'm not sure I understand that part."

To his dismay, Stafford felt his cheeks grow warm at this question. Given the rather unseemly nature of his experience in the thatch the day before, he very much doubted that he could be more specific without embarrassing himself, as well as the boy. "Well, um . . . You didn't *feel* anything, did you, Eddie? Such as something unseen touching you, for instance?"

"Touchin' me?" he echoed blankly.

On the chance that his steward had remained just outside the door—and Stafford considered it a very great one indeed—he lowered his voice considerably as he spoke again. "Yes. You know . . . *kissing* you?"

At this the lad crinkled up his nose and donned an expression that was so conspiratorially mischievous that it almost made Pearce's breath catch in his throat. It was as though little Edward somehow thought him a young peer who had just offered to share some information about the birds and the bees. "What? Kissed me as a lass would, ya mean? On the *lips?*" he inquired with an amazed snicker.

Stafford frowned a bit at his enthusiasm for the subject. "Yes. On the lips, if you like. But, really, anywhere on your person, Edward. I am simply asking if you remember anything of that nature taking place."

The stable boy rolled his eyes and giggled again. "Nay. Never. And, pray believe me, sir, I surely would not have forgotten such a thing!"

Pearce thrust out a palm and shushed him in an effort to keep his voice lowered.

"Why?" the lad inquired in a whisper. "Did somethin' of the kind happen to *you* down there?" he pursued with a smirk which seemed almost mocking.

Pearce met it with a glower, the information he'd sought having already been obtained. "No. Absolutely not, you silly child! And woe be to you, should you ever dare say as much to anyone, mind," he concluded in a growl.

To his credit, the eight-year-old showed the good sense to sober at this warning. "Nay. I won't. I promise. I was just wonderin', was all."

"Well, no need to wonder, Eddie. I have answered you now in that regard. So, that will be all. Thank you for coming to me," Stafford said, his eyes dropping to the paperwork which lay before him on his desk.

"Ya want me to go?" the stable boy asked after several seconds.

"Yes. As I said, lad. That will be all."

To Pearce's surprise, though he again fixed his attention upon the ledgers and such in front of him, his peripheral vision revealed that the child was failing to rise from his chair.

"All right then," he spat, pushing away from his desk and

jerking open its shallow center drawer. "If 'tis money you seek in order to keep the specifics of our little chat a secret, here's fifty pence," he declared, withdrawing three coins and extending them to the boy with an irritated *humph.*

Though Edward looked caught off guard by this offer, Stafford noted that he did spring forward to accept the bribe with lightning speed.

"Why, thank ya marvellous much, my lord," he said with a grin. "But, in truth, that wasn't why I was tarryin' ."

Stafford clucked. "Well, what was the cause of it then?"

The lad pointed to the wall behind his desk. "The butterflies up there. I was wonderin', are they *real?"*

Feeling relieved at the realization that the boy wasn't, in fact, the extortionist he'd taken him for, Pearce turned and glanced back at his framed collection with a prideful laugh. "Of course they are, son. You don't think I would trouble to put fabricated butterflies under glass, do you?"

Edward's eyes grew round with what appeared to be aghastness. "Nay, but . . . but why would you kill 'em? They neither bite nor sting, ya know. They're among the kindest of flyin' creatures in all the world."

"So they are," Stafford agreed, getting from his chair and stepping away from the wall to regard the multicolored display from a broader perspective. "I have never really viewed them in that way, but there is no debating it, is there?"

"So you're not sorry about it, sir?" Eddie asked, continuing to look rather appalled by the extensive collection.

Stafford furrowed his brow in confusion. "Sorry about what?"

"About killin' 'em all, of course They only live for a month, I hope ya realize," he pointed out with a plaintive rise to his voice.

"Now where on earth would you have come to know that?"

"What?"

"How long a butterfly lives."

The stable boy shrugged. "I don't know. 'Twas Selena must have told it to me, I guess."

"Selena?"

Of a sudden, the lad looked as if he'd said something terribly wrong, though Stafford was lost as to what it could possibly have been.

"She . . . she's simply a friend of mine, my lord. No one you would know, I'm sure."

"Oh. A schoolmate of yours, then?"

Eddie continued to appear disconcerted. "Well, nay. More akin to a teacher, I suppose you could say."

"Ah, yes," Pearce replied, circling to the front of his desk and wrapping an ushering arm about the child's shoulders. "Well, do give her my regards, will you?" He began walking Eddie towards the door. " 'Tis quite a treasure of a teacher, indeed, who could succeed in following a *single* butterfly about long enough to determine the length of its life!"

"Aye. She is that, sir."

"Well, splendid," Stafford declared, as they reached the door and he stepped forward to open it for his visitor. "I am truly pleased for you."

Slipping the coins he'd been given into the pocket of his breeches, Edward turned back to whisper something to Pearce in parting. "Pray, none of those in your collection are *Brenna's* butterflies, are they?" he asked with an unmistakable note of warning in his voice.

Stafford couldn't help laughing a bit at the question. "No. Not yet. I fear I have been kept far too busy endeavoring to assume my uncle's duties to have indulged in my hobby at all."

The lad dragged the back of his right hand across his forehead. "Phew. Ah, well, that's good," he exclaimed and hurried off towards the front hall.

Before Stafford could call after him, however, Flaherty stepped out from the shadows of the corridor, his girth blocking Pearce's path.

"What did he mean by that?" Stafford demanded of the steward in a snarl.

The Irishman donned that annoyingly passive smile of his—his lips flattening into a thin broad line across his chubby face, while his eyes remained expressionless.

"By what, my lord?"

"By saying that 'tis good that none of the butterflies in my collection have come from Brenna."

The line of his smile suddenly turned down at both ends. "Hmm. I cannot imagine, sir . . . Unless it has somethin' to do with the fairies."

"The fairies?"

Flaherty chuckled with embarrassment. "Aye. Well, we Irish believe in them, ya see. In their powers to either cure or bless us. And, since all flyin' creatures, be they birds or butterflies, can sometimes prove to be fairies in disguise, I suppose he was simply tryin' to save ya from any harm which might befall ya for goin' huntin' in their realm."

"God's teeth, man! That's ridiculous! I've not heard aught so absurd in all my days."

"Aye, well, there's no denyin' that we are a superstitious lot in this country, sir. Then, too, ya must bear in mind that Eddie is just a lad. And, as ya probably know, lads can be given to all manner of fanciful tales . . . That is to say, he didn't, um, didn't spin ya any other yarns as the pair of ya spoke, did he, my lord?" he went on with an apprehensiveness that was unmistakable on the heels of such feigned jocularity.

Stafford turned from him and headed back into his study. "Now why would he do that?" he asked pointedly.

The steward followed him into the room. "Well, 'tis just that I know you sought to question him about his watch of the thatch, sir, And I, um, I truly hope that all he told ya about it seemed . . . plausible."

Pearce took his place at his desk once more and, folding his hands before him upon it, looked up at the servant with a matter-of-fact expression. "Oh, don't worry yourself, Flaherty. He didn't reveal any of your deep dark secrets. He simply claimed he saw no one stirring down there last night, and I am rather inclined to believe him."

The steward exhaled a relieved breath. "Ah, that's good, sir. I'm glad he struck ya as bein' faith-worthy."

"Yes. But do let us put one of our *men* down there henceforward. 'Tis no place for a lad at night, mind," Stafford added firmly.

"Probably not, my lord. I shall see to findin' a new watch at once then," he declared, turning to leave the room.

"Hold a moment," Pearce called after him. "I do have something more I wish to discuss with you."

The Irishman stopped walking and faced him once more. "Aye, sir?"

"I am wondering about a certain young lady, Mr. Flaherty. That is to say, I do feel it gauche to host a soirée for some of the local gentry and not, at the very least, invite her."

"Invite whom, my lord?"

"My Uncle Prescott's beloved, of course. While I'm well aware that you and the rest of the servants claim not to have known much about her, surely you must have learned such essential things as her full name and address."

For some reason, the steward's cheeks grew lobster red at this line of inquiry. But, perhaps, Stafford thought, his steward's flush was simply due to his sudden directness in making such a query.

"Pray, pardon me, sir, but I wasn't aware that you were plannin' a soirée. Is it that I simply failed to hear ya mention it before now?"

Stafford donned a subtle smile and casually ran an index finger over the bottom edge of his desk's blotter. "No, no, Flaherty. Rest assured. You're far too attentive a fellow for that. Hosting such a party only just occurred to me this morning, in fact. As a means of acquainting myself with those of any importance in this region, you see. There seems no point, after all, in my continuing to feel an unwelcome stranger here in your country, when a few servings of Brenna's fine food and wines could so easily win me some allies. Such tactics worked for my uncle, did they not?"

Though it hardly seemed possible, the steward's blush actually appeared to deepen. "Well, your—your uncle was—" His words broke off and he nervously bit his beefy lower lip.

"Was what?" Stafford fished, his gaze and tone pouncing upon the servant.

"Was, well . . . a very different sort than you are, sir. If ya know what I mean."

"No. I fear I don't," Pearce said evenly. "Please do be good enough to offer some elaboration."

The steward waved his open palms defensively out before him. "Oh, I pray you, do not ask me to draw comparisons between you and the former lord! 'Twould hardly be fair, given how little time I've known ya."

Keeping his eyes fixed upon the Irishman, Stafford eased his way around to the front of the desk and leaned back against its edge. Then he casually crossed his long legs at the ankle. "Well, would you say, for instance, that he was more gregarious than I?"

Flaherty offered a polite shrug. Then, looking as though he was almost as uncomfortable with his tongue-biting as his employer, he dropped his gaze to the floor and began nodding emphatically.

Stafford threw back his head and issued a short laugh at this comically hesitant confession. "So, there, you see? You aren't telling me anything I did not already know about myself. Or my uncle, for that matter."

"Nay, I suppose not, sir. But, well, 'tis important for me to point out that, in order for the local folk to take a likin' to ya, you must also be inclined to like them, and . . . um." He paused and cleared his throat uneasily. "Well, are ya sure that would be your intent in hostin' such a gatherin'? Because I can promise ya that your uncle's betrothed, if, indeed, I am able to find her for ya, would sense any disapproval in ya. I should mention that she was never very fond of those of English extraction."

Stafford furrowed his brow in confusion. "But she promised herself to an Englishman! My uncle was a Londoner, born and bred."

"Aye, well, I shall grant ya that. You know far more about Lord Prescott's beginnin's than any of us do, to be sure, may he rest in peace. But, over time, ya see, I think he became, in his heart, more true to this land than that of his birth. And, well, if that is not also your aim, my lord, I promise ya that you would do well to simply forget about your uncle's affianced. Let sleepin' hounds lie, as it were."

"What is it you're driving at? Could you possibly be trying to tell me that this lover of his is part of the cause, as you always refer to it? A rebel to the Crown?" Stafford inquired, his eyes growing large with consternation. "For I refuse to believe that my uncle would knowingly consort with such a woman!"

The steward's face again flushed brightly, and his suddenly reticent demeanor told his employer that he was finished disclosing what he knew of the woman. "Well, perhaps, your uncle did not do so knowingly, sir. It seems to me that one's political affiliations are often pushed by the wayside when true love comes to the fore."

"Hmm," Pearce replied, folding his arms over his chest contemplatively. Then, after several seconds, a soft smile played upon his lips. "How very intriguing, though, Mr. Flaherty. I, too, rather like my ladies high-spirited, so maybe I would not find this woman as objectionable as you imagine."

The steward lowered his voice to a solemn hush. "But the cause is not mere sport, my lord. I would be showin' ya no loyalty a'tall if I didn't remind ya now what a deadly business it is, indeed. Only a few years past, there were some *fifty thousand* people killed over it in the Great Rebellion at Wexford Bridge. So we had best let the matter rest, don't ya think?" he urged.

"On the contrary, my good fellow. Now that you've told me this much about Prescott's inamorata, I realize that I simply must make her acquaintance! Indeed, it sounds as though she might honestly think herself a worthy opponent for me, and, I regret to tell, it has been far too long since I met a women who dared to challenge me in any sphere. So, do go about finding her address for me at once, will you? In fact, I absolutely insist upon it. I shall not take no for an answer!"

Far from again turning sanguine in the cheeks in those seconds, the Irishman went terribly pale for some reason. Then he gave a nod to this command and left the room as quickly as his feet could seem to carry him.

The request was obviously causing him to reach some sort of breaking point; yet Stafford felt strangely certain that this was due to something more than his concern about a possible flare-up over the local politics.

Five

Selena was just returning from the forest with the additional herbs she needed for her full-moon ritual, when she sensed that her thatch was again being encroached upon.

She slowed her gait as she neared the back of the cottage, and, sliding the handle of her stave basket farther up on her right forearm, she crept around the dwelling's eastern side, towards the door.

There was someone besides Nola inside, to be sure, she acknowledged as she made her stealthy approach; yet the entryway did not appear to be opened, and there wasn't a sound from within. Nevertheless, her heightened powers of perception told her that a large and heavily perspiring male was lying in wait for her.

She crouched and hurried past the thatch's right front window, then, straightening once more, she pulled her magic herb-cutting dagger from her basket and, holding it poised for attack with her right hand, she quietly opened the door with her left.

It was the new lord, she surmised, doing her best to stay calm in those tense seconds before the intruder's identity was finally confirmed for her. It was that blasted Stafford Pearce come to spy upon her once more, *damn* him!

To her surprise, however, she found Brenna's steward standing just within as she entered.

"Mother Mary," he gasped, throwing his arms up over his face in response to her raised weapon. "Pray, don't stab me, Mistress Selena! I've only come to warn ya, after all!"

She let her dagger hand fall to her side with a sigh of relief. "Oh, Flaherty, ya fool! You gave me such a scare! I thought you were that dreadful Englishman skulkin' about again." With that, she closed the door behind her, then walked to one of her hearthside chairs and set her basket upon it. "What are you doin' down here?" she growled, turning back to him. "I don't recall extendin' any invitations."

"Oh, nay, nay. I have not come for a social visit. But, rather, to warn ya, as I said."

With her vision now adjusted to the dimmer indoor light, she saw that he was near hysterical tears. A most uncommon state in this otherwise imperious supervisor, she silently noted. "Warn me of what?"

" 'Tis the new lord, mistress. He's insistin' upon makin' your acquaintance. Says he'll not take no for an answer in the matter!"

"Well, how on earth did he come to know of me?" She narrowed her eyes at him threateningly. "I thought I made it clear to you, as well as your subordinates, that I plan to meet him in my own way and time."

"Aye. That ya did, good lady. And, by truth, we have all complied. 'Tis just that he knew, even before he arrived, that his uncle had a lover here at Brenna, and *she* is the one who he's demandin' to meet now. I've tried to keep him at bay. By all the saints, I truly have," he declared, stifling a sob with a fist. "But how will I ever persuade him to believe that old Prescott's intended simply vanished without a trace after his death? . . . I could go on denyin' that any of us even knew your name, I suppose. But, with him plannin' this grand soirée of his for so many in the county, 'tis sure to slip out sooner or later!"

Selena crossed to the opposite chair, and, after turning it to face him, sank down upon its seat. "A soirée?"

"Aye. To see him properly introduced to the local gentry he says. I—that is, I truly did try to convince him that you are part of the cause and want naught more to do with Englishmen, but it only made him more intent upon meetin' ya, the perverse devil!"

"But why?"

"Because he claimed he would find it challengin', I guess. Oh, I don't recall precisely all he said about it now," he continued, wiping his apparently sweaty palms upon his waistcoat with a whimper. "I only know he fancies the idea of threshin' out the local politics with ya, for some reason. And, pray you, my dear woman, this could all turn frightfully dangerous, if you do not put some manner of hex upon him very soon!"

"Ah, begorra, Flaherty, what a lather ya work yourself into sometimes. You'll likely burst your heart one day with all your frettin'. Then even I won't be able to save ya."

"But what are we to do about this?" he asked, a note of desperation in his voice. "As much as I wish to, I simply cannot continue to keep him away from ya forever!"

"You won't have to."

"What?"

"I shall come to his deuced party. And I will even wear some of the jewels that Prescott gave me."

The Irishman's mouth dropped open in amazement. "You'll what?"

"I shall come, ya daft thing. Have ya gone deaf, for the love of Heaven? I shall come and be introduced as Prescott's affianced and discuss the cause or anythin' else that pompous bugger wishes to."

"But what if ya come to blows, the pair of ya? What if he makes ya cross, mistress? Ya cannot just reduce him to cinders before all those witnesses! Why, we'd not have a hope of concealin' such a thing. 'Twould be the burnin' stake or jail for the lot of us!"

She rose with a confident air and flashed him a calming smile. "Oh, do stop makin' so much of this. No one is goin' to be killed. I shall have a very tight rein upon the situation, you may be sure." She stepped behind the chair with a smooth, seductive motion and began running her fingers over the top of its carved back rail, her expression suddenly wily. "In fact, I have already begun some dream craft upon him."

This revelation did seem to pacify the steward a bit. "Oh, aye? That's how ya won old Prescott's heart, is it not?"

"Precisely," she confirmed with a smile. "So, ya see? You've nothin' at all to worry about. I've full faith that the new lord shall prove quite compliant with my every request by the time he arranges this soirée of his."

"Ah, Sweet Jesus, I surely hope so," he replied with some lingering uneasiness.

Continuing to smile, Selena crossed to open the thatch's door for him. "No. You must not simply hope, you must *know.* For belief is the cornerstone of Celtic magic. And don't ya forget it!"

"Very well," he muttered, as he followed her cue and moved to take his leave. "See ya at the soirée then, I guess."

"Oh, you may be certain of it," she declared, about to shut the door after him.

He remained in the threshold for a moment more, however. "But if ya come to the festivities, mistress," he said guardedly, "please bear in mind that the new lord must not see ya walkin' up to the great house from here."

She clucked with exasperation and gave him a light push out the door. "Ah, God, Flaherty. I'm wise enough to know that I shall need to take a roundabout route. Now, off with ya, before I lose my temper for good and all!"

He obliged her of course. Within the space of a heartbeat, he was down the thatch's front step and she was latching the door behind him.

'Tis not workin', her cat warned in a hush a second or two later.

Selena turned back to face her familiar, where she lay, curled up near the small dining table. "What?"

The dream craft ya told him of. 'Tis havin' no effect upon Stafford Pearce.

"Oh, that's ridiculous, Nola. Of course it is! It must be, for I've never heard of a man who could resist it."

The new lord can, the feline retorted with unsettling certainty.

"Well then, I will simply have to cast it upon him again, won't I," she shot back. "And again and again until it conquers him!"

Nola issued a sigh through her tiny nostrils and set her head back down upon her curving forepaws. *Suit yourself.*

Selena couldn't help clenching her teeth at this mocking response. "And what is that supposed to mean?"

The cat shifted her sharp shoulder bones slightly as though to shrug. *Merely that you can try until ya fall into an exhausted heap, but ya just might never succeed with this one.*

The sorceress folded her arms over her chest. "And why is that, pray tell?"

Nola fixed her gold eyes squarely upon her master. *I don't know. I simply sense that ya may be goin' about this in the wrong way. Perhaps ya were so long with the last lord that you've lost your touch with other men.*

"Ah, now you truly *are* bein' ridiculous. Why, I was castin' love spells before you were so much as a twinkle in a tomcat's eye! And no witch worth tuppence loses her touch with aught as essential as that. I shall simply give it to him twofold tonight. And, what is more, you shall help me! I'll not have ya lost in repose, as ya were the whole while Prescott owned the manor. 'Tis well past time that ya started earnin' your keep again! So, 'tis either that or mousin'."

Her familiar again raised her head, this time to issue a repulsed sniff at so demeaning an alternative. Before she could protest, however, there came a knock at the door and it was clear that she and her master were about to receive another visitor.

Without a sound, Selena stepped away from the threshold and pivoted to face it, so that she could better discern if it was friend or foe coming to call.

It certainly wasn't the villain they were speaking of, she realized with great relief. No. The energy she felt just without was hardly the jaded and somewhat aloof sort which she'd felt pouring off of Stafford Pearce each time he'd come around.

Rather, this was someone who, though also male, was markedly innocent and earthy.

Eddie, Nola declared in a meow.

Yes, Eddie, Selena realized in precisely that same instant. "Eddie?" she said in a welcoming tone, stepping forward and swinging the door open to him.

"Aye, mistress," the stable boy replied, beaming up at her where he stood upon the thatch's front step.

"Don't tell me those dolts have sent ya back down to 'guard' the place again? Not that I dislike your company, mind. But, really, there must be more useful things for a lad of your age to be doin'."

"Oh, nay, mistress. I'm glad to say I've come this time of my own accord. To show ya what the new lord gave me," he added excitedly, digging about in the pocket of his breeches.

Selena reached out and took hold of one of his arms. "Get ye in here then. Let us not hazard Pearce seein' ya speakin' with me."

"Very well," he answered; but he was so lost in his search for his alleged gift, that it was more her strength, than his own, that got him safely out of view.

"Look," he exclaimed, as she quickly shut the thatch door after him.

Her eyes dropped down to the three large coins he now held in his upraised right palm.

"Money is it? My, what a surprise," she said, her voice edged with bitterness at the Pearces' seeming ability to buy nearly everyone's loyalty with their considerable wealth.

"Well, it was to me," Edward retorted, looking up at her with an earnestness that said he'd fully detected the sarcasm in her response. "For, ya see, I didn't ask for them, mistress. I wasn't askin' for anythin' at all from him. I was simply sittin' in his study, answerin' his questions about your thatch, when, of a sudden, he pulled open one of his desk drawers and handed them to me."

Selena looked at him discerningly. "For no reason at all, ya say?"

The boy shrugged. "Well . . . maybe so that I might be better persuaded to keep his secret, I suppose," he conceded after several seconds. "But, aye. In the main, for no reason."

She offered him a disarming smile. "His *secret?* My, my . . . Tell me, Eddie," she began again in her most dulcet tone, "have ya had your luncheon yet?"

"Nay. But 'tis scarcely noon, is it?"

"Ah, near enough, if ya wish to stay and eat with me again. Or you could just have some milk and fruit scones, if ya prefer," she invited, knowing he'd never shown the willpower to refuse her sweetened baked goods. *Two* could play at this business of bribing Brenna's help, after all.

He licked his lips. "Fruit scones, aye."

Selena wisely chose to wait until they were both seated before a plate of the buttered pastries minutes later to resume their talk of Stafford.

"Tasty?" she prompted, once her little visitor had helped himself to his first bites of a scone.

He nodded emphatically.

"Ah, good. You know how I cherish your praise of my bakin' . . . So, tell me, Eddie," she began again with a nonchalant chuckle, "what manner of secret could a man such as the new lord possibly have?"

The eight-year-old reached out with both hands, grabbed the glass of milk his hostess had set before him, and washed what remained of his scone down with it. "I can't tell ya," he replied, a white mustache of the liquid forming around his mouth as he smacked his lips in that instant.

Selena didn't flinch at this refusal. She simply propped her elbows on the table, let her chin come to rest in her upraised palms, and offered him a docile smile. "But why not?"

"Because 'tis a secret, of course. So I gave him my word I would tell no one of it. And, as it happens, he likely isn't the villain I first thought him to be," he added gingerly.

She frowned at this. "So you promised you would keep his secret in exchange for the coins?"

He wiped his mouth on his shirt cuff and took up another scone. "Nay. Those came after I promised him."

"Very well then. Since you've given the man your pledge, you ought not to break it. But, ya know, you could tell me just a wee bit about what the secret was concernin', and maybe I could guess the rest from there."

He knit his brow. "Do ya really think that would be all right?"

"Oh, aye. Of course. We grown folk do that sort of thing quite often."

"Well . . . it had to do with me guardin' your thatch. He was simply wonderin' if anythin' odd might have happened to me down here last night."

"And what did ya tell him?"

He drank more of his milk, then set the glass back down, a slight burp escaping from his lips. "Well, I couldn't very well make mention of my broom ride with ya. Because, even though that truly is odd to most, it would have caused me to have to tell him about *you.* And, since ya said ya don't want him knowin' of ya, I just claimed nothin' strange had befallen me. And then he asked me whether or not I had ever been touched by anyone down here."

"Touched?"

He blushed a little. "Aye. Ya know," he said, rolling his eyes self-consciously. *"Kissed* or anythin'."

Suddenly recalling her encounter with Pearce the afternoon before, Selena found herself having to fight a laugh at this. "And, um . . . what was your answer?"

"Nay, of course. You're not one for kissin' your visitors, and neither is Nola. You've maybe hugged me goodbye once or twice, but that didn't seem to be what he was after in askin' it."

She nodded and donned a subtle smile. "Ah, so *that* is the new lord's precious secret, is it? That he imagines he felt someone kiss him down here?"

"I didn't say that," the stable boy shot back defensively.

Selena took a sip of the hot tea which she'd poured for herself. "Nay. Of course ya didn't, dear child. You promised to keep Pearce's secret and so ya have," she praised. "But ya know, Eddie," she continued, growing very solemn, "you must never become too fond of the outlanders' money. That is how we Irish have been sold into servitude by our own since the time of the Vikin's!"

"Aye, but I wasn't sellin' anyone, mistress. The lord just gave it to me, as I told ya. I was simply studyin' the wall behind him and, bang, there they were. Three shiny gold coins thrust out before me!"

"And why would ya have been studyin' his wall?"

"Because of the butterflies."

"The what?"

"The butterflies he has hangin' behind his desk."

"What? *Real* butterflies?"

"Aye."

Selena felt her heart beginning to race with aghastness. "And they're 'hung'? As from *nooses?*"

He laughed and waved her off. "Nay. Not that sort of hangin'. The framed paintin' sort."

She breathed a sigh of relief and nodded. "Oh, ya mean he has a paintin' with butterflies pictured in it?"

"Nay. Not a paintin'. 'Tis just that they're framed as paintin's would be."

"What are?"

Again he chuckled as though starting to think she meant to tease him with this almost dizzying line of questioning. "The butterflies, naturally! They're real, ya see, though dead, of course."

She gaped with renewed shock. "You mean to tell me he *killed* them?"

Having reached his satiation point apparently, Eddie now sat picking the pieces of candied fruit out of the scone he'd most recently acquired. "Well, he must have, aye. For they were dead, sure enough."

"But why? Who on earth hunts and kills butterflies?"

"Well, he doesn't hunt 'em exactly, mistress. He just collects them, I guess. Anyway, I tried to tell him what a sinful thing it is to do, how they only live to be a month old and they don't bite or sting anyone. But that didn't seem to make much matter to him. In fact, he went on appearin' rather proud of 'em."

In spite of herself, Selena started to inwardly seethe. Now that the initial shock and horror at this new lord's savage hobby was beginning to wear off, her righteous anger was bound to follow, and she wasn't entirely sure she wanted to bridle it as usual. "Just how many of them are there on his wall?" she asked through clenched teeth.

He shrugged. "Ah, faith, I'm not sure. But it did look to be dozens and dozens. He claimed, however, that none of them came from Brenna. So that's good, isn't it."

"Aye," she agreed, though somewhat reluctantly. "Of course 'tis best that it not be *our* fairies he's murderin', Eddie. But that hardly makes what he's done right," she concluded, her tone again warning him against becoming too accepting of this arrogant Englishman.

"Nay. To be sure," he was quick to reply.

"So now, you say they've all been killed and hung in frames somehow?"

"Aye." The boy sprang from his chair and stood spread-eagle before her. "Completely flattened out. Just as I'm standin' now. Only under glass. Their wings are on full display and held by wee pins in all directions."

"What? As Christ on the Cross?" she pursued, her voice cracking with repulsion.

He snapped his fingers, pointed at her, and sat down once more. "Aye. Exactly! Just like crucifixions they were."

Not wanting any of her rage to spill over on her visitor, Selena let both of her hands slip downward, under the table, and she sat digging her long fingernails into the sides of her chair's seat. "Did they appear to be intact? Or wounded by his struggles with 'em?"

"Oh, nay. They were perfectly whole, mistress. As perfect as if they were still alive."

She pondered this. "Hmm. Then he must have suffocated them somehow, wouldn't you think? Caught them in jars quite likely and sealed off their air."

Again her guest shrugged. "Aye. He might have done."

I'll smother *him!* a voice within Selena declared. Godless fairy killer! I shall close him off from the air somehow and see *him* suffer that same horrible death!

But, nay, a more forbearing part of her countered. Why, she had told Eddie just the day before that not even witches should be allowed to claim a human life, and she knew she'd have to obey this primordial law or risk having her magical powers revoked by the Heavens.

Nay, indeed, she thought again, narrowing her eyes and pursing her lips. There certainly were other, far more imaginative—to say nothing of torturous—ways in which to punish Prescott's pitiless nephew for these crimes.

Stafford Pearce had just finished taking a fireside bath in his suite and was settling into bed for the night. An hour or two after his conversation with Edward the stable boy that morning, he'd happened upon a book in Brenna's library on the subject of ghosts, and, given the strange experiences he'd had since arriving at the manor, he was, naturally, interested in reading it.

Not wishing to risk having any of the staff think him crazed for this choice of topics, he'd stowed the volume in his waistcoat and smuggled it up to his bedchamber just before the midday meal had been served. So now, having locked his suite door for the night, he felt safe in withdrawing it from its hiding place, just under the right side of his mattress, and crawling into bed with it.

It was a relatively thin book; but many of its passages were in Latin, he acknowledged with an irritated cluck, as he began thumbing through it. It wasn't that he hadn't been amply schooled in the language. He'd certainly held his own throughout his tutored and university years with this ancient tongue. It was just that he realized now, at the end of what had proven a rather frustrating day, that he simply didn't have the energy for lots of deciphering.

He opened the volume to its beginning. Read its mercifully all-English introduction and what he could of its first chapter. Then, coming upon a long stretch of Latin, he got up and slipped the book back under his mattress with a yawn.

It really hadn't revealed much so far, he thought, throwing off the terry cloth robe he'd donned upon stepping out of his bath. He then extinguished his nighttable lamp and got back into bed. What he'd read of it thus far had merely consisted of a self-indulgent and rather endless exposé on the part of the author, one Andrew Payne, as to why he'd undertaken the task of writing about the accounts of ghosts, which he'd gleaned, purportedly, from years of interviewing those claiming to have witnessed them.

But there was always tomorrow and its far brighter sunlight by which to read farther, Stafford told himself; and, feeling suddenly overcome with sleepiness, he reclined and pulled his propped up pillows down after him. He let his head come to rest upon them, as, naked, he nestled in among the bed's linens.

Slumber was quick in coming. As if he were exhausted by a day of heavy laboring, it enveloped him now like a warm unearthly fog—seeming to promise an entire night of insensibility. And off his spirit drifted, relieved, as it always was in sleep, of the often daunting responsibilities of carrying on his family's good name. He was no longer Lord Pearce, striving to meet his uncle's obligations in a rather inhospitable country, but some nameless soul sailing, as the clouds on a half-sunny day, across the blue nothingness of sky.

And all was well in this land of nod. A trouble-free realm in which he could usually step back from even his nightmares and view then, with as much impunity as if he were merely watching actors in a play.

But, as had sometimes happened to him before, he suddenly became aware of the same mood, sights, and sounds as had been contained in his dream of the previous night. And his wonderful obliviousness began to fall away from him, like a Yorkshire pudding caving in at its center.

It was that damnable Irish peasant again! The one he'd felt so compelled to lust after in his sleep the evening before. Only this time, it was not him after her, but the opposite—her otherwise diminutive form somehow stretching now so that she not only lay over the entire length of him, but was pinning his ankles and wrists to a forest floor!

Still naked from his bath, he could feel the cool moist soil squishing beneath him, as, to his dismay, the brunette bent forward and kissed his lips. Her mouth tasted of some distillation of cherry juice. Seeming to be half perfume and half liqueur, it trickled down his throat with each of her tongue's probing strokes.

'Tis *poison,* he thought, beginning to feel panicky as its potent warmth streamed into him, its strong intoxicating scent overwhelming his nostrils. But, no, it couldn't have been, he realized, for it was clear that she'd been drinking it, too, and it certainly had not weakened her in any way. Indeed, she seemed as strong as an ox as she continued to hold him fast amidst his struggling to break free.

"What do you want of me?" he managed to choke out, as she finally lifted her smothering lips from his.

"Supremacy, of course," she answered with an Irish brogue.

Then, throwing her head back, she let a wicked laugh escape into the night's darkness.

Her hair was what caught Stafford's attention in those seconds. Thick and black it was and straight as a Chinaman's, where it flowed down well past her shoulders and over her chest. And, all at once, he also became aware that she no longer wore her loose-fitting crofter garb of the night before, but was as naked as he—her firm well-rounded breasts seeming to dance with the motion of her torso as she continued to laugh at his query.

"But why?" Stafford pursued with as much presence of mind as he could summon, given the eroticism of his circumstances.

She didn't answer. She merely stared down at him once more, her eyes no longer those of a woman, but glittering and gold, with the daggerlike irises of an enormous cat! She wasn't *human,* Stafford realized with renewed panic running through him. It wasn't a peasant who held him captive now, but, God help him, some sort of *creature!* And, as if to confirm this, her next utterance came forth in a feline hiss.

"Because this land is not yours! Indeed, it never shall be!"

"Let me up," he ordered, doing his best to sound masterful.

She chuckled again, this time with her glowing hypnotic eyes looking squarely down into his. "Nay."

But he mustn't show fear, a voice within him suddenly counseled. If indeed this was some manner of animal he was dealing with, his long experience with hunting hounds and horses had, at least, taught him that much. "Let me up at once, wench," he shouted again, "or I swear I shall see you lashed!"

"And I shall see you raped, Stafford Pearce," she retorted in an equally threatening voice, "just as you invaders have come raping Erin's women for the past one thousand years!"

He shut his eyes against her mesmeric gaze. Then, arching his back, he thrust his pelvis upward in another adamant attempt to throw her off of him.

It was to no avail, however. As if somehow able to anticipate this move, she parted her thighs in that same instant, and it was by his own foolhardy force that he found himself rammed up into the sucking depths of her—as vulnerable to her carnal claiming as any Irish maiden to a conquering chieftain!

"No, damn it," Stafford heard himself cry out, and, as if awakened by the sound of his own voice, he suddenly became aware that he was not truly being held upon a forest floor, but still back in the safety of his spacious bed in Brenna Manor.

He heaved a sigh of relief as his eyes fell open to the familiar moonlit shapes of his chamber. His armoire, his wardrobe, the two camelback chairs near his west window—they were all present and precisely where they should have been. And he again acknowledged that he'd simply fallen victim to the seeming reality of a mere dream.

He sighed once more and decided to roll onto his right side and give sleeping another try. Now that this ludicrous nightmare had returned and played itself out in his mind to its apparent conclusion, he reasoned that he'd be rid of it for good and all.

As he moved to curl into fetal position, however, he discovered that part of the bad dream remained. While he was no longer lying in soil, but upon the warmed linen of his bed, his wrists and ankles were *still* splayed out spread-eagle as they had been in his incubus, and, despite his best efforts now, he couldn't move a single one of them so much as an inch in any direction!

He grunted in the darkness, fighting with all his might against whatever invisible force was holding him to his wide mattress.

Pinned. *Pinned,* he thought peevishly, *like one of my butterflies!* Though why such an analogy should occur to him at so harrowing a moment, he would never know. In fact, it seemed more someone else's thought than his own.

What on earth was fixing him there? he wondered again, looking anxiously over at each of his wrists, but seeing absolutely no binding about them in the moon's dim light. Oddly, he felt no bindings either. Not the wetness of some sort of glue on the backs of his hands, nor the invisible grasps of any phantom who might have followed him out of his dream.

There was only a queer sort of pricking sensation in the center of each of his palms and the backs of his heels. It was as though someone had driven a pin through these points on his body and that they alone were what held him fast.

But that was *impossible,* he told himself. Nothing so insubstantial could ever fasten a fifteen-stone man to a mattress!

Again he fought against the bondage, gritting his teeth and jerking up on each of his limbs by turns until he was forced to sink back upon the bed in total exhaustion.

He'd have to call for Flaherty, he sorrily concluded. He would simply have to swallow his pride and scream out for help, before the diabolical force which held him began causing further injury.

But no, he thought. Trying to rouse the steward would only lead to inadvertently waking some of his other servants, and it would hardly do to have everyone in the household learning of this mortifying development. In fact, if Brenna's staff was half as given to gossip as the one his father employed in London, word of it would be spread throughout the entire county within just an hour or two!

He would simply have to wait until morning, he stoically resolved. He would have to stay awake and guard against any further harm to his person until sunrise arrived and his absence at breakfast caused Mr. Flaherty to come up and knock on his suite's door.

After that, Stafford would just have to pray that the steward would obey his order to bring no one else in with him as he entered, and that there was presently enough cash in the Pearce coffers to keep the Irishman's mouth shut regarding what he was about to behold!

Six

Just as Stafford had surmised, it was indeed his absence from breakfast that prompted Flaherty to come looking for him. Having lost his battle to sleepiness shortly before dawn, the steward's loud knocking awakened him now.

Pearce started at the thunderous noise. "What?" he called out groggily, lifting the right side of his face from the mattress to discover that it was still the only appendage he *could* lift.

" 'Tis I, sir. Mr. Flaherty," the Irishman answered in a concerned tone. "I was simply wonderin' if you would prefer to take your mornin' meal in bed today for some reason."

Stafford raised his head an inch or two more and coughed slightly, his immobile state having caused his throat to become congested over the past several hours. Though he'd finally dozed off, he wasn't in the slightest bit rested. Indeed, it felt as though his pinned limbs were the only parts of him that had actually managed to fall asleep!

"No, Flaherty. Just come in here now," he said loudly in reply.

"What?" the steward asked, clearly unable to hear him well enough from where he stood outside the adjacent sitting-room door—the only entrance to Stafford's suite.

"I said, 'Just come in here,' " Pearce shouted; and to his relief, his outcry was followed by the sound of the door's handle being tried.

Dear God, it was *locked*, he realized. He remembered now that he had locked it the night before in order to avoid having anyone catch him in the act of reading that infernal book about ghosts.

"Ah, Christ's Church, 'tis locked," he acknowledged aloud.

"No matter," the Irishman yelled back. "I've a full set of keys in my pocket."

"Be sure that you enter alone," Pearce bellowed.

"I will. I am . . . alone that is, my lord."

"Shut it behind you," Stafford hissed to him, as the sitting-room door swung open a second or two later.

The steward obediently did so, then came to stand on the threshold of his superior's bedchamber with a cocked head and a scowl. "Why are ya lyin' that way, sir?" he asked worriedly.

"With my wrists stretched out at my sides as though I were about to be flogged you mean?" Pearce asked bitingly.

"Aye."

"Because I'm stuck here, you fool. Can't you see that?"

Flaherty moved hesitantly towards him, continuing to tilt his head to the right that he might take in the Englishman's full form where he lay spread-eagle beneath the bed's covers.

"Well, how could ya be? I see nothin' holdin' ya there."

"But something is, nevertheless," Stafford growled. "Can you honestly think that I would *choose* to have you come in here and find me this way?"

"I suppose not," the steward replied, shaking his head and continuing to look speechless at his employer's plight.

"Naturally not, man. Now get me up from here! At once!"

Having grown markedly pale, Flaherty went on keeping his distance, and it was clear to Stafford that he feared it might be some sort of contagious affliction which had put him into such a helpless state.

"Get over here, you dolt! You have my solemn vow that I am not sick with anything."

The steward began wringing his hands. "Perhaps I should send for the doctor, nonetheless, sir."

"No," Stafford thundered, fighting to sit up on his own. "Ab-

solutely no one is to see me this way or, I swear, you shall be discharged for it!"

"Oh, all right," he tentatively agreed, beginning to head towards the bed at a snail's pace. "I'll have to do what I can for ya on my own then, I guess."

His hands were positively atremble when he finally reached the mattress several seconds later. Stafford could feel the motion in them, as well as the frightened chilliness, as the poor servant made a couple admirable attempts to pull his left hand free.

"Why, it *is* quite stuck, isn't it," he noted. He stared down into Pearce's face with increased concern.

"Yes," Stafford snapped. "What do you think I've been attempting to tell you?"

"Do they hurt at all, I wonder? Your hands and feet, I mean."

"No. Not in the least. In fact, I lost all feeling in them about six hours ago."

Flaherty drew a pained breath in through his teeth and shook his head. "Oh, that cannot be good, can it."

"Please, I pray you. Kindly stop trying to deduce the cause of it and simply help me up!"

"Hmm," he said rather absently, again reaching out and attempting to lift Stafford's left hand. " 'Tis—Well, forgive me if this sounds daft to ya, sir, but, actually, it appears that our best course is to cut the mattress and its cover in the spots where your hands and feet are upon it. For, ya see, the mattress lifts when I raise your hand thus. Which must mean that's all you're attached to and, luckily, not the frame of the bed! So, have ya a knife or a pair of scissors in one of these rooms?"

Not wanting to send the steward off in search of a cutting tool elsewhere and, thereby, risk having him discuss the situation with some of his staff, Pearce racked his brain for where such an instrument might be found amongst his belongings.

"Ah, yes. In the sewing basket, which one of the maids left on the top shelf of my wardrobe. There must be some scissors in there surely."

"Indeed. Let us have a look then," Flaherty declared, hurrying off to the closet.

To Stafford's relief, he returned to the bed a couple minutes later with a pair of shears. Then, muttering something about not having seen the like of such a predicament since Wexford Town's former constable was found naked and shackled, with his own irons, to a whorehouse bed several years past, he proceeded to cut Pearce's left hand free.

Stafford instantly reclaimed use of it, bringing his palm over to his face and moving his fingers about in an effort to stimulate some feeling in them. Then, taking care not to uncover too much of his employer's nakedness in the process, the steward proceeded to clip his remaining limbs loose as well.

"There ya go, my lord," he said brightly, clapping the flats of the scissors' blades to his chest and stepping back to admire his handiwork. "Now we've only to peel those pieces of pallet off of ya and you're as good as new."

Not willing to have this bizarre experience again shrugged off by the Irishman, Stafford seized the opportunity to lunge and grab him by the throat with his mattress-coated hands.

"*What* is happening in this place?" he demanded in a near-murderous snarl. "This is the spark in the powder barrel for me, Flaherty, as God is my Witness!"

Looking shocked out of his wits by this unprecedented show of violence by the new lord, the steward fought to catch his breath.

Pearce loosened his grip so he might offer an answer.

"Saints preserve us, sir, I don't know! I swear it!"

Stafford's hold once more became strangling.

"All right. All right," the Irishman managed to choke out.

Again Pearce slackened his grasp.

" 'Twas the fairies probably, my lord. At least that's my best guess."

Stafford let go of him and, pulling the bed linens up over his privates, sat back on his heels. "The fairies?"

The portly servant took a defensive step or two backward.

"Aye. It could very well have been, I suppose. What with ya pinned out that way, as are the butterflies on your study wall."

Pearce squinted at him astutely. "Why, that was one of my first thoughts when this state befell me last night, man. That I was pinned in just the same manner they are."

"Well, there, ya see, sir. It *must* have been the work of the little people then, for they usually seek to teach us humans lessons with their deeds. That likely bein', in this case, that they simply don't approve of your collection."

"Ah, God, that's absurd! Do you truly expect me to believe that a pack of fairies stole into my locked suite last night and did this to me?"

The Irishman shrugged.

Stafford shook a down-covered finger at him. "No, no, no. I'll not permit you to blame all that has happened to me since my arrival on anything as quaint as that! Even if such a ridiculous belief could explain this last outrage, what cause would the fairies have had to poke me in the eye through my telescope and leave that mark on my neck? To say nothing of that welt which formed on my—" His words broke off as he realized that he mustn't further humiliate himself with a full listing of his mysterious afflictions.

"On your what, sir?" the steward gingerly prompted.

"Just answer my question! How do you explain those occurrences?"

Flaherty dropped his gaze. "Faith, I'm not sure I can, my lord."

"Well, I, sure as the devil, can!"

He looked up and met Stafford's gaze with great trepidation. "Aye, sir?"

"Yes. The place is haunted! There is some sort of Irish ghost in this house, and I, being the only Englishman here, have undeservedly become the object of its wrath."

For some reason, Flaherty appeared rather relieved at this deduction on Pearce's part. "Well, aye. I suppose 'tis possible," he conceded. "That is, if one believes in the existence of ghosts."

"Well, I do not understand how you can go about believing in such rubbish as fairies and not, in turn, believe in ghosts! Hauntings are, after all, a far more widely accepted phenomenon."

"Aye. Well, there's no denyin' that, my lord."

"So, then, just *who* might this spiteful spirit be? Who would have reason to come back to Brenna from the afterlife?"

"Um, I don't know, sir. The truth of the matter is that your dear uncle is the only one to have passed away here in nearly a decade, and you are the only one ever to have complained of feelin' haunted at Brenna. So, perhaps, the two events are linked somehow."

"Are you suggesting that Uncle Prescott might be doing all of these awful things to me? How preposterous," he exclaimed, waving him off. "Why, that man held me in the highest possible regard. He never was heard to say a word against me . . . No. I refuse to believe him capable of such deeds, be he dead or alive!"

"But, maybe—And, mind ya, I am simply puttin' this forth for your consideration, my lord. But, perhaps he resents havin' died, and he's findin' himself a wee bit jealous that you're overseein' things here now."

"Well, am I doing so any differently than he did?"

"Um. Nay, my lord. I guess not. But ya just never know how matters might appear from beyond the grave. Could be he's a trifle confused or somethin'."

"So you expect me to believe 'tis my uncle vexing me thus?"

"Oh, 'tis not my place to expect anything of ya, sir. I'm simply suggestin' that it might be possible."

"Well, let me tell you something," Stafford angrily replied. "I am not nearly as interested in possibilities as I am in getting to the truth behind all of these attacks against me. And, towards that end, I have sent to London for a metaphysical investigator of many years' experience."

The Irishman scowled confusedly. "A what, sir?"

"A metaphysical investigator, for want of a clearer title. A gentleman whose specialty is solving mysteries that involve ghosts and the like."

"Oh," the steward replied simply; but Stafford took satisfaction in noting that there was a markedly threatened waver in this single syllable from him.

Within two weeks' time, the date of Lord Stafford Pearce's soirée finally arrived. In accordance with Flaherty's request in the matter, Selena stood before the full-length mirror in the back of her thatch, studying herself in the beautiful ivory-colored gown she planned to wear to the festivities. Like most of the formal dresses of the day, it was a very low-cut Empire-waisted garment with tight, wrist-length sleeves that puffed out at her shoulders. Added to this was an elegant train of dark green brocade, which tied just beneath the gown's bodice and trailed out a full four feet on the floor behind her. It was a regal costume to be sure; and the emerald-studded tiara, which Prescott had bought her to be worn with this ensemble, made her appear all the more majestic in it.

"What do you think, Nola?" she inquired, turning towards her cat to give her a head-on view of the dress.

Her familiar woke from her nap and slowly ran her gold eyes over the witch—from the crest of her upswept coiffure, down to the tips of her satin slippers.

You look as shamelessly wealthy as old Prescott always intended you to in buyin' ya such things, she answered with a disapproving sniff.

"You're jealous, aren't ya," Selena observed. "You're cross at not bein' invited. Do you wish to have me change ya to a mouse? Ya know, somethin' that could slip into the great house along with me, yet go unseen."

The cat raised a whiskery eyebrow at her. A mouse? *Hon-*

estly, Selena! And have to pass the whole of the evenin' tryin' to escape the notice of the manor's scruffy cats? Surely ya jest!

The witch issued a soft, slightly embarrassed laugh. "Aye. Well, maybe a mouse was not the best of suggestions. Perhaps I could simply make ya invisible for the party. What say ya to that?"

It won't be necessary, mistress. Thank ya just the same. I would rather ya not squander your powers tryin' to keep me out of sight, when I'm so certain you'll be needin' them to keep that bad temper of yours in check.

"Mother Mary, why is everyone so fearful that I'll cause a row at this gatherin'? First Flaherty and now you. Why, ya know perfectly well that, short of the dream spells I keep castin' to win Stafford's heart, I've not done one angry thing to him in nearly a fortnight."

Well, that is only because you've heard nothin' of him. He's not come down here much, and no one's been by to tell ya of what dead creatures he's lately hung upon the great house walls. But, given an hour or two in his presence, Selena, you're very likely to find cause for lashin' out at him again.

The sorceress laughed and shook her head. "Nay. I am glad to say that I'm in grand and kindly spirits today and—" her words broke off as loud knocking was suddenly heard at the cottage's door. "Not Stafford surely," she said anxiously to her pet. "Not with so many guests to receive in just an hour."

Nay. 'Tis not his scent, the cat shot back with a shrill meow; and, after sniffing towards the threshold for several seconds herself, Selena found that she had to concur.

"Mr. Flaherty," she greeted loudly, as she lifted her heavy train and crossed to open the door an instant later.

"Good day to ya, mistress. May I come in?" he inquired. He looked nervously back at the manor, as though he feared being spotted by his employer.

"Of course," she replied, waving him inside, then swiftly shutting the door behind him. He, meanwhile, stood heedfully wiping the soles of his shoes on her threshold mat.

"What is it?" Selena inquired, noticing his troubled expression. "Has somethin' gone awry with this evenin's arrangements?"

"Well, na—nay," he stammered. " 'Tis just that, as it happens, there will be a rather unexpected guest there. One whom I felt compelled to warn ya of, my good woman."

"And who might that be?" she asked with a complacent smile.

"A fellow the new lord has hired. A metaphysical investigator I believe he's called."

"A what?"

"A metaphysical investigator. A man who Lord Pearce claims can scout out ghosts."

"Ghosts?"

"Aye. For, ya see, that is what he thinks *you* are. Or, more rightly, what he thinks accounts for the retaliatory things you've done to him since his arrival."

At this Selena snapped open the lacy black blade fan that hung from her right wrist and proceeded to stand innocently breezing her face with it. "Retaliatory things, ya say? I don't recall doin' much of the kind, Mr. Flaherty."

"Beggin' your pardon, mistress, but ya must have. For how else could he have come to be poked in the eye by a telescope and love-sucked upon the neck in an empty thatch?"

Blushing a bit, Selena batted her long dark eyelashes at him. "Oh, aye. I suppose I've placed a wee hex or two upon him since he came here. But nothin' truly harmful, I'm sure."

"Well, nay. Maybe not. But I should inform ya that that business of ya pinnin' him to his bed a fortnight past grew into a real ordeal for him. What with me havin', in the end, to employ turpentine to get all those bits of mattress stuffin' off of his hands and feet. And ya know how that can burn one's skin and eyes."

"Ah, say what ya might, Flaherty, but he was fully deservin' of that particular spell! Crucifyin' poor helpless butterflies as he does."

"Well, perhaps so, mistress," he hurriedly agreed as though beginning to fear that his absence would soon be noticed at the manor at so busy a time as this, "but I've come to implore ya not to engage in any of your craft with this investigator sniffin' about the manor tonight. For it only stands to reason that, if he has a way with flushin' out ghosts, witches cannot be too much lower on his list."

Selena fanned herself again and considered this with a dry swallow. "Hmm. You're probably right. Perhaps I had better set my magic aside for a time. At least until this stranger has left Brenna."

"Ah, now there's a darlin' lady," Flaherty praised, exhaling a relieved breath. "I knew you would listen to reason, for all of our sakes . . . In truth, it was not my plan to bother ya with news of this visitor, though Stafford told me he had sent for him a couple weeks ago. It all seemed so unbelievable to me then, ya see. Who among us had ever heard of a ghost hunter? But, then, begorra, there the man suddenly stood at the great house door this mornin', with all manner of queer-lookin' paraphernalia to be hauled in after him. And I just knew I must steal down here at my first opportunity and warn ya of his arrival."

"Well, that ya have, Flaherty," Selena said soberly. She reached out and gave his left shoulder a grateful pat. "So, now, describe him to me, if ya will. How might I know him on sight this evenin' so as to avoid him?"

"He's a baldin' fellow. And rather short, with piercin' black eyes. Just like a raven's they are, mind. And every bit as good at lookin' straight through a person. Mr. Horatio Brownwell he's called . . . Oh, you'll meet him well enough," he added, waving her off and turning back towards the door. "He's sure to stay at the new lord's side for most of the evenin', if this afternoon has served as any example."

"Hmm. Not a churchman then, is he?" she asked uneasily.

"Nay. I think not. At least, no mention has been made of any holy affiliation thus far. And he's certainly not a priest, because, even without their cassocks, I can recognize 'em right off. I was an altar boy in my youth, ya see," he said under his breath, "so I learned early not to let 'em sneak up on me . . . Well, I had better be off. You know how my maids are. It seems I can scarcely trust 'em even to pour a glass of water for anyone these days, much less to make decisions about a formal table's presentation. As I've said, I simply wanted to caution ya against any hocus-pocus with this new hound about," he finished, opening the door to take his leave.

"I thank you again," she whispered after him.

"Aye, and don't forget about takin' an indirect route in comin' up, mistress," he called back in a low voice, before moving towards the adjacent trees and making his surreptitious return to the manor.

Ah, God help us, a "ghost hunter" now, Nola exclaimed with a tsk, once Selena had closed the door after him.

"Better than a witch hunter, though, ya must admit."

I don't believe I've ever heard of such a thing. A man goin' about huntin' ghosts. What do ya suppose he does with them once he finds 'em?

Selena did her best to push down her misgivings on the subject. "I haven't the vaguest notion. It—it all sounds rather laughable to me actually."

Maybe. But, then again, Catholic or not, perhaps the fellow knows a thing or two about exorcisms. And that can't be good news for us.

The sorceress crossed back to her looking glass and resumed her coifing. "Ah, twaddle, Nola. What use would an exorcism be against you or me? There's no Devil in possession of either of us. Why, until the Christians came to this country, no one here had ever even heard of Satan. Yet, if we refused to worship the Church's God, we were, without question, assumed to be worshippin' the Antichrist! . . . Nay, I'll not be fearin' a splash of holy water and a 'be thee gone' from some pompous ghost hunter at this late stage in my life! How ridiculous," she concluded with a melodic little laugh.

Even so, you had better watch your waters with this man tonight. Until we've had the opportunity to assess his abilities, in any case.

"Never ya fear, dear cat. You have my word that I shall do my best to steer clear of him. Besides, with all of the dream spells I've sent Stafford these past several nights, he's sure to be far too in love with me to allow this pryin' visitor to come between us."

Her familiar didn't respond. She simply set her chin back down between her forepaws and issued a sigh—one which said she definitely did not share her master's certainty in this.

Seven

Having long since decided to arrive at the soirée stylishly late, Selena rode her broom to the main roadway at the stroke of seven. She'd tied a scarf about her perfectly arranged hair; and, seeking the cover of the treetops all along the way, she reached her rendezvous point with the coachman, whom she'd hired, some five minutes later. It was a well-chosen meeting place, a relatively deserted stretch of highway, which was nearly a mile to the north of the route the rest of the guests would most likely be taking to Brenna.

"Ah, Paddy, always so prompt," she greeted windlessly, as her besom touched down next to the livery vehicle. "I hope I haven't kept ya waitin' too long."

The jovial coachman smiled broadly and hurried down from his driver's box. "Not at all, mistress, I only just got here myself. Will you be takin' your broom in to the party with ya?" he asked as he reached her.

Still keeping her gown's train draped over her right arm, Selena dismounted the besom. "Nay. 'Twould raise the new lord's suspicions, I fear. In truth, I was hopin' ya might be persuaded to keep it in the coach for the evenin', that I might ride back to my thatch when ya return me to this spot at the end of the night. Would twenty pence be enough for its keepin'?" she inquired, delving into her cloak pocket for some coins.

He reached out to take hold of the broom, where it still hovered beside them. "Ah, ya know Wexford Livery will be takin' no money from you, dear woman. Not with all the good turns ya do for us townsfolk year after year. Just ye get yourself inside now," he continued, walking her over to the vehicle's door and pulling down its passenger step, "and I'll look after your broom for ya."

"Thank you, Paddy. You're too kind."

Once she'd arranged herself comfortably upon the coach's back seat, he handed the besom in to her; and she propped it up beside her with the same reverent care that she accorded to all of her magical implements.

"Pray, tell me, before we ride in, have ya met Stafford Pearce yet?" the liveryman inquired.

She smirked and carefully removed her silk head scarf. "In a manner of speakin'. But we have not been introduced, if that is what ya mean."

Paddy reached down and brushed some of the road's dust from the formal attire which Selena had requested he wear. "So, ya don't know if 'tis true, what they're sayin' about him in town."

"And what would that be?" she inquired, leaning forward on the seat to peer out at him with great interest.

"Only that he's not as affable a man as was his uncle. And that, well . . ." He paused and lowered his voice considerably, as though he feared he might somehow be overheard. "And that he is a bit odd about the edges. Collects *butterflies,* 'tis said. Then there's that other Englishman who's just arrived with all his strange paraphernalia in tow. Equipment that can only be compared to things one might find in a laboratory. And I know that much for a fact, since 'twas one of my boys who was hired to drive him here from town this mornin'. Now, please don't tell me young Pearce fancies himself a man of science. How utterly daft!"

"I really couldn't say, havin' not yet gotten to know him. But ya do have my word that, if he truly is seekin' to become a student of Nature, I shall, sure as fate, be teachin' him a thing or two about Her!"

He exhaled a relieved breath, then grinned once more. "Ah, that's our Selena. I've every faith ya will. We knew ya could be counted upon to keep this new lord as reined in as the last."

She withdrew a tiny mirror and comb from her cloak pocket and began to touch up her scarf-mussed hair. "Oh, aye. I've a good hand on him already, Paddy Murphy, so no need to fret about it."

"Well, enough chattin' then. You've an Englishman to bewitch, and I've a few deliveries to see to before I come back for ya at evenin's end. I was just curious about him, was all."

Selena nodded and offered him another grateful smile for his services. "And quite understandably, too."

At that, he shut the coach door after her, returned to his driver's box, and they proceeded to traverse the less than one mile which still separated them from the manor's front entrance.

While en route, Selena repinned her tiara to the crown of her head. Then she combed every hair back into place, brushed off the formal slippers she wore, and reapplied her lip rouge. Thus, by the time Paddy brought the vehicle to a slow and stately stop before Brenna's front walkway, she felt ready to face the night ahead.

She tucked her hand mirror, comb, and tin of rouge back into her cloak pocket. Then she straightened her posture and donned a confident smile as Mr. Murphy opened the coach door for her.

"Go get him, lassie," he whispered, while aiding her descent.

"That I will," she declared with a cosmopolitan laugh, her stride that of royalty as she made her way up to the entrance and was ushered inside by a male servant.

Nothing could have prepared her for the wave of melancholy that rushed over her as she stood removing her cloak in the entrance hall seconds later. Though everything in view looked the same as it had when old Prescott had owned the place, it all seemed so different now.

As she handed her cape to the servant, her eyes traveled up

the broad staircase to its first landing and the vase of fresh flowers which always adorned the Queen Anne tea table that stood there. She remembered a time, several years earlier, when Prescott had pulled the fresh blooms from that same vase and handed them to her, that she might be the bride with bouquet and he the groom in a make-believe wedding which he wished to enact with her.

They'd both been wearing nothing but nightclothes at the time, with the servants having all gone off to Sunday Mass; and thus it had been one of those all-too-rare occasions when they'd had the run of the place and the privacy to enjoy it.

How glorious it had been to play with Prescott! What a warm jolly laugh he'd had. What a sweet, tender smile. And what a curse always, in the end, Selena thought, swallowing back a sorrowful ache in her throat, for her to have outlived all of the men she'd ever loved.

What a curse to possess such merciless longevity!

"Mistress Selena?" she suddenly heard the servant inquiring, as though seeking to rouse her from her reverie.

Realizing that this was hardly the time for such sentimental recollections, she snapped out of her daydream. She hadn't come here to become betrothed to yet another mortal, she reminded herself hearteningly. Where was it written, after all, that a sorceress *had* to fall in love with a man in order to make him fall in love with her?

She had simply come to this party at Flaherty's request, she silently confirmed. Merely to help put an end to Stafford Pearce's curiosity about her, and thereby to prevent him from doing any further sniffing around where she was concerned.

That was all and it would likely be fairly easily accomplished, she decided once more, offering the servant a collected smile and letting him lead her on to join the rest of the new lord's guests.

* * *

Though nothing had yet been said by way of introduction, Stafford somehow knew his uncle's fiancée as he spotted her in the doorway of Brenna's ballroom a couple minutes later.

She was a slender, though somehow sturdy-looking woman, who appeared, on first sight, to be neither old nor particularly young.

Seasoned, he thought, continuing to gaze up from his polite conversation with three of Wexford's most eligible maidens. She was precisely as Prescott would likely have preferred his lovers: experienced, yet just fair enough of complexion to appear strangely untouched. Like a fresh snow in the dead of winter, there seemed a glow about her, an almost angelic quality which somehow offset the worldliness that flashed in her large eyes.

She hadn't been introduced, her name not yet called out by the steward or butler. But then, Stafford realized in that fateful moment, her arrival didn't need to be announced. Not two seconds after he'd caught sight of her, did almost everyone else in the crowded ballroom seem to do the same, and such a silence fell over the huge chamber as to cause one to think that the highest ranking woman in all of Ireland had just entered it!

"Dear God," Stafford exclaimed under his breath. Then, hurriedly excusing himself from the women, he began making his way through the crowd to where this latest arrival still stood in the room's main doorway.

" 'Tis Miss Selena Ross," Mr. Flaherty informed him in an undertone, the steward rushing to flank him as the guests quickly cleared a path for their wealthy host.

Not slowing his pace in his drive to be the first to welcome her, Pearce whispered back to him, "Yes. I gathered that much."

"She's lovely, isn't she," Flaherty pointed out.

"And a great deal more than that, it would seem, to have everyone so tongueless at her entrance."

Despite his obvious efforts to break away from his dogging

steward, the Irishman managed to step out before Stafford as he came within a few feet of his uncle's lover.

"Lord Stafford Pearce," Flaherty said officiously, "pray permit me to present Miss Selena Ross."

The steward finally moved aside and Stafford was, at last, able to close the distance between himself and this honored guest.

He greeted her with a smooth "How do you do?" and a kiss to the back of her right hand. As he brought it up to his lips, he noticed a large emerald sparkling on her ring finger, and he knew in a glance that it must have cost its purchaser a small fortune. That had, no doubt, been Prescott, he concluded.

"Very well. Thank you," Selena said in return, her tone as aloof as a French princess's. "How do you do?"

Her cool manner prompted Stafford to relinquish his hold upon her hand. "Far better now that I am finally being given the opportunity to make your acquaintance, my lady. How very good of you to have come." This certainly wasn't going to be an easy woman to plumb, a voice within him cautioned.

"Aye. Well, I'm told it was at your *special* request." She looked right past him, her eyes scanning the walls of the ballroom. "I must say, it does seem as though ages have passed since I was last in this house."

When she focused upon him once more, her gaze was so challenging that it made Pearce gulp.

"I hope ya have not seen fit to change it much," she added.

"Well, no. Not—not much," he replied, inwardly scolding himself for stammering like a damned schoolboy. Why on earth did it matter what changes he'd made to the place? Every inch of it was *his* now, after all. His solicitor had assured him, more than once, that because this woman had failed to marry Prescott before his death, she held absolutely no legal claim to it.

Nevertheless, she had Stafford rather ruffled, for some reason. In fact, he found himself forced to lock his hands behind him, in order to keep her from seeing their slight trembling.

"In any case, my dear, you are even more beautiful than I

imagined you would be," he declared, hoping that his renowned charm with women might help him through this tense discourse. He simply could not afford to show much vulnerability, with most of Wexford's gentry watching.

To his relief, she smiled. Unfortunately, however, he was soon to learn that this was more out of coyness, than any sense of having been complimented.

"Oh? Well, then, pray tell me, Lord Pearce, have ya *much* of an imagination?"

Though he did his best not to reveal it, he silently damned her for succeeding in turning his own words against him. Then, as if by divine intervention, a suitable retort popped into his mind. *"Enough* of one for such things, I suppose," he replied, raising a roguish brow at her.

A whisper of a smirk fluttered over her lips. "Very good, sir. I was wonderin' when ya might savvy me."

Stafford couldn't help taking in her high cheekbones and the elegant line of her nose. She was, without question, the most indomitable-looking woman he had ever set eyes upon. And, as it was turning out, one of the most sportive as well. "Oh, but I fear I've only just begun to, my dear lady," he replied in his most winning voice. "So, would you permit me to show you about the first floor for a few minutes, that I might better get to know you while you see for yourself how little I have, indeed, altered Brenna since my uncle's passing?"

"Ah, nay. Thank ya, sir, but I do not wish to take ya from the rest of your guests."

"Oh, you wouldn't be," he assured. "Well, not for long, in any case. It will only require a few minutes, as I've said."

Despite her invincible air, he somehow found the mettle to punctuate this invitation by extending an arm to her.

The awful silence in the room seemed to grow even more vacuous, as he awaited her reply, all the while knowing every eye was still upon them.

To his further dismay, she did not respond immediately, but

simply offered him an unreadable expression. He, in turn, couldn't seem to avoid meeting it with a rather imploring gaze.

Then, mercifully, some unspoken language began to pass between them, one which said it would hardly prove fitting for her to play the shrew in refusing him, nor for him to be needlessly humiliated by her doing so.

"Very well," she replied, pursing her lips slightly and taking hold of his elbow with the most reluctant of grips.

"You did not like that, did you," he noted under his breath, once they were well into the adjoining hallway.

She didn't turn to look at him as she answered. She merely stared straight ahead, as he began leading her towards the parlor. "Like what? Your takin' charge of matters just now by offerin' me a wee tour of the place?"

Her dangling emerald earrings and the slight backward breeze against her soft tendrils of black hair were what caught Stafford's eye as they continued walking. She managed to capture his sense of smell, too, as he suddenly noticed a most exquisite scent wafting from the vicinity of her bare neck and shoulders. It was a perfume of honeysuckle or, perhaps, lily of the valley, he deduced. "Precisely."

"Well, is that not what you Englishmen do best? Take charge? Haven't ya a grand talent for orderin' us Irish about?"

He stopped walking and fixed her with as pleasant a look as he could seem to muster. "But I did not order you to come with me, my dear, and you know it as well as I. I merely asked."

She nodded, as if in agreement. "Oh, aye. Just as ya 'asked' that I come here tonight by havin' your steward search *the whole of the county* for me."

"Again, nothing more than an invitation, Miss Ross. I hardly had the authority to summon you," he said with a suave laugh. "So I do wish you would stop implying that that is what has occurred."

She narrowed her eyes at him. They were two beautiful, almond-shaped orbs with centers so deep and green that Stafford could almost imagine himself drowning in them. And, all at once, he became aware that she was extracting some piece of information from his mind.

There was something she sought to know about him with every bit as much curiosity as he felt towards her; yet he couldn't imagine what it might be. Her gaze was simply too hypnotic for him to feel anything but numbed by it.

Blast it, Selena inwardly exclaimed in those same seconds. He wasn't enamored with her yet! In spite of the dream craft she'd repeatedly worked upon him, he'd somehow managed to remain fairly unaffected. In fact, it appeared as though he didn't even recognize her spirit as being the entrancing entity who'd been coming to him in his sleep.

She would have to start all over again, she angrily concluded. It was, most certainly, back to the cauldron for her, where she would have to conjure up something far more potent.

She had thought, because her dream spells had proven so immediately effective on his uncle, that they would be well matched to this junior Pearce as well. But she realized now just how wrong that assumption had been.

"Miss Ross?" she heard him query; as, in her aggravation, she'd dropped her gaze, inadvertently letting him slip out of her brief mesmerism.

"Aye?" she answered downheartedly.

He began leading her towards the parlor once more. "I'm sorry, but I seem to have lost my train of thought. In truth, I can't remember what I was saying to you just now."

"Only that ya wanted me plain on the fact that you did not summon me here this evenin', but merely invited me."

"Right," he said brightly. "Oh, and, now I remember what more I wished to tell you. That is, I just want you to know that I hope it was not much trouble for you to come. Do you live quite a distance from Brenna now?" he fished.

Dear Jesus, Selena thought, doing her best not to let her irritation with the situation show, *here begins his barrage of nettling questions!* "Nay. Not far," she said simply.

"What? You mean, just in town?"

"Aye," she lied, thinking this as safe a response as any.

"Oh. At a family residence then?"

She nodded, weighing her next words. "Aye. 'Tis a modest abode, but certainly one long held by my kin."

"Well, I've no doubt you come from very fine lineage, given my uncle's impeccable taste in women. Tell me, did you know one another for many years?"

"Aye."

"Then, might I be so bold as to ask why—"

"Why we never married?" she finished for him, now finding his line of inquiry not only painfully predictable, but unabashedly patronizing.

"Ye—yes," he faltered, as though sensing this resentment in her.

"I don't know," she fibbed. Then, again realizing that he was definitely the sort to press for more of an answer on so crucial a point, she offered, "I suppose 'twas because we grew complacent. Prescott had always been in good health and young for his years, as ya probably know. So we thought we had more than enough time left to us for nuptials. Then, too," she added, having finally managed to call to mind a most convincing excuse for their inaction on the matter, "we were of different faiths, as ya might have guessed."

Just *how* different she was sure he couldn't have guessed! But she was, of course, content to let him believe it was Catholicism, rather than Druidism, which had dissuaded their union.

"And neither of us seemed willin' to convert for the other," she concluded.

"Ah, yes," he replied, dropping his gaze just long enough to make it appear that he genuinely felt badly about how matters had turned out between her and his uncle . . . When, in truth, Selena thought, *he* was the one who had most benefited from it all.

"Well, I quite understand," he went on, meeting her eyes again. "I would not have agreed to become a Catholic either, had I been in Prescott's stead."

Though Selena had, naturally, never been overly fond of some of the teachings of Ireland's Church, she was suddenly struck with the urge to see him smacked in the back of the head for having made so tactless a comment. Especially to a woman who was clearly still in mourning over his uncle's passing.

Such spellcraft would be too obvious, though, a sagacious voice within her warned. It just wouldn't do to call forth such a hexing action with that ghost hunter fellow on the premises. So, after giving it a few more seconds of consideration, she settled for simply making one of her host's polished boots skid out from under him as they continued to walk along the well-buffed marble floor of the corridor.

In the space of a heartbeat, Stafford's right ankle had turned beneath him and he was lying face-down just before Selena.

She bit her lower lip in an effort to keep from laughing aloud. Then, feigning a gasp, she padded around his long, sprawled form and bent from the waist to stare down at him with an expression of great concern. "Dear me," she said softly, cocking her head. "I truly hope ya haven't hurt yourself, sir."

He looked up at her just long enough to roll his eyes as though roiled. Then his long, muscular arms pushed his torso upward and, bringing his legs forward, he rose on his knees and sat back on his heels.

"Deuced maids," he snarled. "Forever laboring to keep these floors scrubbed to a high gloss! They're *floors,* for the love of God, not mirrors!"

"Oh, well, do let me help ya up," she declared, stepping in front of him and extending one of her pale, bejeweled hands downward.

"No. 'Tis all right." He cupped a palm to the right wall of the corridor and struggled up to his feet on his own. "I'll simply have one of the maids discharged because of it, and I'm sure 'twill make me feel a great deal better."

"Oh, ya won't," Selena exclaimed, clapping a hand to her mouth as it began to dawn on her what hardship she might inadvertently have just caused for one of Brenna's servants. "Pray tell me ya won't do that, sir!"

He flashed her a questioning look, as he began limping forward once more. It was as though he couldn't imagine why she might care about one of the servants being sacked. "Very well then," he said tentatively. "If you really feel so strongly against it, I won't. I shall simply have the dumb wenches sprinkle these halls with sand henceforward against anyone else slipping to his death!"

"Ah, you're just angry because it hurts, most likely," she returned gently.

He squared his jaw and donned a stoic expression. "No. 'Tis all right. We Pearces are rather impervious to pain actually."

Selena, in response, brought her unopened blade fan up from her right wrist and pressed the top of it over the smirk she was fighting. "Oh, aye. I've no doubt. Even so, I'm sure it must have smarted a little. What with it havin' been so thunderous a fall. Why, please take no offense, sir, but ya did sound a bit like a great overripe melon hittin' the floor."

He paused, as they finally reached the parlor, and offered her a scowl which said he welcomed no more talk of the mishap. "No offense taken," he said in a near growl. Then, waving her into the room before him, he returned to his former gracious tone of voice. "You see," he declared with a broad sweep of his right arm. "I can't be so bad a chap, can I? Not when I've kept everything in here exactly as my uncle left it."

Selena ran a careful eye over the chamber from one of its ends to the other. "Nay, now, hold a moment, Lord Pearce. I believe I do see a wee change to this room."

"And what is that?"

"Why, this," she answered, striding over to the telescope, through which she knew he'd been surveying her thatch off and on in the past several weeks. "This is new, is it not?"

Stafford hobbled after her as she finally reached the device and bent to peer into its eyepiece—her well-rounded posterior protruding alluringly out behind her. "Oh, yes. So it is. I had the steward purchase it for me in town."

"What? To observe the Heavens?" she asked innocently, continuing to look into it.

He drew up next to her, still feeling a bit on edge as he always did whenever anyone toyed with his belongings. "Yes, in fact. That is precisely its purpose"

"Hmm," she said, drawing her eye away from it and turning to gaze at him with an artless flutter of her dark lashes. "Why then is it not pointed at the stars, I wonder? All I see out of it is that seaside cottage. Pray, do not tell me, sir, that ya sometimes use it to spy on those about the grounds," she said with a gasp.

"Oh, no, no," he denied, quickly tilting its far end upward. "It simply must have been bumped out of position. Perhaps by one of the maids when they were dusting in here."

Selena pressed her folded fan to her chest and continued to gape at him. "Well, let us hope that is the case. For we wouldn't want ya to be deemed a peepin' Tom! Why, a man could wind up in jail for such an act, couldn't he now?" she asked, her tone striking Stafford as so strangely knowing that it almost seemed she was issuing a slight threat to see that Wexford's constable was told he'd been engaging in just that. "Surely ya take my meanin', don't ya? Usin' it, for instance, for catchin' sight of one of your servant lasses undressin' or bathin' in yon quarters to the south. And—"

"Oh, yes, Miss Ross," he interrupted. "Your words carry my full understanding with them. You needn't say anything more on the subject," he concluded, nervously giving the telescope's main tube another push skyward. "Now, let us move on to the next room, shall we?"

He again took her arm and off they went, across the corridor to his study.

Selena did her best not to show her repulsion as his heinous collection of dead butterflies caught her eye upon their entrance. "Begorra, how dishonest you're provin', Lord Pearce, when here, in this room as well, there is such an obvious change before me!"

He strode farther into the study and turned back to her with a puzzled smile. "And what is that?"

She pointed to the wall over his desk and his gaze followed her finger.

"Oh, my collection, you mean? Ah, well, 'tis a small addition really. But I do feel it has lent some much-needed color to the room, don't you?"

She pressed her lips together in an effort to hide her clenched teeth. "What I feel, sir, is that the things of Nature belong in Nature. Out-of-doors, where everyone, and not merely *English lords,* are allowed to admire 'em!"

He gave forth a light laugh as though taken aback by her anger on the subject. "Well, yes. But I have only claimed one of each type I've encountered. 'Tis not as if I have hunted any of them into extinction, mind you."

"Nevertheless, I feel compelled to inform ya that I find such displays barbarous! Deer heads, stuffed birds, dead butterflies, the whole horrible lot of poor creatures you men feel ya must—must *crucify* in order to show your supposed power!" With that, she turned on her heel and flounced from the room.

"Miss Ross?" he called out in befuddlement, hurrying after her as she fled into the corridor and out onto the nearby terrace.

She was leaning against the far balustrade as he caught up to her several seconds later; and his profile view of her in the dim light of dusk told him that she was almost gasping for breath. It was as though she'd somehow grown nauseous indoors and had found herself in desperate need of fresh air.

"Miss Ross?" he said again, coming up next to her. He didn't know why, but he was finding himself feeling not only moved, but strangely aroused by the vulnerability which her fleeing had seemed to indicate.

To his further surprise, she turned in response to his nearness and flashed him a look that was so scornful that he instantly drew away from her.

" 'S'death! Are you all right?" he queried softly.

She directed her gaze back out at the sea and, throwing open her fan, began waving it before her face with great rapidity. "I'll be fine. Thank you."

"You know, my dear," he began again in a honeyed voice. " 'Tis not disregard for butterflies that has moved me to collect them thus, but my great admiration for their beauty."

"Ooh, Saints preserve us! I can only pray ya never find *me* as comely!"

Stafford laughed at this seeming witticism on her part, only to realize that she didn't, in the least, appear to have uttered it in jest.

"Honestly, Miss Ross," he went on with renewed sincerity, "as difficult as this may be for you to believe, I am probably no more fond of seeing buck heads mounted in people's homes, than you are. In truth, I can even understand your aversion to stuffed birds. But, though I try never to argue with my guests, I must point out that butterflies *are* insects. And, while Mr. Flaherty has been good enough to inform me that you Irish think them somehow capable of turning themselves into fairies from time to time, I do hope you'll bear in mind that, being an Englishman, they are, nevertheless, simply insects to me and likely always will be."

She turned her gaze slowly from the sea, one beguiling green eye and then the next fixing upon him with such intensity that he felt suddenly lashed where he stood. "Lord Pearce, has it never occurred to ya that we humans might often seem like mere insects to God? Indeed, some days I think it a very sound wager that we do, and you don't see Him usin' this as carte blanche to pin any of us to some great wall in His Kingdom on high!"

Stafford drew back his head, stunned at this most unlikely comparison. He'd known, since the day he'd asked Flaherty to invite his uncle's fiancée to this gathering, that she probably wouldn't share his views on many things. Nevertheless, he hadn't planned on having to parry with such a wit. "While that is an extraordinary observation," he said after several seconds, "I should note that I hardly think of myself as being anywhere near as benevolent as God!"

"But you think yourselves gods, nonetheless, don't ya? You English noblemen, comin' to this sacred isle to rule over its natives!"

Again she had him nonplussed. "Well, I—had never thought of it in such terms. I simply inherited this manor from Prescott, as you know, and I—"

"Whisht," she interrupted, suddenly realizing that all she'd likely do in pursuing this topic with him would be to utterly alienate his affections—if, indeed, she had much chance of winning them. "Pray, let us not argue, my lord," she went on, her tone now ingratiating. "May I simply inquire instead as to why it is you asked me here tonight?"

"That I might finally meet you, of course."

"But why? Prescott is gone now, and, as I am sure you're aware, I've no lawful claim to Brenna. So, what business have we between us?" she concluded, running a provocative eye down the length of him, from his chin-high white collar to the cuffs of his formal knee-length breeches. In this light from the doorway's lanterns, she could study him so much better than she had on the few occasions when he'd visited her darkened thatch; and her breath caught in her throat as she acknowledged how much he resembled her dear Prescott. He had the same enticingly dark eyes, the same square and strangely invincible jawline.

So much of his sweet uncle was here before her again, and yet, to both her dismay and her secret delight, it was all contained now in the well-built body of a much younger man.

"All right," he began again, looking rather surprised by her unrestrained scanning of his form. It was as though he'd never encountered a woman who had so straightforwardly surveyed him. "I must confess, I suppose, to having at least one small aim in inviting you this evening."

"And what is that?" she asked, a smile tugging at the right corner of her mouth.

"Well, I thought that, because my uncle fared so well here with you at his side, I might become more widely accepted by the local folk if I befriended you as well."

"Hmm," she replied, pressing the top of her closed fan to the base of her chin, then running it slowly, suggestively down her neck to her cleavage. "That's an interestin' supposition, my lord. But I feel I should remind ya that Prescott and I were a great deal more than friends."

To her satisfaction, this made his cheeks flush. Vulnerability and boyishness, she thought triumphantly. How she loved those qualities in a man!

"Oh, yes, yes," he replied. "I am well aware of that, and I—"

Before he could finish, however, they were interrupted by the call of a short balding gentleman who was clad in somewhat less formal attire than theirs.

The ghost hunter, Selena realized in that instant, as both she and Stafford turned to face him. And, as her eyes fixed upon the stranger's and she saw that they were every bit as dark and piercing as Flaherty had claimed, she knew that she was absolutely right in this assumption.

"Pardon me, Lord Pearce," the fellow said with a clumsy chuckle, "but your steward asked me to come out and inform you that the evening meal is very soon to be served."

"Oh, yes. Thank you, Horatio," Stafford returned. "May I introduce Miss Selena Ross?"

The little man hurried out to where they stood and, taking Selena's right hand in his, pressed an obligatory kiss to the back of it. She couldn't help noticing that his lips felt nearly as chilly as his fingers as he did so.

She met his penetrating gaze unflinchingly, all the while doing her best to offer him a smile. What a repulsive weasel he was, she thought, not caring whether his probing eyes were, indeed, capable of reading her thoughts.

"Miss Ross was my Uncle Prescott's intended," Stafford explained.

"Aha," Brownwell drawled meaningfully, continuing to stare at her. "The former lady of this manor then. Correct?"

Selena couldn't seem to keep from frowning, as she eased her hand out of his grasp. "Well, I would have been, had Prescott wed me." She then directed a questioning expression at Stafford.

"Oh, I am sorry, Miss Ross, for not finishing my introductions. This gentleman is Mr. Horatio Brownwell. A—friend of mine from London. He's simply come for a visit, haven't you, Horatio?"

Brownwell flashed her a thin smile. "Quite right."

And what a *right* fine liar you are, Stafford Pearce, Selena thought in those uncomfortable seconds. He's no friend, but simply one more of your hirelings. And worse yet, help meant to sniff out the likes of *me!*

"Shall we go in to supper, then?" Stafford asked.

"Perhaps the young lady should head in before us," Brownwell suggested gingerly, "for I need a word with you, if 'tis all right."

Selena stepped away from them with a suddenly detached air. "Fine by me, gentlemen. I shall see ya at table then."

With that she walked back inside. Unruffled, unrushed, her posture ramrod straight. This was certainly not the first time she'd had some sort of witch finder on her trail, and she positively refused to be disturbed by him.

Damned little pry! If he tried anything with her, she'd turn him into a plateful of the cook's famous escargot!

Eight

"What is it, Brownwell?" Stafford snarled in a whisper, once Selena was well inside the house.

"Well, only that I thought it important, Lord Pearce, that I share a couple of my observations thus far with you. They are concerning Miss Ross, and, once I learned from your steward that she will be seated next to you throughout supper, I thought it best to steal a word with you beforehand. That is to say, I can hardly speak in private with you about her, if she's at your side all evening."

"What is it then?" Pearce repeated, heaving an impatient sigh.

"Simply that I felt you should know that she is some sort of healer. I've been eavesdropping upon your guests. All the while appearing to be mingling, of course," he hastened to add. "And there is some talk which indicates that she has treated the wounds and illnesses of several of them, as well as those of their children."

"That *is* interesting," Stafford agreed, his irritation with the investigator's interruption abating.

"Isn't it though. When I learned from Mr. Flaherty that this woman, whose arrival brought such an apprehensive silence to your ballroom, was your uncle's affianced, I began listening round about her, as I've said. And I thought it important that you know what I've learned, before you continue to speak with her."

"You found my guests' silence upon her arrival 'apprehensive'?"

"Indubitably, sir. Didn't you?" he asked in amazement.

"Now that you make mention of it, I suppose it was a bit so. Yes. But that doesn't really stand to reason, though, does it? Not given how peacefully she and my uncle were said to have reigned over this region, and not if she truly is a healer, as you have heard tell. On the contrary, I should think everyone here far more inclined to embrace her than fear her."

"Yes. But perhaps it was not simply she who made them ill at ease, but you, sir, as well. If you'll forgive my suggesting so."

"Me?"

"Well, yes. You conversing with her, you see. Though you might become good friends, now that you have met, we cannot overlook the fact that 'twas she who stood to inherit Brenna, had she and Prescott only married."

"But I was just discussing that very topic with her before you came out here, and she didn't appear in the least bit rankled by my having fallen Prescott's heir."

The investigator raised a professorial finger to him. "I am sure that is true. But a man in my field quickly learns, my lord, that he must never be too swayed by appearances. Things are often not as they look to be, after all. So, given that 'tis possible that your uncle's ghost could be behind your vexing experiences in this place, I do feel 'tis necessary to learn all we can about his intended."

"As I've told you, Brownwell, I truly don't believe Prescott is haunting me. But I will concede that you are the expert where such matters are concerned. So, if you wish to spy on Miss Ross, very well. Provided you are careful not to be caught at it, of course. You know I *am* determined to see an end put to whatever or whomever is nettling me."

"And so we shall," Brownwell vowed, before they both went back indoors.

Selena was already seated in her appointed place to the right of the head of the table, as Stafford and his "friend" from London entered the formal dining room minutes later. She had been leaning to her right, suggesting some recipes for catarrh liniment to the female guest who sat beside her; but she fell silent now, as the new lord of the manor finally took his place at her left.

"Miss Ross," he said, smiling broadly at her, as he motioned for Flaherty to begin the pouring of the dinner wine, "I am so sorry for Horatio's interruption out there. Please refresh my memory. What were we last speaking of?"

Selena remembered the subject all too well, of course—just as she suspected her host did. But, since it suited her purposes, she obliged him. "I had just asked ya what it is you were seekin' in invitin' me here tonight."

Continuing to beam at her with admiration, he leaned forward slightly. "Ah, yes. Now I recall it. And I answered by saying that I hoped to be more readily received by the people in this area if I befriended you as my uncle did. And then . . ." He paused and laughed lightly. "You pointed out that you and Prescott were certainly a great deal more to one another than friends."

"That I did," she replied, offering him a calculating smile.

"How is it that you came to meet? You and my uncle, I mean."

"Hmm," she replied, pretending to be trying to remember. The truth of the matter, however, was that it had been such a lusty first encounter that she thought it both too embarrassing and too incriminatory to recount.

But, yes, indeed, she remembered it. All too well. The night Prescott had been traipsing through the forest to the north of the manor house, not two days after he'd first come to live at Brenna. She realized later that he must have been suffering from one of his frequent bouts of insomnia at the time. And what should he stumble upon in his restless quest for sleepiness, but a *naked* witch whirling about a clearing in the woods with a dagger in hand!

Selena had been performing a full-moon ritual at the time, in what she had always before found to be an amply secluded cluster of oaks.

Upon becoming aware of his presence, she'd, of course, attempted to make herself invisible to him. But, having spotted her, he charged in her direction—in the end, showing her the advantage of sexual relations with older men. Ultimately, to her great satisfaction, he had served as flesh and blood proof of the claim that males of advancing years, while perhaps more difficult to arouse than their juniors, were gloriously gifted with long-lasting rigidity.

And what an *enduring* lover he'd truly been, old Prescott, she acknowledged again with a secret smirk. The wind-swept upper boughs of the ancient oaks, that had surrounded them, certainly hadn't done any more rocking about than she had at his passion-crazed thrusts on that warm summer evening!

No, indeed. Prescott hadn't been a tough one to seduce and make fall in love with her. She'd only had a mere couple days of difficulty with him, before her dream-spell work had made him hers completely. And, given the intensity of their first meeting, she supposed this really wasn't surprising.

But then, realizing that her host was still awaiting an answer from her, she sobered a bit and said simply, "We met one night at a social gathering."

"Oh," Stafford replied, looking as though he found this response disappointingly bland. "Well then, my dear," he went on, his voice growing considerably lower, as the pouring wenches finally reached Selena's glass and then his, "would it be too presumptuous on my part to inquire as to whether or not *I've* any chance of ever becoming more than a friend to you?"

She didn't look away from the spicy gleam in his eyes in that instant, though she knew he probably expected her to do so. Such was the response of virgins and dowdy widows, however, she acknowledged, and she saw no advantage in pretending to be either with him.

"Anythin' is possible, I suppose," she answered, taking a sip of the pleasingly tart rosé which she'd just been served.

He again met and held her gaze, his eyes sparkling warmly. "Well, I must say that is good to hear . . . Will you excuse me again for a moment? It seems Mr. Flaherty is signaling to me that it is time I stood and offered a welcoming toast to everyone."

"Certainly," Selena replied, her eyes locking upon him, as did everyone else's, as he got to his feet.

He paused just long enough for his many tables full of guests to grow quiet. Then he launched into what struck Selena as a fairly unrehearsed speech.

"On behalf of all of us at Brenna Manor, I would like to thank all of you for coming here tonight. While I know that we are still in mourning over the death of my good uncle, I am hoping that I can serve well in his stead and that you might eventually come to hold some measure of the respect and good will for me that I know you always did for him." With that, Stafford raised his glass to toast the gathering, only to see one of the local bankers, who was seated at the opposite end of the table, rise on cue to do this for him.

"To the new lord of Brenna," the fellow said loudly, lifting his wine and smiling all around.

To Stafford's relief, the rest of his guests were mercifully quick to join in, noisily pushing up from their chairs and repeating the banker's words.

They'd been the best five pounds he would ever have Flaherty spend for him, Pearce thought with a relieved sigh, as he reciprocated the gay expressions that shone all about him, then gave the banker an appreciative nod.

After several seconds, the assemblage was again seated and Stafford, sinking into his chair as well, returned his full attention to Selena.

"Very well said," she praised, lifting her glass to him once more.

"Why, thank you, my dear."

"And how nice that our good banker was so quick to extend his welcome in response," she added, raising a pawky brow at him.

He swallowed dryly at her uncanny perceptivity. First there had been her seeming certainty about his having used his telescope for the purposes of spying, and now the inexplicable awareness that the banker had been paid to offer his toast. But, determined to give her no confirmation of what she suspected, he continued to smile evenly at her.

"So then," he hastened to say, "where were we?"

She rolled her eyes up towards the right, trying to recall. "Oh, aye. You just asked me if I thought 'twould be too presumptuous of ya to inquire if ya might ever become more to me than a friend, and I told ya that I suppose anythin' is possible."

"Ah, yes," he murmured, looking as though he wished to reach out and take one of her hands in his.

Selena, however, thought it best to sit back from him at this point, given the tenor of her next words. "I feel I should tell ya though, that your uncle was loved by Wexford's natives more for himself, Lord Pearce, than his association with me. Prescott fared well here because he permitted all those around him to do the same. And I must confess to bein' a bit disappointed in ya for thinkin' it could have come about in any other way."

"Well, in truth, Miss Ross—Selena. May I call you that?" he asked, his cheeks coloring once more.

She gave him a nod.

"In truth, Selena, I cannot imagine what I might do in Prescott's stead that could be construed as not permitting all those around me to fare well."

"But there are so many things really, aren't there? You would have only to follow the example set by the many Englishmen who have come to Ireland before ya. You might, for instance, burn the thatches of those crofters on your land whom you don't feel are payin' ya enough of their profits. Or ya might keep raisin' their rents until they have barely enough money to sustain themselves in exchange for their endless laborin'. Ha! Need I go on? The injustices committed by outlanders upon these shores date back all the way to the time of the Norse raiders. Erin has always been an isle besieged, and I must confess to bein' surprised that such a presumably educated man as yourself does not know that."

Stafford took a long drink of his wine, then leaned back in his chair. "Well, I suppose I was aware of some of what you're telling me. Lest we forget, my dear, my own England was also raided by Vikings at the same time in history. So my people were likely every bit as besieged as yours. And certainly, any fair-minded person cannot hold us responsible for the sorry conflicts that you Catholics always seem to be having with this country's Protestants."

Selena grew quiet again as the first course, a beef consommé and warm dinner rolls with butter, was served. Then, once the maids were well away, she dared to reply, her left hand beginning to close angrily about her linen serviette where it rested in her lap. "Lord Pearce," she said in a low, warning voice, "do not think for a moment that the conflicts in Ireland are about religion, for, indeed, they are not!"

He laughed, which only caused her to grow more incensed with his insouciant ignorance in the matter. "Well, what are they about then, if not for the Green versus the Orange?"

"That is simply an English lie, don't ya see? Meant to keep us Irish fightin' amongst ourselves, whilst you gentry are busy stealin' our land out from under us. Then drivin' us into the unfarmable bogs to starve. They are about us Irish wantin' you English the devil out of our country, of course! And I will thank ya not to say any more on the subject until you have somethin' of intelligence to say!"

Not knowing quite how to respond to this show of anger from her, Stafford merely gave forth a startled laugh. He then made a hasty attempt to finish chewing the large piece of roll that he had just bitten off. "Well, I am sorry to have been misinformed. But I don't know how you can deny—" He was about to say that there seemed no denying that the Catholics and Protestants in this country were genuinely at odds, when, of a sudden, he discovered that he couldn't get his upper and lower back teeth apart! In his rush to see his last mouthful swallowed, the dinner roll had somehow *glued* his jaw shut, and he found he couldn't utter anything more now than a panic-filled grunt!

Nine

"Are you all right?" Selena asked in response to his look of fear. She hurriedly brought her napkin up to her lips, stifling her urge to laugh at him.

He shook his head emphatically. Then, apparently deciding that he preferred to seek assistance from his ghost-hunter friend, he turned to where Brownwell sat at his left and clamped an entreating hand to his forearm.

"What troubles you, Stafford?" Horatio inquired with great alarm. "You look as if you've been poisoned. Are you in pain?"

Pearce shook his head once more, still unable to reply with anything but the most humiliating of sounds.

"Is he in pain?" Brownwell called across to Selena, obviously assuming that, because she had just been conversing with him, she should know.

She shrugged. "I am not sure. He simply fell suddenly silent."

The investigator pushed away from the table and sprang to his feet. "Well, Good God, woman, let us get him up! He could be choking!"

Selena obediently rose as well—meanwhile, silently uttering the words to reverse the spell. Much as she wished to continue to watch her host squirm in return for his dangerous naiveté about the local politics, she knew she had truly overstepped her bounds this time. She'd simply had no business hexing Pearce with his hired ghost hunter sitting just across from her. She had, after all, assured both Nola and Flaherty that she wouldn't indulge in such shenanigans at the soirée, and she knew now that she must do her best to make it appear as though she'd kept her word.

Even as she reached Pearce, therefore, his mouth was once again in good working order, and he was both fighting Brownwell's attempts to lift him from his chair and waving off those guests at the table who were rising to come to his aid as well.

"Are you all right?" she asked Stafford again before going back to her seat.

He opened his mouth widely and worked his jaw. "Yes, yes. 'Tis passed now, whatever it was."

The investigator expelled a relieved breath. "Well, thank Heaven. You had us frightfully worried, you know . . . What happened?" he went on, bending to whisper into his ear.

Pearce answered him in an equally hushed voice. "I don't know. I was talking to Miss Ross and I suddenly found that I couldn't get my mouth open for some reason. It was as though the back halves of my jaw had been glued shut! Most disconcerting, to be sure." He reached up and ran his fingers over his chin.

"I'll warrant it was," Brownwell replied sympathetically. "I don't believe I've ever heard of such an occurrence."

"Nor have I," Stafford hissed back, now focusing upon the great number of his guests who sat gaping at him over the incident. "But let us speak of it later. It seems we have already created enough of a fuss."

"Are you sure you're all right?" Selena asked yet another time, as the investigator finally returned to his chair. Having bitten the inside of her right cheek until it was bleeding in order to curtail her urge to show her amusement, she felt safer at this point in attempting to address the matter with him. She even punctuated her feigned concern by reaching out and placing a hand upon one of Stafford's wrists.

"Oh, I'm fine, my dear. Simply a bit of food going down the wrong passage, I think."

She nodded consolingly at this lie. "Aye. It happens to the best of us."

Pearce took another long drink of his wine and continued to try to collect himself. "So it does. And I would be most pleased, Selena, if you would call me by my Christian name, as well."

"Very well then . . . Stafford," she added with a girlish titter. Admittedly, girlishness was not her way, but, given how iniquitous she had once again just proven herself to be, she felt the need to atone.

"Are you all right, my lord?" Flaherty interrupted them, suddenly appearing at Pearce's left side. "One of the maids just told me you looked as if you'd taken ill a couple minutes ago."

Stafford waved him off. "Yes, yes. I'm fine. As I was just telling Miss Ross here, I simply swallowed in the wrong way."

"Aye, well, I am most relieved to hear it was nothin' more than that! The lass said it appeared for a moment as though you were sufferin' heart trouble."

At this Pearce scowled and turned more fully to him. "I am fine, I tell you. So kindly continue about your business and stop embarrassing me with talk of it!"

Hearing these growled words, the steward reflexively took a step back from him. "Very well, sir. We were simply worried is all."

"Well, no need to be. Now off with you, Flaherty," he concluded in a slightly louder voice.

Selena was just cutting into the evening's entrée of spiced salmon as the steward finally hurried away and her host returned his attention to her. "Tell me," she said calmly, "why were ya so rude to him?"

Stafford furrowed his brow in confusion. "To whom?"

"Mr. Flaherty, of course. It did seem to me, after all, that he was merely concerned for your well-bein' in makin' those inquiries of ya."

He continued to look befuddled. "Well, I wasn't rude, was I? What would make you think so?"

"Oh, simply the way ya snarled at him and the way he, in

turn, stepped back from ya. These do not strike me as bein' signs of an amicable exchange."

Pearce again swallowed uneasily. What a singularly *unnerving* woman she was proving to be! He was truly beginning to wonder how his uncle had endured her for so many years. "He's a servant, for Heaven's sake. Naturally there are times when we will not be in accord on certain matters. Why, you must have learned, during your years here at Brenna, that a manor's lord is often at odds with his steward's point of view."

"Ah, but there is no need to be discourteous about it, is there? Servants are human bein's too, are they not?" she asked in a sweet tone.

He pursed his lips. "I don't remember making the claim that they aren't."

She winked at him, then returned to cutting her salmon. "Well, not all of what one says is spoken, Stafford."

I'd like to say *good night* to you, my dear, he thought, his nostrils flaring. But, having been raised a gentleman and still hoping to win whatever local support she might lend him, he wisely chose to move on to another topic.

"It is rumored," he began again cheerfully, joining her in starting to cut into the evening's main dish, "that you are a healer of sorts."

To his chagrin, she said nothing in response to this. She simply scowled at him.

"Oh, I do hope I haven't been misinformed about that as well."

She continued to look uncomfortable with the subject. "Nay. 'Tis just that I'm wonderin' precisely *who* it was did the informin' in this case."

"Um. I don't know," he stammered. "I simply overheard some of my guests speaking of it before your arrival," he fibbed.

"Well, 'tis true," she conceded. "But I generally do not advertise my services," she added with a certain sternness.

Though it was clear to Stafford that he'd once again stumbled upon a subject that might prove unsettling for them both, he pursued it for want of any other ideas. "Oh. I see. Well, but, now that I already know of it, might I inquire as to exactly what afflictions you heal?"

She slanted him a provocative smile. "What is it that ails ya?"

"Me?" he retorted defensively. "Why, nothing, my dear. I was not asking in order to solicit your services. I was merely wondering if you have a specialty."

"None that I can think of. The local folk send for me due to all manner of maladies. I've even some facility with impotence, if the truth be told."

He appeared, for an instant, stunned by this disclosure. Then he donned an expression of sudden understanding. "Oh. You mean the feebleness of body that comes with illness and old age."

She looked him squarely in the eye. "Nay. I mean the sort ya first thought I meant. The kind pertainin' solely to men."

As if to spite him, the white lie that he'd told both her and Flaherty about his locked jaw earlier seemed to come back at him now—as he did, indeed, find his initial bite of salmon slipping down the wrong passage in response to her jarring candor.

Gasping, he quickly reached out and took up his wine in an effort to wash the food back.

"Faith, what a night you're havin', Stafford," Selena whispered, leaning towards him. "Do ya need me to come round and strike ya on your back?"

He gave his head a forceful shake. "Absolutely not," he said hoarsely. "I have already called enough attention to myself this evening, thank you."

"Oh, I know what it is," she declared, continuing to keep her voice low. "I've shocked ya, haven't I? You're likely not accustomed to women speakin' of such private matters."

Pearce coughed loudly, finally managing to clear his throat. "Well, not at table, in any case."

She gave forth a light laugh. "Ah, of course not. How very thoughtless of me. I sometimes forget, ya see, that there are men whose sensibilities are offended by such talk . . . Of course, they are usually the ones with the greatest difficulties in such areas—"

"I am *not*—not suffering from that disorder," he declared in a low growl. "Not now. Nor have I ever!"

"Oh mercy, of course not. And pray forgive me if it did seem I was implyin'—"

"I am simply," he interrupted again, "astounded to hear that a man would even consider taking such a problem to a woman!"

"But now pray think on it for a time, will ya? And, if ya do, I promise 'twill be takin' such a problem to a *male* that will seem the more unnatural course."

He glared at her, but, somewhere beneath it, he couldn't help imagining what intriguing ministrations such an emerald-eyed angel might devise for so intimate a dysfunction. And, in this very imagining once again lay his proof that he was never likely to need such aid. "So, what does Wexford's doctor think of your healing abilities?" he asked, the quaver in his voice half betraying his arousal.

"We have never conferred, I'm afraid. For I am often sent for, once he has declared that there is no hope left for a patient. Thus I rarely rival him for a fee, ya see. And I've found that is exceedin'ly important to men: that women not collect the money they feel should go to them."

"But 'tis as it should be, don't you think? That is, when one considers that the needs of entire households are placed squarely upon the shoulders of males."

She laughed to herself. "Well, might I remind ya of all the impoverished widows in this world who can say the same? And ya don't see many people rushin' to set those situations right, now, do ya?"

He smiled and shook his head with slight amazement, "Tell

me, do you think it even possible that I will ever say aught with which you won't feel compelled to take exception?"

She returned his smile, again realizing how overbearing she was being with him. "Aye. I do, Stafford," she replied, her eyes twinkling with sincerity. "I think whatever kind words ya might utter about Prescott will always be well received by me."

He was surprised to see what affection shown on this shrewd woman's face in that instant. She'd honestly loved his uncle, he silently noted. And, judging by the tears that welled in her green orbs now, she honestly mourned him as well . . . Perhaps she was not the treasure seeker he'd assumed she was.

"Why couldn't you save him?" he asked in an undertone. "From dying, I mean. With your healing skills."

She drew back from him a bit, her posture straightening. "Ah, faith," she choked out, "it all happened so quickly. While he was sleepin' and, consequently while I was as well."

To her surprise, he reached out in that instant and took hold of her left hand, his large warm palm gently closing about it. She simply hadn't expected such a sympathetic gesture from one who had otherwise struck her as a wholly self-serving man; and it caused her breath to catch in her throat.

"I'm sorry," she said tearfully, "but I just do not think I can speak of it this soon."

"We shan't, then," he replied, giving her hand a consoling squeeze; and they finished their meal while making nothing more than light, pleasant conversation. They spoke of Wexford's weather and what local sights Pearce should be sure to see.

By nine o'clock, all of his guests returned to the ballroom and the music of a fiddler, violoncellist, and fipple flautist began. They started with a sprightly reel, which had both the male and female dancers up on pointed toes, their arms arched above them as though they were circling a May pole.

Selena looked on, as Stafford strode away to resume the obligatory mingling he'd been doing before her arrival. Though he'd left her with a promise that he would return shortly to dance with her to a slower-paced tune, she began to wonder if it might not be best for her to simply steal out one of the doors before her presence provoked more talk of her amongst the guests. While almost all of those in attendance knew better than to cross her, she couldn't help believing that the less Stafford was told of her by others, the better.

She felt torn on this point, however. While part of her knew that making herself scarce was probably prudent, another part felt riveted by the festivities. She was compelled to stay at least long enough to bask for a few minutes in some of the lovely memories she and Prescott had made in this very room.

It was just as her fiancé had left it. Its outer walls were still draped with yard upon yard of grayish blue satin, while the arched and double-columned openings of its inner wall allowed half of the huge chamber to serve as a dance floor and the other half a sitting room for those who preferred to simply relax and chat.

Her eyes traveled up to one of the large brass chandeliers. Its four tall glass chimneys twinkled with the white light of bright flame, and she suddenly saw it as it had been on so many holidays past: adorned with a thick garland of evergreen sprigs, which were decorated with four enormous crimson velvet bows.

Many had been the Christmas and New Year's she'd spent in this happy place, with her friends and neighbors gathered so merrily about her, as they were again now. And she couldn't help wishing that she could cast herself back into those days, when Prescott was still alive.

Time marched on, however, she glumly reminded herself, and, unless she wished to have Brenna, and all the land around it for as far as the eye could see, fall into the sole control of Prescott's obviously acquisitive nephew, she had to keep marching along with it.

"Miss Ross?" she heard someone say, her vivid memories suddenly melting from view like ghosts.

She turned with a start to see that god-awful Mr. Brownwell standing just to the left of her. "Aye?" she answered guardedly.

"Might I have a word with you?"

"Concernin' what?"

He donned a casual smile, obviously in the hopes of disarming her. But it was to no avail. She saw right through him and knew instantly that he'd come to quiz her about Prescott.

What could he want to know that Stafford could not tell him, though? she wondered.

"Concerning your late affianced."

"Prescott?"

A snide smirk flickered over his lips. "But, of course. Who else could I possibly mean?"

"No other, naturally," she returned in a steely tone. " 'Tis simply that I do not understand what one of Stafford's *friends* from London would need to know about Brenna's former lord."

He did his best to look sheepish at this retort. "Well, in truth, fair lady, I am not just Stafford's friend."

She arched a brow at him. "Oh?"

"No. You see, I am also one of his solicitors, and I'm afraid there are a few still-unanswered questions about Prescott's holdings that remain to be addressed."

"Really?" she asked with a surprised rise to her voice. "And what might they be?"

He shook his head. "Oh, they're a bit too trifling for me to detail for you, I fear. Let us merely allow it to suffice for me to say that I simply wish to pose one or two easy questions to you."

She took a step back and snapped open her fan to breeze the scent of him away from her. He was clearly the intense and work-enslaved sort who most needed frequent baths, but found far too little time for them. "And what would they be?"

"Well, to the best of your knowledge, was Prescott of sound mind at the time of his death?"

She again knit her brow, not at all sure where this line of questioning was headed. Were Brownwell less repulsive, she might have gone on trying to read his thoughts. But her desire to be free of his unwashed smell, in these hot and crowded quarters, dissuaded her. "Aye."

He appeared neither pleased nor displeased with this response.

"Well, then, Miss Ross, can you tell me if he was prone to shows of anger? With you or any of his friends, for instance."

"He grew cross from time to time, of course, Mr. Brownwell. I would, in fact, find it impossible to name a man who doesn't."

"Of course you would, my dear. I simply meant, was he given to violence of any kind? Or would you have sometimes thought of him as, say, prone to playing pranks?"

"Playing pranks?"

"Yes. You know, given to trickery upon others?"

"What sort of trickery might ya be referrin' to?"

"Well, such as affixing a house guest to his mattress while he slept here at Brenna."

She frowned, hoping it would keep her sudden understanding of his questioning's aim from showing. It was not simply a ghost they were after in trying to account for the spells she'd cast upon Stafford thus far, but specifically *Prescott's* ghost.

"Most assuredly not," she answered, with what she felt was just the right measure of indignation in her voice. "How on earth could you or Stafford think him capable of so demented a deed?"

Though she was certain he saw the anger in her eyes in that instant, the impudent bugger scarcely flinched at it.

"I was merely curious was all, my lady. There have been rumors of such pranks circulating amongst Stafford's servants, you see; so I thought it best to try to get to the bottom of them."

"Well, they are plainly ridiculous. So, now, if you will pardon me, I think I will go and see if my coachman is waitin'."

With that, she made a hurried retreat out of the ballroom's main door, and, to her relief, the ghost hunter was not following her as she stole a glance backward seconds later.

Now free of him, she decided it was best to say good night to her host before leaving. She made her way to the chamber's other entrance and tried to catch Stafford's eye where he stood on the right edge of the dance floor, speaking to a tall blond woman, whom she had never met.

With some concentration, Selena did manage to make him look up at her; though he seemed far more enthralled with the beautiful stranger than she would have preferred.

He whispered something to the blonde, apparently to excuse himself, then hurried over to where Selena stood. His expression was both puzzled and troubled as he stepped into the light from the corridor.

"What is it, my dear? Please do not tell me you are leaving so soon."

She nodded. "Aye. I ought to, really."

He looked surprisingly disappointed at this news. "But why?"

"Because I—I've a patient with childbed fever to look in upon yet tonight," she replied, this explanation being somewhat accurate. The truth was she suspected that the young mother in question was fairly well out of the woods, but it certainly seemed wise to check on her within the next twenty-four hours, in any case.

Stafford reached out and firmly took hold of one of her hands. "Oh, no. Please don't leave just yet. Not before I've danced with you, anyway. I shall go and ask for a slower tune at once," he declared. "We English haven't the facility with jigs that you Irish do, I'm afraid."

"Ah, very well," she agreed, thinking it far too impolite to refuse.

He smiled back at her broadly as he drew her along through the crowd, en route to the musicians.

Though she scowled all about at how the guests stopped and watched the new lord lead her forward, she could see in their faces that they were pleased with Stafford's apparent attraction to her. And, as the waltz-like music, which he requested, began a moment later, the guests even went so far as to clear the dance floor for the two of them.

"My," Stafford murmured, as he took her into his arms and began leading her about to the lilting melody, "how silent they become whenever you enter a room."

"Ah, nay," she whispered back. " 'Tis not I they revere, but you, my lord," she replied, knowing this was only partially true. " 'Tis, after all, your first dance of the evenin', is it not?"

"Yes. I suppose there's no denying that it is."

Selena fell silent. She was suddenly aware of the great warmth he was imparting to her with his large encircling arms and body. How confident he was in his movement, how natural at guiding her about. And, all at once, she realized that she was experiencing something she hadn't in ages: a sense of being protected and sheltered. The feeling of being looked after in a way that poor Prescott's old body could never have afforded her. And while it was, admittedly, a somewhat foreign sensation, it was also unmistakably pleasurable.

She *needed* this somehow, a small voice within her sorrily acknowledged. She craved such a strong, virile man in her life. Yet, she had to assume that it was the fact that she had lived for so long without one that had caused her to forget how important it was to her. She had obviously spent too many years ministering to others to have taken her own needs into account nearly enough.

"Stafford," she began again in an undertone.

He continued to meet her gaze, as she went on trusting his feet to guide hers safely about the floor. "Yes?"

"I—I am sorry for havin' been so difficult to talk with this evenin'. For havin' been so . . . I don't know—*righteous* with ya on certain subjects."

"Not at all," he gallantly excused.

"Oh, but I have been. I have treated ya as just another loathsome Englishman who is simply beyond redemption, when the very fact that you're Prescott's nephew should have told me there's some hope for ya."

Stafford bit his lower lip, trying not to laugh at this half-hearted apology. "Oh, you are far too kind, my dear," he managed to say.

"Nay, nay. I really have been officious. Especially when I scolded ya for dressin' Mr. Flaherty down. Now that was truly hypocritical of me, considerin' that I've been known to speak sharply to him myself on occasion. He's simply the sort who invites that kind of treatment, steward or not, isn't he?" she noted, fighting a laugh as well.

"Yes. He does, rather."

"In any case, I do want ya to know that I will be your friend, as ya requested earlier, and that ya should feel welcome to ask for my counsel on local matters at any time. Flaherty knows where to find me."

"Why, thank you, Selena. You have my promise that I will." Before he could say anything more to her, however, a misstep on his part caused them both to lurch noticeably.

Her eyes grew round with concern. "Stafford?"

He winced and brought their dancing to a halt. "Oh, 'tis nothing, my dear. Simply that fall I took in the corridor earlier, I think. My ankle is acting up is all."

"Well, you must get off of it at once. What if it's broken and you're wrong in thinkin' it merely sprained?"

"No. 'Tis all right," he maintained, looking embarrassed now by all the attention that their sudden stillness on the dance floor was drawing to them.

She caught hold of his right hand, as his arms fell away from her. "Nay, now I insist that ya come out of here with me and let me have a look at it in better light!"

He smiled at again seeing such forcefulness coming from so diminutive a lady. "Very well. If 'twill make you happy."

"It will," she confirmed, and off she led him, out of the room, past a chorus of murmured questions as to where they were going and what strange malfunction had befallen the new lord this time.

A couple minutes later, Stafford was seated upon one of the

parlor's settees, his ever-vigilant steward struggling to get the long boot off of his right foot, as Selena looked on.

"Ooof, careful," she directed, "ya don't want to do that poor ankle even more harm!"

Abandoning the head-on approach with an exasperated cluck, Flaherty set the injured limb down and turned his back to his employer. He then resumed the task by bending at his waist, straddling Pearce's right leg, and bringing it up towards his own crotch. As he did so, he flashed Selena a look that said that, despite any promises she might have made him about not using her witchcraft at this function, a little "loosening" spell would be very much appreciated now.

She, in turn, assumed that he understood that such sorcery would come into play immediately. He apparently didn't, however. Indeed, his first tug in this new position proved so strong that it, combined with her unseen effort, sent him hurling at a dangerous speed towards the piano, which was situated on the opposite side of the room.

"Jesus, Mary, and Joseph," she gasped as his head hit the arm of the keyboard. "Now I've *two* of ya to tend to!"

She rushed over to the Irishman and helped him straighten back up to his full height. "I thought ya were ready for me," she whispered, so that Stafford could not hear.

Dropping the boot, the steward raised a hand to the resultant cut in his forehead with a groan. "Well, ya could have nodded or somethin' to tell me it was comin', woman," he returned in an equally inaudible hiss.

"Ah, Flaherty, ya great silly hedgehog," she said, just loudly enough for Stafford's benefit. She withdrew a small linen handkerchief from one of her gown's sleeves and pressed it to his wound. "What ye won't do for the lords of this fair manor!"

After making certain that he had a hold of this makeshift bandage, she hurried back to Pearce with a slightly flustered smile. "I hope you weren't hurt as well in all of that."

He shook his head, doing his best not to laugh at the mishap.

"No. Only stunned to see myself so suddenly freed of the deuced thing."

She knelt before him and began gently removing his right sock; and, though he tried to fight it, he reflexively locked his eyes upon her very bare cleavage. He couldn't help marveling at how this exquisitely elevated view of the bulging ivory flesh of her chest helped to quell the pain in his ankle.

"Well, let us see, my lord," she said, carefully lifting his foot with one hand and running her other softly up and down the swollen joint. "It's puffed up on ya to be sure, hasn't it."

He nodded, but her gaze remained dutifully fixed upon her task.

Then, suddenly, Stafford became aware of a strange sort of warmth flowing about the injured area, one clearly generated by her fingers and palms—though he was not at all sure how this was possible.

Those emerald orbs of hers traveled up to look hypnotically into his face. " 'Tis not broken," she declared.

He felt half-dazed for some reason. "No. I thought not."

She donned a smile that was, at once, knowing and serene. "And how's it feelin' now?"

"What?" he asked blankly.

She issued a light laugh. "Your ankle, of course."

He shook his head, as though to wake himself from a daydream. "Why, fine. *Fine.* 'Tis as if a numbing balm has been spread all about it. Under my skin, I mean. Into the bone."

She gave his heel an affectionate squeeze, then bent to press a playful kiss to the top of his big toe; and he knew that, even if just for that instant, she'd somehow claimed a part of his heart. Indeed, he felt as rapturous and vulnerable as a lovesick adolescent, as she set his foot back down upon the floor and returned to a standing position. Oddly, however, this sentiment seemed to leave him just as quickly as it had come.

"Well, no need to bind it then, I guess," she declared. "And I shan't embarrass ya by bedriddin' ya for it, with all your guests still here. But tomorrow, mind," she added sternly, shaking a finger at him, "I want ya on crutches, to take your weight off of it."

"Did ya hear that, Flaherty?" she called behind her, only to see that the steward had settled, rather unsteadily, upon the piano's stool.

"Aye, mistress. Crutches it will be," he replied in a still-pained voice.

"Faith," she said, turning back to Stafford with a grimace. "I should check to see if he'll be requirin' some suturin' before I go."

"Yes. Please do. We hardly need yet another calamity tonight. And rest assured that I shall pay you for all your services."

"Nay. I'll not accept one pence for 'em."

"Oh, but I insist that you be remunerated."

"In that case," she replied without hesitation, "I shall take Brenna's seaside thatch as my payment, kind sir."

Pearce's mouth dropped open at this, and he looked across the room to see his steward gaping with equal shock. "What was that?"

"You heard me, Stafford," she answered, as if she were asking for nothing more from him than a new gown or hat. "I want that thatch to be made my lawful property. I miss the manor and, therefore, wish to dwell near it from time to time."

"But it could bring me many, many pounds of rent money each year, my good woman. Surely you cannot think your healing services of just this evening equal to that!"

She bent forward, her palms coming to rest upon his respective knees, and her beautiful green eyes were both spellbinding and uncompromising as she spoke again. " 'Tis what I want in exchange, my lord, and, *if* ya wish to live here as peacefully as Prescott did, you shall grant it to me."

"Ver-very well," Stafford stammered, somehow convinced in those unnerving seconds that this was one of the wisest concessions he would ever make.

Ten

"Mother Mary, mistress," Flaherty exclaimed in a low voice, once Stafford had gone back to the ballroom, "how, in the name of all that is holy, could ya have asked him for such a thing?"

"Because he was foolish enough to inquire as to what I wanted! Ya heard the conversation as well as I," she snapped, starting to dab his wound with some of the brandy he'd fetched at her request.

Flaherty winced. "God, that stuff stings like the blazes! Why do ya press it to every wound ya come upon?"

"Whisht, will ya, and hold ye still! I've told ya countless times how the Wise Ones taught that it kills the peccant spirits who come to dwell in your blood whenever your skin is torn. Why, they would claim the whole of your body quite likely, if not for this stuff, as ya call it."

He clucked. "Peccant spirits, floatin' about unseen. Begorra, what will ya be askin' me to believe next?"

"Oh, ye think 'tis rubbish, do ya? You who believes in fairies and pucas. Well, let me ask ya this, mister; how many of those I've treated have fevered and died?"

"None, I guess," he answered reluctantly.

"There ya have it then. Let my successes speak for themselves . . . Anyway, Flaherty," she continued, reapplying her handkerchief to his cut, "I did not truly break my promise to ya, because I had to place him under a spell to mend his ankle, ya see. So, since, he was already under my influence, I just thought I would take it a wee bit further and ask for what I really wanted as payment. Ah, Lord, in very truth, 'tis best for all of us if I'm not forced to keep sneakin' about my own cottage this way. Just think of the lies 'twill save you and your servants with him henceforward."

"Well, I can't argue with that, I suppose."

"Of course ya can't. And, you shall see, 'twill prove best," she assured, offering him a wink and a smile. "Now, I should take my leave. I fear my tarryin' will only provoke more talk of me amongst the guests, and Stafford has already learned as much from them as I dare allow."

"Pray, let me see ya to the door and get your cloak, mistress," he volunteered, finally getting up from the piano stool and removing her kerchief from his wound. "I'll have this laundered and sent down to ya," he promised, clumsily stuffing it into the pocket of his tailed, cutaway coat. "So, what do ya think?" he continued sotto voce, as they both proceeded out of the parlor and down the adjoining corridor. "Is the new lord smitten with ya yet? For what 'tis worth, he did appear to me to be, once or twice, while ya were seein' to his ankle. But then, that enamored look seemed to fade, if you'll forgive my sayin' so, when ya told him ya wanted yon thatch."

"It didn't fade exactly," she countered. "It simply dimmed temporarily. 'Tis to be expected, of course, with me havin' so obviously tread upon the one thing he holds dearer than love. That bein' money, naturally. The English are a greedy lot, as ye certainly know."

"Aye. Well, whatever it was caused his amorous smile to fall, I sincerely hope you can make it return."

"Of course I can, ya hand-wringer! What sort of witch do ye take me for?" she snarled. But, as they passed by the ballroom en route to the front door and she again spotted Stafford speaking to that blond stranger she'd seen him with earlier, a sense of doubt began nipping at her stomach like the tip of a dancing flame.

"Who was that woman I just saw him with?" she asked

Flaherty, as they continued walking to the manor's entrance hall.

"I know not, mistress. But I shall find out her name if ye wish it."

"I do," she replied, as the male servant, who'd seen her in earlier, hurried off to get her cape.

She sensed great trouble ahead for all concerned, if Stafford was allowed to spend too much more time with that fair-haired outsider; but she'd be damned if she'd let her fears show.

Nola was curled up by the fire as Selena stormed into her thatch a short time later and slammed its door behind her.

Why are you so cross? the cat inquired, raising her velvety black head from her paws. *He granted ya this place, did he not?*

Selena propped her broom up beside the threshold and began untying the laces at the neck of her cloak. "I suppose you were watchin' me through my crystal ball all evenin'."

Her familiar pushed her tiny shoulder blades upward, as if in a shrug. *Off and on, aye. So, what of it?*

"Then you should also know he is not in love with me yet," she said in a bitter tone.

Faith, Selena, I knew that before *ya left for that silly party! 'Twas simply your deuced pride kept you from seein' it. Sure, you can get your little spells to work on him. Such as makin' him fall in that corridor tonight and gluin' his jaw shut.* Nola tsked at her and shook her head with an expression of great disapproval. *'Tis just the most important witchcraft ya can't seem to make work.*

Continuing to fume, Selena strode back to her dressing partition and began to shed her fineries. "Well, anyway, I did succeed in gettin' this thatch from him, as ya said. Fair and square, with Flaherty actin' as witness, Stafford granted it to me. So 'tis not as if he were unbendin', Nola. And, once I'm out of this damnable gown and corset, I want ya up on your feet to help me make him mine for good and all!"

The cat looked uneasy about this, as Selena peered at her over the partition.

By what means, pray?

"By every means known to witches! By dried apple blossom, mugwort, red heather, and rose. By elder, mint, sandalwood, and hawthorn flowers."

Hawthorn? her familiar exclaimed. *Selena,* nay! *Ye know full well what that does to a man!*

"And I shall hazard it. I'll not let the silly fear that he'll grow too lusty for me keep him from gettin' caught in my net this time. I want his heart in my hands forevermore! Now go jump up on my herb shelf and start battin' down all of the pouches I've named. You know how crucial cats are to love spells."

Issuing an anxious sigh, her familiar uncurled and slowly pushed up to her feet. *As ya wish, mistress. But I do pray you'll be changin' your mind about the hawthorn!*

Stafford's injured ankle was still surprisingly free of pain, as he and Brownwell retired to the parlour with their glasses of claret after the soirée.

"Congratulations to you, my lord! I think your gathering was a great success," Horatio declared, as they sank into the wing chairs on either side of the room's hearth.

"Thank you," Pearce replied, putting his feet up on the footstool before him.

"Certainly. 'Tis my most sincere belief that a good time was had by all."

A contented smile spread over Stafford's lips and he settled back more comfortably upon the upholstered seat. "Excellent, for I may need my neighbors' graces as the years unfold for me here at Brenna."

"Now, if it would not be too much bother, sir," the ghost

hunter began again in a businesslike tone, "I welcome any more facts you can offer about that incident at the table a few hours back. You know, when you told me you were unable to get your mouth open for some reason."

Pearce's satisfied expression sank. "Oh, yes. It was the strangest sensation. Almost as if all of my back teeth had been glued together! And then it passed, nearly as quickly as it came."

Horatio sat studying his face with great interest. "And you were talking to Miss Ross when it occurred?"

"Yes."

"Do you recall what you were saying to her?"

"Oh, I don't know. We spoke of so many things really. 'Tis difficult to remember precisely what subject we were on when it happened . . . Why, Brownwell? What possible bearing could that have upon it anyway?"

The investigator shrugged. "None, perhaps. But ghosts are sometimes spiteful, as I've likely told you, sir. So I simply wonder if you might have been discussing something to which your late uncle may have objected."

Stafford searched his mind, then shook his head. "No. I think not. Indeed, if there was anyone who objected to my opinions, it was Miss Ross herself."

"Oh, really? And what opinions, if I may ask, were those?"

"They were about the local political affairs in the main. She seemed rather adamant in her belief that I am ignorant of the Irish sentiment towards us Englishmen."

"And what did she claim that to be?"

Pearce chuckled. "That we get out of their country and *stay* out, of course. That it is not so much Catholic against Protestant that causes trouble here, but the Irish against England."

"And that is all you differed about?"

"I guess so. I think that was when she told me to shut my mouth, in any case."

Brownwell raised an amazed brow at him. "She told you to *shut your mouth,* my lord?"

"Well, not in those words, precisely. But, yes, she said she welcomed nothing more from me on the subject."

"And *that* was when you found your jaw would not open?"

Stafford considered this for several seconds, then snapped his fingers. "Yes. Now that you make mention of it, I believe it was."

"There you have it then," the investigator said triumphantly.

"Have what?"

"Well, don't you see? This shows that it truly must be your uncle's spirit haunting you. What with your having annoyed his affianced and then finding yourself so swiftly chastised for it."

Stafford knit his brows. "Do you really think so?"

"I feel certain of it. 'Tis exactly the sort of reprisal I would expect from a vexed ghost. In truth, I've heard tell of such retribution on the part of apparitions more times than I could possibly count through the years," he declared, shaking his head grimly.

While Stafford found his companion's suddenly grave expression almost comical, given the outlandishness of his field, another, more sober part of him held no doubt that the realm of the dead could become pretty baneful indeed.

"In any event," Brownwell went on, "I feel that, for your own sake, sir, I must be bold enough to warn you against seeing Miss Ross much in future."

"But why?"

"Because of your uncle, of course. He clearly still feels very protective towards her, to have gone to such lengths against you on her behalf."

"Yes, but, lest we forget, we do not know for sure if 'twas on her behalf that that—*jaw lock,* or whatever one might call it, befell me. That is to say, most of the pranks I've suffered here occurred over a fortnight ago. Well before I met Selena Ross."

Brownwell shook his head again. "Nevertheless, sir, I do feel that your safest course would be to avoid her."

Stafford laughed to himself. "Well, I don't know how much

luck I'll have in that. Not with her coming and going from Brenna's seaside cottage henceforward."

Horatio scowled. "But why would she be doing that?"

"Because I gave it to her," Pearce answered with a nonchalant shrug.

"You what, sir?"

"I gave her the place. You see, I had a bit of a fall in the corridor before supper this evening, and I sprained my ankle in the process. So, in return for examining it for me, she asked that I give her that thatch."

Brownwell looked, for an instant, stunned by this. Then he nodded, as though with sudden comprehension. "Oh. You agreed to lease it to her, you mean."

"No. As I have just said, I *gave* it to her."

The investigator's mouth dropped open. "An entire thatch? As payment for merely looking at your ankle?"

"Yes," Stafford shot back somewhat indignantly. "She seemed very much to want it, and I reasoned that it might work to appease everyone concerned, you see. Not only my uncle's spirit, if indeed that is what we are dealing with here, but my neighbors as well. As you yourself pointed out, Horatio, Miss Ross did seem to command a great deal of respect among my guests tonight. And, given her obvious healing abilities, it just struck me as wise to have her on the premises from time to time. To tend to the health of my servants and such, you understand," he added in an effort to better anchor his argument for the investigator. While part of him was still aware that granting Prescott's intended so much in exchange for a couple minutes' service could be viewed as an irrational act, he couldn't bring himself to look the fool now by admitting it.

"Well, be that as it may, my lord, were you not curious as to why she would ask for such a thing? Is it possible, do you suppose, that your uncle's death has left her without a home?"

"Oh, no. I'm sure not. For I distinctly remember her telling me that she lives in town, in a house long held by her family.

She simply said she misses Brenna and that the thatch would enable her to visit the manor whenever she wishes."

"Well, I hope that will not be often, sir, for I must confess to finding her spirit rather threatening."

"Her what?"

"Her spectral being. In all modesty, I must say that we ghost experts grow quite good at assessing people's spirits, whether they've left their carnal forms yet or not."

"And you didn't like her?" Stafford asked, a note of surprise in his voice.

"Well, pray take no offense at this, my lord. I know she was to be your uncle's wife, after all. But, no. If the truth be told, I did not like her in the least. In fact, she struck me as being—oh, I don't know. Almost inhuman, I guess."

Stafford gave forth an amazed laugh. "Inhuman? Oh, I do think you exaggerate, Brownwell."

"Perhaps. But there was just something . . ." Again he paused, obviously to search for the right word. "Impenetrable about her."

Pearce laughed again, this time with a provocatively arched brow. *"Impenetrable?* Good God, man. You wouldn't be saying that if you'd danced with her as I did. On the contrary, I believe that, given a bit of privacy, penetration would be the least of a fellow's problems where she is concerned!"

The investigator sniffed at him and moved to rise. "If you're going to turn my professional observations into nothing more than bawdy remarks, sir, perhaps we should resume this conversation when you can be more sober-minded."

Stafford reached out to him. "No, no. Stay, Mr. Brownwell. At least until you've finished your claret. 'Tis simply that I have had rather a trying day, you see. What with my concern that tonight's festivities would not go as smoothly as they did."

To his relief, the investigator settled back into his chair at this urging.

"All I meant to say just now," Pearce continued, "was that,

though I'm aware of Miss Ross's somewhat aloof manner, I could not help growing rather fond of her the more we spoke."

"You're not enamored with her, are you, my lord?" the ghost hunter asked, with just a tinge of horror in his voice.

"On, no, no. In truth, 'tis blond women I'm most drawn to. But, even if I were taken with Miss Ross, there really would be no unseemliness to it, now would there. She never did actually become my aunt. And, even if she had, 'tis not as though she's too old for me. Why, she looked to be a few years my junior, in fact . . . Se-leen-a," he said reflectively after a moment, admiring the lovely musicality of it. "Yes. Now I recall where I had heard that name before meeting her this evening."

"And where was that, sir?"

"From one of Brenna's stable boys. He said it to me a couple weeks ago, when we were discussing the butterfly collection in my study. Selena had, apparently, informed the lad that butterflies only live for about a month; and I remember wondering who she was and just how she had come to learn so much about them." He paused to chuckle. "By God, you would not believe how greatly these silly Irish folk object to a fellow collecting butterflies! You would think I had committed murder, the way that stable hand, and then Miss Ross tonight, fretted over it! They think them fairies in disguise or some such thing."

"Ah, yes. Wasn't that what Mr. Flaherty told you when you were pinned to your bed a fortnight ago? That it was probably retribution for what you had done to your butterflies."

"Yes. The fairies' revenge, Mr. Brownwell. Have you ever heard of aught so absurd?"

Horatio did not reciprocate his amused grin. " 'Twas Prescott's work again; I've no doubt."

"Oh, pray you, desist, man. My uncle was not fool enough to believe in 'the wee folk.' "

"No, but the woman he most held dear in this world obviously does. And you may mark my words, sir, if you chance to cross her, you are crossing your uncle's ghost as well. Which is why I shall point out to you again, Lord Pearce, that you are paying me for far more than exorcising whomever is haunting you. You have hired me to offer my most acute instincts in this case, and I assure you that they are shouting to me now that your uncle's affianced should be avoided at all costs!"

Selena was roused just after sunrise the following morning by loud knocking at her thatch's door.

"Sweet Jesus," she snarled, as she rose from her bed in the cottage's loft and threw on her robe de chambre. *"Who* has taken ill at this desperate hour?"

Though she didn't attempt, in her sleepy state, to use her powers to answer this question, her descent to the door quickly revealed that it was just Brenna's steward who had come to call.

"Begorra, Flaherty, how can ya possibly be upon me this early with all that revelin' still to clean up after?"

"I'm sorry, mistress," he apologized, hurriedly gesturing for her to let him slip inside, "but there are a couple matters I felt I should inform ya of at once."

Yawning, she stepped back so he could enter and close the door behind himself. "Well, they had better be pressin', because ya know full well the trouble I have fallin' back to sleep once I'm up."

"Oh, that they are! Indeed, I can give ya the sum of it in just a pair of sentences, if ya wish."

Selena closed her robe more tightly about her and ran a hand back over her now-braided hair. "I do," she said drowsily.

"Very well. That young lady ya asked after last night. The blonde we saw speakin' to Lord Pearce—"

"A pair of sentences, remember?" Selena interrupted with a weary sigh.

"Aye, well, she's English," the steward blurted.

Selena felt a frightened chill run through her at this revelation. *"English?"*

"Aye."

"But how can that be? I thought Stafford only intended to invite the local gentry to the soirée."

"Well, he did. But the lady in question, a Miss Carolyn Barnes I believe she's called, is presently a house guest at the O'Dugans' estate. She's one of their cousins. And they couldn't very well have left her at home alone all evenin'. So they took the liberty of bringin' her along. And, sadly, mistress, I fear ya left us too soon last night, for Lord Pearce spent a goodly share of the rest of the party talkin' and dancin' with her."

"Ah, mercy, I should have guessed she was English! None of the local women would have dared oppose me by sparkin' with him so. By the Saints, I shall tear her hair out," Selena concluded in a growl, now fully awakened by this possibly ruinous turn of events.

"Nay, now, calm yourself. Please," the steward directed. "We don't want ya all wrought up with Lord Pearce on his way to see ya."

"He's coming down here? At *this* hour?"

"Indeed he is. He claims he saw the smoke from your hearth just a few minutes ago, and he said that he had better get dressed and come to speak with ya at once. Thus I raced down to warn ya of it."

Selena winced at being reminded of this oversight on her part. Ever since Stafford's arrival at Brenna, she had unfailingly extinguished her fire before retiring each night, for fear that Pearce might spot smoke coming from her chimney by the next morning's light. She had been so upset upon returning from the soirée, however, that this task had slipped her mind. Intent upon casting the most powerful love spell possible, she'd thought of nothing but fully capturing Stafford's heart, until she'd finally drifted off to sleep.

"What does he wish to speak to me about?" she asked apprehensively.

"I'm sorry to say that I don't know. I inquired, but he wouldn't tell me."

"Oh, Hell's fire, ya don't think he's comin' to announce that he's changed his mind about grantin' me the thatch, do ya? I *knew* I should have required that he put it in writin'!"

"Well, he can hardly break his word, can he? Not with me havin' been there to hear it all said between ya."

"I fear our many years with Prescott must have muddled your thinkin', Flaherty. When will ya learn that the English are never to be trusted? Why, they've been lyin' to us Irish for centuries."

"Well, honest or not, the man is likely headed here even as we speak. So, havin' now forewarned ya, I must creep back to the great house with the fervent prayer that you'll not kill him, unless ya find it absolutely necessary!"

"Off with ya, then. And thanks for heraldin' his arrival," Selena whispered after him, as he slipped back outdoors and hurried off around the sea side of her thatch.

Though it required Nola's help, Selena was ready for Pearce when he knocked at her door a few minutes later. Having made all of her furnishings vanish, she greeted him in a pretty, if utilitarian day gown, with her waist-length hair now unbraided and neatly combed into a girlish mane down her back.

"Lord Pearce," she said with a grin as she opened the door to him.

Though he reciprocated her smile, he couldn't seem to help looking a trifle taken aback at discovering that she was indeed *already* in residence.

"Selena, my dear. I was hoping it was you who had lit the hearth."

She knit her brow. "You were?"

"Oh, yes. You see, I half feared our trespasser had returned and I thought it best, on the chance that it was you down here, that I come and warn you of him."

"Of whom?"

"Of the person who's been encroaching upon this thatch off and on for the past few weeks."

Selena felt both relieved at this news and touched by the chivalry that he was displaying in conveying it. She did her best not to let either of these emotions show, however. "Encroaching?"

"Yes. Flaherty and his stable hands keep trying to convince me that I'm imagining things, but I tell you, I am not. There's been someone coming and going from this place since my arrival, and it suddenly occurred to me this morning that I failed to warn you of it last night. What could I have been thinking?" he asked with obvious concern, reaching out to give one of her hands an endearing squeeze. "Why, I shudder at the thought of what you might have walked in upon down here! Uncle Prescott's soul would simply never have forgiven me, if some harm had befallen you due to such an oversight on my part."

"And that is why you've come?"

"Yes. And to welcome you. Provided, of course, that 'twas *you* I found herein."

Selena extended her arms out at her sides with a playful cock of her head. " 'Tis I, indeed, Stafford. Do you wish to enter? Well," she went on with a laugh, " 'tis not as if I have some of my sweetie scones or tea or even a chair to offer ya, but you're welcome, nonetheless."

"All right."

He looked, Selena thought with satisfaction, a trifle bashful at this invitation.

"You make sweetie scones?" he inquired with interest, as she opened the door more widely and he stepped inside.

"Aye. Do ya like 'em?"

He smiled. "Indeed. As did my uncle, no doubt. We Pearces have a fierce appetite for all things sugary."

"Then I shall bring ya up a batch. As soon as I'm settled in here, that is," she added, catching herself.

His dark eyes fixed upon her face with an almost reverent sincerity. "Yes. I would like that very much."

A silence fell between them. The sort that plagues tongue-tied young suitors, Stafford thought with some annoyance at himself; and his eyes searched the small dwelling for something upon which to remark.

"Is that your cat?" he asked, catching sight of Nola, where she presently sat, looking down upon them from the top of the loft's stairs.

"Aye."

"Oh, I feared she was simply one of those from Brenna's barn, come to pester you on your first day back here."

Selena's familiar responded to this slight by issuing a piercing and toothy meow. She'd always held a low opinion of the manor's feline population, and this was more than evident now in her shrillness.

"Nay, nay. Nola has long been mine."

"Well, 'twas not my intent to imply that you had taken her from here, my dear. Believe me, the place has more than its share of such creatures as it is," he said with a forbearant roll of his eyes. "And none of them too fond of the hounds I brought from England either, mind."

"Aye, well, cats and dogs, unless reared together, are often incompatible. Don't you find?"

"Quite."

Another clumsy silence ensued, and Stafford again found himself searching for something upon which to focus. Something. *Anything,* but her entrancing green eyes.

"Listen," he began again after several seconds, "might I offer you some furniture for this place? I'm sure it would prove a great deal easier to see some pieces moved down from the manor, than for you to haul chairs and such all the way from your home in town."

"Oh, nay, Stafford. I can't take aught more from ya, not with you're havin' already been generous enough to give me this thatch. Indeed, it was probably too much for me to have requested in the first place; but, missin' your uncle as I do, I'm eternally grateful to ya for it. 'Twill take some of the heartbreak from his passin', ya understand."

"Yes. Well. I feel certain he would have wanted you to have it."

This time it was clearly Selena's turn to fill the gap in their conversation, though she knew she would have been equally content to simply let herself continue to study the lulling effect her magical presence seemed to be having upon him.

"So, how was the rest of your soirée? Was it as enjoyable as I found the first couple hours to be?"

"I think so. At least it appeared that everyone was having a good time." *Bedroom* hair, an enticing voice within him suddenly whispered, as his eyes traveled down from her face to take special notice of her silky black mane.

Only little girls and Gypsies let their tresses hang so straight and free . . . Oh, and *inamoratas,* of course, he acknowledged again with a dry swallow. How he envied his old uncle now for having succeeded in bedding this one as often as he must have.

"And what did you think of the maidens who attended?" Selena fished. "Were ya taken with any of them?"

He offered a quick shake of his head. "Not really, I guess."

Ya lyin' heap of cow dung, she thought. Flaherty's already told me of the Englishwoman! And, as she stood trying to read Pearce's memories through his large brown eyes now, Selena could see that the scoundrel had even taken matters so far as to invite the blonde out for a carriage ride late in the coming week. Nevertheless, she did her best to remain sweet and unthreatening with him. More flies were taken with a drop of honey than a ton of vinegar, she reminded herself.

"In any case," he began again, seeming to want to move onto a more comfortable subject, "I um—I brought this for you," he declared, pulling a pistol from his cutaway-coat pocket and extending it to her, handle first.

She accepted it with a puzzled smile. "Did ya now? But why?"

"Well, because of the trespasser I spoke of earlier. You shall need some means of protection, should he come round again."

"A Londoner givin' an Irishwoman a *gun,* Stafford?" she asked in a salty tone. "Tsk, tsk! In a country where English landlords are in season year round? Now, what would your King say to that?"

He laughed under his breath. "Well, we needn't let him know of it. In truth, 'twas worry for your safety that woke me this morning," he confessed, growing solemn, "so I do hope you will put it to use, should it be required."

She reached out to give it back to him, her palm still open. "Nay, dear man. Thank ya just the same, but I truly won't be needin' it. There is no one in Wexford I fear."

He gently closed her fingers about the weapon. "No. Keep it, Selena. I insist. If not for your own peace of mind, then for mine."

Though she was touched by this gesture, she could see in his eyes that it was more out of viewing her as his uncle's survivor, than out of affection for her that he offered it. He thought her attractive, to be sure. But, *blast it all,* though she'd brought him close to it a few times, he still did not love her! That bloody blonde was getting in the way somehow!

"Very well," she agreed, unable to hide the disappointment in her voice, "if 'twill humor ya."

"Good," he replied, giving her now-closed hand the sort of patronizing pat a grown son might offer his mother. "And I shall also be sure to have one of my men look in on the place from time to time . . . I say, would you care to join my friend Horatio and me for breakfast? It is very soon to be served."

Had the ghost hunter not been part of the invitation, Selena would have accepted it in the space of a heartbeat. But, not wishing to subject herself to further questioning by him and afraid he'd notice the stupefying effect her magic sometimes had upon Stafford, she donned a thoughtful smile and shook her head. "No thank you, my lord. I fear I've too much yet to do down here."

He shrugged. "Suit yourself. I am simply glad, in any case, for this chance to tell you how very happy I am that you shall be staying here," he concluded, turning back towards the door as if about to leave.

"You are?" she asked hopefully.

"Oh, yes. Of course. In fact, I was just telling Horatio last night, that 'twill be most convenient having a healer about the place. One never knows when someone at Brenna might take ill or be injured, after all. Good day to you, Selena."

And, with that, he was gone. Heading back to the manor while whistling a cheery tune—as if he had just driven a good bargain with the local smithy or dry-goods merchant.

"By the Saints, I've never seen the like of it," Selena whispered up to Nola as she shut the door after him and pressed her back against it. " 'Tis as if he were a greased hog dartin' about a pen! One moment I could swear I have his heart in my grips. Then, in the next, he slips away from me again!"

'Tis because you don't really want him, mistress, her familiar observed, in her most sagacious tone. *Sure, ya want command of him, but not* him *as he stands.*

"Ah, God, that's ridiculous, cat! He's a handsome young man who reigns over all I hold dear. The manor. Its servants. And, with that blond outlander now vyin' for him, the futures of nearly every tenant farmer in this part of Wexford! Of course I want him!"

Then why did ya not accept his invitation to breakfast?

"Because of that ruddy Brownwell, of course. He'd only pelt me all the while with more questions about Prescott and such. That's who he thinks is hauntin' the great house, of all the crazed notions!"

Nola clucked. *Well, I don't feel sorry for ya, havin' a ghost hunter to contend with as well now. If you'd only made Stafford fall in love with ya from the first, rather than simply puttin' your angry little hexes upon him, he would never have had cause to think Brenna haunted!*

"Oh, do stop chastisin' me, ya damnable creature, and make yourself of use in helpin' me reckon why he's not yet smitten with me," Selena shot back with a note of desperation in her voice. "Likely I simply failed to use enough hawthorn in our spell last night."

Nay! Not more of that, Nola said pleadingly. *In truth, we've no way of knowin' what so many of those ruttish blossoms might do to him!*

"Then 'tis a risk we shall have to run, for I will not and cannot abide losin' him to an *English* woman!"

Eleven

Within a few minutes, Selena again had her ceremonial cauldron arranged, as it had been the night before, for another love spell upon Stafford. It rested on her dining table, which served as her altar on such occasions. Inside it was a flaming candle, which had a wide pink ribbon tied about it, the rosy glow it emitted providing the amorous energy that was so crucial to such white magic.

Summoning all of her strength of will, she tapped her wand upon the cauldron's rim with each verse of her incantation: "One tap to fetch him. One tap to bind him. One tap to make him put all other hearts behind him. A second pinch of hawthorn blooms to pique his lust for me. He will love me and not leave me and so it shall be!"

With that, she raised her wand from the edge of the kettle, never once suspecting what she'd just caused to rise on her recipient's end.

Stafford was sitting down to breakfast with Mr. Brownwell a short time later, when hot arousal struck his loins—the front of his breeches suddenly filling with the most precipitous display of manhood he had ever experienced.

He looked up from his plate in an effort to determine what might have caused this most unexpected state in him.

But, no. He saw in a glance that none of Brenna's maids were anywhere in sight. Not a peripheral glimpse of a long skirt rushing past or a flash of a serving girl's cleavage at the other end of the table to account for what had just happened. What was more, he was quite certain that his thoughts had not been focused upon anyone of the softer sex.

As with most of his tumescences, he welcomed the sensation at first. It made him feel more fully alive and softened his normally staid morning disposition. When he failed to return to flaccidity by early afternoon, however, his cheerful mood began giving way to great concern.

Once the following evening approached and his repeated attempts to deflate this most intimate part of him had failed, he knew that he should probably send for Wexford's physician. The condition was making it increasingly difficult for him to pass water, and he was beginning to fear that he had caught some sort of strange plague in this still-foreign environment, particularly with him having so recently surrounded himself with such a great number of its natives at his soirée.

He was, naturally, hesitant to suffer the embarrassment of having to tell the doctor of this mysterious state. But, by the time Brenna's clocks chimed the hour of seven, genuine fear was starting to outweigh his discomfiture, and, claiming to have been struck with sharp stomach pains, he retired to his bed and sent Flaherty off for medical help.

Within the hour, the town's physician, a Dr. Ahern Mahony arrived. He was a tall thin balding fellow, whose face was lined with what appeared to be years of experience in his field; and Stafford took instant comfort in seeing that his eyes shone with unmistakable empathy, as the steward ushered him into the lord's bedchamber.

"That will be all, thank you," Pearce said firmly, as Flaherty lingered curiously in the threshold of the room. And, in spite of an immediate inquiry from Mahony as to Stafford's exact symptoms, he waited, until he heard both his bedroom and his sitting-room doors close behind the steward, to respond.

"Loose as a goose are ya, sir?" the doctor prompted again before Pearce could answer.

In spite of himself, Stafford couldn't help being amused by this most descriptive inquiry. He'd never before heard diarrhea referred to in such a manner. English physicians were simply more reserved than those in this country, apparently. "No," he replied, his smile fading as his thoughts returned to the humiliating disclosure that still had to be made. "I fear 'tis not as simple as that."

Mahony, having remained a respectful few paces from the bed, walked over and perched upon the end of it now, his leather medical bag coming to rest in his long narrow lap. "Well then, what is it that troubles ye? Have ya a need for some purgative, do ya suppose? When was your last expulsion, if ya please?"

Stafford lowered his voice as he spoke again. "In truth, Doctor, I must confess that 'tis not my stomach that ails me. I simply told my steward that in order to get you here, so that I could inform you of my real problem personally."

"And what would that be?"

Unable to think of a better course, Stafford seized this opportunity to avoid having to put the matter into words. He pulled down his bed covers and eased up his night chemise, so that the physician could see his condition for himself.

To Pearce's chagrin, however, Mahony responded to this display by jerking back as though he'd just been struck in the face with a rock. Then his cheeks went crimson with either abashment or rage. Stafford couldn't be sure which.

"Lord Pearce," he said scoldingly, "whatever is the matter with ya? Callin' me all the way out here to play at such perversion, when I've so many truly sick patients to tend to! Why, I should report ya to the constable!"

"No, no. You don't understand," Stafford blurted, pulling the bedclothes back over himself, "it won't *go away!* I have been in this state, without respite, since yesterday morning!"

The physician's graying brows knit with perplexity. "What?"

"Yes. You heard me correctly. It won't return to normal! And 'tis making it increasingly difficult for me to piss, as I am sure you can understand."

"Aye," he replied, looking a great deal less offended now. "Does it hurt at all?"

"No."

"So no redness or discharge?"

"No. Indeed, 'tis its very lack of discharge that worries me, Doctor," Stafford replied, his voice edged with exasperation.

"So then, I gather you've tried to—to *rid* yourself of it?" Mahony stammered. "Um, . . . manually?"

"Of course. Countless times, it seems. But to no avail," Pearce concluded, unable to hide his desperation.

"And what of your thoughts, sir? Could it be you're fancyin' some young lady and 'tis your ruminatin' upon her that affects ya thus? If so, I might recommend your picturin' cow droppin's or somethin' equally as revoltin' for a time."

"No. Now that you make mention of it, that is one of the oddest features of this condition. It does not seem linked to any of the women I know or have lately met. In fact, I am fairly sure that love and attraction have nothing whatsoever to do with it."

The physician shook his head as though baffled. "Saints preserve us, I have seen many maladies in my time, but this one wins the laurels! . . . Do ya suppose you might need to enlist a female's help in relievin' it, nevertheless?" he suggested, continuing to appear ill at ease. "As ya likely know, they can inspire a gent in a way in which he simply cannot himself. Unless, of course, 'tis the company of *men* ya prefer," he went on in a forbidding whisper.

"Oh, no! I'm drawn to women and women alone, I assure you. 'Tis just that, being so new to Wexford, I have not yet met any whom I would dare solicit for such—such services."

"I could send ye out a strumpet," Mahony volunteered. Then, seeming to realize that he'd been far too quick in making this offer, he hastened to add, "Well, 'tis not that I visit them myself, mind ya. 'Tis just that, given the nature of their business, they're often in need of doctorin', ya understand."

"Yes. I imagine so," Stafford replied, excusing the man's blunder with a sympathetic nod.

"In any case, that would be my first recommendation to ya, Lord Pearce. Then, if that should fail, I fear I shall have to begin correspondin' with some of my colleagues in search of another cure. Because, plainly put, ya have me quite confounded. 'Tis the most endurin' rammer I have ever heard tell of! Were it any other part of ya, we might consider simply loppin' it off before it grows gangrenous or somethin'. But," he added, shaking his head once more and rising from the bed, "a man really should not be without one of those."

"Oh, I couldn't agree more!"

"So then, if you'll come to my office round the hour of ten tomorrow mornin', sir, I shall have ya serviced."

"Serviced?" Stafford asked apprehensively, the horror of imagining the physician's last suggestion lingering.

"Aye. By one of Wexford's courtesans, whom I know to be free of disease. That is, unless you would rather hazard bein' seen goin' into the brothel; for, upon second thought, 'tis probably best that none of them be seen comin' to Brenna."

"No, no. Your office will be quite satisfactory, Doctor."

"Oh, by the way, my lord," Mahony added, as he reached the bedroom door, "have ya a preference? Blonde, brunette or redhead? The ginger-haired ones can be very lovely, if I do say so myself."

"Blonde," Pearce replied without hesitation. "Definitely a blonde, thank you."

There was, indeed, an attractive blonde waiting for Stafford as the physician directed him into one of his examining rooms the following day. Buxom and beautifully clad in an aqua gown and matching bonnet, she sat in the far corner of the small chamber, casually paging through a book, as Pearce made his rather sheepish entrance.

"Miss Pauline McGinty," Mahony introduced, before hurriedly taking his leave and closing the door firmly behind him.

The young lady looked up at Stafford, her garishly shadowed eyes fixing on him as if he were a choice apple she was about to pluck from a tree. "Aye. But you need not give *your* name, sir, for the doctor has already seen to payin' me."

Though Pearce issued a very audible sigh of relief at hearing that his anonymity had been preserved, he did not move in those seconds. He merely scanned the room and, to his embarrassment, his eyes immediately lighted upon a small bed, which was situated far to his right, just opposite the prostitute.

He instantly took his gaze from it. Though that was, of course, where he and Miss McGinty would end up together, it seemed rather tasteless to have her catch him focusing upon it too soon. He, therefore, locked his eyes upon the tops of his boots and continued to stand beside the room's only exit, with his hat hanging respectfully from his hands. Due to his nagging awareness of his condition, he'd made a point on this particular occasion of wearing the longest waistcoat he owned. But, given the short, cutaway jackets of the day, the added, crotch-level concealment, now afforded by his high-crowned chapeau, seemed equally necessary. He remained thusly shielded and at this safe distance, until he could confirm that the young lady had been adequately informed of the nature of his ailment.

"You know what you must seek to accomplish with me then?" he inquired, again looking up at her.

Her rouged and very fleshy cheeks grew rounder yet, as they gave way to a perfect, crescent smile; and Stafford was pleased to note that there didn't appear to be a jot of bashfulness in her.

"Aye," she answered in a teasing tone. " 'Tis, in truth, no different from what I seek to accomplish *and do* with most all of my customers."

"Yes. But the doctor should have told you that this is somewhat . . . somewhat different," Pearce faltered.

"Aye. That he did," she replied, rising and removing her bonnet with a practiced sort of grace. "He said 'tis like a cat up a tree. It won't come down. But, don't ya fear, sir," she continued, reaching back and beginning to unbutton her dress with a cocksure wink, "I'll bring it to ground faster than a game fowl rifle. Just ya wait and see!"

In spite of this brave declaration, the dear lady was proven sorrily wrong. After roughly ninety minutes of doing battle with Stafford's privates, she collapsed over him in an exhausted heap, with the breathless claim that she'd already more than earned her usual fee.

Though Stafford offered to double that amount, if she'd only stay with him a while longer, she flatly refused; and, feeling quite winded and sore himself by this point, he made no further appeals to her.

"Are we right again?" the doctor inquired hopefully, when Stafford stopped by his desk a few minutes later to see him paid for the arrangement.

Pearce frowned, looking around to make certain there was no one else present to overhear their conversation. "I'm afraid not."

Mahony shook his head in disbelief. "Ah, faith, you're jestin', aren't ya? Why, she's one of the best in the whole of the county, and the pair of ya were in there for what seemed hours!"

"Nevertheless, Doctor, I am the same as when I arrived here."

"Oh, Mother of God. Perhaps a redhead would have been a better choice after all."

Stafford bent down to whisper, as he passed him an ample number of silver coins for the servicing. "No, Mahony. She used upon me every weapon known to womankind. Her tongue, her hands, and every reasonable orifice. Indeed, I think it a sound wager that her courage would have brought a tear to your eye. I've heard tell of men in battle with less daring. Thus I hardly think that the color of her hair had much bearing upon it."

The physician leaned back in his desk chair with a discouraged sigh. "Well then, 'tis to my colleagues I must turn for suggestions now, I'm afraid. Again, with no mention of your name being made, of course . . . I'm frightfully sorry, my lord."

"Believe me, Doctor, no more sorry than I."

"If 'tis of any comfort to ya, sir—That is, until such time as I learn of some remedy for it, I've many a male patient who complains of just the opposite problem. Though, if the truth be told, my best guess is that excesses of spirited drink are to blame in most of such cases. I only wish the cure was as simple for you," he finished sadly.

"So do I," Stafford replied in parting; and, though he did his damnedest not to let it show, he felt deeply discouraged as he climbed back into his waiting coach to return home.

He realized later, however, that there truly was some measure of comfort to be taken from Mahony's final words to him. It was, of course, impotence to which he'd been referring, and this caused Pearce's thoughts to travel back to the last person who'd spoken to him of that very same condition. *Miss Selena Ross.*

In fact, she'd even gone so far as to claim that she knew how to treat it. None of that "best guess" rubbish which Wexford's doctor had tendered on the subject. She obviously prided herself upon obtaining tangible results in her practice, and, that being the case, perhaps she had an antidote for the other extreme.

It took two days and, of course, the ever-throbbing tenacity of Stafford's unmentionable state, for him to finally work up the nerve to pay Brenna's latest resident a visit. By noon of that Tuesday, however, he did so—once more clad in his longest waistcoat.

The new lord is headed back down here, Nola warned, where

she lay, near the cottage's door. *Do you want to make the furnishin's vanish again?*

Selena looked up with a start from her herb grinding. "Nay. I suppose he'll believe I've had long enough now to fill the place thusly. Ah, good," she continued in a triumphant tone, setting her pestle down on her dining table and reaching up to brush the wisps of stray hair from her forehead, "it's finally taken effect, Nola. You shall see. At last our spells have made his heart mine and he's comin' down to declare as much."

Her familiar met this with a skeptical glare. *Let us not count our chickens before they've hatched. Don't ya wish to change your clothes before he gets here?* she added anxiously.

Selena gazed down at her gauzy drawstring chemise and matching beige skirt. "Nay. I think 'twill do him good to see me this once as I'm usually dressed. Besides, men like cloth they can almost see through on a woman."

Suit yourself. But ya do look the peasant.

"I'm willin' to hazard it, thank ya even so, cat," she snarled in return. "Why, Stafford," she greeted with a wide smile a moment later, as his knock finally came at her door, "pray don't tell me ya've grown weary of the cook's fare already."

He gave forth a soft laugh. But, to Selena's disappointment, he appeared a little too ill at ease for a fellow who'd come to announce that he'd just discovered he'd fallen head over heels in love with her.

"No, my dear. I'm happy to tell I still find it quite palatable."

"Well, with it so near the luncheon hour, I thought perhaps ya'd come to dine with me."

He raised an interested brow and scanned the space behind her as though in search of what she might be cooking.

She waved him off, continuing to smile. "Nay. I'm merely toyin' with ya. I've nothin' in the makin' at present, save a bowl of bitter herbs."

"For your medicines?" he inquired, with, Selena noticed, an immoderate amount of enthusiasm in his voice.

"Aye. Do come in," she invited, opening the door more fully to him.

He looked all about the place as he entered. "You've already furnished it."

"Aye. However humbly. Simply a few things to make it serve as my second home, ya understand. I do hope you approve."

"Yes. Of course. I am only sorry ya troubled to move all of this from town. My offer of some of the great house's furniture was not merely a courtesy, I hope you realize."

She gestured for him to have a seat at the table. "Oh, nay, now, my lord. Let us not go round about that again. Not when I've already told ya how forever in your debt I am for givin' me this thatch in the first place. May I pour ya some tea?" she asked, her tone brightening with this change of subject.

"Yes. That would be wonderful. Thank you."

"I truly hope you're not sick with anythin'," Selena declared, as she walked over to her stove.

"No. Not at all," he denied.

"Well, I'm most relieved to hear it. The reason I ask, ya see," she continued, using her apron as a pot holder to carry her spouted copper kettle to the table, "is that word about the manor has it you were sufferin' some stomach pain a day or two ago."

He rolled his eyes with disgust. "Christ's Church. A man has no secrets about this place, does he."

Selena chuckled as she hurried back to the stove's shelf to fetch two of her china cups and some tea leaves. "Very few, I'm afraid."

"Well, I am fine now, sweet lady. So you needn't worry about me."

She feigned dejection with an exaggerated frown, as she returned to the table. "Nay. Not after ya paid Wexford's doctor to do so."

He looked a trifle embarrassed. "Oh, you learned of his visit here as well?"

"That I did. Ya must bear in mind, after all, Stafford, that it has been years since anyone at Brenna has sent for him, what with *me* about the place. So, naturally, word of his comin' to call spread like wildfire."

"And it offended you, didn't it," he acknowledged, his large dark eyes growing larger still with what appeared to be genuine remorse.

She sat down opposite him and turned her attention to placing the tea leaves on her silver strainer and pouring the boiling hot water over them. "Perhaps, a bit . . . But," she continued, looking up at him once more with conspicuous amorousness, "I figured ya had your reasons. What with some of the feelin's that seem to run between you and me when we're together. Well, I assumed ya weren't entirely at ease with the thought of my wee hands probin' your bared stomach and such."

Though he tried to fight it, a surge of even greater arousal swept over his loins at the provocative images her words conjured up for him. Oh, that he had felt even half so eruptive with the blond strumpet he'd paid for in Mahony's office, he was certain now that she would have succeeded in making him climax in no time at all.

How very odd, though, he thought, that Selena's mere utterances could affect him even more profoundly than a naked prostitute's grasping limbs and recesses!

He cleared his throat with a clumsy cough before attempting to respond. "Yes. I suppose that did have some bearing upon my decision to send for the physician."

She smirked with a knowingness that made a titillating chill run through him. "Well, just don't do it again, my lord," she said, her voice teasingly stern. "For it pains me to think that ya don't feel you can trust me with each and *every* part of yourself. The other men at Brenna do, so why not you?" she asked, reaching out and placing one of her soft delicate hands over his.

He gulped, and, though half of him sensed that the only prudent course of action was to pull away from her seductive touch at once, he knew he would simply offend her further by doing so. "Oh, yes," he choked out. "Indeed, I am well aware of your ability to comfortably address virtually any subject with a male patient. Why, as I recall, we even spoke of impotence the other evening, did we not?"

"That we did. And there, you see? We've, neither of us, died of chagrin by cause of it, now have we."

He took a sip of the minty tea. "No, no. Of course not . . . Which brings to mind a question I've been pondering off and on ever since," he continued, in what he hoped was an amply offhanded tone.

"And what is that, pray?"

"Do you suppose 'tis possible for a man to be struck with just the opposite problem? In your many years of healing experience, have you ever heard tell of such an affliction?"

"The opposite of impotency, ya mean?"

"Yes."

"What? A perpetual state of, shall we say, readiness?"

"Yes. Precisely. That is precisely my meaning."

She laughed, rather more lustily than she probably should have. "No. I've never heard of such a condition and, to be frank with ya, I rather doubt that most men would deem it an affliction, as ya call it, were it to happen to them."

"Oh, but it is," Stafford suddenly heard himself saying in a plaintive voice. Then, catching himself in this slip, he quickly amended it with, "It *would* be trying, I believe."

"But why?"

He shrugged, "Well, I don't know. I simply imagine it would be. Concealing it, for instance. Now that, in itself, would prove troublous," he pointed out, his cheeks growing warm with embarrassment, despite his hostess's insistence that there was absolutely no call for such feelings.

"I suppose you're right. I hadn't thought of that."

"Oh, yes. I cannot help but believe 'twould prove a great bother to a fellow after awhile."

'Tis the hawthorn, *damn it all, Selena,* Nola hissed, from where she still lay near the door. *I told ya you used too much*

of it, and, if you could only look up at his lap, as I can now, you'd see for yourself that he's got a ramrod on him from here to Tipperary! Faith, 'tis his very self to whom he's referrin'!

Stafford couldn't help flinching at the cat's sudden sputtering. "S'death! I'd half forgotten she was here with us," he said, clapping a palm to his chest. "I do hope I didn't frighten her somehow."

Selena gave forth a light laugh, doing, she thought, an admirable job of not betraying how surprised she was by her familiar's revelation. "Oh, nay. She simply woke from a bad dream again, I've no doubt. Crazed creature! Whatever shall I do with her?" she asked rhetorically, bending to glower under the table at the cat.

Her eyes told Nola, in the instant that followed, that she was more than happy to hear that their love spells had had at least this much effect.

Nay, her pet shot back with a shrill meow. *Lest 'tis his intent to use it on you, we must bring it down at once. We cannot have him courtin' that English lass in such a state later this week!*

"Ah, very well," Selena whispered grudgingly. But, as she concluded her covert conversation with her familiar, her eyes lit upon her visitor's lap, and the surprise of seeing that he appeared even better endowed than he'd felt on the day she'd groped him in this very dwelling, caused her to lurch upward and hit her head resoundingly on the underside of the table.

"God's teeth," Stafford said with concern, as she sat up in her chair once more. "Did you hurt yourself?"

"Nay. I'm fine," she fibbed, reflexively pressing a hand to the throbbing point of impact. "I was simply concedin' to Nola's demand to be let out. Bothersome beast!" With that she rose and proceeded to rush the cat outdoors in the hopes of making it all look like a matter of course. "You were sayin'?" she prompted, as she shut the door once more and came back to the table.

Pearce knit his brows. "Hmm. What *was* I saying, indeed? . . . Oh, yes, I guess the long and the short of it is that I was wondering about your cure for impotency. Could there possibly be one that has an opposing effect?"

" 'The long and the short of it'?" she repeated, trying not to laugh at this obviously unintended pun on his part.

He shrugged, clearly failing to see any humor in the subject.

Selena grew serious as well. She now sorrily agreed with Nola's assessment that she would be endangering all concerned, if she failed to suggest a reliable remedy to him; so she began at once to search her mind for one. "A pinch of white heather might work, I suppose," she said after several seconds. "That's good for quellin' passions. And I should think, given the condition ya describe," she continued, quirking a brow at him and lowering her voice to a temptress's murmur, "that 'twould be best made into a salve and *rubbed* onto the—the afflicted area."

Pearce gulped again, this time quite audibly. "Rubbed, you say?"

She donned a coquettish smile. "Aye. With great *vigor.* And, of course, for as long a time as is required to see matters returned to normal, as it were."

"Oh, God," he exclaimed under his breath.

"What was that?"

"Um. Nothing."

She cocked her head at him with an apologetic expression. "Oh, dear. I've embarrassed ya again, haven't I."

"No, no. 'Tis entirely my fault I'm afraid. Questioning you about such a preposterous ailment. And what good would your sound and commendably quick answer do the likes of me, in any case? Why, I would not know white heather, if it grew in my very own garden."

She reached out and gave his hand a pat. "But that is what healers, such as myself, are for, ya dear man. I'd know white heather if I came upon it blindfolded. And, of course," she went on, gently drawing his forefinger away from his others and beginning to rub it in a most suggestive manner, "I'd gladly fetch some for ya. That is, if I thought for a moment that you could possibly be in need of it."

"Oh, Lord, well, I suppose I'd better be going now," he blurted, pushing back in his chair and bolting to his feet. Another few seconds of her enticing touch and he knew, without a doubt, that he'd humiliate himself for all eternity by confessing that his questioning was anything but hypothetical! What was more, he'd seriously begun to doubt the wisdom of getting romantically involved with her. Given her obvious influence with the citizens of Wexford, it was possible that she could stir up a great deal of trouble for him, should any amorous relations between them sour.

She was best kept at arm's length, he concluded. Despite his growing attraction to her, it was better that she remained a mere friend, than be allowed to become a possibly spurned lover.

"Leavin' so soon?" she was asking beseechingly, as his thoughts returned to the present moment and he found himself headed for her door.

"Yes. I'm afraid I really must get back to the great house. Flaherty and the cook are sure to be wondering what has become of me so near the time luncheon is served. That is, I have just remembered that I neglected to tell either of them I was coming down here."

"Well, suit yourself, my lord," she said, getting to her feet and rushing after him, "but you are welcome to eat here, if ya wish. I've some game-fowl pie, which I could heat for ya in a twinklin'."

He turned back to her before making his precipitous exit. The midday sun shone through her sheer chemise, revealing a bosom that was, at once, ample, yet surprisingly pert; and, as his gaze traveled upward in an effort to escape this almost irresistible sight, it met her eyes in such a way that he knew he would ravish her with abandon, if he dared stay an instant longer. "God, no! I cannot," he called after himself as he hurried outside. "I'm sorry, my dear, but I promise we shall visit at more length one day soon."

"Ah, bleedin' Hell, and I so very nearly had him in hand this time," Selena said in a desperate whisper, as she lingered on the thatch's threshold, watching him dash away, across the grounds.

Nola, who'd taken refuge beside a nearby bush, stared over at her with a chastising meow. *Well, if not by hand, by* mind, *mistress, for, if we hazard leavin' him in that state, there might be a* full-blooded *English child as heir to this place, come nine months from now. And I needn't tell ya that such will most certainly be the end of us!*

Twelve

"White heather, Flaherty," Stafford bellowed, as he came rushing through the manor's terrace entrance seconds later and caught sight of his steward. "Have we any about the place?"

Flaherty scuttled down the first-floor corridor towards him, looking flustered by this odd inquiry. "White what, sir?" he asked windlessly, as he finally came within a few yards of his employer.

"White heather. Pray do not tell me it can't be found in Ireland," Pearce snapped, still feeling wrenchingly drawn towards the woman whose beckoning body he'd just so narrowly managed to escape.

Flaherty fought to catch his breath, his heft having made his sprint down the hallway quite an accomplishment. "Um—Aye. It grows here, to be sure."

"Well, what is it? A weed or an herb or what?" Stafford demanded, waving his hands about with an irritable cluck.

" 'Tis a shrub, I think, sir . . . Aye," he said more confidently after a second or two. "I believe 'tis referred to as a shrub."

"And have we any of it at Brenna?"

"I don't know. Shall I ask the gardener for ya, my lord?"

"Yes. Do. And the sooner the better!"

The steward's brow continued to be furrowed at this most unlikely request. It was clear that he couldn't imagine what Pearce would want with such a plant.

"For my stomach problems," Stafford snarled. "I'm told 'twill make me feel better."

"Hmm. I've never heard that said of heather."

"You are my steward, man, not my physician. What care I what you've heard of herbs? Just get it for me at once!"

The Irishman recoiled. "Very well, my lord," he said, as Pearce pushed past him and hurried on down the corridor.

Though Stafford couldn't explain why, he knew he must keep moving forward—away from that damnable thatch—or risk being mysteriously pulled back down there, as if he were a hapless water bug slipping into a whirling tide pool.

"I shall be in my bedchamber, so please have my luncheon brought up when 'tis ready."

"White heather, sir?" his resident ghost hunter asked a second or two later. Having been in the study, he came darting out at Pearce now, like an eel from the cracked hull of a sunken ship. He was in step with Stafford within the space of a heartbeat.

Pearce could feel himself starting to bristle at this additional questioning on the subject. "Yes, Brownwell. As I was just telling Mr. Flaherty, 'tis said to ease stomach pain," he fibbed again, continuing his speedy gait.

"Yes. Well, I most certainly hope so, sir, for it seems you have spent most of the past four days sealed up in that suite of yours. So, how am I to continue with my investigation, when I'm never allowed to consult with you?"

At this, Stafford stopped dead in his tracks and turned back to him with a glower. "You're being paid for every day you are here, so what does it matter *when* I find time to meet with you?"

"Lord Pearce," he countered with, Stafford was surprised to note, almost equal vehemence, "I've other cases to attend to back in London, so I certainly cannot remain at Brenna indefinitely, however good the pay or fine the accommodations. But, more to the point, sir, has it not occurred to you that this stomach trouble which has befallen you might also be the work of a ghost?"

Pearce took a step back from him and pulled down on his waistcoat—a self-conscious habit he'd developed of late. Indeed, it had *not* occurred to him that his mortifying state might have been brought on by the spirit world, and he now found that the very suggestion of it sent a frightened chill running up his spine.

What sort of depraved apparition would even think to do such a thing to a man? Not the uncle he'd so respected all of his life, surely! "No," he replied in a quavery voice. "I suppose I simply was not aware that ghosts could cause illness."

"Ghosts, my lord, can cause *anything*. Pray, believe me in that."

Stafford swallowed uneasily and again tugged downward on his vest. "Well then, should the heather which I have requested fail to help me, you and I will just have to try another course, won't we."

There really was no arguing with this retort, and, to Pearce's great relief, the investigator did not try. So, offering him a placative, "You shall be the first to know the results," Stafford hurried on, reaching his suite in record time and locking its door behind him.

His noonday meal was delivered to his room within fifteen minutes, and the requested shrub shortly thereafter.

"I wasn't sure if you wished to take it as a tea or sprinkle it upon some food, my lord," Flaherty explained, when he came to Stafford's door with a pouch of the heather. "So I simply had one of the maids grind it up for ya."

"That was the perfect choice," Pearce praised, snatching the tiny bag from his hands, before the steward found cause to enter the suite. Given the manner of administration that Selena had recommended, *privacy* was truly all else Stafford would be requiring for a good while to come.

Looking, at once, radiant at the new lord's rare compliment of his decision-making and rather befuddled at not being allowed to enter and retrieve his now-emptied lunch dishes, the Irishman stepped back from the door.

"I shall be drinking it down with a glass of water from my bedside pitcher," Pearce offered, hoping to ward off any further inquiries on the subject.

The servant moved towards him once more. "Then, pray, let me refill it for you, so that 'tis fresh and cold."

Stafford continued to block his passage through the partially opened door. "No, no. That won't be necessary. Thank you, Mr. Flaherty. 'Tis fresh and cold enough . . . In truth," he added, pretending to yawn, "I am in terrible need of a nap."

This declaration, as was true with all of Pearce's references to bodily requirements, seemed to finally sink in with the overly attentive steward, and, vowing to keep this wing of the manor especially quiet so Stafford could sleep, he hurried away, down the upstairs corridor.

Pearce instantly locked his suite, and, proceeding to one of his night tables, he withdrew a tiny crock of skin cream from its drawer. In lieu of a more medicinal compound, this would have to serve as the salve that Selena had recommended.

He removed the lid from the crock and, opening the drawstring pouch, added the pinch of ground heather which she'd prescribed. Then he began the delicate task of stirring the two ingredients together with his forefinger.

It was a messy gritty mixture, to be sure. But no more distasteful, he acknowledged, than having to go on trying to conceal his unspeakable condition.

If this worked—and he prayed to all that was holy that it would—Miss Selena Ross would immediately, and without fail, become his new physician!

After Stafford had made his precipitous exit from her thatch, Selena began at once to prepare the white heather salve she'd prescribed to him. Then she selected a curse doll, which most closely fit his description, from her collection.

It was, of course, a male effigy, and a dark-haired one at that. Its trouser-clad cloth body was equipped with a crotch-level silken tassel, meant to render it anatomically precise. She'd never before found need for this intimate detail, and had thought the Wise Ones' recommendation of its inclusion rather ridiculous at the time she'd created her dolls. But, on this particular occasion, she was infinitely thankful for it. With her love spells having gone so awry of late, there seemed no telling what her attempts to add such an appendage to the effigy might do to poor unwitting Pearce!

So, over to her fireplace she carried her cushiony embodiment of the handsome new lord, along with a tiny earthenware jar of the white heather salve she'd concocted. Then she set the doll down upon the hearth rug and proceeded to rekindle the flames of the night before in the logs that rested upon her andirons.

Though she had not succeeded in persuading Stafford to stay, she was determined that this treatment of him, represented in the doll, would be the same in every aspect as if he had remained for it, rather than fleeing to the great house.

She hurried up to her loft, dotted drops of her favorite perfume upon the base of her neck and at the backs of her wrists and knees. Then she returned to the first floor, took a candle from one of the shelves near her fireplace, and stuck it into an engraved copper holder—copper being the metal that most favored love spells.

She withdrew a punk from the tinderbox which rested on her hearth's upper ledge. Then she lit it from the fireplace's flame and used it to ignite the wick of her taper. Once it seemed lastingly aglow, she carefully centered the candle upon the hearthstones before the fire.

Then she returned to her curse doll, and, kneeling beside it, embraced it with fervor. Feeling like a love-struck young maiden clutching her bed's pillow to the length of her, she hugged it with every ounce of the great desire she already felt for Pearce.

She sank to a sitting position, and, lovingly cradling the effigy's torso in one arm, she used her free hand to begin applying the white heather salve to that unmentionable part of him.

"See me, Stafford," she whispered, locking her eyes upon the dancing flame of the candle, as the movement of her hand quickened in its task. "See me, smell me, hear me, feel me. *Feel* me. As though 'twere me, indeed, who brings the long-sought relief you requested."

Pearce heaved a passion-filled gasp, his thighs tensing upon his mattress as the final convulsions of his private act ran through him. However, it was not only that he'd remedied his condition that made the experience so spectacular, but the remarkable images that filled his brain as he'd done so.

It was as if he had agreed to let Selena treat his condition personally. Amidst the post-climactic exhaustion that swept over him, every detail of it still seemed so very real. The feeling of her cradling his head and upper body in her lap, the tickling sensation of her long hair streaming over his face and neck, as she stared down into his eyes. Even the hand he'd felt upon him, working to bring him release, had not seemed his own, not large and coarse and masculine—but silky and small and so very, ecstatically tight with its tiny grasp.

What was more, the lily-of-the-valley scent she'd worn on the night they'd met was unmistakably surrounding him now. It was as though it had somehow been applied to his bed linens in his absence, and, yet, he was positive that he had not smelt it there when he'd first reclined minutes earlier.

Dear God, how was it possible to have experienced her so fully, when she was nowhere in sight?

He rolled over towards his washbasin with a slight groan. If he didn't know better, he would say he was *in love* with the woman! How else could he account for the flood of goodwill towards all mankind which filled every part of him? Not only could he not remember ever feeling this relieved, he couldn't recall having ever been filled with such a warm, magical glow! It was an odd mix of exuberance and gratefulness, which made him know genuine compassion for every person and creature who was less fortunate than he. In fact, if allowed to run rampant for much longer, this heart-smitten cast of mind might even cause him to do something truly rash. Something utterly fool-headed, such as donating some of his money to charity—of all the insane notions!

She'd done it! That remarkable lady, who'd been his uncle's lover for so many years, had actually succeeded where a professionally trained doctor had failed!

Stafford was plainly dazzled. So impressed as to want to go racing about the manor, praising Selena's name to each and every soul in residence. But, given the nature of the dysfunction she'd advised him about, he knew he had better keep his jubilation to himself . . . Dear Lord, because he had not confessed to Selena herself that his questioning was anything but theoretical, he couldn't even tell *her* how very indebted he felt.

He would find a way, however, he silently vowed, as he rose to clean up after himself. Somehow he would let her know how tremendously impressed he was with her healing abilities, and how wonderful he thought it was to have her once more dwelling on Brenna's grounds!

I still think there was no call to put white heather in them, Nola said critically, as she sat by the fire that evening, licking and preening.

Selena went on placing the sweetie scones in question into her serviette-lined picnic basket. "Ah, I baked nothin' more than a pinch of it into 'em. Not nearly enough to sicken a man of Stafford's size. Besides, as ya said yourself, cat, we simply cannot hazard havin' him courtin' that English woman with his cannon incessantly primed."

But he used the salve ya recommended. Ya saw for yourself in the crystal ball when he was preparin' it. And, then, with ya havin' done an incantation towards that same end, don't ya think that hawthorn trouble is behind us?

Selena cocked her head at her brimful basket of scones, assessing whether they were stacked as neatly as she could manage. Then, finally satisfied with the arrangement, she carefully tied the four corners of the linen napkin about them for conveyance to the great house. "Well, when it comes to the matter of savin' most of Wexford from the tyranny of an all-English rule, we just cannot be too careful, now can we. In any case, the dash of heather will likely just give him the trots, should it do him any harm at all. And that can only work for the good, where foilin' his carriage ride with the blonde is concerned. Nothin' like diarrhea, after all, for spoilin' a tour of the countryside."

Pray beware that ya don't become too spiteful in this, mistress. Remember what the Wise Ones taught about unnecessary cruelty. I can already see in your mind that you're not entirely adverse to arrangin' rather a grave accident for this Carolyn Barnes of his.

Selena clucked at her, as she ran a smoothing hand over the skirt of the sky blue satin gown she'd donned for her call upon Stafford. Then she gathered up her basket and headed for the door. "Nay, now, dear familiar. You must know, after all these years of servin' with me, that I shall prove a good deal more subtle than that!"

"Sweetie scones for Lord Pearce, Flaherty," Selena explained, extending the basket as the steward greeted her at the manor's terrace door minutes later.

The Irishman reached out and stole a peek at the basket's contents, as if suspicious they might be somewhat less innocent than the witch claimed. "So they are, mistress," he said with great relief. "Then the pair of ya are gettin' on well?"

"Well enough, thank ya. Might I see him then?"

"Aye. I suppose he'll agree to receive ya. He was once again bedridden with his stomach disorder this afternoon. But he did come down for supper and has gone into his study now. So I imagine he's well enough for a visit, if you'll wait here while I ask him," he concluded gingerly.

"Certainly," she replied, pulling her basket back into her arms and sauntering off towards the terrace's sea-view rail.

"Selena," she heard Stafford call out to her a moment or two later in a voice that was so winning that it made a great welcoming warmth rush over her. "How wonderful to see you again!"

She turned back and reciprocated his broad smile, as he walked to where she stood.

"Are you cold out here? Do you wish to come in and join Horatio and me in partaking of some brandy-wine?"

She shook her head, still determined to avoid the meddlesome ghost hunter. "Oh, nay. I simply brought these sweetie scones up for ya, as I said I would the other day."

He accepted them from her, continuing to beam. Then, pulling upward slightly upon the enwrapping serviette, he drew in a long, appreciative whiff of the pastries. "How generous. You are an angel!"

She dropped her gaze at this compliment. "Oh, that's truly makin' too much of me, sir. But I did remember your sayin' ya were fond of 'em. So there ya are, two dozen. Still warm from my oven."

He reached out with his free arm and, wrapping it about her shoulders, pressed her to him as if she were a long-lost sister.

She studied his eyes at this close range. His feelings towards her were very positive, she silently noted. Indeed, even worshipful in nature. But, sadly, having now been relieved of his state of arousal, he was not particularly amorous.

"God bless you, darling Selena," he continued. "How indispensable you're proving to me."

She could only conclude that this sudden effusiveness towards her was due to her having helped him rid himself of his tumescence—however much she regretted doing so now. "Well, take care not to eat too many of 'em in one sittin', mind," she replied, starting to feel a bit guilty over putting the dash of heather into them. "With Mr. Flaherty havin' just informed me that your stomach was painin' ya again this afternoon, I can't imagine that sweets are the best thing for ya."

He laughed softly at her concern, all the while looking terribly grateful for it. "Ah, what would we do without you here, dear lady? . . . You've changed your clothes since last I saw you. What a lovely gown. How beautiful you are in blue! And in such heavenly light, too," he finished, lifting his arm from her to point up at the sky.

"Aye. The moon. 'Tis my medium, I guess. I was named for it, after all."

He smiled. "Oh, so you were. Selena. I had half forgotten 'tis Greek for 'moonlight.' It suits you. How very wise your parents were in choosing it. I do hope they're still alive," he said thoughtfully, joining her in sitting down upon the stone rail.

She shook her head. She'd never known her father, though he was said to have been quite high-ranking among the Druid population; and her mother had died two centuries past. So, obviously, she didn't dare say much on the subject.

"Oh, what a shame. I am truly sorry for you."

"Aye, well . . . one learns to carry on, nonetheless."

"Yes. Especially a woman as skilled and charming as you are."

If I'm so damnably charming, why won't ya at least kiss me? Selena thought, shooting him an alluring sideward glance. I could have serviced ya like the most dearly bought courtesan this afternoon. I could have and *would* have, and yet ya fled as if you were a frightened child!

She could see in his eyes, however, that her gift for conveying her thoughts without aid of speech was not working with him. He simply went on grinning rather stupidly at her, as if she were the matron saint of visiting Englishmen.

"I should go, I suppose," she said, pushing up to her feet with the realization that she might very well lose patience with him again, if she remained much longer. There seemed no point, after all, in wasting any more of her magical powers on petty hexes. "I'm sure your friend Horatio is waitin' for ya."

"Are you certain you don't wish to come in?" he called after her, as she began heading down the terrace steps to the lawn which lay beyond them.

She waved back at him. "Another time, perhaps. Thank ya, Stafford."

Pearce watched for several seconds, as she strolled off across the back grounds. Dressed, as she was, in the blue of the moon's light, she did indeed seem strangely one with it, as her gracile figure grew smaller with her retreat.

There was something eternal, maybe even sacred about her, he acknowledged. Something peaceful and sagacious and breathtakingly in harmony with the mix of azure and black tree shadows that surrounded her now.

He rarely met a person whom he thought more right with God than he himself was. Why, the life of wealth and luxury that Heaven had seen fit to bestow upon him since infancy seemed evidence enough of his favored status with the Creator. But, he realized, in that silent, almost eerie moment, that he'd finally encountered someone who was even more divinely prized.

Thirteen

So, did he appear to be any more in love with ya than he was when last ya saw him? Nola asked, as Selena returned to her thatch minutes later.

"Nay," she answered calmly. "Less so now, in fact, what with that salve havin' done the trick."

How strangely at peace ya seem with it. Do ya think it will put him off Miss Barnes as well?

Selena gave forth a mischievous laugh. "Nay. When I get done with the pair of 'em, 'twill be *she* who puts him off, I promise ya!"

Nothin' too baneful now, mistress. Pray give me your word!

"I'll not harm a hair on either of their heads, dear cat. You have my vow."

Stafford could feel his face flush as Carolyn Barnes entered the O'Dugans' front hall in order to accompany him on the agreed-upon carriage ride that Thursday afternoon.

Here, in the full light of day, she was even more beautiful than he had remembered her being, and he felt, at once, aroused, yet tongue-tied by it.

She wore a bright pink day gown, which rivaled the hues of the lushest English rose, and, as she strode towards him now, she was fastening the narrow ties of its matching bonnet into a perfectly balanced bow beneath her chin.

"Why, Lord Pearce," she said in greeting, "how commendably prompt you are."

"Am I?" he asked, seizing this excuse to look down at his pocket watch, so she wouldn't see how his face had colored at her loveliness. "Oh, yes. I guess it is just the stroke of two."

Smiling as she reached him, she looped an arm into one of his with an ease which surprised him, given that she was so many years his junior. Though it couldn't have been long since she'd attained adult age, she was clearly already accustomed to being courted by men of title.

He stole another look at her, before turning to lead her towards the door. How like his elegant mother she was with her regally high cheekbones, melting blue eyes, and gleaming blond hair, which was parted so impeccably down the middle.

She was, in every physical sense, the woman of his dreams, and he silently thanked God now, with his palms so moist at her radiant presence, that she had simply taken hold of his arm and not one of his hands.

He scoured his mind for a suitable topic of conversation, as he helped her up into his carriage minutes later. Unfortunately, however, he couldn't seem to think of anything less banal than the weather. " 'Tis a fine day for this, isn't it?" he asked. "That is, when one considers the fact that it might have rained this afternoon."

She smiled and directed her bonnet-framed face skyward, as he climbed up next to her on the vehicle and took the reins.

"Well, I don't see how it could have. There isn't a cloud in sight."

He issued a nervous laugh, silently damning himself for somehow botching so innocuous a subject. While he found himself savoring the refined ring of her English accent, after so many weeks of having been exposed to the locals' careless dropping of their *g's* and such, this retort struck him as far more caustic than he remembered her being. He hadn't realized, when he'd met her at the soirée, that he was dealing with such a literalist. Perhaps that evening's wine had made her more affable than usual. But, whatever the case, he concluded, he would obviously have to choose his words more carefully with her henceforward. "Yes. I know. I merely meant it *might* have. In theory, that is."

"Oh? Does it rain much in Wexford this time of year? I was not aware of that. I certainly haven't seen a drop in the seven days I've been visiting here."

In his annoyance at how badly their interaction was going, he gave the reins a much harder snap than he should have. His horse bolted in response. Then it began pulling them down the carriage drive at breakneck speed, a cloud of *rain-starved* dust being stirred up all about the vehicle in the process.

He managed to bring them to a skidding stop, but not before his comely companion found cause to begin coughing and waving her hand before her face at the squall.

"God's teeth," she exclaimed. "Perhaps you should have brought along your coachman."

Stafford couldn't help taking offense at this. "For what reason?" he asked coolly. "I have been driving my own carriage for years, and I've never once suffered a mishap."

Everything would have been fine. Sufficiently smoothed over, he assured himself in that trying instant, if not for the fact that he involuntarily concluded this declaration with an indignant snort—the volume of which would have rivaled that of one issued by a bull!

It was one of the oddest sounds he'd ever heard, let alone produced; and he could tell, given the young lady's stunned expression, that she found it equally mystifying.

She raised a hand to her chest and nervously began fingering the long, beaded necklace she wore. She looked as if she considered his emission disquietingly bestial in retrospect. "Perhaps we should try this another day."

"Nonsense," he replied, his tone, to his relief, once again collected. "We've simply made a poor start of it, is all. You will have a good time, once we get going. I promise you."

"Well . . . all right," she said tentatively.

He offered her a reassuring smile, beginning to feel like himself again, and off they rode, down the rest of the long driveway and out onto the road.

"So, are you still enjoying your stay with your cousins?" he inquired after a moment or two.

"Very much. But I miss London, of course. As I'm sure you must, my lord. I fear this part of Ireland is a trifle too bucolic for me."

At last, Pearce thought with both relief and enthusiasm, a topic on which they were in fairly total agreement. Still interested in possibly wooing her, however, he knew he must try to minimize the drawbacks of life in Wexford. "Yes. I must confess to finding it that way myself from time to time. One cannot help but crave all that the city has to offer, when away from it for too long. But it must be said that the Irish countryside is some of the loveliest in the world."

His passenger looked all about her as they continued to ride at a leisurely pace. "Yes. I quite agree . . . And so fragrant at this time of year, too," she added, shutting her eyes and drawing in a long, appreciative breath.

To Stafford's horror, his body chose that same instant in which to give forth a loud belch! What was worse, it was so distinctive a sound that there seemed no point in attempting to attribute it to any other source.

Carolyn's eyes fell open with shock. "Are you unwell, sir?"

His cheeks were now so hot with embarrassment that they felt as though they might burst into flame at any moment. "Well, I was suffering with some stomach trouble earlier this week," he replied, deciding it was best to take refuge in the little white lie that he'd been telling everyone else of late. "But I thought it had finally passed."

"You could take me back to my cousins' manor," she suggested again, this time in a tone that said it was much more for her sake she was doing so, than for his. "I would understand entirely if you wish to take our jaunt on another day. When you are feeling better perhaps."

His first thought was to respond to this with a stoic and firm "I'm fine," and continue driving the horse forward. Instead, however, he decided to steer the carriage to the side of the road and make an honest and heartrending appeal to her. If properly delivered, he reasoned, it would very likely serve the dual purpose of flattering her and winning her sympathy. To his surprise, he even managed to grow slightly teary-eyed as he turned to address her. "In truth, Carolyn, I do not want to take you back just yet. For, if I do, I fear you will not agree to go out with me again. And, since you are, by far, the most comely woman I have ever set eyes upon, it would break my heart to lose this precious time with you to a bit of stomach upset. Indeed, I have likely only been ill due to missing our dear England, and, because you seem to me to embody all that is beautiful and noble and gracious about Her, I do beseech you to give me just a little while longer in your presence."

Looking not only deeply touched, but rather dumbstruck by this outpouring, she offered him a whisper of a smile. "All right."

It appeared that he had succeeded in swaying her to her very core, and he felt fairly certain now that he would wheedle at least a kiss from her before they returned to the O'Dugans.

Having thusly charmed her, he returned her smile and directed his horse back onto the road. She was one of his own kind, he silently reminded himself, a sense of gratification running through him. She was educated, well-shod, and of gentle birth; so it was only natural that he'd been able to regain her trust.

They rode for a while in comfortable silence, Stafford breaking it now and then in order to offer her the details about the orchards and estates they passed along the way. Though he'd traveled this stretch of road several times since his arrival in Wexford, he'd required Mr. Flaherty to furnish him with the specifics of both its history and the families who owned the land all about it, and the steward had done quite an admirable job.

The culmination of this casual tour was to be a walk along the fairly deserted seashore to the north of Wexford Harbor; and, apparently still appeased by his poignant entreaty earlier, Carolyn offered no protest as he finally steered the carriage to the beach side of the road and circled around to help her down from it.

He had an almost overwhelming urge to be so bold as to wrap his large hands about her slim waist and lower her to the ground. Fortunately, however, he managed to resist it, letting the discreet offering of one of his hands suffice.

Her grip was amazingly delicate, and, once she lifted her skirt to negotiate the carriage step, Stafford couldn't help hazarding staring at her slipper-clad feet and slender ankles. They were absolutely perfect in their shape and diminutiveness, and he found himself so caught up in imagining what the niveous flesh above them might look like, that he drew a complete blank as she addressed him again.

"What was that?" he asked with a flustered chuckle, as he suddenly became aware of the interrogative rise of her voice.

"I was merely wondering how far you wish to walk."

"Oh, just a little way, my dear. That is, if you don't mind."

She looked, for the first time since he'd met her, rather blushful as he continued to stand so near her.

Their eyes locked, hers half inviting him to kiss her, and so he did. Taking hold of her shoulders, he gently pressed her back against the side of the carriage, and, to his delight, she fully reciprocated. Her lips parted and her tongue began intertwining quite readily with his.

God, how heavenly she smelled, he thought, as their kiss grew more and more heated. Her floral perfume filled his senses. He felt urged on by the warmth she was generating beneath his palms, to say nothing of the soft, yet seething sound of the excited breaths she was drawing through her nostrils, as he continued to keep her mouth fully occupied. And, the next thing he knew, he was taking the enormous risk of moving his right hand down to the low-cut bodice of her dress.

Though he felt certain she was aware of this improper advance on his part, she made absolutely no effort to stop him. Indeed, he was just beginning to revel in this victory, to savor every thrilling second of it, when, to his astoundment, he heard himself whisper, "I want to *swive* you, dear Carolyn. Pray let us do it right here in the sand."

Now, even as a lad, Stafford had known that it was acceptable for a fellow to be entertaining such thoughts on a first outing with a lady. But to have actually given voice to one of them was nothing short of an outrage. And he was very quickly reminded of this important truth, as his pretty companion stepped back from him and delivered a stinging slap to his right cheek.

"How dare you say such a thing to a woman of my station! I demand that you return me to my cousins at once, you lecher!"

Feeling almost as appalled as she seemed to, he backed away from her. "But it was not my intention to utter anything of the kind, my dear. You must believe me! 'Twas as if I were possessed by some evil spirit as it left my lips! Why, I myself would never even dream of saying such a thing to *any* woman, much less to one as magnificent as you are!"

"Nevertheless, you clearly have," she declared, turning on her heel and hurrying back up into the carriage. "Now, come take the reins this instant or I shall see myself home!"

Certain that she intended to act on this threat, if he didn't make haste, Stafford hurried over to his side of the vehicle and sullenly began guiding the horse back out onto the road. He wanted, with his whole heart, to offer her more words of explanation for his dreadful behavior, but he sensed that, true to their stern English code of conduct in such areas, he would only anger her further by doing so. He, therefore, kept his eyes fixed solely upon the way ahead, as he continued driving. And, it wasn't until his stomach was suddenly seized with the burbling pain, which usually preceded the worst diarrhea, that he felt compelled to speak again.

"I must stop," he muttered, when they were within a mile or so of the O'Dugans.

She turned and flashed him a suspicious sideward glance. "Why?"

"Because, as I told you earlier, I have been unwell of late. And it seems I am that way again now."

"All right," she replied with a put-upon sniff. "But do be quick about it!"

Knowing he had caused her more than enough displeasure for one day, he rushed to comply. He whipped the horse to a gallop, his eyes searching the road ahead for a suitably dense grouping of trees or bushes.

When he finally spotted an amply tall hedgerow off to the right, he brought his carriage to a halt a tasteful several feet from it and dashed off to seek its cover.

He felt as if he might explode in the seconds that followed. It was one of the most bowel-bursting experiences he had ever known. But, though it took several minutes for his body to fully relieve itself, his agony quickly subsided thereafter; and he began to take comfort in the belief that he could travel the rest of the way to her cousins' estate without having to stop again.

Just as he was beginning to clean up after himself, however—with the silken handkerchief that would now be condemned to be left behind in this deserted place—he heard Miss Barnes calling out to him in the scathing tone of the sternest governess.

The voice, which only an hour before had sounded like a choir of angels to him, cut right through his being now with its shrillness.

"Stafford Pearce, you blackguard, what is keeping you so long? This is just another of your ploys to have your way with me, isn't it! You want to force me to come back there after you, whereupon you will pounce on me. Well, I will have no more of your wily ways. I have waited long enough," she shouted; and, before Stafford could even raise the waist of his breeches from his ankles, he heard his mare race off down the road at Carolyn's loud slap of the reins.

He realized in those harrowing moments that this had easily become the most disastrous afternoon of his life. Not only had he dishonored himself with what had seemed the ideal woman, but his having to return to the O'Dugans' manor in order to retrieve his horse and carriage seemed to guarantee that everyone in County Wexford would learn all about it!

Fourteen

As always, Stafford failed to escape being greeted at the door by Flaherty, when he returned to Brenna roughly two hours later.

"How was your carriage ride with Miss Barnes, my lord?" the steward asked with a smile.

"Catastrophic," Pearce replied simply, having had to stop twice more en route home from the O'Dugans' by cause of his stomach disorder. "Pray you, do be so kind as to make no further inquiries about it," he added, not pausing in his drive to flee to the privacy of his suite. "And please see that my bath is prepared at once."

Likely having spotted the at-his-wits'-end look in Stafford's eyes in those fleeting seconds, Flaherty mercifully chose to satisfy both of these requests without rebuttal. And, within the hour, Pearce was sitting up to his chest in soothingly hot bath-water, fully enjoying the solitude he'd demanded.

With all traces of his humiliating case of the runs finally washed from him, he could only wish that the rest of his be-smirching outing with the O'Dugans' house guest could be just as easily eradicated.

He reached out to one of the large terry towels, which lay upon an adjacent wicker footstool, and, taking it in hand, rolled it up into a bolsterlike pillow. Then he placed it behind his neck and slid down in the water until it cushioned his nape against the back rim of the tub.

He shut his eyes, doing his best to put all thoughts of his

afternoon with Carolyn out of his mind. Considering his high station in Wexford, it was possible, he supposed, that the locals would give him the benefit of the doubt, should Miss Barnes or her cousins decide to speak ill of him. Carolyn was, after all, one of the enemy English, while he must surely have already been granted some of the honorary Irish status that his Uncle Prescott had always seemed to enjoy.

What was more, since she hadn't insisted upon bringing a chaperone along on their ride, it truly would come down to her word against his, Stafford told himself hearteningly. And, because his only real offense against her had merely been a verbal one and—he would maintain to his grave—wholly unintended, her physical person could bear no evidence against him. Neither now nor nine months hence—thanks be to God!

He exhaled a long, relieved breath at this reassuring truth, and tried again to clear his mind. Given both his mortifying experiences with Carolyn and with the courtesan whom Dr. Mahony had prescribed for him, it would probably be a good long while before he braved the risks of seeking female companionship again.

The embarrassing truth of the matter was that, with the powerful effect that the white heather had had upon him, he wasn't likely to be in need of such company for some time. Not for sexual purposes, in any case.

But, perhaps, for the sake of consolation, a strange sweet voice suddenly whispered in his head. And, in that same instant, all of his worry about Miss Barnes hurting his reputation seemed to magically give way to infinitely comforting images of meadow flowers and great stretches of rich green grass bathed in warm sunlight. And there, reclining in the midst of this pastoral scene, as though she were as indigenous to it as the bright yellow blossoms which surrounded her, was Selena Ross.

Dressed in a green gown, which blended with the verdant growth all about her, she lay with her long black hair flowing out behind the crown of her head.

She was humming a tune, a haunting lulling melody that sounded much like some sort of hymn. It seemed to rise from her closed lips and nostrils and be carried along by the passing breeze.

She was at rest. Utterly at peace with nature. And somehow beyond the reproach of gentry and peasantry alike in this country, which was still so unwelcoming to Stafford in many ways.

Selena could testify to his gentlemanly nature, he realized. Who better than a woman, to whom he had just granted so generous a gift as a newly roofed cottage, to bear witness to his kindness toward the softer sex?

Yes! If it became necessary, she could, indeed, attest to the fact that Stafford had not only given her a second home, but had taken measures to make certain she was safe from any prowlers there.

And she'd been so amicable in return, Pearce happily reminded himself. So attentive and unselfish with her time in baking him so many of her delicious scones.

After the nightmarish hours he'd just endured, what warm, sympathetic company she would be for him.

He's comin' down here again, Nola warned, as Selena sat beside the fire, brushing the remaining moisture from her freshly washed hair.

"I know," she said, a smile playing upon her lips. "I beckoned him."

So, do ya not wish to put somethin' else on? her familiar asked in a critical tone.

Selena cast a glance down at the yellow dressing gown she wore and shrugged. "My heart might have invited him, but my words did not. And, since this is rightfully *my* thatch now, he will simply have to see me in whatever state I'm in, when he happens by."

That carriage ride with the English girl has left him in a worse mind than ya realize.

"Faith, why must ya always be so nigglin' with me, cat? The crystal ball shows ya a few passin' moments of discomfort in anyone at my hands and, next I know, you're carpin' at me as though I'd beheaded someone. I told ya I would do neither of them any real harm, and I kept my word, while still drivin' that snooty wench off. Now, what more can ya ask of me? Besides," she added, rising from her Carver chair and crossing to the dining table with a brusque gait, "I found their little jaunt quite humorous, if the truth be told."

Upon reaching the table, she set her brush down on the seat of one of its chairs. Then she reached out to the vase of wildflowers, which rested in the center of it, and snapped off three of the thick bouquet's bright yellow blooms.

Stooping to see her reflection in the round mirror, which hung upon the thatch's eastern wall, she carefully slipped the flowers' stems into the right side of her thick hair. "And, to my credit," she went on firmly, "it must be noted once more that I did, indeed, caution him about eatin' too many of my scones. If you were gazin' into the ball on the evenin' I carried 'em up to him at the great house, ya must have seen and heard me warnin' him."

That I did, mistress. 'Tis just that I worry about how much sufferin' we've cast upon him thus far. I cannot help thinkin' that the gods might have some retribution in store for the pair of us because of it.

"Lest ye forget, however, it has all been in the name of preservin' Irish justice."

From what? Stafford hasn't shown himself to be particularly tyrannical or greedy.

"Oh, but he will, given more time here. I've yet to meet an Englishman of title who hasn't. Save for my dear Prescott, of course. And that was only because I succeeded in winning control of him before he could cause any real damage."

Shushing her, Nola leapt away from the door and up the loft stairs. *He's just outside now!*

Selena allowed Pearce to knock a few times before she responded. Then, picking up her hairbrush once more, she resumed her coifing while walking to the door at a leisurely pace.

"Stafford?" she said, feigning flusterment as she greeted him. "Oh, do forgive my appearance, will ya? I fear ya've found me just comin' out of the bath."

To Selena's secret delight, he couldn't seem to resist looking her sheerly clad form up and down.

"You *bathe* in here?" he asked, his jaw dropping.

She couldn't hide her amusement at his shocked expression. "Aye. Have ya some objection to it, my lord? If 'tis my use of the well's water that concerns ya, I could put out a cistern to collect rain for such purposes."

He shook his head. "Oh, no. 'Tis not that at all. I—I simply hadn't thought of you *bathing* down here," he stammered with boyish discomfiture.

She issued a teasing gasp, her eyes growing wide. "Well then, the truth is out. In fact, I must confess to even havin' slept here once or twice in the past week or so. That is, ya did grant me this cottage that I might do as I wish in it, did ya not?"

Again mindful of how he would need her character testimony against any besmirching which Miss Barnes or her cousins might do, he nodded emphatically. "But, *of course.* Naturally, I have no complaint as to your use of the place. I guess I simply assumed that you wished only to pass a few hours a day here for some reason. You know, in order to paint or read or gaze out at the sea. Or some such thing," he concluded with an awkward gulp.

"You do not wish to have me spendin' nights on Brenna's grounds then?"

He swallowed loudly again, baffled as to how he'd managed to put her on the defensive with so few utterances, when, in truth, it was his sheer appreciation of her that had prompted him to come calling in the first place. "Good gracious, my dear lady, if I have implied anything of the sort, I am eternally sorry. Indeed, I could not be more pleased that you are here, whatever the hour."

"Why? Has someone fallen ill?" she inquired, though her keenly accurate sixth sense told her he sought something far more personal than medical aid for someone on the grounds. It was never wise to seem too knowing with mortals, however, she inwardly cautioned herself. Far better, in this case, to compel him to actually voice his needs.

He scowled, suddenly filled with dread that his disastrous discourse with Miss Barnes might somehow have been contagious—that he might now prove equally adept at offending Selena, when this was absolutely the last thing he wanted to do.

"Oh, no. Not at all," he insisted. "I—I simply came to make certain that you are faring well down here. No signs of our encroacher, I mean."

She reached out and patted his left shoulder. "Not a one, ya sweet man. How kind ya are to keep frettin' over my safety . . . But now ya look a bit wrought-up over somethin', if ya don't mind my sayin' so," she went on, with a sympathetic tilt of her head. "Would a cup of tea and a chat be of any comfort to ya, Stafford? As your beloved uncle might have told ya, I can be counted upon to keep a man's confidences, no matter what the natures of 'em."

He couldn't help flashing her a heartened smile at this invitation. What a relief it was to realize that he hadn't alienated her completely. Some nagging part of him knew that the most chivalrous course at this point would be to offer to come back when her hair had fully dried and she'd had time to don a proper dress. But, fearing that she might take him up on this suggestion—leaving him to go on wallowing in his mortification over his failed outing with Carolyn—he simply replied with, "Yes. Thank you. Some tea would be splendid."

He slipped inside. "Odd, isn't it," he remarked, "but I've just come from bathing as well."

Selena bit her lip, fighting the urge to laugh at her memory of her crystal ball's images of his bout of diarrhea while in that despicable Englishwoman's company. "Oh, aye?" she returned innocently. "This must be a good day for it then."

Stafford again caught himself staring helplessly at her. This time he focused upon the bright yellow flowers which adorned her raven hair. They looked just like the ones he'd pictured all about her in that imaginary meadow earlier, he marveled. And he knew, in that instant, that, whether she'd been ready for callers or not, he'd made the right choice in coming to her. This was, after all, the sort of coincidence that one could only attribute to divine intervention.

Selena smirked at his entranced expression and let her right hand drift up to feel about the side of her head, at roughly the point where he seemed to be staring. "Ya think me simple, don't ya?" she asked, again pretending embarrassment. "Puttin' fresh flowers in my hair, when 'tis the dear-bought gilded ones that are truly in fashion for us ladies these days."

"Oh, no. Not in the least. On the contrary, I'm struck by how lovely they are against your beautiful black mane."

"Really?" she asked, a bit taken aback by the great depth of feeling reflected in his tone. She'd believed that, sooner or later, her love spells would draw him to her; she just hadn't expected him to grow quite so senseless with infatuation in the process.

She wasn't about to rush matters, however. It had taken far too long to catch him in her net for her to risk losing him now.

"Oh, yes," he said in a reverent whisper.

"Well, let us go sit by the fire then," she directed, trying to shake him from his worshipful stare. "We two bathers, as the chill of evenin' approaches," she added with a laugh. "And I shall put on the kettle."

"Oh, yes. That would be grand"

"Grand, is it?" she asked, turning back to him with a smile, as she led him to one of her hearthside chairs. "By the Saints, Stafford, you're startin' to speak as we Irish do."

"Am I?" he asked, with a note of concern in his voice.

She waved him off as he sat down. "Don't sound so disappointed. That's good, after all."

"Oh," he said rather blankly, as she headed off to her stove.

"So," she began again in a loud, bracing voice, "how is your stomach these days? No more trouble with it, I hope."

"Yes. A bit more, I fear," he admitted. "But I have reason to believe 'tis passing now."

Again, Selena bit her lip to keep from snickering at this. "Excellent. But I do have a remedy or two to recommend to ya, should the pain return."

He rose from his chair just long enough to turn it away from the fire and more towards her. Then he sat down again and looked at her with great interest. "Do you?"

"Aye. An elixir or two of my very own concoctin'," she said proudly. "And then, of course, there is always the simple layin' on of hands. Ya know? As I did with that ankle ya turned at your lovely soirée. That is, if ya wouldn't mind my touchin' your middle," she added with a slightly teasing wink. "You'd have my vow, of course, that my hands would not stray from it."

Ah, God, Stafford thought, that was absolutely the *last* promise he'd seek to receive from her at this point! Indeed, a reconfirmation of his manhood might be precisely what he needed. "Oh, yes. Well, I suppose there's a chance that that would prove aidful to me. We could always give it a try, I guess."

She raised a sportive brow at him, as she finished kindling the flame beneath her teakettle. "What? *Now,* do ya mean?"

He shrugged. "What harm could it do, really? I must confess to not having had the easiest of days with it."

Not wishing to give him the chance to change his mind in the matter, Selena bustled back over to where he sat and knelt at his feet.

The next thing Stafford knew, her healing hands were, indeed, upon him—methodically unbuttoning his waistcoat and easing his shirttails out of his breeches. Then her two soft palms slipped in under these garments and traveled up to a point just below his ribs.

As if able to sense every inch of his soreness, her fingertips began gently pressing down upon his flesh, tracing the snaking path of his intestines from side to side, as surely as if there had been a map of them drawn out for her upon his vest.

"God's wounds! How do you know just where it hurts?" he asked in an awed murmur.

She shushed him. "Shut your eyes, pray, and let me heal ya. We shall speak further when I have finished."

Though still rather ruffled by her touch, Stafford decided to obey. Heaving a relieved breath, he closed his eyes and let his head rest against the chair's high back.

In spite of the fact that his luck with women of late had been atrocious, he felt oddly certain now that, come what may, all would go smoothly with this one. Were it not for the use-worn tenderness of the area she was touching, he thought it even possible that he might actually be relaxed enough to fall asleep amidst the soothing feel of her ministration.

To his disappointment, her velvety fingers did finally reach the waist of his breeches once more, and, true to her word—blast it all—she withdrew them from him and slowly rose to her feet.

"Feeling any better?" she asked softly.

He opened his eyes to see her smiling down at him. "Yes," he said with mild surprise. "As a matter of fact, I do. Thank you. Thank you very much, my dear."

Though she continued to grin, she shook a stern finger at him. "And no more of those sweetie scones for a while. I believe I felt more than your share of them just now, as I traced my way down that gullet of yours."

He chuckled at this ridiculous claim and shook his head. "Caught irrefutably at my gluttony, am I? I suppose there would be no point in my trying to deny it."

Her hands dropped down to rest on each of her hips. It was the classic Irishwoman's fighting stance. "Absolutely none."

"All right. I promise. No more sweets for me for a time."

"Capital choice," she replied, reaching out to run a tousling hand through his hair as if he were one of the youngsters she doctored. "Now, over to the table with ya, and let's have our tea."

Stafford, of course, obliged her, anxious to let the warm, soothing beverage take over where her healing fingers had left off upon his stomach. *"You're* the Selena whom Eddie spoke of a fortnight past in my study," he acknowledged with a broad smile, as he sat down to be served. He hadn't thought about this since the night of his soirée, when he'd mentioned it to Brownwell; but it came rushing back to mind now. Perhaps because he wanted so much to keep his conversation with her going.

Looking puzzled by this declaration, she made her way over to him with the requisite cups and saucers. "What was that?"

"I say, I have just recalled that *you* are the one who told Eddie the stable boy that butterflies live for no more than a month."

Stafford noticed that she frowned upon hearing this, and, without a word, she returned to the stove to get the kettle and tea leaves.

"Eddie told ya that?" she asked, as she rejoined him.

"Yes. I remember it quite clearly, because, as you know, I am a great admirer of butterflies, and I couldn't help thinking how remarkable it was that anyone had been able to gather such information . . . Well, I suppose, one might do so, if he or she kept them in captivity, from chrysalis to death. But captivity could hardly be similar enough to the conditions under which they live in the wild, now could it. That is, when one considers the probability that such a creature would die far sooner in confinement than in nature. So, in any case, Selena," he added, reaching out and placing a palm over the steadying hand she now rested on the table, as she poured the boiling water through the tea strainer and into their cups, "what I am attempting to say, in my bungling way, is that I'm in awe of you, if you have, indeed, succeeded in obtaining such knowledge."

She continued to look ill at ease with this topic. "You're

quite right of course. One would have to consider the likelihood of early death in captivity." Slipping her hand out from under his, she pushed his cup of tea over to him. Then she sat down before her own. "And it is for that reason that I troubled to observe them only out-of-doors."

"But how could you have? I've hunted them long enough to know just how elusive they are, and I feel certain I could not keep one of them in my range of sight for even an hour, much less an entire month."

She took a sip of her tea. "Well, that is just it. You *hunt* them. You seek to kill them. While I merely seek to study 'em."

"So, what is your meaning? That they somehow know the difference in our ends?" he asked with an incredulous laugh.

How absurd, Selena heard him add in his mind, as he lifted his cup to his mouth. Though, to his credit, he proved polite enough not to actually voice it.

Nevertheless, she responded to his slightly demeaning look with a steely one of her own. "That is precisely what I mean to say. How, by truth, can ya think otherwise? Have ya never, with all of the hounds and horses ya own, come at one of them with a will to lash out for some disobedience? And has the animal not, in turn, sensin' this sentiment in ya before you've even said a word, cringed or run away?"

"Well, naturally," he conceded. "But 'tis commonly known that horses and hounds are a good deal brighter than butterflies."

She cocked her head at him. "Really? But how, when you would find it so difficult to learn the length of their lives, Stafford, could anyone have possibly come to measure their intelligence?"

Though he continued to appear jocular, he narrowed his eyes at her impregnable wit. "They are *not* fairies, woman, and, pray you, understand that you shall never persuade me to believe they are."

She threw up her hands, issuing a light laugh of her own. "Ah, Mother Mary, man, I'm not tryin' to. I'm only sayin' I've had occasion to observe *many* of them, from caterpillar to carrion, and one month is all they live, and there's an end to it! Now drink what remains of your tea, before it grows cold!"

As she lifted her cup to her lips again, in order to follow her own good counsel, she saw him fighting his amusement at her sudden bossiness.

"You are trouble," he said under his breath.

"Why? Because I know what I know, and I use my learnin' to help others?" She shook her head. "Nay, Lord Pearce, you'll never see that brought against me. Besides, your good uncle always fared well here with me at his side, did he not?"

"As far as I know."

"Oh, aye. I swear to ya, he was a most contented soul as master of this manor. Which is a good bit more than can be said of you. And don't ya bother tellin' me I'm wrong on that score. I saw your face minutes ago, when ya first came down here, and ya looked as though ya hadn't a friend in the world. So, pray tell, what is it that burdens your heart?" she asked, her tone turning genuinely sympathetic.

He stared down into his nearly emptied cup. "Oh, I don't know. But, because you did say you would keep my confidences earlier, I suppose I can hazard telling you that you're right. Many things have gone awry for me since I assumed Prescott's position." He gave his head a shake, half wondering why he had told her even this much. But then, she was very similar to Wexford's physician, he supposed. Healer or doctor, what was the difference really? Both had to be trusted with everyone's secrets or they would not have remained thusly employed. And, God knew, given how daunting Miss Barnes had been as a conversational partner, Selena couldn't help proving far easier to talk with.

So, bearing all of this in mind, he drew in a bolstering breath and tried to be more specific in response to her still questioning expression. "I am not—not myself. That is, I say and do things sometimes which seem entirely apart from my own will. Why, just today, I fear my words greatly offended someone. A young lady of some import, I am sorry to tell."

"Would it have honestly mattered to ya less, had she been a peasant?"

He clucked with annoyance at the trenchant way in which she'd made this inquiry. "Please, my dear, let us not lock horns again about how inconsiderate you think me of lesser beings. You have my assurance that you've made your point where that is concerned. I am merely saying that I uttered things this afternoon which I should not have, and which, I swear to you, I never intended to say. And it would ease my mind tremendously if you would agree to speak out on my behalf, should the need arise."

There was suddenly a coquettish glint in her eye. "And say what, Stafford?"

"That I am a gentleman, of course."

"Hmm. But how would I know that in such case? You've not come courtin' me, as I'm sure ya must have been her."

"Well, I suppose I was wooing her in some measure," he admitted. "But you must believe me when I tell you that I never, ever intended for matters to go as far as they did."

To his dismay, his hostess looked quite intrigued by this. What was worse, she sidled over in her chair, closing the space between them as she began speaking to him in the hushed tone of a town gossip. "Ya mean to say ya propositioned her?"

He scowled. "Um, ye-yes. *How* did you know that?"

She sobered a bit. "Oh, I didn't. I merely guessed is all."

He continued to frown. "You are a terribly good guesser, as it happens."

"Ah, 'tis nothin'. It simply comes from years of listenin' to people's troubles. Anyway," she continued, again looking intrigued with his recounting of his afternoon with Miss Barnes, "what is it exactly that ya didn't intend to say to her, yet did? If I'm to speak out for your honorable character, which of course I will, I really should know the precise nature of your *faux pas*."

Though he was inwardly taking great comfort in her willingness to come to his defense, Stafford shook his head woefully. "Believe me. It does not bear repeating."

She leaned towards him once more, her next words flowing into his ear in a hot stream. "Did ya say ya thought she would have the tightest of love sheaths?"

In spite of the fact that this query caused him instant arousal, he pulled his face away from hers with an appalled gasp. "Dear God, *no!*"

She laughed softly at his aghastness. Obviously unswayed by it, she beckoned him to incline his ear towards her again with a curling forefinger.

When he failed to do so, she laid one of her warm palms upon his left thigh. "Did ya say that ya wanted to press your cock between her creamy breasts?" she pursued in another heated murmur.

Again he was seized by an impassioned tingle, which ran from his left ear all the way down to his groin. "Most certainly not!"

He reached up and brushed some stray locks of hair from his now seemingly feverish forehead. "S'death, Selena," he exclaimed, glowering at her. "Whatever is the matter with you? How completely depraved!"

To his further astonishment, she didn't bat an eye at this scolding. She simply removed her hand from his leg, rose from the table, and began clearing it of their cups.

"Ah, perhaps," she said, in a suddenly matter-of-fact tone, "but I *have* succeeded in makin' ya feel better on the subject, now, haven't I? Why, just think of all the truly indecent things ya might have said to her! It could have been far worse, I've no doubt. And, consider, too, if ya will, what secret pleasure ya just derived from my havin' shown ya as much."

"I'm shocked," he maintained, as she carried the dishes to her washbasin.

She smiled over her shoulder at him. "No, you're not. In fact, I wager ya found it wildly titillatin', just as your uncle always did. Believe me, 'tis usually more than sweets that men of the same clan love in common."

"I am flatly speechless," he declared, as she returned to the table.

"Well, were I some village virgin, I could understand your bein' so. But I'm not. I am a woman of experience and I have never pretended to be aught else. If, however, you now find my company too objectionable to continue abidin', do feel at liberty to take your leave. I'll not hold it against ya," she concluded with a shrug.

Their eyes locked in those tense seconds, hers unyielding in her conviction that she'd done nothing wrong in venturing a couple of guesses as to what he'd said to Miss Barnes.

Then, finally, to her relief, he threw back his head and issued a hearty laugh. "You're quite wicked, you realize," he declared, wiping some chuckle-induced tears from his eyes.

She smiled down at him. "Aye. But ya must admit that I have succeeded in makin' ya feel better in every regard."

"So you have," he agreed, suddenly unable to resist doing something outrageous to her in return.

Before she could possibly have had time to move away, he reached out and grabbed her by the hips. Then he turned her about and pulled her down to a sitting position upon his knees—as though she were nothing more than a passing serving wench at a public house.

It was Selena who gasped now, as she found herself wrapped in his muscular arms and planted upon his lap.

"Stafford Pearce! Just what is it ya fancy you're doin'?"

"Whispering to you," he answered in a hush, as his lips traveled around to her right ear. "Even as you did to me. I want to swive you."

She gasped again and tried to pull away from him. It seemed the only respectable thing to do; yet he held her fast.

"No," he went on, shushing her. "That is what I said to the young lady I offended. You seemed so eager to know that I thought I'd better tell you."

"Oh," she replied with a somewhat relieved sigh. "I thought you were sayin' it to *me.*"

He brought his mouth so close to her ear, as he spoke again, that Selena could actually feel it brushing her flesh. She shut her eyes in response, and the innermost part of her began to melt.

Nearly a kiss, she thought. Almost.

She had waited so long for this moment that she could only thank the Heavens now that it had come at a time when her face was turned away from him, so he couldn't see how deeply grateful she was. How very hard she'd been working toward it.

Then, praise be to the gods, it finally came: that soft, moist puckering of his lips at a point just beneath her earlobe. That act that could not possibly be explained away by him later as anything but a kiss.

"Is this all right," he asked in a low, heedful tone, before attempting to do it again.

Though she did her best to keep it steady, her voice was aquiver as she answered. "Aye."

In the space of a heartbeat, his mouth was upon her once more, kissing her with far less reserve now. His lips and tongue dotted a seductive trail down the right side of her neck.

As he brought his hands up to her breasts a moment later, she couldn't help letting herself fall heavily back against his broad chest.

"She was daft, ya know," she said in an undertone.

He replied in an equally dreamy whisper. "Who was?"

"The woman who refused ya today."

He sounded even more breathless with passion than she was, as his fingers massaged the hardening peaks of her breasts through the sheer cloth of her dressing gown. "Do you think so?"

"I *know* so," she answered, no longer able to resist turning upon his lap and pressing her lips to his. "I—I would never have said ye nay," she managed to purr between kisses.

Something snapped in Stafford upon hearing this. Any small

voice of reason which he could have hoped to rally against the risks of having relations with his uncle's former lover, was stifled by her seeming adoration of him; and, the next thing he knew, he was gathering her up in his arms and carrying her over to her hearth rug.

It was mercifully darker there, away from the stark sunlight, which was streaming in through the kitchen's windows; and, as he set her down beside the glow of the fire, he noted that she had the most bewitching eyes he'd ever seen in a woman.

You *must claim him, remember,* Selena heard Nola warn her in a meow from the direction of the loft. *'Tis you who must do the mountin' if ya swive, or your love spells won't hold!*

I know, I know, Selena shot back to her telepathically. *And, if you'll kindly be quiet, I'll try to see it done so. Jesus, Mary, and Joseph, cat, it has taken me weeks to get him this far. I dare not scare him off now!*

"I'm afraid of this," Stafford confessed, as he went on kneeling at her side.

She reached up, and, firmly taking hold of his cravat, pulled his face down towards hers. Her voice had the quality of thick dark honey dripping from a dipper as she replied. "Don't be, love, for I swear that you shall find me the finest ally a man could ever require."

Fifteen

Stafford was not given the chance to say anything in response to this. His mouth was overcome by Selena's, as she suddenly sat up and began kissing him with fervor, her grip traveling upward to grow ever tighter upon his neck scarf.

He felt a certain shortness of breath at her hold, but, as her other hand raced down and, with thrilling adeptness, found the very tip of his manhood through his breeches, he hesitated to say or do anything which might discourage her obvious intention to pleasure him.

She was magnificent! The sensation of her tight massaging grasp absolutely exquisite, and, in spite of himself, his torso grew weak as he continued to kneel beside her.

"Oh, *Selena,*" he choked out, between her deep kisses. "Even given our conflicting opinions, I've such tender feelings for you. I have since the night we met. 'Tis as if there is nothing in the world I cannot say to you."

"There isn't," she assured, her voice so soft and winning that he thought he might burst then and there for want of her.

He *had to have* her, he realized in that instant. It wasn't her dear delicate hand that he had so longed to erupt into, but her sweet warm body.

Unfortunately, however, this masterful call to action, this urge to free himself of his breeches and she of her gown and simply claim her in those seconds, ended in her throwing herself upon him and shoving him backward, onto the rug. This, in turn, made his head hit the floor with a dizzying thud.

It was the second time that day that a woman had caused him physical pain. First there had been Carolyn's slap across his face, and now this. Fortunately, though, his present discomfort seemed due to his being desired, rather than repelled.

A second later, Selena was sitting astride him, the skirt of her garment pushed far up upon the lengths of her niveous thighs. And, though she had relinquished her almost strangling hold upon his cravat, she was tearing at his trousers' buttons now with such zeal that he actually heard the front panel of the garment rip.

"Selena," he exclaimed under his breath, "how will I explain this upon my return to the great house?"

Continuing to struggle for access to his privates, she let her face drop down to his right ear with a seductive growl. "You're clever enough to contrive some innocent excuse for it. Are ya not, my lord?"

"I suppose so," he answered, fighting his way back up to a sitting position. "But you don't understand," he continued through clenched teeth. He took hold of her upper arms with a firmness that surprised her enough to halt her efforts to ravish him for a second or two. And, in that brief pause, to her dismay, he gained the upper hand.

"Pearce men are not swived, my sweet," he declared, rolling her onto her back with alarming speed. "Rather, 'tis *we* who do the swiving!"

This certainly hadn't been true of his uncle, Selena thought, as she stared up into his smoldering dark eyes. On the contrary, when it had come to their first joining, Prescott had succumbed to her spellbinding aggressions without a word of protest, enabling her to hex him all the more. But, being at least twenty-five years his junior, Stafford had his own code of conduct apparently, and Selena was finding herself too overwhelmed by his strength and lustful will to contend for very long against him. Not without aid of her magic, in any case.

He was pushing up her gown now, and, knowing there was no time to spare, she mouthed the last line of an immobilizing incantation and every part of him froze as though he were an enormous stuffed bird sitting over her.

She seized the opportunity to slip out from under his weight. Then, when she was safely away from him, well into her kitchen, she took refuge on the far end of the dining table and freed him from her paralyzing spell with a nod of her head.

"Selena?" he said, staring down at where she had been lying beneath him with a befuddled expression.

"Over here," she gingerly replied.

"But what—what are you doing over there? You were here just an instant ago."

"Aye. But don't ya remember? Ya let me up to pour a glass of water for myself. I was so very thirsty, as you'll recall."

"Oh," he said blankly. "So, have you now drunk?"

"I have."

Donning a welcoming smile, he got back up to a kneeling position and opened his arms to her. "Then come back to me."

She shook her head, remaining safely behind the table.

He quirked a brow at her, suddenly looking rather wolfish by the dancing firelight. His tone was half provocative and half threatening as he spoke again. "Oh, so 'tis sport you seek?" he asked, slowly getting to his feet.

She swallowed nervously, poising to run in either direction, depending upon his approach. "In a manner of speaking, I suppose it is."

"Selena Ross, you should be spanked for leading a fellow on this way," he said tauntingly, as he began stealing towards her. "Why, I cannot imagine my uncle tolerating such flightiness from a woman."

"Perhaps not. But 'tis different with you, sweet Stafford. For you're far younger than he and, therefore, possess the stamina to give chase."

Apparently having already had his fill of this game, his slow, cautious approach gave way to a desirous lunge, which brought him so close to her that she had no choice but to hex him again.

This time, she caused him to slip on the kitchen floor and crash, face-first, into the edge of the dining table.

"Ruddy Hell," he exclaimed, as he lifted his head once more to reveal a bleeding cut at the side of his lower lip. "I swear I shall thrash you, once I'm around this accursed thing! You're certainly experienced enough to realize how mad you are driving me with this sudden coyness, and we all know that a madman cannot be held to account for his deeds."

He raised his hand to his injured lip and, upon seeing the blood it left on his fingers, he looked all the more angry with her evasiveness.

Selena, in turn, began easing away from the table.

"I thought you wanted me to make love to you," he began again, his large eyes suddenly brimming with entreaty.

In spite of herself, Selena felt her resolve to take charge of their joining softening. "I—I do."

He furrowed his brow. "What? With a table between us? Well, perhaps I don't know how 'tis done in Wexford, but, in England, lovers must come a good deal closer to one another than this in order to achieve such ends."

Though still tense about trying to gain the advantage with him, she couldn't help tittering at this remark. She hated having to admit it to herself, but she'd always found a humorous wit terribly seductive.

"Ah. So it *is* the same in Wexford, is it?" He reached across the table, extending a conciliatory hand to her. "Well then, do come along now, my dear, and let me show you how fond I've grown of you . . . You cannot imagine what a dreadful afternoon I've had. How coldhearted the woman I was squiring was to me," he continued, when she failed to respond. "Indeed, I came to you expressly to find comfort in your company. I simply knew, without having to be told, that you are wiser and kinder than most ladies could ever conceive of."

He must have been wielding some magic of his own, because, instead of continuing to step out of his range, she simply froze at this touching appeal. "Oh, Stafford, I—"

Before she could choke out another word, however, he dove under the table and grabbed her by the legs! Then, rising to his full height once more, he slung her over his right shoulder and carried her back to the hearth—one of his large palms delivering a swat to her derrière, before he again deposited her upon the rug.

"I'm a gentleman, to be sure, my dear," he said in a growl, as he positioned himself over her a second or two later. "But never one to be trifled with regarding such a serious business as this."

Showing even less restraint with her than she had with him, he wasted no time in shoving the skirt of her dressing gown up to her midriff. Then he hurriedly undid what buttons she hadn't torn from the front flap of his breeches.

Upon seeing the true length and breadth of what he freed from the garment, Selena couldn't help wincing a bit in anticipation of the initial pain she knew it would bring her. It had been so many weeks since she'd lain with a man, let alone one as well endowed as Stafford, that she wondered now at her presumptuousness in trying to have her way with him.

She squeezed her eyes shut, knowing that to offer any further resistance now—supernatural or otherwise—would probably be to drive him away for good and all.

He was clearly still angry; obviously pushed to his limit by both Miss Barnes' rebuffs and her own seeming indecisiveness. She sensed that a smack on the bottom wasn't all she'd suffer as a result.

He slipped his upturned palms under her well-rounded posterior, and she continued to cringe in anticipation of his forceful entry of her. Instead, however, she found herself shocked to feel him kissing her stomach. Wet, warm, and surprisingly gentle, his lips slowly made their way downward from her navel to the secret place which awaited him between her legs; and, with great skillfulness, he began readying this private part of her for their merging.

Though his large hands continued to hold her in place, she

managed to arch her back slightly at the titillating feel of his tongue. Playful, yet demanding, it wriggled over her love knob, then plunged inward to lap at the most sensitive reaches of her.

How methodical he was as he repeated this sequence again and again. How torturously teasing!

She could see in his gleaming eyes, as she stole a glance down at him, that he fully meant to castigate her in this way, for having been arrogant enough to try taking the lead with him in what he apparently viewed as a solely male domain.

They were, even in so ardent an act as this, keen competitors beneath the flesh; and it wasn't until she cried out minutes later, at not being able to bear any more of his tongue's work, that he was finally merciful enough to replace it with his tumescence.

As they began to make full-fledged love, she heard her familiar scolding her with a yowl for not succeeding in initiating their coupling. She was so transported by the ineffable sensations that Stafford was causing within her, however—so overwhelmed at having such a young strong man servicing her, after so many years in Prescott's frail arms—that she had no hope of offering any defense for herself.

She was flatly stunned that two people, who, only moments before, had been fighting for dominance and who likely couldn't agree on even the simplest of governmental policies, could now be bringing such ecstasy to one another.

Perhaps it was merely the passion of the moment clouding her perception, but in a full two centuries of life, she could not remember having experienced a more satisfying lover! It was as though they had been created for one another. The scent of him, his heat, as he glided over her. His timing and his every move within her—all of it seemed so suited to her that it was as if she had always known him, had always been meant for him and he for her. They were like two halves of a broken sword finally being forged back together, after eons of separation.

His arms traveled up to close about her shoulders, as the

culmination of their act seemed to near; and he held her as though he never wished to let her go.

He wanted her, *needed* her, would somehow have been diminished without her. She could read all of this so clearly in his thoughts now, that it was as if their minds were one.

Stafford couldn't believe what pleasure his motion within her was bringing him. He had never known anything like it. Each thrust into her sweet secret depths was like a tiny climax which sent chills running up and down his spine. With every inch of himself that he surrendered to the sublime vortex within her, it was as though his very spirit was being hoisted heavenward; and his mind was filled with divine images of gilded autumn leaves falling from the trees of what seemed an enchanted woods. Gleaming red and orange as blaze itself, they drifted and whirled to the ground, settling at the feet of oaks which appeared to have wise old faces etched into their rippled trunks and whose uppermost branches sparkled against an evening sky, as though lit by the flashing glows of a thousand fireflies.

It was absolutely unworldly! Unlike anything he'd ever known before, but now would be hungry to see again for the rest of his days.

It was sheer *magic;* and, as his body finally began to yield to hers and he could no longer hold back the hot tide he would cause to flow into her, he was so overcome with emotions that he was actually very near tears—and, as he'd been reminded since toddlerhood, Pearce men were *never* very near tears.

"Dear God, I think I love you," he said in a worshipful whisper, feeling he had no choice but to reveal this soul-stirring truth to her.

"And I you," Selena murmured back—to her surprise, meaning every word of it.

Sixteen

They lay, still intimately linked, in exhausted silence for a moment or two, each breathing heavily and laughing a bit at the tempestuousness that had swept over them.

Pearce lifted himself just enough to look down into her face. "Now, you see, love, that was not so bad, was it? Hardly worth running away from me because of, do you think?"

She sighed with utter contentment, her deepest recesses still pleasantly throbbing from his intoxicating thrusts. "Oh, nay. 'Twas wonderful, in fact."

"For me, as well . . . Uncle Prescott would *kill* me if he knew what just happened," he added, chuckling at how trivial this comment sounded after the earth-moving experience they'd just shared.

"Do ya think so?"

"Don't you?"

"Nay. In truth, I think he would rather I gave myself to you, than any of the other lords in these parts."

"Now I understand why he did not visit London as much as we would have liked. He was kept too happy here by your many charms."

"You flatter me, sir."

He propped an elbow to the left of her and shifted much of his weight onto it. Then he reached down and brushed some stray strands of hair from her forehead. "Rubbish. You know full well what a prize you are, and now you've let me know, too . . . I truly hope I didn't hurt you," he continued, looking rather embarrassed about having been so forceful with her.

Donning a subtle smile, she shook her head.

"Ah, good. Because you really are rather small, you know. For all of your fierceness at times, you're surprisingly delicate to the touch. In fact, should you ever let me do this with you again, I think a bed would be in order, don't you?"

"Aye. And I've one here. Up in the loft."

"Do you? . . . Oh, yes. That's right. You did tell me earlier that you spend your nights here sometimes. And, blast it all, I shan't sleep soundly ever again, for wondering when you are here at Brenna and when you are not."

She slanted him a playful look. "Would ya have me throw pebbles at your bedroom window then, to let ya know for certain?"

He shook his head. "You need only leave a lamp burning near one of your windows, and I'll be down here in a twinkling, good lady. That is, if you'll have me."

"I shall. More often than I should, no doubt. But be ye forewarned, Stafford. Tongues will wag at such an arrangement."

He looked concerned by this admonition. "And more to your detriment, than mine of course. I do realize that. So we will have to be discreet. At least until such time as we decide what should be done about the fact that we seem to love one another . . . Oh, Heaven take me, did you hear how readily that came from my lips? 'Tis as though I've had some practice at saying it with women, when, in fact, you are the first to have heard it from me."

This *was* the truth, Selena realized with a touched sigh. She could see it in his mind. He'd praised the beauty of many a female in his time, but she was, quite honestly, the first he'd ever professed to love!

God bless him. She hadn't expected such candor from an English lord—particularly in light of the fact that she wasn't sure her love spells had fully claimed him yet. But she felt certain that she could take him at his word on this.

He finally eased himself off of her. Rolling onto his back, he heaved a satisfied sigh. "I don't want to return to the manor house," he admitted.

After pulling her gown back down over her legs, she rolled onto her right side to face him. Then, placing an elbow on the floor, she let her head come to rest in her upraised right palm. "You needn't. Why not stay a while longer?"

"May I?" he asked rather sheepishly.

"Of course. I've just given ya my very self, after all. Why, then, would I not grant ya more of my hospitality?"

"You've a bed here, you say?" he fished, still feeling ill at ease about inviting himself into it. Nevertheless, there was nothing very comfortable in continuing to recline upon a mere rug, cast over hard hearthstones.

She smiled, pushed up to her feet, and extended a hand down to him. "Aye. Come along then. To where we should have gone from the first."

He did not hesitate to join her, of course. After closing his trousers as best he could around him, he quickly rose and took her hand.

She led him up to the dimly lit loft, and, as he reached the top of the stairs, her cat hissed at him, then skittered off to hide under a nearby hooped-back chair. "Such a serpent's greetin', Nola," Selena scolded. "Is that any way to behave towards a guest?"

As he climbed up into the chamber, Stafford looked all about him. It was a small, though beautifully furnished room, with a four-poster bed which had a ruffled, aqua coverlet spread over it.

His home away from home, he instantly thought. It was so ideal a refuge from the demands of serving as master of the manor, that he couldn't help feeling he'd seen it before—that he'd somehow always known it awaited him.

"Ah, Lord, what savages we were," he said, looking downward. "Why, I did not even remove my boots before lying with you!"

"Well, remove them now then," she said, walking over to the far side of the large bed. Then, with a smile, she turned back to face him and nonchalantly began unbuttoning her gown. "Take off everythin' and come snuggle for a time beneath my warm covers."

Still looking a little unsure of himself, he strode to the far end of the bed's footboard and extended a hand to her.

She reached out and took it in one of hers. Then he raised them both to his lips and kissed the tips of her fingers. "You're truly a lady, Selena. I shall not lose sight of that, no matter what liberties we may feel compelled to take with one another."

Donning a confident smirk, she slipped her hand from his and returned to the task of unbuttoning her garment.

To his surprise, she made no effort to turn away as her dressing gown fell open, baring her ample breasts. It was as though she was totally comfortable being naked with a man. As if she were actually less self-conscious out of her clothes in his company, than in them. And Stafford realized in those arousing seconds what a creature of nature she truly was. How out of character she'd always been in the dresses in which he'd seen her.

She had a glorious body—one which he knew he wouldn't have been able to keep from staring at, even if she had been one to act shy. Her legs and arms were slender, her waist small enough for him to nearly encircle with his hands, and her breasts and hips were perfectly balanced in size.

"Come on. What's keepin' ya?" she asked, as she finally stepped out of her gown and slipped in under her bed's spread.

The discerning look in her eye told Stafford she was completely aware of how transfixed he was at having seen her disrobed.

" 'Tis your turn at it, after all," she prompted again.

"Miss Ross," he returned with an indignation that was only half feigned, "I have never stripped myself for a woman in my life!"

She leveled a glare at him. "Then 'tis time ya did . . . Do

so," she began again after several seconds, "Or be on your way at once, Lord Pearce. This is *my* thatch now, remember, and my word is the rule here."

Realizing that she was, more or less, serious in this demand, he slowly began to comply. He sat down on the unoccupied side of the bed just long enough to pull off his calf-length boots. Then he rose once more and shed the rest of his clothing—all the while aware of her shamelessly relishing regard.

"Ah, good," she said, once he was fully undressed. "Now come lie close and tell me more of this young lady ya so unintentionally propositioned today. I'm terribly jealous of her, I hope ya realize."

He crawled in under the covers and sidled over to where she lay, the length of his nakedness pressing up against hers. "Oh, she means nothing to me," he assured. "I would much prefer we talk of you."

"I do wonder though—that is, if ya don't mind my askin', why you would say come hither to a woman, when ya did not feel that way towards her."

"Oh, I rather felt that way. In the heat of the moment, you understand. I simply had not planned on saying as much."

"Well, perhaps she put ya so at ease that it just slipped out."

He raised a brow at her. "At ease? *Carolyn.* Hardly."

"That was her name then? Carolyn?" she pursued, continuing to pretend total ignorance of the encounter.

"Yes."

She knit her brow. "That's odd. I cannot call to mind anyone by that name hereabouts."

"Oh, she's not from Wexford. She's a Londoner. And 'tis just as well you don't know her. A wholly unpleasant soul, that one! I suppose the best that can be said of her is that she drove me to come seeking you today. Her heartlessness was what caused me to realize that 'twas you I truly craved. So, you see, far from being jealous of her, we both owe her thanks for bringing us together."

"Owe an *English*woman thanks? Never," she grumbled.

"What was that?"

"Oh, nothin'."

He snuggled up more tightly to her and slipped his left arm under her shoulders. "Now, on to speaking of you, my dearest. I really know so little about your life, prior to your taking up with my uncle."

She shrugged. "There is little to tell. I have always lived in Wexford, and, though I am a woman of means, my tastes are very simple. In truth, I feel far more comfortable here in this thatch, than I ever did in the great house, and so I thank ya again from the depths of my heart for it."

He turned his body so he could face her more fully. Then he reached out and ran his fingers through one of her long tresses. "After what you just granted me downstairs, I would give you every thatch I own," he said, his voice brimming with gratitude.

To his dismay, she pounced upon this remark. Turning more squarely to him as well, she smiled and said, "How generous of ya, my lord. Aye, I accept them, and I give ya my word that I shall personally oversee all of the crofters who live in 'em."

His previously contented expression sank to a frown. "Oh, Selena, pray do not be ridiculous. Of course you won't serve as their landlord. Only *I* am entitled to do that."

"But why?" she asked with an innocent bat of her dark lashes. "Why, with all of the demands upon ya here at Brenna, would ya not welcome my aid?"

He gave forth a nonplussed laugh. "Because 'tis not a woman's place. Putting herself in possible peril presuming to come collecting rents from strapping farmers."

She issued an equally baffled laugh. "What is your meanin'? That I need fear their wraths for some reason? *I,* who have helped to bring most of their babies into this world and regularly keep fevers from claimin' their entire clans?"

He shook his head sternly, his dark eyes growing less and less amused with her contention. "Let us hear no more of this absurd topic," he replied, pressing a forefinger to her lips. "Do you not realize I was merely speaking hypothetically about my thatches?"

"Nay," she countered, pulling away from him. Then she sat up and crossed her arms over her chest. "I heard ya offer 'em to me fair and square. And so did my cat."

He tugged playfully on her right elbow. "Oh, do stop this now, love, will you? We were getting on so well, before you misunderstood me."

"But that's just the point, isn't it? I *did not* misunderstand. You said that, after what I just granted ya downstairs, you would give me every thatch ya own."

Stafford groaned. Women could be such excruciating literalists sometimes. He had thought he'd left most of the world's female wranglers behind, when he'd departed England; however, this was, apparently, a trait common to Irish ladies as well.

"But that is where we've missed one another, you see?" he said evenly after several seconds. "I said I *would,* which, you must agree, is a very different word than *can.* There are, of course, many, many gifts a man would make to his lover, but that does not mean he always *can.*"

"Then, perhaps, ya cavilin' bugger, I *can't* be persuaded to ever open my legs to ya again! Now, what say ya to that?" she concluded, using two hands to give his chest a good shove away from her.

Pearce considered the possibility of never being given another chance to experience the life-transforming bliss that her body had imparted to his, as they'd made love; and it quickly became clear to him that some sort of compromise was necessary.

"You'll see to *half* my crofters' steads then, *Delilah,*" he returned grudgingly. "And not a one more!"

Her lips gave way to a grin and she reached out to pull him back to her with an appeased purr. "That's grand, dear Stafford. I just knew you could be persuaded to be fair in this."

"Yes, but I do, nevertheless, insist that you take Flaherty or one of my other men with you when you go collecting."

She nodded, still looking very pleased with the agreement. "That I will."

His eyes narrowed as he continued to regard her. "My uncle was not the first for you, was he?"

She met his squint with one of her own. "Are ya askin' or tellin'?"

"Asking."

"Why? What matter would somethin' of that sort make to ya?"

"It doesn't really. I'm merely curious."

"But why? Can you truly tell me that I was only the second lady you have ever lain with?"

"That is a different matter entirely."

"Why?"

"Because it simply is, Selena. Most men of my station have their first lover bought for them by their fathers. A courtesan of dear papa's choosing, in the hopes of not loosing his lad, fumbling and painfully inexperienced, upon his future bride."

"Is that how it was with you?"

"Of course."

She surveyed the long line of his body with an admiring twinkle in her eye. "Then your father would be pleased to know he chose well for ya."

"Thank you."

She looked suddenly sympathetic. "Was it awfully embarrassin'? Your first time with a total stranger, I mean."

He pondered it, doing his best to recall the details of having lost his virginity. "Not really, I guess. The drapery was drawn in her room, so it was mercifully dark."

"And did ya like it?"

He issued a dry laugh. "Yes, indeed. She was the confident, yet compassionate sort. Much as you are, my sweet. But, sadly, and through no fault of hers, it was over far too soon."

"So she did not let ya stay and have another turn at it?"

"That was not the house's policy apparently, and I was, of course, too bashful about the whole business to request that my father see her paid a second time . . . But now you've again diverted me from my question, my dear. Who was it that taught *you* the ways of love? Not my uncle, surely. Not with those exotically churning hips of yours. He simply was not well-travelled enough to have learned of such maneuvers."

"Perhaps not," she replied, fighting a giggle, "but he certainly enjoyed them."

He clapped his palms to his ears with a kind of mock disgust. "Oh, please, tell me nothing more of his predilections in bed. With him having been my father's brother, 'tis too akin, I fear, to hearing of my own parents' carnal practices."

"Very well then, darlin'. I shall say nothin' more on the subject."

The truth was she was very happily relieved of it, for no mortal could fully understand that, though she, like Prescott, was not well-travelled, and had passed her entire life thus far in Wexford, she'd grown up in a time and among a people who actually encouraged sexual promiscuity. Her kith and kin had, in fact, revered the rich red of holly berries for its resemblance to a maiden's monthly blood and the white fruit of mistletoe for its likeness to semen.

Nevertheless, as had happened to Stafford, she'd lost her innocence to one chosen for her. A Druidic priest many years her senior, whose fully matured body had, despite his efforts to be gentle, torn at her callow, untried form with a lustiness that could not have been ignored. Yet, unlike Stafford's disappointingly brief merging with his whore tutor, Selena's first experience had seemed to go and on forever, leaving her sore for days afterward.

Such was life in a woman's skin, however, she told herself stoically. Such, too, were the rigors of the fertility rites which the people of her faith held most dear. It, nonetheless, had to be noted that, in time, she'd not only learned to enjoy the act of coupling, she had actually come to be quite good at it.

But none of this—not one deuced word of it—could ever be told to Stafford. As fond as she'd already grown of him, she knew that he and his fellow humans could never be expected to understand a Wiccian's ways.

"Let us sleep for a while, my love," she said in a soft hypnotic voice. She placed her right hand on Pearce's brow and, with her magic, rendered his eyelids suddenly too heavy to keep open.

Although she was not always successful in her efforts to alter people's memories, it was her hope that a nap would keep her companion from recalling that he had been seeking to know how she'd come by her sexual expertise.

Stafford woke a couple hours later from the deepest and most refreshing sleep he'd known since coming to Brenna. Selena was still lying at his side. She had her back to him, yet she was breathing so rhythmically that he knew, without seeing her face, that she'd succeeded in falling asleep as well.

The loft was nearly dark now. It was illuminated only by the dim blue light of dusk, which emanated from the downstairs windows; and, not wishing to waken his new lover any sooner than was necessary, he eased himself out of her bed and began feeling his way back into his clothes.

"Must ya go?" she inquired with a yawn, as she rolled over and looked at him seconds later.

"Yes. I really should. Mr. Flaherty and the rest will be wondering what has become of me so well past suppertime, and there seems no sense in causing them to worry."

"Then come back down afterwards, why don't ya," she suggested, blinking drowsily.

"Not again this evening, love," he replied, in a tone meant to soften what she might perceive as a rejection. Indeed, rejecting her was the *last* thing he meant to do, now that he'd come to realize how much he cared for her. He simply needed some time alone during which to sort through the raft of emotions that their impassioned hours together had stirred up in him.

He couldn't think clearly in her presence, he acknowledged. He never had been able to, and, having been so intimate with her was only serving to further cloud his mental processes.

"Tomorrow though, my angel. I shall come down to you again without fail," he promised, his hands working in the darkness to get his chin-high cravat retied.

Upon finishing this task, he slipped back into his boots. Then, fully dressed, he circled around the bed to kiss her goodbye.

Her lips eagerly claimed his; and, knowing from experience that she was entirely capable of seducing him all over again, he placed a hand on each of her shoulders and gently, but firmly extricated himself.

She issued a soft wrenching sigh which threatened to yank him back into her arms; yet he managed to fight his more basic urges and make his way over to the loft's ladder.

"Until tomorrow then," he said, blowing her a kiss, as she purposefully let the bed's linens fall away to reveal her naked breasts. "Stop it now, ye shameless temptress," he added with a nervous laugh. Then he began descending the steps by the light of the dying fire in her hearth.

"I love you," she called out.

"And I you," he shouted up to her, before taking his leave.

A couple seconds later, she heard him close the cottage's door behind him; and Nola, as though relieved at his departure, crept out from beneath the hooped-back chair and sprang up onto the bed.

You should have mounted him, the cat chided, starting to preen rather smugly.

"Aye. And I tried to, didn't I? Ya must have seen how I made him give chase, so I could turn the tables upon him. I did the best I could."

Nay. Ya should have claimed him while ya had him frozen. Or caused him to fall into slumber, then done the deed to him.

"Aha! At last, dear familiar, I remember the laws of our magic more clearly than ye do," Selena shot back triumphantly. "The subject in such spells must be both awake for and aware of such claimin' for true love to ensue."

Nevertheless, mistress, ya should not have forsaken your aim, as ya did, for fear that any more resistance from ya might have driven him away.

"But he seemed smitten enough afterward. Ya heard for yourself how he granted me half his crofters' thatches."

Half? Humph. Prescott gave 'em all *to ya. And on the very first night ya met him, no less.*

Selena squared her chin, refusing to be disheartened by Nola's seemingly unwarranted concern. "Well, he's more reluctant than his uncle, is all. We've known from the first that he's a wilier sort."

Aye. I only wish we could also be sure ya've truly claimed his heart now. We could all rest a great deal easier, if we knew that for certain.

"I shall simply see to it that the next time we make love 'tis I on the top."

That you'd better. For, by the gods, the cat added, her tiny nostrils suddenly widening, then contracting, *I still smell trouble ahead with him!*

Seventeen

Stafford felt as if he were a naughty schoolboy, as he stealthily entered the great house minutes later. Selena had left the front flap of his breeches in such a battle-torn state that he had to keep one hand constantly upon it, so that the garment didn't slip down from around his waist.

To make matters worse, he could tell, even without aid of a mirror, that his thick, long hair was completely sleep-disheveled.

Luck seemed to be with him, however. As he crept in through the terrace door, there was absolutely no sign of his otherwise inescapable steward; and, with no other staff member in sight either, he actually began to hold out hope that he could sneak all the way up to his suite without being detected.

He tiptoed down the corridor which led to the front staircase. Just as he rounded its newel post, however, he came face to face with his second-in-command.

Flaherty gasped upon seeing him. Then he threw one of his pudgy hands over his gaping mouth. "By the Saints, my lord, who dared to do that to ya?"

"What?" Stafford returned, reaching up and self-consciously running a smoothing palm over his hair.

"Well, attacked ya, of course. Why, just look at ya. Your mouth has been bloodied. Your trousers are torn. Faith, forgive me for sayin' so, but ya look as though you've been dragged through a knothole!"

Pressing a couple fingers to his cut lip, Pearce discovered

that it had, indeed, begun bleeding again. He did his best to produce an unconcerned chuckle, however. "Oh, nonsense. I'm fine. I was simply visiting with Miss Ross," he explained, lowering his voice considerably.

Pushing past the steward, he began hurrying up the stairs. The Irishman, of course, followed. Stafford could hear him very close on his heel.

"Ya mean to say *she* did these things to ya?" Flaherty inquired, now speaking in a whisper as well.

Pearce gave forth another nervous laugh. "No, no," he quickly denied, not wanting to tarnish Selena's reputation with the full truth. "I simply slipped on the floor of her thatch, cutting my lip on her dining table, is all. 'Twas nothing. I assure you."

As they reached the door of Stafford's suite, the steward drew up beside him with one astutely raised brow, his expression saying that this response hadn't begun to answer what might have left his breeches and hair in such obviously ravished shape.

"Beggin' your pardon, sir," he began again guardedly. " 'Tis no business of mine, I know; but the pair of ya didn't come to blows, did ya?" His eyes warned in that instant that he considered crossing swords with the healer a most ill-advised thing to do.

"No. Of course not. On the contrary. We are most fond of one another."

The Irishman's face lit up like a radiant dawn, and he enthusiastically clapped his palms together. "Ya *are?*"

Stafford clucked with wonder at this exuberant response. "Yes. In fact, she will be seeing to the collection of half my crofters' rent henceforward, if you will kindly accompany her on such progress," he said, stealing a look about the hallway to again make certain no one was overhearing them. Fortunately, there wasn't a soul in sight. But then, to his dismay, he noticed the ajar door of Mr. Brownwell's suite shutting quite abruptly against his searching gaze. "Horatio is up here?" he asked the steward in a barely audible voice.

"Aye, sir. He has been most of the afternoon, I believe. That is, save for two trips down to the kitchen to inquire as to why we were holdin' supper so late."

"Well, he need not wait much longer, Flaherty. I shall tidy myself up a bit and be down to dine within ten minutes, if you will please tell the cook as much."

"Aye. That I shall, sir. And might I say how glad I am to hear that you and Miss Ross are gettin' on so well these days."

An obviously disapproving ghost hunter awaited Stafford as he entered the dining room a short time later.

"Mr. Brownwell," Pearce hailed with a forced smile, "how are you this evening?"

"Famished," the Londoner answered simply, not hesitating to seat himself in the very same instant his host did so.

As on previous evenings, Horatio sat just to Stafford's right; but now, as though wishing to bridge what little space remained between them, he drew his chair up even closer to Pearce's.

"Because you are failing to grant me the audience I have so repeatedly requested with you, my lord, I hope you will permit me to receive it now."

"Fire at will, man. I sense I could not dissuade you from it by refusing, in any case."

"Very well," he replied, taking the added liberty of splaying his arms out before him on the table, as though planning upon conversing as bluntly as a carpet merchant. "I believe that you and I had better be as aboveboard as possible regarding your acquaintanceship with your uncle's affianced."

Though Stafford inwardly bristled at this topic, he waited until the serving girls had placed their respective bowls of soup in front of each of them and again left the room, in order to respond.

"What of it?"

"Are you enamored with her?"

"Of course not," he lied in an incensed tone. "Why would you ask such a ridiculous question?"

To Pearce's surprise, this hireling didn't even blink at his sudden anger.

"Because you *look* to be, my lord. Though I know your servants haven't the mettle to make mention of it, you have appeared increasingly lovesick of late, and I can only conclude that 'tis our resident healer who has put you in such a way."

"Well, that is absurd," Stafford maintained, bringing one of his fists down heavily upon the table. "I insist that you cease making such accusations at once!"

"But did I not overhear you saying to Mr. Flaherty earlier that you are allowing her to preside over half of your tenant farmers?"

"So, what of it?" he retorted defensively. "Who better for collecting my due from them, than a woman with whom they have entrusted their very lives?"

The ghost hunter sat back in his chair with a somewhat resigned sigh. "Very well. Leaving your fondness for her, *or* the lack thereof, aside for a moment then, sir; I do feel you are entitled to know what I have learned of her."

Though Stafford wasn't entirely sure why, an uneasy lump began forming in his throat. "And what—what would that be?"

"Well, that she hasn't a family home in town, as she told you the night you met."

"Of course she has, Brownwell. She *must.* Where else could she have gotten the chairs and such to completely furnish that thatch I gave her?"

Horatio shrugged. "I don't know. Did she claim that they came from her family's stead?"

Pearce narrowed his eyes, trying to remember. "I don't recall. That is, I suppose I simply assumed that they did. My thinking sometimes grows a bit muddled when I'm with her," he added absently. Then, reminding himself who he was speaking to, he immediately regretted having done so.

"Does it?" his companion replied with a meaningful look. "That *is* revealing, isn't it."

"Mr. Brownwell," Stafford growled, "do stop suggesting that I am somehow senseless with affection for her! I assure you that, whatever my feelings where she is concerned, I still have my wits very much about me."

"In that case, I am confident that you shall hear me when I tell you that there is no family—" His words broke off as one of the serving girls again entered from the kitchen with an uncorked bottle of dinner wine.

"You were saying?" Pearce prompted, as she began to pour for them.

The ghost hunter shook his head and raised a silencing finger to his own lips, as if to warn that no one on Brenna's staff should be allowed to hear what he had been attempting to say.

"Come now. Surely your investigation cannot have turned up anything so unspeakable," Stafford said bitingly, when they were alone once more. "I feel certain my servants can be trusted."

"Well, I do not," Horatio countered. "And, perhaps, when you hear all I have to say, you will understand why. You see, there is no Ross family home in town, as your uncle's betrothed claimed, because there is no Ross family in the whole of Wexford. Indeed, according to the town registers, there has not been for over two hundred years. What is more, days of searching on my part have failed to bring to light even one scrivened fact about Miss Ross's origins or those of her parents. Not so much as a date of birth has been entered for any of them."

Though Pearce was troubled by this news, he did his best not to let it show. He simply nodded thoughtfully, then took a long drink of his wine. "So, what is your meaning? That *she* is the ghost we've been seeking? Are you questioning her very existence?"

Brownwell greeted this with a dry laugh. "Of course not. She is obviously quite real. Why, your hours with her in her thatch this afternoon must have told you that much," he said pointedly.

Stafford glowered at him. "How would you know how long I was with her?"

Horatio fingered the stem of his wineglass. "You are my client, Lord Pearce. You engaged me so that I might defend you against the dark forces of the afterlife. 'Tis, therefore, my business to know your whereabouts whenever possible. I am merely pointing out to you that something seems very much awry with Miss Ross. And, given the dreadful experiences you've had since coming to this place, I should think you would wish to finally get to the bottom of it."

The two men fell silent again, as the maids reentered with platters of roasted pork and boiled vegetables. Then, when they'd been served and were alone once more, Stafford responded with, "In that case, you had better know that, far from vexing me, Miss Ross was the only true comfort I knew today. You see, while I attempted to win the affections of a lass from our own England, who is kin to a local family, I ended by being made such a fool of in her presence, that only our resident healer could restore any sense of assuredness in me."

"What on earth do you mean?"

"Well, I was 'haunted' again, while on my outing with Miss Carolyn Barnes this afternoon. For some reason I found myself saying things I should not even have been thinking, and emitting the most inexplicable noises. And, next I knew, the young lady had had her fill of my behavior and was slapping my face and demanding that I return her to her cousins' manor at once. And, you may believe me when I tell you that I have *never* before given any woman cause to lash out at me thus. Then, upon my return home, who should it be, but the 'villainous' Selena Ross who revived my faith in myself and rid me of the frightful stomach pain I suffered while with Carolyn. So, you see, Brownwell, you have no call whatsoever for casting doubt upon Miss Ross's motives. Even as true-blue Irish as she is, she treated me far better than one from our own land! 'Tis no wonder that my uncle chose her over a maiden of English blood," he finished with a self-righteous lift of his chin.

"And perhaps, by making certain that your efforts to court other ladies go amiss, he is seeing that you do the same."

"So you think it was Prescott foiling my carriage ride with Carolyn?"

"It could have been, I suppose."

"But for what purpose? Why would he want me to have *his* lover?"

Brownwell shrugged. "Out of pity for her maybe. Ghosts are well known for sympathizing with those they held most dear while on earth. Perhaps he simply does not want her to be lonely-hearted."

"So he is driving me towards her?"

"He could be. If, indeed, 'tis his spirit with which we are contending. But, to be frank, my lord I have cause to believe it is not."

"Then whose ghost could it possibly be?"

"No one's."

"No one's, Mr. Brownwell? I fear I'm not following you."

"If you will be good enough to extend your present audience with me to an after-dinner drink in your study, I shall be more than happy to demonstrate what I am saying."

Stafford, of course, agreed to this.

Though it took the ghost hunter several minutes to prepare for his promised demonstration, he finally finished doing so—his entire collection of outlandish spirit-seeking devices now lined up upon the front edge of Pearce's desk.

The first of these was a tiny V-shaped crystal vial, which rested within the upraised metal prongs of a large wooden stand, as if it were a jewel in the setting of a ring.

Into this vial, Horatio poured a small amount of clear blue liquid from another container, which stood next to it on the desk. When the vial's contents looked to measure roughly half an inch in height, he stopped pouring and cautiously backed away from it.

"Why are you moving so lightly?" Stafford asked, from where he now sat behind the desk. "Do not tell me 'tis somehow dangerous!"

"Oh, no. Not at all, my lord. I simply don't want to cause any vibrations in it. You see, 'tis a very special fluid, indeed. One used solely for metaphysical purposes and, therefore, we must both stay as still as possible for the next moment or so."

Pearce, naturally, complied. Staring at the vial as intently as Brownwell was, he froze in his chair and stayed that way for the next several seconds.

Absolutely nothing transpired, however. The mysterious blue liquid remained every bit as motionless as its two observers in the minutes that followed.

"That proves it then," the ghost hunter declared finally.

"Proves what?" Stafford asked, mystified.

"Well, don't you see?"

"See *what?* There is nothing happening."

"That is just my point, sir. Were there a ghost present, we would surely have spied some sort of activity in the vial by now."

"Really?"

"Most certainly. I've done so in each and every case of true haunting that I have undertaken."

Pearce responded only with a shrug.

"But I can tell that you are not yet convinced, my lord."

"No. Not in the least, in fact."

"Well then, let me show you how this next instrument functions. 'Tis a spirit sphere," he said, turning what was, apparently, the front of a large sievelike silver globe around to Stafford's vantage point. "Now, if, indeed, there is an apparition anywhere near, it will be drawn into this aperture which you see here," he explained, sticking his forefinger into the large opening in the face of the sphere. "Pray permit me, if you will, to temporarily extinguish the candles in this room, that I might demonstrate."

"Oh, yes, do."

Brownwell scurried about accordingly. Using the snuffer from Stafford's desk, he put out the flames of the two tapers which burned on either end of the room's upper hearth ledge. Then he returned to where Pearce sat and brought the study to total darkness by bending far forward and blowing out the pair of lamps which flanked the lord's blotter.

Though not usually afraid of the dark, Stafford had to admit to himself that he was finding this exercise much more unsettling than the last. "Tell me, Horatio," he said in a low voice, "just how are we to be able to see what enters this sphere of yours, now that we are in total blackness?"

"Well, it starts to glow when occupied. 'Twill be as clear as day to you, if it comes to pass. Thus the need for darkness, sir."

"And said spirit will enter through the opening you turned towards me?"

"Precisely."

"Ahum," Pearce uttered in response. It was a sound that was half affirmative in nature and half the product of a rather skeptical throat-clearing. Nevertheless, he leaned back in his desk chair and did his best to wait patiently.

When, after what seemed a couple moments, not so much as a glimmer of light could be seen emanating from the direction of the odd globe, the investigator again proclaimed that this was irrefutable proof that no one from the ghostly realm was present at Brenna.

"Well, there is our answer, my lord," he said once more. "Not a soul afoot here." With that, he strode off to the adjoining hallway and returned an instant later, carrying one of the flickering candles from the holders which were mounted on the wall just outside the study door.

"But, I don't know," Stafford replied, as Brownwell hurried about, relighting all of the wicks he'd extinguished. "If ghosts are as cunning as you have given me to believe in the past several days, would they not sense your intention to exorcise them? And would they not, in turn, be disinclined to reveal themselves by way of these . . ." he paused, searching for a tactful term, "these contrivances of yours?"

Having finished returning the room to its illuminated state, Horatio blew out the candle he'd taken from the corridor. Then he perched, half facing Stafford, upon the front of the desk. "Oh, but they cannot be, you see, my lord. For these instruments were designed expressly to draw them forth. While they may appear odd or unattractive to you or me, spirits find them quite irresistible."

"Be that as it may, Brownwell, this manor has scores of rooms beneath its roof. So how can testing this one chamber tell you anything about what might be lurking on another floor or in one of the wings?"

"That is an excellent question. You are quite correct that such tests must be conducted in every part of a dwelling before a conclusion can be reached. And let me assure you that that is precisely what I have been doing since coming here. I have not only employed the instruments I've shown to you, but many many others, again and again, in every reach of this house, and, not once, in all the time I have been here, have I seen any evidence that Brenna is haunted."

"Then what explanation can you give for all that has befallen me?"

"I cannot, I fear. That is, I have my theories, but I will need a bit more time to verify any of them."

Stafford threw up his hands. "But what other causes could there be?"

"Oh, I really should not say, sir. At least not until I have had a chance to investigate the matter further."

"Brownwell, I've already seen you paid quite generously for your efforts thus far, so surely you can tell me what your guesses are at this point."

"Very well then," came his reluctant reply. "I suppose 'tis

possible that you have been cursed somehow by one of the local folk."

"Cursed?" Pearce repeated, his voice rising with disbelief.

"Yes. This is not London, after all, my lord. 'Tis not as if you've inherited entirely amiable circumstances. As you well know, we English are hated here, and, with so many tinkers and Gypsy sorts passing by, who can say what kind of dark powers may have been brought to bear against you or this manor? The Irish are, as you know, a most superstitious lot. Their ancient pagan faith has writings which state that 'by words *alone*' shall they 'smite their enemies and cause them all manner of adversity.' So I'm sure they regularly conjure up their bands of 'wee folk' to work their evil deeds for them."

"Bloody Hell, man! I don't, for an instant, believe in wee folk. So, how can a fellow be cursed by creatures he does not even think exist?"

"Well, many people don't believe in ghosts either, yet I earn a very fair living, year after year, ridding homes of them. One usually cannot see them, but, when they choose to make nuisances of themselves, one will pay a goodly sum to have them driven out."

"But, even if you can prove there has been a curse put upon me or this place, is there anything you can do to remove it?"

"I will certainly try. I am considered, by those who know me best, a man of many resources, and you have my promise that I will do all in my power to vanquish whatever or *whomever* is vexing you!"

Eighteen

A priest, *mistress,* Nola exclaimed, while gazing into their crystal ball the following afternoon. *Why on earth would Lord Pearce have sent for a priest?*

Selena, who was hunched over her dining table reading an ancient spell book, sat bolt upright at this alarming question. "Are ya certain that is what you're seein'?"

Dead sure of it. Who else wears a cassock, but a man of the Church?

Selena set the volume facedown on the table in order to mark her place in its pages. Then she hurried back behind her folding room partition, where she kept the presageful crystal hidden from the view of visitors.

Having leapt up on the small table upon which the ball rested, Nola was staring into it with the intensity that most cats would dedicate to a kettle of fish.

"Lord, it *is* a priest, isn't it," Selena acknowledged, bending down to look into the crystal as well. "Why, it appears to be Father Purcell, in fact," she noted, as she watched the steward ushering the clergyman down the great house's first-floor corridor and into the new lord's study.

Faith, 'tis that ghost-hunter fella greetin' him. Do ya see? Nola asked.

"By God, so it is. Could it possibly be he's a Catholic?"

A Londoner. Hardly.

"Then why is he receivin' him with such enthusiasm? If

someone on the grounds has grown ill enough to need a priest, you would think Flaherty would have come seekin' *me* by now."

Nay. 'Tis not by cause of sickness, mistress. Look there what Purcell is takin' from his pocket. 'Tis the paraphernalia of exorcism!

"Sweet Mother Mary, that villain Brownwell has engaged him to clear the place of evil spirits or some such thing!"

Nola shook her head and went on staring at the ever-changing images in the ball. *Oh, faith, we can't have that! What if he continues on to this thatch? Nay, nay! We simply cannot have a man of the cloth rummagin' through our belongin's! 'Tis far too dangerous for us,* she concluded in a panic-filled voice.

Selena reached out and gave her pet's back a pat. "Don't be worryin' yourself so. We'll think of somethin', if he heads our way . . . Simply keep a watch on him and call me back here again, should anythin' important come to pass."

Having just uttered this reassurance, however, Selena herself gave a terrible start as her return to her reading was interrupted by a sudden knock at the door.

"Ah, God, 'tis *Stafford,* isn't it?" she whispered back to Nola.

Aye, mistress, the cat confirmed. *Catchin' ya in nothin' more than a workin' frock again, I fear.*

"Well, not if I have aught to say about it," she replied; and, within a twinkling, she had her book of spells hidden away in a secret hollow behind a removable hearth stone. Then, with a mere sweep of her hand, her magic reattired her in a gorgeous emerald green day gown.

"Stafford?" she said, pretending surprise as she swung the door open to him seconds later.

"Selena," he returned, smiling and running an admiring eye down the beautifully clad length of her.

She smiled as well, though not as fully. Then she met his gaze with an innocent look. "And what brings you here on this fine, sunny afternoon?"

He rolled his eyes at her. "Ah, God's bones, pray don't tell me you are one of those heartbreaking ladies who makes the most passionate love with a fellow one day, then acts as though she scarcely knows him the next."

Continuing to smirk coyly, she turned away from the door and wandered over towards her dining table, leaving him to see himself in. "Nay. 'Tis simply that I thought there might be some specific aim in your comin' down. Perhaps that someone has taken ill and needs my help?" she fished, still curious about the priest's visit.

He stepped inside, shutting the door after himself. Then he wasted no time in coming up behind her, where she stood in the kitchen, and wrapping his arms about her waist.

As if possessing some presaging abilities of his own, he brushed the loose tendrils of her upswept hair aside and began kissing the back of her neck—the one overture that Selena had never been able to resist from a man.

"Well, yes, in fact," he whispered. "I must confess that someone is indeed in need of your healing at Brenna. 'Tis I, you see. I desperately require your aid in relieving me of this awful swelling here," he finished, bringing one of her hands back and placing the palm of it upon his ready loins.

Though she couldn't help chuckling at this adolescent ploy, she managed to grow sober, as she turned about to face him. "Ah, so, 'tis white heather ya seek from me, is it?"

He moved his arms up to her shoulders and hugged her closer to him. "No. In truth, I was hoping for a slightly more *personal* remedy. Do you suppose you could think of one?"

"Given some time, I fancy I could."

He planted a kiss on her forehead and relinquished his hold upon her. Then he strolled over to the hearth. "Far be it for me to rush you, good lady. I've all the time in the world, when it comes to one as enchanting as you are."

"Have ya?" she replied, walking towards him with an equally nonchalant air. "And what of your torn breeches and such last evenin'? I do hope your steward and the rest did not tease ya too terribly over that."

He turned back to face her, as he reached the fireplace. "As a matter of fact, Mr. Flaherty did express a bit of concern over it. He seemed to think you and I had gotten into a tussle for some reason. Can you imagine?" he continued in a probing tone, "a Pearce man coming to blows with a lady? What on earth would make him think such a thing? Don't tell me you and old Prescott used to be driven to wrestling one another on occasion."

"Oh, faith, no! Your uncle was forever the gentleman, Stafford. Ya must have known at least that much about him."

He propped an elbow on the hearth's upper ledge, then leaned back heavily against it. "Yes. I suppose I did. In any case, my dear, Flaherty seemed to believe I would be most unwise to cross you."

"And he said as much to ya?" she asked, unable to hide her surprise at this insinuation.

"No. 'Twas simply the warning look in his eye that conveyed it, as I recall."

She was very relieved to hear this. "Oh."

"So, what have you?" he began again, with a provocative smile. "A wicked right thrust of which I should steer clear? Or was he merely thinking of your obvious sway with the local gentry?"

"Aye. That must have been what was in his mind," she quickly confirmed.

A silence fell between them and Stafford seized the pause to glance about the place. "You know, I just cannot help marveling how beautifully you have furnished this cottage. 'Tis as if these chairs and such were *made* for it. Designed with an eye to settling them in this very dwelling."

"Why, thank you," she returned tentatively, unsure of where this praise might be leading.

"You're quite welcome." He began running his right forefinger along the smoothed edge of the hearth ledge, doing his best to continue seeming as though he was speaking offhandedly. "So, um, where was it you said it all came from? Your family's home in town?"

"I don't believe I did say. But you may be sure that I came by it honestly, if that is what concerns ya."

He issued a forced laugh. "Concerns me? Oh, no. Gracious no. It never once occurred to me that you stole it, love! What on earth would make you think I suspected that?"

She shrugged, "I don't know. Ya simply seemed a bit too curious just now."

"Too curious? No, no. Not at all. In fact, many of my acquaintances back in London used to remark that I am the least questioning fellow they know. Which is why my friend Mr. Brownwell has seen fit to come to Brenna, I suppose. Now *there* is a gent who is filled with questions! Indeed, do you know what he was asking me about just the other day?"

"I cannot imagine," she replied, refusing to join in his stilted jocularity on the subject.

"Well, he was asking why, in all of his searching of Wexford town's records, he had not come across your family's name. Save for some entries made over two centuries ago."

"And what did you tell him?"

"What did *I* tell him?"

"Aye."

"Well, Selena, what could I have told him? I know nothing of your kin, except for the snippet or two you have offered me regarding your parents."

"And why would Brownwell need to know more?"

"Oh, he doesn't. Not in the least. He was likely just making small talk with me over it, was all."

"Well, do be good enough to inform him for me that this is not London and we citizens of Wexford are not interested in wastin' all our days and nights scrivenin' every detail of our lives into our public records, as you English do! Thus the omissions of my family name, I assume."

Feeling quite relieved at having finally extracted this explanation from her, Pearce fought the urge to laugh at her outrage at the ghost hunter's prying. In the space of just a few seconds, her cheeks had grown bright red with anger, and she looked as if she were capable of carving Horatio up for supper without an ounce of compunction.

Hers was, Stafford was realizing, one of the fiery Irish tempers of which his uncle had often warned him. It had to be remembered, however, a voice inside him hastened to add, that old Prescott had also always been quick to say that the local folk were, in the main, the most affectionate people he'd ever encountered. So they were double-edged swords, it seemed.

"Please," he began again, crossing to her and taking her into his arms once more, "do not be offended by Horatio's findings. He's a bit meddlesome, I know. But he truly means no harm."

Despite the fact that Selena very rarely resorted to employing a pout with men, she did make the concession of letting her lower lip protrude slightly now. "All right," she agreed in a childlike voice, "but keep him away from me and from this thatch. Though I know he's a friend of yours, I must admit to finding him quite distasteful."

Pearce hugged her to him with a soft laugh. "Just a week or two more, my angel, and then I promise to send him home to England. Meanwhile, let us not spoil another moment of our precious time together with talk of him," he concluded, punctuating it with a kiss.

Selena reciprocated. Filled with renewed hope that his obvious love for her could continue to be manipulated in her favor, she opened her mouth to his with abandon.

Although the urge to sink to the floor with him and again make love was nearly overwhelming for her, she somehow managed to draw her face away from his seconds later, with a higher purpose in mind. "Do ya trust me, Stafford?" she inquired gingerly.

He looked, for just an instant, taken aback by this question. "Yes. Of course."

"Ah, so ya don't object to my puttin' that trust to a bit of a test then?" she asked, lowering her voice to an enticing murmur.

He smiled, seeming shamelessly eager to take part in just about any sexual act she might suggest. “And what have you in mind, my dear?”

She wrapped her hands tightly about each of his wrists and drew them back behind him. “I wish to blindfold ya.”

Despite the fact that he appeared rather caught off guard by this, he continued to smile. “For what purpose?”

She brought one of her hands upward and wagged a finger at him. “For a purpose you shall understand, once I’ve covered your eyes and not before.”

“Very well,” he answered, his voice beginning to betray some uneasiness.

Having finally obtained his consent, she reached forward and, with what struck Stafford as surprising effortlessness, she undid his cravat and slowly, savoringly slipped it out from behind his neck.

Then she moved around to the back of him once more, and, warning him to close his eyes, placed the neckband of the long tie over them and knotted it firmly about his head.

“This is a game you used to play with my uncle, isn’t it?”

“Nay. There was never any need for it, ya see. For, unlike you, he trusted me completely.”

“As do I,” he maintained.

“Nay. Ya don’t entirely. But ’tis my hope that ya will, once I’ve finished with ya.”

He cleared his throat, largely to mask his continued disquietude with being thusly handicapped. “This hasn’t to do with hot candle wax, does it?”

She laughed again. “Nay. Nothin’ of the sort.”

“Ah, good. I’ve never much cared for being burned, you see.”

“But I thought ya told me at your soirée that you Pearces are fairly impervious to pain.”

“Did I? Well, I was mistaken then. I must have forgotten how I feel about burns.”

"Whisht with ya now," she ordered, with continued amusement in her voice. " 'Tis not my plan to burn ya, as I've said."

Though he did his best not to let it show, he took tremendous comfort in being assured of this again. Nevertheless, he had to admit to himself that some primitive part of him was finding the uncertainty of letting her take total charge of him strangely exciting "So, just what is it I am to do, now that I can't see?"

"I'll simply have ya walk with me," she answered, circling back around to the front of him and taking one of his hands in hers.

Her fingers felt like those of a young girl to him now. Tiny and seemingly so weak, when compared to the largeness and sinew of his. Yet every inch of him was aware that she was anything but weak. Indeed, she was, in some way he might never be able to fix upon, one of the most formidable people he would ever have the pleasure of knowing.

"Walk? Up to your loft, you mean?" he asked hopefully.

"Nay. A wee bit farther than that, I'm afraid."

He began to experience misgivings once more. "Farther, you say? Well, just how far can we go in this little thatch?"

"Oh, but we're leavin' it."

"Leaving it? You mean, we're going out where one of my servants might catch sight of me this way?" His voice was edged with horror and he jerked his hand out of hers.

She just as quickly reclaimed it, however. "Nay, Stafford. No one will see ya. I promise. We're just goin' off into the woods."

"With all of those hare holes and tree roots? But how will I know if I'm about to trip or turn an ankle?"

"Well, that is where your trust in me enters in, isn't it?" she asked in an exacting tone. "You will simply have to rely upon my eyes to work for us both, now won't ya?"

He let her lead him towards the door, then grew hesitant as they were nearly to it. "But why the woods? What could you possibly wish to do with me there?"

"Show ya somethin'."

"What?"

"A *dead* body," she returned in a menacingly low voice.

Before Stafford could even fully experience the shocked chill that ran through him at this response, she let go a burst of uproarious laughter.

"Oh, you *are* enjoying this, aren't you, my dear," he noted grudgingly. "This golden opportunity to try to frighten me."

"Aye. 'Tis great fun, I must confess. But, remember now, that ya did bring it upon yourself by allowin' that beastly friend of yours to go sniffin' round about my family name."

"But that was strictly in the line of duty, as I have explained."

"And so is this, you may be sure," she retorted, stopping just long enough to shut the cottage's door behind them. "For, lest ya prove your trust in me thus, I believe I won't be able to go on givin' myself to ya, Stafford Pearce."

This threat made the undertaking suddenly seem worthwhile to him. "In that case, lead on, my beauty."

They walked for what struck him as an interminable length of time. He was, however, able to see a foot or so of the ground before him, as they proceeded, through a slight gap at the bottom of his makeshift blindfold. And this, fortunately, served to prevent any missteps on his part. Then, too, Selena, being of smaller size than he, possessed a mercifully slower gait, as she led him along.

They were, just as she had claimed, in the woods now. Stafford could see how the ground was strewn with broken twigs and the vines extended from the trunks of some of the older trees they passed. And he was duly comforted by it. Thusly cloaked by the enveloping forest, he could stop dreading the possibility of being seen by any of his staff at what might have appeared a moronic game of blindman's buff.

When, at last, they reached what looked to be a row of large grayish stones, Selena turned back to him, and, pressing her palms to his chest, brought their mysterious hike to a halt.

"Where are we? May I uncover my eyes now?"

"Not just yet," she answered in a saucy voice, stepping closer to him and beginning to unbutton his waistcoat.

"Are you disrobing me?" He was filled with mixed emotions at this prospect.

She bent towards him and began kissing his chest, as she bared it from beneath his shirt—each of her pecks followed by a wet stroke of her tongue. "You're a clever lot, you English."

"But what if someone happens upon us?"

"No one will."

"How do you know that?"

"Because this is *my* place. A secret place which only I know of, and no one ever comes here."

"I don't think I like this," he said with renewed trepidation, as her hands moved downward and began undoing the front flap of his breeches.

"Oh, but you will," she assured, her voice now sounding like an unearthly mix of feline purr and siren's song.

If any part of Stafford doubted his hearing in this, what he experienced next told him he shouldn't. As her hands slipped behind him and eased the seat of his trousers down to his thighs, it was not a human tongue he felt licking the sensitive tip of his manhood, but, seemingly, that of a *cat!* It chafed over him as if it were coated with sand, the friction it created so arousing that he was forced to reach down and place a bracing palm upon one of her shoulders, where she now knelt before him.

"Dear God," was all he could seem to choke out, a nearly climactic shudder running through him. He closed his eyes at the ecstasy of it, his desire to keep peeking through the opening at the base of his cravat vanquished by the compulsion to shut down all of his other senses and simply savor this extraordinary tactile experience. "*How* are you doing that?" he whispered after several seconds.

She withdrew her mouth from him just long enough to answer. " 'Tis magic," she said in what seemed a jesting tone.

"And ye must never question magic, love, lest ya scare it away for good and all."

"Magic. What a silly pixie you are."

"I suppose I am," she replied, peeling his breeches the rest of the way down to his ankles. "But, if a woman is foolish enough to reveal to her lover all of her tricks in winnin' his heart, she hazards losin' him, doesn't she? Now, slip out of those shoes, and let me show ya somethin' you shall find even more delightful."

He chuckled with disbelief and shook his head. "I hardly think that possible."

"Oh, but it is." With that, she took a step back from him, and, as he again looked downward and spied her green gown falling to her feet, he realized that she was undressing as well.

"Then you wish to make love here, in the woods? And that is your surprise?"

"Nay. 'Tis somethin' better still."

With his curiosity piqued, he removed his shoes, as she'd requested, then stepped out of the nest that his trousers had formed at his ankles. "Naked, at last," he announced, "save for this confounded blindfold, of course. May I remove it now as well?"

She reached out and took hold of his right hand. "Not just yet. But only a step or two more, I am glad to tell."

He moved forward accordingly, his bared feet sinking into the dark, moist soil of the forest floor. "Christ's Church, woman, this is the maddest thing I have ever done!"

"Ya poor soul," she replied, a note of genuine pity in her voice. "What a sad, barren boyhood ya must have known. 'Tis a shame *I* was not your nanny or governess."

He threw back his head and chortled. "Indeed! But I must say that I am not entirely adverse to compensating for it now. If the truth be told, however, one look at you, and I believe my dear father would have decided to discharge you as my governess and keep you entirely to himself!"

"Well, let us remove this now," she declared, stepping around to the rear of him to untie his blindfold. As she did so, she made a point of rubbing her naked form up against his. Her breasts straddled the side of him, at roughly the level of his ribs, as she slipped behind him.

Just like a *cat,* Stafford thought in response—that feline analogy again popping into his head, as if apart from his will. He'd never been much of a keeper of cats, far preferring the company of hounds, but he'd certainly been around the barn variety enough to know how they often went out of their ways to rub up against the humans they walked by—as if stealing the petting they sensed would otherwise go unoffered.

In that same instant, Selena slipped his silky necktie away from his eyes, and these thoughts were replaced by his astoundment at what he saw just inches before him.

"Good Lord, a hot spring," he exclaimed.

"Aye."

"But in the midst of the woods?"

"Aye. Bubbly and wonderfully warm, love."

She circled back around to face him, and he saw that she was every bit as naked as he.

"Do ya like it?" she prompted, when he went on staring down in wonder at the large circle of stone-framed water.

"Well, of course. 'Tis simply that I cannot imagine how it came to be here. A natural bath in the midst of nothing but trees and black soil?"

She stepped up onto the smooth, yet rounded rocks and dipped a big toe into the steamy water. "But that is just the point, Stafford. 'Tis because folks would not expect to find it in such a place that I have been able to keep it a secret. From all, save you now. So, pray, let it remain thus."

"As you wish, my dear." He leaned forward and peered cautiously down into it. "And just what is its depth?"

She didn't answer. She simply jumped in, splashing him terribly as she did so; and Stafford noticed in that instant that the droplets which struck his face did not smell of sulfur or minerals, as he'd expected, but, inexplicably, of rose petals.

"This depth," she answered finally, turning back to face him with the water lapping about her neck. "Get in. There's plenty of room for us both."

He was certainly inclined to, her splash upon him having borne out her claim that the spring's temperature was luxuriously warm. But, rather than risking hurting her by leaping feet-first into it, he sat down upon the rocks and slid himself slowly downward.

"Ah, Lord, you were right," he said with an appreciative sigh, as his feet reached the muddy bottom of the bath, "it is quite wonderful, isn't it? I am amazed that no one else has learned of it."

She smiled sweetly. Then, pushing off from her side of the large bath, she reached out and embraced him. "Nay, Stafford. 'Tis ours alone."

He wrapped his arms about her as well, continuing to relish the marvelous heat which swirled all around him. "So you were the one who encircled it with stones?"

"Naturally."

"Quite a bit of labor for such a slip of a lady."

"Aye. But, as ya must know, the strength of one's will can far surpass that of one's body. And I had a most powerful will to make this spring perfect in every way."

"It seems you've a will to do something else now as well," he retorted with a grin, as he felt one of her hands slip around to the front of him and again begin to provoke his arousal.

He didn't fight her, as she slowly pushed him backward, up against his side of the bath. He knew precisely where matters were leading, as her arms closed about his neck and her legs around his hips; yet he possessed absolutely no will to again insist that he be the one to do the claiming.

Though he was aware that maintaining sexual dominance with her probably should have been important to him, it simply wasn't, for some reason. Indeed, he felt as though he had just drunk far more than his usual share of brandy-wine—as disinclined towards a fray with her as a babe in a womb.

He shut his eyes, unable to fight a pleasure-filled moan, as her secret sheath closed over him an instant later. If he failed to be admitted to Heaven after death, at least he would now always know that he'd experienced the next best thing.

As had happened the first time they'd made love, he found himself unable to imagine how he had ever been moved to argue with this angel of a woman. As her wet body glided over his and the depths of her brought him an ecstasy that finally made him cry out at her ever-quickening movement, some part of him silently swore that he would never say or do anything which might drive her away.

"Are you *mine* now, Stafford?" she whispered into his right ear, as their act was finally brought to a thoroughly satisfying, if leg-weakening, close.

He hugged her tightly and bent to kiss the side of her neck with an emotional quiver in his voice. "Yes. Of course."

"Forever and for always?"

He gave forth a soft laugh at this rather unreasonable request. Nevertheless, he raised his face so he could look her in the eye with earnestness. "Yes. I believe I am."

She uncoupled from him and made her way slowly to his right. Then, turning to face the opposite side of the bath, she wrapped an arm about his shoulders. He reciprocated, slipping a hand around her waist and pulling her even closer to him.

They basked in the water. Its churning undercurrents went on shooting bursts of heat up against their legs and torsos and its intoxicating floral scent rose, with its steam, to fill their nostrils. Now confident that her having mounted him had finally made his heart hers, Selena shut her eyes and savored the lingering feel of how thoroughly he'd just filled the carnal core of her.

He was so well endowed and possessed such lustful prowess that it was difficult to believe he was actually Prescott's nephew. As much as she'd adored the old man, what bliss it was to, at last, find herself loved by a fellow who had the physical strength to protect her from others—should that ability ever prove necessary.

Though she'd always prided herself on being independent,

some bestial part of her truly liked having a paramour who could act as her champion. What was more, any misgivings she'd had about falling in love again with a mortal, after Prescott's tragic death, had somehow faded away when Stafford had lain with her the day before.

She was genuinely ready for romance once more—as open to all of its possibilities as a young maiden, and she honestly craved this new inamorato's companionship for what might prove the rest of her life.

"So, now," she began again in a low voice, "havin' not found yourself burned by hot candle wax in lettin' me lead ya here, do ya trust me more fully?"

"Oh, yes. And I'm very grateful to you as well."

"For what?"

"For bringing me to this marvelous bath, of course. Tell me, is it on my land?" he inquired with a greedy edge to his voice. "Or do you suppose the midst of these woods marks the boundary of the neighboring manor?"

Selena emitted a contented sigh and leaned more heavily back against the stone ridge behind them. "Oh, what does it matter? No one else knows of it, as I told ya."

"Yes, but what if word of it gets about? I don't want folks traipsing here from far and wide to overrun this place. Particularly if 'tis mine."

"Can ya not simply take pleasure in it without frettin' over its ownership?"

"No. It seems I can't."

She laughed to herself. "Then I would advise ya to learn to, my sweet, for this bath is *mine* and no one else's, as I've said. 'Twas I who discovered it and framed it thus."

"Yes. But, in the eyes of the law, anything that is found upon my grounds belongs to me, my dear."

She turned and glared at him, not believing that such an acquisitive spirit could rise up in him so soon after their mutual professing of love for one another. "Ah, for mercy's sake, why is possessin' everythin' so important to you English?"

"It's not."

"It most certainly is! Why, next I know, you'll be tellin' me that ya own a length of the Irish Sea, as well, just because your land ends at it."

"Nonsense. Landlords don't own water, they own land. Thus the title."

"Very well, then. Be ye now officially informed that the body of water, in which we are soakin', is mine."

He chuckled. "Well, if you want it so much, I shall make a gift of it to you."

Her glare turned to a glower of such intensity that he couldn't help recoiling a bit in response. "How dare ya presume to grant me what's of my own makin'! Get out," she ordered, taking her arm from around him, then using both of her hands to shove him away from her.

"What?"

"You heard me well enough, ya miser. Get yourself out of my bathin' pool at once, lest I lose all patience and try drownin' ya."

He stared at her for several seconds, stunned by this demand. "But I just told you you may have it. What more can you ask?"

"That is precisely the point. This bath is not, nor shall it ever be, yours to give. Now, *get out* and dress yourself and be gone from this place!"

"No," he retorted, folding his arms over his chest. " 'Twas you who invited me into it, and I shall bloody well stay for as long as I please!"

Her eyes remained locked upon his. Widening with rage, they had an almost paralyzing effect upon him, which he secretly found unnerving. He, nevertheless, refused to flinch.

The next thing he knew, she'd savagely splashed him in the face with a great sweep of water and she was scrambling out of the bath.

"Where are you going?" he asked, wiping his eyes.

"Well, I'm certainly not stayin' here with you, ya great greedy cow pat! If you won't show the decency to leave, as I've requested, then 'tis I who will away."

"Oh, Selena, stop this now," he commanded, catching hold of her right ankle, as she finally hiked herself up onto the surrounding ground. "I promised myself, as we made love, that I would never again give you cause to grow cross with me and flee, and I mean to keep that pledge."

She jerked her foot free of his grasp and hurried over to where she'd left her gown. "Aye, well, don't be too disappointed if you should break that vow to yourself. There's no one can put faith in the word of a money-hoardin' Londoner. Not even himself! You English lords are all the same. You'll let a woman into your lives, perhaps even your hearts, but never, may God forfend, into your precious purses! For *that* is where the true essence of you is to be found, isn't it?"

This accusation stung Stafford to his very soul—perhaps because he suspected it was true. "Oh, Selena," he said again, this time more imploringly. "I do apologize if that is how I seem to you. Please, what can I possibly say to cause you a change of heart?"

Now half dressed, she yanked the bodice of her garment up over her chest and forced her still-wet arms down its sleeves. "You can swear to me that you will be just in determinin' the share you shall take from your crofters each year."

"God's blood, the crofters again, is it? Why on earth have you so much interest in my dealings with them?"

"They are my people. My patients and friends. Therefore, their interests and mine are the very same."

"Not if you wed me, they won't be."

To his surprise, this allusion to a possible proposal of marriage from him seemed to do nothing to lessen her anger.

"Wed you? When has a word ever been spoken concernin' my weddin' ya?"

He offered her a gentle smile. "But you would, would you not? If I asked for your hand, I mean."

She stepped back into her slippers. "Not unless I approved of your share to the crofters."

"Very well then. Though I must inform you that it violates

my beliefs to seek your approval of my business practices, I was thinking along the lines of a ninety-eight and two percent split."

"By thunder, you're even more rapacious than I thought! How is it possible?" she asked, directing her gaze at the heavens as if seeking some divine answer to this, before flouncing off.

"Ninety-six and four?" he called after her, as she strode away.

She stopped walking and turned back to him, her lips pursed with fury. And it was in that same instant that Stafford became aware that the previously hot water all about him had grown inexplicably cool.

"No, damn it, Stafford," she bellowed. "You must agree to a fifty-fifty split or, I swear, you shall never again set eyes upon me!"

"Fifty-fifty?" he echoed, obviously horrified.

"Aye. 'Tis the only fair division."

"But *why?*"

"Because your crofters do all of the work. They sow, they tend, they harvest. They look after your sheep and such. And what, by contrast, do you do to see all of this accomplished?"

"I give them cottages in which to live and the land to farm."

"Oh? And how did ya go about earnin' that land, pray tell? Did ya sweat and bleed upon it and watch your kin be buried in it whenever a fever or famine swept through? Nay. Heavens, nay! Ya simply waited about in London for your old uncle to finally die! . . . *Fifty-fifty,* Stafford," she concluded, shaking a finger at him with such vehemence that she almost seemed to be putting a curse upon him, "Or I shall personally see to it you rue the day ya came to Brenna!"

"But no landlord of sound mind gives his crofters half."

"Some do, I'm told. But, if you are so very sure you would prefer the extra profit over me, so shall it be."

Pearce felt an unbearable ache growing in the middle of him as she again turned and began heading away. Though it had otherwise been a still day, an odd chilly wind stole up on him suddenly, causing the water all about him to ripple and gooseflesh to rise on his shoulders and neck. It was as though Nature herself was decreeing that she'd aligned irrevocably with Selena.

"All right. Very well," he shouted after her.

To his relief, she again stopped walking.

"But, by God, woman," he continued loudly, "this had better be the last of your demands upon me. I will not be the victim of such female extortion for the rest of my days!"

She turned, donned a radiant smile, and came dashing back to him. "As ya wish, sweet Stafford. No more of such requests. I promise ya."

As she returned to the edge of the spring, Pearce noticed that the breeze, which had begun blowing over him, again gave way to stillness and the bath's water no longer seemed cold. Harmony had somehow been restored all the way around. He once more felt safe and appreciated and at peace with Selena and his surroundings; and, after weeks of finding himself beset and lonely in his new home, such contentment seemed worth any price she had asked.

They spent the rest of the day together in the loft of her thatch. Again making love, then dozing off in one another's arms. As night began to fall, however, Stafford knew that he must rise, as he had on the previous evening, and leave her to go back to the great house. Until he succeeded in making her his bride, there was no respectable way to bring her with him to his bed as he so yearned to do. And, though it had enjoyed one of its longest reigns of the year on that midsummer day, the setting sun actually struck him as mournful at this fact, as he made his way westward to his manse a short time later.

He had once heard that true love often affected a fellow in such a way. That if a gent's amorous feelings for a woman were genuine, he could expect to see her everywhere he looked. In the treetops and the sea, the sun and the moon.

There was simply no denying that Selena Ross was in all of these for him now. Indeed, she seemed as crucial to his existence as the very air he breathed.

Nineteen

"Good afternoon, Mr. Brownwell," Stafford said with a wide smile, as he looked up from the ledgers he was filling out at his desk and saw the investigator standing in his study doorway. Pearce usually was not so effusive with Horatio, or anyone else for that matter, but his growing love for Selena was leaving him in an increasingly benevolent humor.

"Good afternoon, my lord."

"Do you wish to come in?"

"Indeed I do."

"Come along then. By all means," Stafford replied, waving him to one of the camel-back chairs which were situated in front of his desk.

Not returning his employer's glad expression, the ghost hunter entered and shut the room's door behind him before proceeding to the indicated seat.

Pearce pushed his ledgers aside and folded his hands in front of him. "What is it?" he inquired pleasantly.

" 'Tis in regard to my visit with the priest several days ago, sir. I felt I should finally come to you, now that I have had the time to look into some of his claims."

"Yes. I meant to ask you how he fared with his exorcism. I trust he freed Brenna of any demons who may have been lurking."

Brownwell frowned and shifted in his chair as though unable to get comfortable. "Well, my lord, I feel certain he would have, had there been any to exorcise. He seemed a competent and fair man, as Catholics go. But, apparently, 'tis not demons or evil spirits with which we are dealing here. Rather, Father Purcell seems to think 'tis witchcraft."

Stafford gave forth an astonished laugh. "Witchcraft?"

"Yes."

"Oh, how daft, man. I thought all of the world's witches were burned or hung centuries ago. Why, I remember reading somewhere that the Spanish alone put nearly one hundred of them to death each day for years."

"Nevertheless, sir, it does seem that at least one of them may have survived."

Still not believing this assertion, Stafford couldn't help smirking. "And who, pray tell, would that be?"

"Purcell and his colleagues are not sure. The Church has long suspected the practice of sorcery in this area, but they have been unable to determine the source of it. However, since most of your episodes with whatever is vexing you have taken place here at Brenna, I believe *I* can venture a very good guess."

"Yes? And?" Pearce prompted, growing a bit impatient with his evasive manner. "Is there a maid you would advise me to discharge? Some wench curdling fresh milk with naught but a glance or the like?"

"No, sir. I fear the situation is graver than that."

"Yes. So? *Who* is it you suppose is to blame? Out with it, please."

"Well, after—after doing a goodly share of research into the matter," Horatio stammered nervously, "I am sorry to say that I believe it is Miss Ross, my lord."

"Selena?" Stafford threw back his head and laughed. "What a joker you are, Brownwell. I had not realized until now that you're so given to jest."

"But I'm not jesting, sir. On the contrary, it pains me very deeply to have to come to you with such news."

Pearce frowned as it began to dawn upon him that the investigator was actually serious in making this accusation.

"Well, it had better pain you. For the woman of whom you speak is soon to be made my betrothed. That is, if she will have me."

Horatio gasped. "Your betrothed? S'death, Lord Pearce. How disastrous! I knew that the pair of you had grown close, I just did not realize that you'd taken matters that far!"

"Well, I've not proposed marriage to her yet. Indeed, given the seriousness of your claim against her, 'tis happening that *you* are the first I've told of this intention. But, yes, matters, as you call them, have progressed to such an extent between us."

The ghost hunter leaned towards him, continuing to look terribly worried. "Then you have already lain with her?" he inquired in a hushed voice.

"How dare you ask such a question," Stafford thundered, bringing a fist down upon his desk.

Horatio sat back at this outburst. "Well, perhaps I was a bit out of line with it. But I do feel I must inform you, sir, that, whatever has or has not taken place between you and Miss Ross, you must make very certain that, when it comes time for such an act, 'tis *you* who does the mounting."

Pearce knit his brow with continued shock and confusion. "Good God, my ears are aflame at your bluntness! What possible difference could it make whether I mount her or she me?"

"All of the difference, my lord. For, you see, the books I have consulted in the matter state that, for a witch to truly claim a man's heart, she must first claim his body."

Stafford fell silent and leaned back pensively in his chair. Though he could honestly say that, in the end, it was he who had done the swiving the first time with Selena, he would not soon forget the tussle he had gone through with her in order to accomplish it. Never before had he seen such precipitous resistance in a young lady, who had, at first, seemed so willing. He also recalled how readily she'd taken the sexual lead with him in her bath in the woods the following day. He'd learned through the years that it was a very rare woman who seized such opportunities with so much abandon. He'd thought, at the time, that it had simply bespoken her obviously considerable experience with males, but now it occurred to him that it might have held an even greater significance. He narrowed his eyes at the investigator. "And this applies only to the *first* time between us, you say?"

"I believe so. Therefore, please, do take this counsel to heart. And, just to be safe, I would also advise you to continue holding the reins with her, as it were, the next couple of times thereafter."

Not wishing to in any way betray the fact that those times had, in truth, come and gone for Selena and him—thereby besmirching her honor—Stafford nodded in response to this and declared that he would be sure to do so. Nevertheless, the damage might already have been done, if, indeed, there was any truth to Horatio's outlandish contention.

"I do want you to know, however," Pearce began again sternly, "that, while I find this information of passing interest, I do not, for one instant, think Miss Ross a sorceress!"

"Naturally you wouldn't, my lord. The bewitched rarely know how they have come to be smitten."

Stafford emitted a dry laugh. "Have you not seen the woman, Brownwell? Why, one glance at her ivory skin and emerald eyes should tell you how I came to feel as I do. There seems to me no magic in it."

"Yes, but that is the rub, isn't it? While I agree that she is beautiful, *I* feel no amorousness towards her. Thus her visage cannot be the sole cause of your affection for her. Now, maybe you are truly in love with her, and then again, it could be 'tis the result of a spell. And, were it mine to do, sir, I would certainly want to know which it was before taking her to wife!"

"This is all very trite of you, I hope you realize. Just because she possesses the gift of healing, one cannot conclude that 'tis sorcery she employs in it. Why, Christ Himself was a healer, and I am not aware of any such charges being brought against Him."

"I'm perfectly aware that not all healers are sorcerers, my lord. But, ask yourself this, if you will: since becoming close to this particular healer, what vexing experiences have you had? Is it possible that, now that Miss Ross feels certain she's won your heart, she sees no advantage in continuing to attempt to control you with her curses?"

Stafford swallowed dryly. Once again the investigator had touched upon an unnerving truth with him. The fact of the matter was that, since making love with Selena for the first time the previous week, he had not suffered a single mishap. The only curious thing he'd experienced was the sudden chilliness of her spring bath, once she'd removed herself from it; and that, at the time, had seemed to have far more to do with the forces of nature than with those of any black arts.

"Then," Horatio went on, "having answered that for yourself, sir, I would also counsel you to take a full accounting of any concessions you may have made to her, which did not otherwise seem true to your will. Please do pardon me for saying so, but your naming her the overseer of half your crofters a week or so past did strike me as excessive."

Pearce couldn't help frowning at this observation. Putting Selena in charge of some of his tenants was hardly the worst of it. If Brownwell got wind of the fact that he'd actually agreed to a forty-eight percent decrease in his rents at her demand, he would denounce her to the Church at once as the definite source of the spellcraft they suspected. "Brownwell," he replied with a snarl, "may I remind you that she was my late uncle's affianced for many, many years? How could she possibly be a sorceress when they were together for so long? How could something so momentous have evaded Prescott's notice over all that time?"

"Perhaps she succeeded in bewitching him before he could come to question her behavior, as you and I are now. Maybe he was so blinded by love for her that he could never see beyond it. He certainly would not have been the first man to have fallen prey to such enchantment."

"But Selena claims that she has dwelt in Wexford all of her life. How has she kept such practice a secret from the local folk in the course of over two decades?"

"Oh, Lord Pearce, you've seen for yourself what a high esteem your neighbors here have set upon her. She has probably saved too many lives to be accused of anything so vile. And, because she's true-blue Irish, as you've said, 'tis not likely that she or the dark powers she might use are at cross purposes with any of them."

Stafford knit his brow and leaned towards him to speak in a whisper. "You mean to tell me they might all know about her witchery, and are simply protecting her with their silence?"

" 'Tis possible, I suppose. All, save for the Church, of course. It has been trying to drive out the practitioners of native magic in this country for over one thousand years by my count. Which is probably why the priest has been the only one I have questioned who has mentioned sorcery to me as the likely cause of your difficulties here at Brenna."

Pearce leaned forward, fixing him with a scrutinizing stare. "But you, in turn, did not mention that you think Miss Ross the perpetrator of them, did you?" he asked from behind clenched teeth.

"Oh, no, sir. I would never have done such a thing! I am in your employ at present and no one else's. And I shan't lose sight of that."

Stafford eased back in his chair, taking far more comfort in this assurance than he cared to reveal. "Yes. Well, see that you don't! I happen to *love* Selena Ross, regardless of what you may believe she is, and I do not want her coming to any harm over this! . . . What is more," he continued, calming himself after several seconds, "though your accusation may seem to fit on a few counts, you have yet to prove to me that 'tis true."

"I believe I can, though, sir, if you wish to have me do so."

"How?" Stafford asked in a challenging tone.

"Well, I have taken a few days to think of a test, and now I feel I've got one. Tuesday next is the summer solstice. 'Tis, as you likely know, the longest day of the year; and, being descendant of centuries of sun worshipers, no Celtic witch would let that date pass without properly observing it. Furthermore, I have read that sorcerers believe that herbs gathered on that day possess far greater powers than those cut on any other. So I propose to you that we secretly keep a watch of Miss Ross's activities from dawn to dusk on the twenty-first, and see for ourselves if she acts the part of a witch."

"But, if she is one, won't she be able to sense that we are spying upon her?"

"Maybe. But I believe that that is something we simply must hazard, if we are to learn the truth."

A tense silence fell between them, as Pearce steepled his fingers beneath his chin and pondered this course of action. The very thought of directing such underhanded attentions toward his beloved made him feel rather nauseated.

"After all, my lord," the investigator began again tentatively, " 'tis altogether possible that such a test is just as likely to prove her innocent as guilty. And why not see her exonerated, before doing anything as irreversible as pledging your troth to her?"

Stafford continued to consider this for several seconds longer, Horatio's last question ringing in his ears. "Very well, then," he said finally. "Because I've every faith you are wrong in this, Brownwell, I shall take you up on your suggestion. Let us put *your* doubts about the lady to rest once and for all!"

As planned, the ghost hunter quietly roused Pearce just before dawn on the following Tuesday, and the two men set off for a clump of oak trees which were a few hundred yards to the west of Selena's thatch. At Horatio's insistence, they carried with them a satchel, which contained a loaf of bread, a brick of cheese, a skin of water, two grass-green capes to help camouflage them, a spyglass, and a couple of books to entertain whomever was not on watch at any given time.

As they settled behind the wide trunks of the cloaking trees, Stafford directed a cursory look at the western side of his lover's cottage. Then he opened their satchel, withdrew one of the capes from it, and rolled it up to serve as a pillow upon the cold, root-furrowed ground. "Since we are going to this trouble to satisfy your curiosity, rather than mine, Brownwell, you may conduct the first lookout, while I finish my slumber," he declared with a yawn.

Then, turning towards the north, so that the rising sun was not as likely to shine in his eyes, he reclined and went back to sleep with surprising ease.

Roughly four hours later, Horatio woke him with the request that he take his turn at watching the thatch. Pearce groaned and, brushing a seed tuft from where it had settled upon one of his eyelashes as he'd slept, he slowly rose to a sitting position. "Nothing thus far, right?" he asked, almost rhetorically.

"Right," the ghost hunter admitted. "But there is much day ahead yet, sir."

Stafford heaved a weary sigh at this response and began rummaging about in their satchel for the water skin. Brownwell, meanwhile, took the liberty of creeping off to the nearby woods with the claim that he needed to relieve himself.

"This is quite ridiculous, I hope you realize," Stafford grumbled, once Horatio had returned. Visoring his eyes against the glare of the sunlit sea, he stared down at Selena's humble dwelling and clucked. "She is, I can assure you, far more angel than witch."

"Then you have absolutely nothing to fear in this, do you, my lord," the investigator retorted rather smugly, before rolling up his own cape and lying down to sleep as Pearce had.

Though Brownwell's pertness caused Stafford to be seized with the urge to jab a knee into his back, as he turned away to nap, he resisted it and directed his attentions instead to the food they'd brought along from the great house.

Within the space of an hour, his boredom with the situation led him to finish off their entire loaf of bread and most of the brick of cheese. He also managed, in that time, to read a full chapter of one of the books on witchcraft, which Horatio had packed, do a fair amount of bird watching, and slip off to the woods to urinate twice. Though he did dutifully survey the cottage every few minutes, he had discovered that he was most comfortable with his back up against one of their concealing tree trunks. He, therefore, found himself stuck having to crane his neck over his shoulder each time he wished to check on it.

This was, by far, he thought, the greatest waste of a morning he had ever suffered through—his mind racing over the scores of matters he'd set aside at the manor in order to engage in this espionage. But, he told himself stoically, if it ultimately served to bear out his belief that his dear Selena was no more a sorcerer than he was, he supposed it was worth his while.

He was well into chapter three of Brownwell's book on spellcraft when the ghost hunter finally woke. Not wishing to appear to be shirking his duty, Pearce clapped the volume shut and whirled himself around on his derrière, in his cross-legged sitting position, so that he would again be fully facing the dwelling in question.

"You haven't been watching," Horatio accused.

"Yes—yes I have," he fibbed.

Brownwell propped himself up on an elbow and pointed just to the south of the seaside thatch. "Pardon me, my lord, but you couldn't have been, else you would have seen the lady where she goes there."

Pearce followed the ghost-hunter's finger to see a dark-haired figure heading into the woods behind the cottage. He could also see with his naked eye that whomever it was was draped from the neck down in a flowing white cloth and had a large basket in hand.

He groped behind himself for the spyglass, so that he might have a better look; but the investigator beat him to it. As if totally unaware of this encroachment, Horatio sat up and raised the telescope to his right eye.

"Is it she?" Stafford inquired anxiously.

"It certainly appears to be."

"Oh, God, what shall we do?" he asked, feeling totally at a loss.

The ghost hunter wasted no time in springing to his feet and throwing on his green cape. "We put these on and follow her, of course. 'Tis the only way to learn anything more, I fear."

"But what if she sees us?"

"She likely won't. Heaven knows we're already far enough behind her to keep ourselves out of her line of sight."

"But what if she's going off to bathe? That is, it won't do for either of us to be gazing upon her in nature's own."

Brownwell scowled at him. " 'Off to bathe?' In the *woods,* sir?"

Stafford bit his lower lip, remembering how he'd given Selena his word that he would tell no one of her hot spring. Then he stood up and threw on his cape as well. "Yes, um, well, perhaps there is a creek therein."

"We shall avert our eyes in that case, my lord. Now, please," he continued, bending to pick up the spyglass again, then frantically waving Pearce on, "she's getting away from us. There's no more time to spare!"

Though it was one of the most degrading things he'd ever done, Stafford stayed close at the investigator's heel in the minutes that followed. Like a pair of hunted squirrels, they darted from tree trunk to tree trunk, seeking cover with every three or four strides, as the white-draped figure was seen rushing past each tree, far to the east of them.

"We're even with her now anyway," Brownwell said windlessly, as they hid behind the bole of yet another towering oak. "She shouldn't be able to give us the slip from here on."

"How comforting," Pearce replied with a sarcastic roll of his eyes. "But I meant what I said earlier," he added sternly. "We are turning back, should she begin to undress! I will not dishonor her, even if she is unaware of us!"

"As you wish, my lord. Lo! Come along, pray. She's getting ahead of us again."

They hurried southward for a while longer. Still hundreds of yards to the west of her, they came flush with her once more. And, to both Stafford's relief and dismay, it did seem that they were well past the point where he remembered her hot spring being . . . So, if it wasn't bathing his lover was about in her voluminous white robe on this fine summer day, a wary voice within him queried, just exactly *what* was her aim?

After a few moments more, it seemed he was about to have his answer. Stopping in a clearing where the sun shone down on her from the treetops like a celestial shower of gold dust she set the basket she'd been carrying upon the forest floor.

"No picnic luncheon in there I'll wager," Brownwell remarked in a low snide voice, as they drew even with her once more and he again studied her through the glass.

Stafford reached out and jerked it from him with a snarl. "Bloody Hell, man, give me that thing! Thanks to you, I've yet to get a good look at her."

He was sorry as he did, though, for the magnifying lens confirmed for him that it was indeed his Selena who was kneeling to withdraw a knife of some kind from her basket now.

"Aha! There, you see?" Horatio asked triumphantly. "Her ceremonial dagger!"

Pearce gulped, having already read about such implements in the investigator's book on the practice of witchcraft. He lowered the glass and glared at him. "So, she has come to cut some herbs in the woods," he countered, squaring his shoulders. "What healer does not from time to time?"

Even as he spoke these words, however, he realized that they were balderdash, for the way in which Selena was presently holding the weapon out before her was nothing if not ceremonial. Its blade flashed in the noonday sun, as she raised it skyward with a slow gracefulness which indicated that she was definitely paying homage to someone or something.

Stafford's breath caught in his throat and he said nothing more. He simply went on watching as his lover again knelt down and began removing some other objects from her basket.

"And 'tis also perfectly natural, is it, for her to grind them right where they are found?" Brownwell asked with a critical sniff, as she got back up to her feet and crossed to a nearby boulder.

It appeared, from where they watched, to be more an altar than a naturally occurring stone, and, as she proceeded to set her dagger, a cluster of dried plants, and some other tiny metal object down upon it, Pearce sensed that herb grinding was likely the furthest thought from her mind.

"Bishopwort," Horatio said decidedly.

"What?"

"Is it purple in color, the herb she's carried there?"

Pearce strained to get a better look at it. "Well, 'tis difficult to say from this distance. But I must confess that it does seem to be more purple than green."

" 'Tis bishopwort, then, sir. If she sets fire to it upon the rock, we shall know for certain that that is what it is. Sorcerers always burn it at summer solstice, for they believe it will bring them protection and purification in the coming year."

Stafford breathed a sigh of relief as he continued to watch and no flame was evident upon the scene. Rather, Selena simply knelt, her hands propped up on the boulder before her in a prayerlike position.

"No. You see? She is merely saying vespers or some such thing. Most Christians do. One need not be in a church, you know, in order to pray."

To Pearce's horror, however, he saw what was, unmistakably, flame breaking out before his lover as she went on kneeling. The second metal object she'd brought with her was, apparently, a flint striking steel, and the herbs now began to burn upon the rock.

"Oh, dear God," he exclaimed, thrusting the glass back to the investigator and dropping his gaze to his feet. "I believe I would rather have found her with another man, than anything as sinister as this!" He lowered his voice to an aghast whisper. "It has been *her* all along, hasn't it? Causing my jaw to lock at the soirée table, because she did not agree with my views on the local politics. Making me behave as if I were an animal with Miss Barnes on the carriage ride, so that I would be thusly spurned. Then compelling me to come down to her thatch just afterward, that I might receive consolation from her . . . Since reaching manhood I've searched for my ideal mate, a woman of beauty, wit, and charm. And, Heaven take me, now that I have found her, 'tis revealed that she's a *witch!* I can watch no more," he concluded, his voice cracking with heartbreak, as he pushed off from the tree trunk and began heading back towards the manor.

The ghost hunter came rushing after him a couple seconds later. "Lord Pearce, please. 'Tis not as though we need see her put to death because of it. There are other courses we can take to stop her influence upon you. Ones which, given the local folks' reverence for her, would not cause you further trouble."

Stafford felt almost too despairing to respond. "Such as what?" he croaked finally, picking up his pace as they continued to retreat.

"Such as secretly hiring another sorceress to nullify her magic. You know, to make certain you are released from any love spells she may have cast upon you. And to restore your free will, if indeed it has been stolen."

Pearce stopped walking. "But you don't understand, Brownwell. 'Tis not simply a matter of my possibly having been hexed by her. I *love* the woman! I'm smitten with a Devil worshiper, of all the unthinkable occurrences!"

"Well, now that is painting the matter a bit darkly, my lord, if you will forgive my saying so. In truth, I have read nothing which indicates that Celtic sorcerers worship Satan. In fact, there is much evidence to show that 'twas the Church which first made that claim against them, and that they had no knowledge at all of the Devil, until Christianity was brought to these shores. Rather, it seems they derive their magic from the forces of nature. From fire, air, earth, and water, you see."

"So, you don't think her truly evil?" Stafford asked, with some hopefulness in his voice.

"Given her healing abilities, I don't feel she is. But 'tis, nevertheless, doubtful that her ends are well aligned with yours. And, if she has indeed bewitched you somehow, I firmly believe that we should seek help in ridding your spirit of her spell-craft."

"And you are certain that you can see this done in the strictest of confidence and without any harm coming to her?"

"I am," the investigator answered with a nod.

"Very well," Pearce agreed after several seconds. But he sensed that, no matter how competent the sorceress they were about to hire, she would not be able to quell the ache he now felt in his heart.

Twenty

A strange uneasiness ran through Selena, as she concluded her summer solstice ritual and was returning her dagger and flint-striking steel to her basket.

She pivoted slowly on the balls of her feet, scanning the forest in all directions. Someone was watching her! She felt certain of it, and yet it appeared that, except for the birds and other creatures of the wood, she was completely alone in this sacred place.

Nevertheless, she sensed a human presence very nearby. Somebody had been watching her, *spying* upon her as she'd conducted her ceremony, and she'd simply been too enthralled in the business of calling up the gods, to bless her and her loved ones in the coming year, to have been aware of it until now.

She bent to stow her magic paraphernalia in her basket. Slipping its handle onto her forearm, she slowly rose back up to her full height—her ears alert to any telltale sounds. But, as with her eyes, she perceived nothing which confirmed what the mystical soul of her so deeply sensed. There was no snap of twigs beneath an intruder's feet, nor rush of birds at the creeping form of a spectator.

From the looks and sounds of things, she could only conclude that she was alone. And perhaps, she silently conceded, that was true now. But it hadn't been just minutes earlier. She'd been observed as she'd burnt her traditional offering of bishopwort. Someone had seen her doing it, and she felt very sure that either Father Purcell or that deuced ghost hunter from London was responsible!

"Dear God, Brownwell, why must I meet with her? Can she not just wave her wand near my door or some such thing and see me freed of Miss Ross's influence?"

"I'm sorry, my lord, but no," Horatio whispered, gesturing for Stafford to keep his voice down as well. "She's just out in the corridor, mind, so please let us avoid being overheard by her. It has been miserable enough, has it not, having one witch's wrath stirred up against you? You hardly need hazard angering two."

Pearce gave forth a resigned sigh, where he sat at his study desk. "Oh, very well then. See her in. But," he added, leaning back in his chair and crossing his arms over his chest, "I've absolutely no intentions of drinking any foul brews which she might concoct for me; so you may as well tell her as much here and now."

"Hopefully, that won't prove necessary," the investigator returned sotto voce, before heading back to open the study door to the waiting sorceress. "Madam Katrina Kerry, my lord," he introduced, as he ushered her in an instant later.

Though he resented feeling obliged to do so, Stafford rose just long enough to offer her a slight bow. "A pleasure to make your acquaintance, ma'am."

The old woman swept over to his desk, as though to get a better look at him—her Gypsylike apparel dripping with fringe. Though Stafford found her appearance rather frightening, he did his best not to reveal it. This was not only in the hope of not offending her, as the ghost hunter had requested, but also because Pearce men did not show fear in the presence of others.

"You're afraid of me, aren't ya?" she accused with an air of satisfaction.

Despite his resolve, Stafford couldn't help flinching at this question. Her black eyes were so beady, her long, crooked nose so beaklike, that he felt as though a huge ravenous hawk had just been loosed upon him.

"Nonsense," he replied with a gulp, finding himself unable to believe that this excruciatingly ugly woman and his beautiful Selena could be one in the same sort of creature.

She emitted what could only be described as a cackle, and this, in turn, prompted Brownwell to rush back to the door and see it again firmly closed to any passersby. Their meeting, as he'd promised Pearce, had to be kept as secret as possible.

Their guest proceeded to jab a long fingernail in Stafford's direction. "You *are,*" she said victoriously, "so don't be denyin' it. And I shall tell ya somethin' else about yourself, sir."

Pearce raised his chin defiantly and tried to look her squarely in the face. "Yes? And what would that be, pray tell?"

"You're squeeged, sure enough. Aye. 'Tis one of the worst cases of it that I have ever seen. So your Mr. Brownwell was most wise to send for me. Rest ye assured of that!"

Stafford knit his brows. " 'Squeeged'?" he repeated confusedly.

She began strolling about the room, stopping to pick up a knickknack here and there, as though assessing their worths. "Ah, 'tis merely witch-speak for smitten, my lord. Ya know, made to fall hopelessly in love by cause of one of our spells."

"How can you tell that by simply looking at me?"

" 'Tis in the eyes. There is always a sad and dreamy spot just in the center of a squeeged man's pupils."

"Well, it is not that I believe in such hocus-pocus, mind you. It was Horatio here who sent for you, madam, and not I. But, if these spots, as you call them, truly were in a fellow's eyes, how might he go about ridding himself of them?"

As she reached the room's hearth, she turned back to face him with a slightly sadistic smirk. "Well, we could place leeches upon your eyelids and let them suck them out. That is what the sorceresses of my mother's day used to do. But, fortunately, for you, sir, I am of a more progressive mind, and feel we should begin with somethin' less invasive."

Stafford directed his gaze at Brownwell. *"Where* did you find this woman?" he asked, his words rising with incredulity.

"I am not a woman," she answered for herself, her voice brimming with indignation, "I am a witch, Lord Pearce. A very powerful witch from the North, who, as it happens, is somewhat sympathetic to English interests in this country. And, lest ye relish the thought of findin' your privates turned to powder, I will thank ya to never again speak of me as though I were not present, when, in fact, I am!"

Stafford bolted to his feet. "How dare you threaten me!"

Before he could say a word more, however, Brownwell threw himself between them.

"Now, now, my lord," he entreated with his palms thrust out at Pearce. "Let us not forget that Madam Kerry was good enough to travel all the way from Londonderry to come to your aid . . . I beg of you, do not anger her," he silently mouthed in conclusion, his face contorting as though he feared that her ire might bring the world to an end, if Stafford spoke another cross word to her.

"Oh . . . Very well," Pearce replied with a cluck. "If, indeed, 'tis aid she has come here to render, then let us get on with it."

"Not until you give me your word that you will never again behave so rudely towards me," Katrina put in, one of her raven eyes peering out from behind where the investigator still stood between them.

"See here," Stafford retorted, leaning his head far to the right in order to better focus upon her. "I was hardly the one who threatened to do something horrid to *your* privates!"

"Be that as it may, I insist upon an apology from you, else I shall leave ya to your own devices with whomever has so mercilessly squeeged ya!"

Brownwell sidled to the left just enough to again block Pearce's view of her. Then he raised his brows in an expression of total beseechment.

"Oh, all right," Stafford replied with an exasperated puff

after several seconds. He sank back into his chair. "I shall not prove discourteous to you again."

The ghost hunter heaved a sigh of relief and, after flashing his employer a grateful smile, turned to offer the same to Katrina. "Splendid. Now that 'tis agreed that we are all allied in this effort, we can get on to the particulars of it."

"Not just yet," Pearce declared, getting up again and walking out from behind his desk. "There are a couple of questions I would like you to answer for me, madam, before we proceed."

Apparently now content to believe that the pair of them intended to deal with one another peaceably henceforward, Brownwell was good enough to step aside and allow Stafford to look directly at the witch.

She offered as much of a polite smile as her frightening features seemed able to accommodate. "Aye, sir?"

Pearce perched upon the front edge of his heavy desk. "These spots or dots or whatever it is you claim to have seen in my eyes, are they not present in the pupils of every man who is in love?"

"Well . . . aye," she admitted.

"Then how can you know that I've been squeeged, as you call it? Could it not simply be that I am truly enamored with the lady in question?"

"Aye. I suppose that is possible. But, if such enamorment was preceded by any times when you seemed to lose consciousness with her or, if you remember her hummin' in such a way as to induce a trance in ya, 'tis likely due to witchcraft, as Mr. Brownwell has alleged."

"Humming?"

"Aye. You know. A tune of this sort, for instance." Her words gave way to a low, hymnlike resonating from within her closed mouth.

Stafford felt a sinking sensation in the pit of his stomach, as she continued. Not only did the string of mesmeric notes she was producing seem to match the one he remembered his image of Selena humming as he'd bathed after his disastrous outing with Miss Barnes, but this information from Katrina caused him to remember that he had indeed suffered what had seemed a lapse of consciousness, just before he'd made love with Selena the first time.

He recalled now, in vivid detail, how he'd been atop her, poised to enter her one moment, and then she'd magically appeared in the adjoining room the next.

"Oh, yes," he replied with a dry swallow. "I guess I must confess to having experienced both of those occurrences with her."

"There is your answer then. 'Tis witchcraft, if ever I've heard tell of it."

Pearce shook his head sadly and dropped his gaze to the floor. Since having spotted Selena at her pagan ritual four days earlier, he'd come to feel that the only thing worse than discovering that his love for her might not be real, was that the same was probably true of her professed feelings for him.

"But ya need not fall prey to it forever, you know," Madam Kerry went on hearteningly. "That is to say, there are several ways to rid ya of the lady's manipulation."

"*Without* harming her?" he inquired in an insistent tone.

"Aye."

"Very well. Let us proceed with it then."

"Right, sir," the sorceress began again brightly. She strode towards him with such enthusiasm, that he couldn't help getting to his feet and starting to slip back behind his desk, for fear that she intended to hug him.

"Nay, my lord. Here," she said with a soft laugh, lifting one of her many long necklaces up over her head as she reached his desk. "I simply wish to have you wear this."

He knit his brow. "Jewelry? Oh, no, I couldn't. That is—it, um, looks so much better on you. Don't you think?" he stammered.

" 'Tis not for adornment, ya daft thing. 'Tis worn for protection."

"From love spells?"

"From anything which threatens, really. They are amethysts, you see," she continued, extending the chain of purple gems to him. "Stones meant to ward off any who would seek to trouble ya."

"Oh," he replied, plucking them from her palm as though fearing he might catch the plague from her at such close range. "This is most generous of you, madam. But, in truth, I simply cannot picture myself in them."

She clucked. "Then wear them under your shirt. No one need know ya have 'em on."

"So, all I have to do is don them and I will no longer be in love with the woman who has squeeged me?"

She smiled at the skittish way in which he continued to hold the necklace.

"If she's worth her salt as a witch, I fancy we shall need to do a bit more to cast her off. But 'twill be makin' a start, anyway."

"All—all right," he replied, setting the necklace down on his desk and, beginning to untie his cravat, so that he could slip it on under his clothing.

"And then," she paused as though reconsidering her next words. "Well, am I to assume you are utterly averse to the leeches on your eyelids?"

Stafford glared at her as if she were rather unhinged. "You are."

"In that case, we shall have to wait until we have collected enough cow urine in order to take matters any further."

Pearce hoped to God he had not heard her correctly. "Cow *what?*"

"Cow urine. We shall need enough for ya to bathe in."

"Oh, no. No, no," he replied, casting a scathing look at Brownwell. "That is out of the question. I have never heard of anything so disgusting!"

"Well, we will reheat it for you, of course, once 'tis all gathered," the sorceress hastened to add. " 'Tis not as though I'm expectin' ya to lower yourself into a cold tub of it."

"Are you crazed? Can you possibly believe that 'tis the temperature of the stuff I would find most objectionable?"

"What else can it be? 'Tis a pure enough liquid, if that is what concerns ye. The people of India have been washin' in it for centuries."

"But it stinks, you ridiculous wench! Have you never been in a barn long enough to know that much?"

She pursed her lips and raised a scolding forefinger to him. "Whisht, now! Don't be forgettin' your promise to me. No rudeness!"

"Yes, yes. Well, I'm sorry. I should not have called you ridiculous, but I don't know how I can make it any more plain to you that I simply have no intentions of placing any part of myself in cow piss!"

"Is there no other way?" Brownwell interposed, beginning to wring his hands in the manner of the intermediary he'd made himself in bringing this feisty hag to Stafford.

"Oh, I don't know," she snapped. "Apart from the leeches, 'tis likely the best course. But, if you are goin' to prove so uncooperative, Lord Pearce, I suppose I could consult my spell books and see what else they might recommend."

"Yes. Please do," he said firmly, slipping her necklace over his head and directing its cool chain down beneath his collar. "For I believe I would rather be made my inamorata's slave, than to find myself up to my chest in anything so vile! Some magic, that," he went on critically, under his breath. "There seems no trick to staving off a lady when one reeks to the Heavens!"

"I beg your pardon," the witch demanded.

"Oh, nothing," he answered grudgingly, still determined to keep the peace as he'd promised to do.

Continuing to look irritated by his obvious disapproval of her, however, she fixed him with another glare. "While I've no doubt that you'll continue to claim that 'twas Mr. Brownwell who has engaged me to take the squeege off ya, sir, I want ya to hear, from my own lips, that my fee for it will be twenty-five pounds."

"What? Have you taken leave of your senses? Why, that is more a ransom than a fee!"

"A ransom, is it? Might I remind ya that *I* am not the sorceress who is holdin' your heart hostage?"

"But are you much better than she? Asking such a fortune for your services?"

She threw up her hands in exasperation. "Faith, ya live as if ya were a ruddy king in this manse of yours. What is a mere twenty-five pounds to ya, when just one of the wee, dust-gatherin' statues in this room alone is likely worth more than that? . . . Sweet Jesus, you are a greedy beast! 'Tis no wonder some local witch has chosen to hex ya!"

"Of all the impudent—" Stafford barked in response; but, before he could say a word more, she resumed her tirade.

"Can ya truly believe that powers such as mine can be found anywhere at all? On any street in any town? As easy to call forth and buy as kitchen or stable help? Well, if that is what ya think, you've got the wrong pig by the ear, ya frugal bugger! Your Mr. Brownwell did very well in sendin' for me. And my talents, to make no mention of my reverence for my patrons' needs for secrecy, are worth every penny I ask!"

Pearce slammed a fist down on his desk. "All right, then, you harpy! Twenty-five pounds it is . . . if that is what is required to keep you quiet about this matter."

"Very good, my lord," she replied, her tone amazingly pleasant, given how virulent her previous words to him had been. "You had better show me to my quarters then, Horatio. It seems I've some studyin' ahead of me, if I'm to arrive at some amply potent alternatives to the cow urine."

"Keep her away from Flaherty and the rest," Stafford whispered after the investigator, as he moved to follow her out of the room.

"Oh, I will, my lord," he assured. "No one, save you and I, shall be given the opportunity to speak with her."

Pearce drew a tense breath in through his teeth. "They had better not, lest we hazard news of her getting down to *you know who!"*

A few minutes after Stafford retired to his parlor with his usual after-supper glass of brandy-wine that evening, his steward came and stood before the wing chair he occupied.

"Yes?" he queried, setting down the newspaper he'd been reading and looking up at the servant.

"Sorry to bother ya, my lord, but Miss Ross has come to see ya."

Pearce took a long swallow of his drink in the hopes of masking the fact that he was caught totally off guard by this announcement. "Oh, I—I don't know, Mr. Flaherty," he faltered. "I'm really not feeling up to a visitor at present. I fear I'm a bit drowsy from eating too much of our evening meal."

"So you're turnin' her away, sir?" he asked in a forbidding hush, his eyes growing round enough to silently communicate the fact that this sort of thing was simply not done to their local healer.

"Well, I—I hardly think you need phrase it in that way. Just tell her 'maybe another time.' "

The steward winced slightly. "If that is all there is to be said, my lord, perhaps *you* would be good enough to convey it to her. That is, she flatly refused to tell me what her call is concernin' when I inquired just now . . . Surely, sir, you can spare a moment or two for her," he concluded with a note of desperation in his voice.

"Oh, very well, you craven," Stafford growled, realizing that he would have to face Selena again sooner or later. "Show her in."

His palms were already wet with nervous perspiration as their resident sorceress was led into the parlour a couple minutes later. Out of courtesy, he rose as she entered. Then, fully aware that his uneasiness was less likely to show if he was seated, he sank down in his chair once more and simply gestured for her to take the matching one to his left.

"Thank ya, Mr. Flaherty," Selena said dulcetly, as she sat down beside her host. "And would ya kindly shut the room's doors after ya as ya leave?"

"That I will, mistress," the servant replied, quickly complying.

"So, Stafford," she began with a wavering smile, once they were alone. "What has become of ya these past several days? I had begun to worry at not havin' seen ya in so long."

She certainly was a direct one, Pearce thought in those strained seconds, inwardly admiring the courage it must have taken for her to come to him this way. He also couldn't seem to help admiring her provocatively shadowed cleavage, framed as it was now by the flattering rose-colored evening gown she wore.

"Oh, I'm afraid I have simply become engrossed with some matters here in the great house. I must have lost track of time."

She fluttered her eyelashes at him and smiled again. "So ya haven't been missin' me then?"

How disarming she was, an aching voice within him acknowledged. How disarming she'd always been . . .

But he must not give in to his deeper feelings with her, another part of him warned. There was simply no excuse for it now, having finally learned what she truly was beneath that extraordinarily alluring façade of hers.

"Well, I did not say that, my dear. I simply stated that I've been quite busy. You, of all people, must know how much work a manor and its land demand."

Her lower lip slipped forward, giving way to one of the pouts he found so irresistible. "Aye. But surely ya could give me an hour or two. Perhaps for another dip in my spring bath on one of these hot summer days."

He cleared his throat, still doing his level best not to lose the reins in this conversation. "Yes, well, that is an agreeable suggestion, isn't it. Perhaps I can find some time to slip down to the woods in future."

"With me, of course," she put in with an awkward giggle.

"Um. Yes. I suppose that is what I meant."

"Ya 'suppose'?" she asked pointedly. Then she leaned far towards him, more of her creamy breasts being revealed in the process. "Come now. What's afoot with ya, love? Could it be that you are precisely what ya accused me of bein' a week or so back?"

He scoured his memory, but found himself unable to place this reference. "And what was that?"

"The heart-breakin' sort who makes the most passionate love with a body one day, then pretends to hardly know her the next."

"Of course not. I know perfectly well who you are." *All too well, in fact,* his mind silently interjected. " 'Tis just that I have been immersed in other matters, as I've said. Now, thank you for coming by, Selena," he concluded, rising abruptly to show her out. "Please let us speak at more length when I am feeling a little less overfed. I fear I ate too much at supper, you see."

She stood up as well, but to Pearce's dismay, he instantly sensed that this wasn't so she could leave. "Oh, your stomach is painin' ya again, is it?" she asked with a look of great concern. "Then let me soothe it for ya, as I have in the past," she continued, rushing over to him and pressing her palms to his middle, before he could stop her.

He grabbed her wrists and, not sparing any strength, pulled her hands away from him. "No, now, thank you," he said with a clumsy smile, "but I would rather you did not help this time, if 'tis all the same to you. I simply feel that getting to bed soon will be cure enough."

Though he'd succeeded in freeing himself of her seductive touch, he couldn't seem to avoid being lashed where he stood by her hypnotic green eyes.

"What is the trouble, Stafford?" she whispered, clearly near tears. "Have I done somethin' to drive ya away from me?"

He swallowed loudly, rended within by this sudden show of vulnerability from her. He'd always thought of her as invincible. And even more so, once he'd learned what dark powers she had at her command. Yet, for some reason, she seemed every bit as pregnable as he now; and he knew, in his soul, that she deserved much more of an answer to this question than he'd been giving.

"I just—I simply feel that matters have been progressing a bit too quickly between us," he replied, his voice as hushed as hers. "You do understand, don't you?"

"What? You mean you're no longer sure 'tis love ya feel for me?"

Releasing her wrists with a tormented sigh, he let his hands slide forward and close about hers. "Yes, well, one truly ought to be certain of such sentiments. Don't you agree?"

"But how can you make certain?" she asked, her voice cracking with emotion. "By stayin' away from me until we both die of heartache? 'Tis not a very good plan," she added, slipping one of her hands out of his and reaching up to wipe a tear from the corner of her right eye.

He gave forth a sad chuckle and continued to look into her beautiful face. "No. Not that long. I promise."

He was so transfixed that he scarcely felt it as she took her hand from her cheek and casually let it come to rest upon his chest. Not an instant later, to his great surprise, she jerked it away as though she'd just touched a live coal.

"Faith, what is that under there?" she exclaimed.

"What is what?" he asked, having forgotten about the amethysts that Madam Kerry had given him.

"I felt somethin' restin' beneath your shirt just now. Pray, what is it?"

His face grew warm with abashment. "Oh, 'tis simply some jewelry which someone gave me for safekeeping."

"About your *neck?*"

He laughed again. "Yes, well, apparently this friend of mine felt that I've a very well-protected body."

"Gems, are they then?"

"Yes. As a matter of fact."

"Ah. What kind?"

"Amethysts."

"Oh," she replied simply, taking a step back from him.

"Did they hurt you somehow?"

"No," she denied. "Why do ya ask?"

"Well, 'twas the way you removed your hand from me. I thought you'd been cut by them or something."

"Not cut. Nay. Merely pricked, I fear," she lied. "One of the prongs in the settin's, no doubt."

"Oh, I'm terribly sorry, my dear."

"Nay. Don't be. I am just fine now."

"Good."

An uncomfortable silence fell between them. Then Selena finally spoke again.

"Do ya not think it best, Stafford, to put the necklace in the manor's repository until your friend returns for it?"

"I suppose it would be. Yes. I merely forgot about it, was all."

"Even so. You should probably lock it away. 'Twill be safer for all concerned, don't ya think?"

"Yes. Likely you're right. I shall have Flaherty see to it once you've left. In the meantime, might I steal a good night kiss?" he asked, his expression, at least to her perception, slightly taunting.

He *knew,* she realized in those harrowing seconds. He'd somehow discovered that she was a witch, and he'd learned how to keep her from getting too close to him!

"Oh, aye," she replied, carefully avoiding his chest as she leaned forward just far enough to deliver a peck to his right cheek. "Good night to ya, love. And may your dreams be filled with me."

She turned away from him and headed for the door.

"Good night, sweet Selena. Rest ye safe and warm in your very own thatch."

"Oh, and, Stafford," she added, facing him again before leaving the room.

"Yes?"

"Take care with those stones, as I've said. All gems have powers, ya see. Some for healin' and some, unfortunately, for doin' injury. And I fear a novice in that realm, such as yourself, might not know when he has undertaken too much. 'Tis a very perilous thing indeed to underrate unseen forces," she declared, her eyes narrowing admonishingly. "Mind ya, 'tis simply for your own good that I'm warnin' ya thus. I know that amethysts are lovely when the sun shines through their purple depths. But, just because somethin' is beautiful does not mean 'tis without its defenses."

"Oh, I'm quite sure you're right," he replied, knowing—as she obviously intended him to—that she was actually referring to herself with this last statement.

Twenty-one

"Blast," Selena hollered, as she returned to her thatch minutes later and slammed its door shut behind her.

Nola, who'd been curled up asleep beside the hearth, woke with a start. *What is it, mistress? Mercy, I believe ya just scared me out of one of my nine lives!*

"He *knows,*" Selena exclaimed, folding her arms over her chest and leaning back heavily against the door.

Her familiar blinked sleepily. *Who knows what, for Heaven's sake?*

"Stafford knows I'm a witch!"

Oh, that's impossible. How could he? No one in Wexford would dare tell him.

"No one had to. 'Tis my own foolish self who is to blame! I sensed that I was bein' watched Tuesday last, when I slipped into the woods to observe the solstice. But the realization came to me too late. Whoever saw me told Stafford of my ritual, and one thing must have led to the next."

How do ya know this for certain? Did he say as much when ya went up to call upon him?

"Nay. But you've seen how he has kept away from me since the twenty-first. Not once has he come down to visit, even though our thatch's lights have shone every night. And, when I went to touch him this evenin', I felt somethin' searin' hot beneath his shirt. So, naturally, I questioned him about it, and he said that he was wearin' a string of *amethysts!"*

"Amethysts?"

"Aye. And hexed ones to boot. It must have been the work of another sorceress, else why would they have burned me?"

Nola gave her head a befuddled shake. *Nay. They should not have, right enough. Not unless they'd been hexed, as ya say, by one whose magic is at least equal to ours.*

"Aye. And the only reason Stafford would have to acquire such jewelry from a witch is that he now believes *I* am one . . . Bloody blazes, Nola," she continued, storming over to her dining table and pulling out one of its chairs for herself with thunderous force, "what sorceress would dare to cross me thus? For centuries we've striven to steer clear of one another's territory."

Aye. But perhaps 'tis not an Irish witch who has intervened. Maybe Pearce sent to London for her.

Selena waved her familiar off, then sat down. "Nay. Ya know as well as I that English magic has never been as strong as ours."

They both fell silent for several seconds. Then the most probable answer occurred to them simultaneously.

" 'Tis someone from the *North,*" they said in unison.

"Joseph and Mary, 'tis that mercenary beast Katrina Kerry I'll wager," Selena declared.

God, ya may be right.

"Of course, I am. Who else would have agreed to travel all the way down here? Riskin' life and limb by traversin' all those other witches' grounds en route? Only Crafty Katrina would do that for an Englishman's coins. The whore!"

The shrew, Nola added.

"The bloodless bitch!"

Why, she'd sell her own children into slavery, for the right price!

"Aye. So, just imagine what she's inclined to do to us! . . . Well, I simply will not have it," Selena declared after several seconds. "This is our bailiwick, and, if she thinks I'll let her sorcery prevail here, she has another thing comin'!"

Even as this threat emanated from behind her clenched teeth, a flash of lightning could be seen from outside the thatch's windows and Brenna's grounds shook with the thunder that her rage had obviously evoked.

Now, now, mistress. No ill tempers, pray! Remember that 'tis only she and not the whole of Wexford Town ya want to smite with your wrath. Let us not have the sea sweepin' up to swallow us, as we did the last time you were as roiled as this!

Though she knew it was in vain, Selena drew in a long breath and tried to calm herself at this warning. "To the crystal, Nola," she ordered. "We are goin' to scan every corner of the great house and servants' quarters until we find Katrina Kerry. She's here somewhere. I can *smell* her on the wind, and I shall not rest until we've driven her out!"

Minutes later, Stafford was standing before one of the parlor's east windows, watching as the violent and most unexpected storm seemed to roll in from the sea.

" 'Tis a humdinger, my lord," he heard his investigator say from somewhere behind him.

He looked back just long enough to nod in greeting, as the ghost hunter stepped farther into the room. "Yes. That it is. And so sudden, Brownwell. Don't you agree? As the sun set half an hour ago, there wasn't a cloud in the sky. And now, just feel that thunder. 'Tis as if a score of cannons were being fired by turns down on the shore!"

Horatio came up behind him and began staring outside as well—Selena's warmly lit cottage the only thing visible in between the illuminating flashes of lightning. "And you think Miss Ross is causing it, don't you?"

Stafford didn't answer at first. He was still too troubled by the tenor of the conversation he'd had with Selena half an hour earlier, to risk letting his voice betray how deeply he still felt towards her.

"I don't know," he said finally. "I just wish that I could go back to the time before I learned what she was. It was so peaceful when she and I were in accord."

"She came up to visit you a short while ago, did she not?"

Pearce didn't bother to ask how he knew this. He'd long since accepted the fact that the indefatigable investigator was keeping watch over almost everything that went on in his life. "Yes," he answered simply. Then he turned back and offered the ghost hunter a nippy look. "And you should be pleased to hear that Madam Kerry's necklace did its work."

"Oh?"

"Yes. As Miss Ross moved to touch me, she jerked her hand back as though it had been bitten," he explained in a joyless voice.

Stafford returned his gaze to the window and saw Brownwell's grinning reflection in its glass.

"Ah, that is wonderful, my lord. 'Tis exactly the response we were hoping for. And it does seem to confirm that we did well in hiring Katrina."

Pearce's tone was once again sullen. "Yes."

"So, do you feel any less in love with Miss Ross?" Horatio asked hopefully.

"Absolutely not. In fact, she seems to be tugging at my heart all the more now."

"Well, that is likely only because you just saw her."

"Perhaps."

"Oh, yes. I feel certain of it. And, you must admit, my lord, that we've scarcely given Madam Kerry a chance with this case yet. Considering her many, many years in the business of sorcery, I'm sure she has far more potent methods in store for you."

"Uh-huh."

Neither of them spoke in the seconds that followed. They simply stood watching the surprisingly severe rainstorm.

"You know, sir," the ghost hunter began again in a low thoughtful voice, " 'tis only natural that you should feel somewhat resistant to being made to fall out of love with the lady.

Enamorment is pleasurable, after all. That is why most of us seek to experience it. But please try to remember, if you will," he continued more gingerly, "that she probably does not love you, no matter what she may have claimed. Witches generally avoid becoming too fond of mortal men. 'Tis said to weaken their magical powers. So, however painful, we must again conclude that she is merely endeavoring to use you for her own ends, mustn't we? Just as she did with your good uncle."

"Yes. Well, obviously, Brownwell, 'tis not at all an easy truth for one to accept . . . She knows, though," he added, his voice trailing off.

"Knows what, my lord?"

"That I know she's a sorceress. I could see it in her eyes when she came up to visit. She knows and she warned me, in her way, not to cross her."

Horatio's voice rose with surprise. "She threatened you?"

"No. She simply implied that it would be most unwise to oppose her. And, seeing these fireworks she has conjured up, I cannot help but believe that they are meant to underscore that warning."

"On the other hand, it could just be the act of nature which most storms are, sir."

"I think not," Stafford gasped, as a bolt of lightning arched across the sky and appeared to touch down squarely upon one of the servants' lodges, just to the north of the great house.

The investigator leaned far forward, clearly straining to make out what was happening amidst the obscuring downpour of rain. "Dear God, 'tis aflame! And in the very corner where I quartered Madam Kerry for the night!"

"We had better get down there," Pearce declared, pushing away from the window and heading towards the front hall to get his rain-cloak. "I won't have anyone's blood on my hands over this outrageous clash of witches!"

As they reached the building in question several minutes later, Stafford spied a group of its former occupants rushing to take refuge from the storm in the nearby stable. While the fire appeared to have been already snuffed out by the rain, the lightning-struck portion of the lodge was still emitting a stream of dark smoke.

Pearce rushed into its front hall without hesitation and Brownwell followed closely. "Down the corridor and to the left, may I assume?" he inquired of the investigator as they hurried onward.

"Precisely, sir. She is in the last room on the right."

"Madam Kerry?" Stafford called out in a worried voice, when they reached the indicated door.

It swung open widely with nothing more than a slight push of his knuckles, and Katrina was immediately visible by the light of the room's two oil lamps.

"Aye. My thanks to ya, sir, for comin' down to check on me," she replied, rising from where she'd been sitting at the writing desk and reaching up to give the top of her still-smoking nightcap a couple of brisk pats.

Pearce gaped in horror. "Are you all right?"

"Oh, aye. A wee bit singed is all. But the spell book I was readin' when it struck . . . Well, dear me, have a look," she said, giving her head a sorry shake and turning back to the desk just long enough to lift up the leather-bound volume from it. "Defunct, I'm afraid." She tsked and raised it farther upward, so that her visitors could see the light from the desk's lamp shine through the large hole which had been burned down into the last half of its pages and out its back cover. "But not before I memorized a few of its better incantations for removin' squeeges, thank the Heavens!"

Brownwell sighed with relief. "Well, that's good to hear."

"She knows right where I'm to be found, however, this sorceress of yours, my lord, So, if 'twould not be too great an imposition, I do think it best if I passed the rest of the night in your room."

Stafford's mouth dropped open once more. "My room?"

"Aye. I should be out of harm's way there, since we witches seldom succeed in killin' the men we choose as lovers."

"What? In my—my *bed,* you mean?" he choked out, finding this the most nightmarish proposal he'd had put to him in memory.

She gave forth a soft laugh. "Nay. But in the same chamber, if ya don't mind. Lightnin's a ticklish medium, ya see. Very touch and go. So I doubt that she will try it a second time with you lyin' anywhere near."

Pearce reached under his dripping cloak and hurriedly began untying his cravat. "Perhaps, if I just returned your necklace, 'twould prove protection enough for you."

She raised a halting palm to him. "Nay. Sorry, but I insist that ya go on wearin' it. Amethysts are not much good against storms, anyway."

"Yes, sir. I'm sure she's right. Keeping her with you is probably the wisest course," the ghost hunter interposed.

Katrina nodded. "Aye. Then, come dawn, we'll begin work on the spells I committed to memory. The sooner I've cured ya and can get out of Wexford, the better, of course."

Stafford issued a perturbed cluck. "Well, put something on over your nightclothes, woman. 'Tis pouring rain out there, as you can see."

"That I will," she cheerfully agreed, sidling away from the desk and crossing to the traveling trunk she'd left open on the floor at the foot of the room's narrow bed. "She's a hotspur, this sorceress of yours, gentlemen," she noted, shaking her head with apparent wonder, as she knelt to withdraw the clothing she would be needing for the trip back to the great house. "I understand all too well now why ya seek to be rid of her influence. 'Tis a most ungovernable weapon, that self-made lightnin'. Why, she could have struck anyone of us in this lodge, if her angle had been even a hair's breadth askew!"

"Yes. She's dangerous, to be sure," Horatio concurred. "And, though you have our words, madam, that we did not tell her of your arrival, she seems somehow to have learned of it."

"That is why we're called witches, Mr. Brownwell," she returned with a sagacious wink, as she got back up to her feet, her arms draped with garments. "There isn't much that escapes our notice."

She stepped over to the bed and set the clothing upon it. Then she withdrew a long black cape from the pile and put it on. After that, she gathered the garments up again and, crossing to Stafford, looped an arm into one of his. "Stay close to me, if ya please, sir, as we walk back up to the house," she directed—the necessity for this being punctuated in that same instant by yet another blast of thunder.

Seeing how much heavier the rain had become as they reached the main door of the servants' lodge, Pearce stopped to untie his cloak and pull the top half of it up over his head. Handing her bundle of clothes to Brownwell, Madam Kerry followed suit. Then, apparently considering it pointless to thusly hood himself while carrying Katrina's garments, the investigator simply chose to use them as a makeshift hat en route.

Into the storm the three of them dashed. The sorceress again cleaved to Stafford, and Horatio stayed close at his other side all the while, as though believing that Selena Ross would have little more compunction about trying to strike him with lightning than she had this rival witch from the North.

They ran abreast, as best they could in the downpour, the blend of murky dusk and driving rain making it impossible to see even two feet ahead of themselves.

It was then, amidst their struggle to traverse the puddle-dotted back lawn, that Stafford suffered the misfortune of nearly colliding headlong with his drenched and panting steward.

The fat pink face of the Irishman suddenly became visible before him. Then, apparently in an attempt to avoid the collision, the servant went hurling to the ground at Pearce's feet. An act which, given his heft, sent alarming quantities of water and freshly cut grass flying in all directions.

"For Christ's sake, Flaherty! What are you doing out here?" Stafford blared—as annoyed at being caught with the house guest he'd been trying to keep hidden, as he was concerned about the Irishman possibly having injured himself in the fall.

The steward got back up to his feet with surprising agility, so much rain dripping down his face that he looked as if he had just submerged his head in the adjacent sea. "The lodge, my lord. I was just told that it was struck by lightnin' and that a fire had started."

" 'Tis out now, man," Stafford responded calmly. "But most of the servants fled to the stables. So please go and see to getting them returned safely to their rooms."

With that, he stepped past Flaherty's blocking form, pulling Madam Kerry along after him in an effort to get away before any questions could be posed about her. The near-drowning conditions seemed not to dissuade the steward, however.

"And this is one of your friends then, sir?" he called after them.

"No. One of Mr. Brownwell's," Pearce replied, continuing to stride forward.

"Whom you quartered with the servants?"

"Well, obviously! Can you honestly believe we are out in this freezing soup because we wish to be?"

"But where will you put her, my lord? Perhaps I should return with you now and arrange a guest room."

"No, damn it," Stafford hollered back at him, scarcely able to believe that he possessed the will to continue conversing under such treacherous conditions. "Just go and see to the servants, as I have requested!"

They were greeted at Brenna's terrace door seconds later by a maid bearing a mound of blankets. One glare from Pearce, however, was sufficient to cause her to step back and let them proceed, unquestioned, down the ground-floor corridor and up the front stairs to his suite.

After locking the three of them inside his sitting room, Stafford's first order of business was to fetch a stack of freshly laundered bath towels from his room's linen cabinet. "Well, madam," he began, as he handed the towels out to his drenched companions, then started to dry himself, "I'll sleep on one of these settees and you may have my bed."

"Oh, rubbish," she said sharply. "I have never inconvenienced a patron, and I never shall. Then too, we must stay much closer together than that or your witch friend will likely try for me again. Nay. You shall take your bed as always, and I will sleep on the floor beside it."

Stafford rolled his eyes at Brownwell, silently conveying the fact that he considered this almost as cozy a prospect as curling up with a viper for the night.

"Now, come mornin', you will have to steal this sorceress's familiar, my lord," Katrina went on, slipping out of her soaked cape and beginning to pat her nightclothes dry with one of the towels.

Pearce returned his humorless gaze to her. "Her what?"

"Her familiar, of course," she said impatiently. "You know, her pet. All witches have one. A cat, dog, bird, or ferret who helps them work their magic. And your task will be to see her relieved of whatever creature it is."

"She has a cat, yes. But I have never heard her address it as anything but an animal."

"Well, she wouldn't, naturally. Not with you present. But, aye. Cats are the most oft chosen for our work."

"So you want me to kill it?" Stafford asked in repulsed disbelief.

"Nay. I am not askin' that at all. I'm simply sayin' that you must catch it and hold it captive for a time. Until I've had the chance to cast a spell or two to free your heart from this sorceress, in any case. She'll prove a great deal more defenseless against me, I promise ya, without her familiar at her side."

"Catch it?" he queried again, his voice still filled with incredulity. "But it's in the lady's thatch all the time. 'Twould have to be more an act of stealing, than catching."

"No, sir," Brownwell interjected. "Pray pardon me for saying as much, but she does let the cat out most afternoons. Around the hour of one . . . I've kept a close eye on the place, you see," he added, somewhat sheepishly. "Well . . . for the obvious reasons."

Stafford shook his head. "Oh, I don't know. I fear I have never been much good with cats. The creature will likely smell my hounds upon me and flee, if I get too near."

"But surely it must have come to know you by now, my lord. That is, when one considers all of the days that you've spent—" Horatio's words broke off abruptly as Pearce glowered at him. It was a silent reminder that there was no need to discuss the particulars of his relationship with Selena in this outsider's presence.

Brownwell, in turn, cleared his throat and began again in a much more amenable tone. "Well, perhaps 'tis safe to assume that the cat has come to know and trust you better than you think."

"Perhaps," Madam Kerry agreed. "But do be forewarned, my lord, that familiars are often as second-sighted as their masters. So you will have to take great care not to seem as though you are stalkin' the animal. Usually a fish or a dead mouse can be used to lure 'em to one in such instances, however."

Stafford tried to think of a way to counter this, but, failing, simply shut his eyes and shook his head with a moan. The very thought of skulking about outside Selena's cottage in broad daylight was just too mortifying for words.

"Why me?" he asked at last with an almost-pitiful sigh. "Why can't one of you capture the beast?"

"Because 'tis too dangerous of course, sir," Brownwell answered without hesitation. "Why, you just saw for yourself what your witch is willing to do to Madam Kerry for taking part in this. And, having met the woman at your soirée, I cannot believe that I would fare much better at her hands, if caught in such an act. Whereas you, my lord, would have reason to be seen near her cottage. She has come to expect a visit from you now and again."

"Ah, God save me," Stafford grumbled, throwing down the towel he'd been using to wipe off his head and arms and walking into the adjoining room to flop back upon his bed.

"Nay. I'm sorry, sir," Katrina called after him with a dry

laugh, "but I'm afraid that, in this case, 'twill be you havin' to help save yourself."

"Oh, let her keep my heart," Pearce replied forlornly. "What care I *how* she won it. She simply has."

At this, Horatio came and stood in his bedroom doorway, his eyes wide with apprehensiveness. "But never to know the truth, my lord. Never to know whether your feelings for her are genuine or merely begotten of some spell. Can you honestly wish to live out your days with such uncertainty? Do you not owe it to the lady, as well as to yourself, to learn the answer to this before any vows are spoken between you?"

"Dear Christ, I suppose so," he said with a groan. "But," he continued, sitting up slightly and shaking a stern finger at the investigator, "the pair of you had better conceive a plausible pretext, should she spy me at this humbuggery. 'Twill take far more than a string of amethysts to save me, if that happens!"

Twenty-two

Stafford and Brownwell hid in the woods behind Selena's thatch the following afternoon. As the hour of one came and went, they waited to see if she would let Nola outside, as Horatio had claimed she'd done on so many other occasions.

The investigator gazed down at his pocket watch after a time. " 'Tis ten past," he announced. "Much longer and I fear 'twill have to be our second plan you carry out, my lord."

Pearce let a pained breath escape through his teeth and leaned back heavily against the tree before which he stood. He had his butterfly net and a paper-wrapped fillet of salmon in one hand, and a bouquet of garden flowers in the other.

Brownwell was right, he acknowledged. If Selena failed to let the cat out within the next twenty minutes or so, they would probably have to abandon their plan of having Stafford go after the animal, with the excuse—if spotted at it—of having wandered into the cottage's yard to catch butterflies. Thwarted in this course, he would have to proceed directly to Selena's front door with his ingratiating arrangement of roses extended before him and hope that she would view it as ample atonement for his having neglected her so much in the past fortnight. After that, he would somehow have to see that Nola was allowed to slip outside, so that Horatio could lay hold of her, while Pearce kept her owner sufficiently distracted.

He closed his eyes and offered up a silent prayer that Selena's pet would soon appear at one side or the other of the thatch. According to Horatio, if she followed her usual progression, she would immediately head for the cottage's backyard to hunt for mice and the like.

"Oh, 'tis no good," Pearce remonstrated under his breath to the ghost hunter. "I cannot think clearly when I'm in Miss Ross's presence of late. Why, last night, when she came to call, all of the wetness in my mouth and throat seemed to pour out through my palms. Such was my concern that she could read my thoughts as we spoke!"

"Well, witches can, to some measure, sir. But, please remember what Madam Kerry told us. 'Twill happen only if you permit it. If, however, you concentrate on thwarting such penetration, she should believe your claim that you have come to warm matters up between the pair of you, after your recent estrangement, and she shall welcome you into the place, thereby allowing you to let the cat chance to dart out-of-doors."

"But this isn't a village virgin we're speaking of, man," Stafford began again more vehemently. He set all he was holding down and reached out to grip Horatio's shoulders for emphasis. "This is a full-fledged sorceress, for the love of Heaven! The sort of temptress who lured ancient Greek ships to shore to be dashed to bits upon unseen reefs. The kind of woman who can drown a gent in her eyes and play his heartstrings as if they were drawn tight upon a harp! I feel utterly bereft whenever she is away from me, Brownwell. As though my very soul were about to curl up and blow away, like a leaf in autumn! I ask you, have you ever known a lady to possess such power?"

The investigator looked dumbstruck at this uncharacteristic outpouring of emotion from his employer. "Christ's Church, my lord, please get a hold upon yourself, for all of our sakes! Just do not look into her eyes, should you encounter her, and there will be no risk of drowning in them. I say this not facetiously, mind, sir," he continued, gently peeling Pearce's fingers from his shoulders, "but for your own survival. You *must* take command of your thoughts and will, as you set about this, lest you prove forever a lost man! . . . Heigh, look what goes there, sir," he began again brightly, pointing at the thatch. " 'Tis a black cat, sure enough, creeping towards Miss Ross's backyard in search of prey!"

"By thunder. So it does look to be," Stafford agreed, picking up the spyglass, which Horatio had set down at their feet, and directing it at the animal.

"Is it Nola?" Brownwell asked hopefully.

"Indeed. And thanks be to God for that, as I would much rather face her, than her owner," Pearce replied, handing the glass back to him and quickly bending down to gather up his net and fish. "All right, then. I'm off to seize the creature, before she can be missed," he proclaimed, hurrying away towards the cottage.

"Stay low, sir," the investigator whispered after him. "And please remember that 'tis crucial to keep your voice down."

Stafford stopped just long enough to glare back at his companion's statement of the obvious. Then he began rushing forward once more, tucking the long handle of his net under his left arm, so his hands were freed to unwrap the salmon en route.

The cat stopped moving upon spotting him emerging from the woods seconds later. Still in her creeping posture, she locked her golden eyes upon his face, as though instantly suspecting that he was up to no good. Her dagger-like pupils seemed almost as able to plumb his mind as her mistress's always were.

"Kitty, kitty," he called out to her in an undertone, stooping down with the fish extended before him. "Come along now, Nola darling, and see what I've brought for you."

His inviting smile began to sink after a moment, as the creature remained where she was. Only the tip of her long tail was moving. It waved slowly back and forth, as if to say that she had no intention of allowing him to get the best of her in whatever game he had in mind.

Stafford rose back up to his full height after several seconds and began moving towards her once more, his odorous offering still well out before him. "Kitty, kitty, kitty. I won't hurt you," he assured, continuing to speak in a low voice. "Just take some nice salmon, you see." He tore off a bit of the fillet and flung it in her direction.

Unfortunately, however, it appeared that she was not to be so easily bought. Instead of going after the bait, she simply went on staring at him with those large shining eyes, as if thinking him unhinged.

He came to another halt. Smiling and cooing at the pet, he pointed at the scrap he had just tossed to her.

Once again, however, she failed to do anything but go on waving that tail of hers like a taunting battle flag.

"Nola, 'tis I, your good friend Stafford. Come with a gift which I feel certain you'll enjoy." He took the risk of throwing the rest of the salmon over to her.

To his relief, though he hadn't really expected much of a trajectory from the limp, raw fish, it landed just half a foot from her front paws. And, after a couple of seconds of sniffing and contemplation, she pounced upon it and began eating, as he'd hoped she would.

He now knew he didn't have an instant to lose. Likely being as particular as cats were said to be, there was no way of gauging how long she would partake of the salmon, so he wasted no time in dashing to her and throwing his net over her body.

She stopped eating and looked up at him with unmistakable indignation. It was as if she believed that he'd simply committed an error in judgment, that he'd somehow mistaken her for a butterfly or some such thing. Then, as it seemed to dawn upon her that she was indeed his quarry, she snarled and swiped up at him with a fully clawed forepaw.

"Now, Nola," he said in a consolatory hush, "I mean you no harm. I merely want to take you to the great house for an hour or two."

Even as he spoke these words, he was scouring his mind for some way to transport her there in the net.

His cutaway coat, he concluded. He would remove it and

use it to seal up the opening of the net, so that the cat would be adequately trapped inside it as he hurried off with her.

Having decided this, he stepped down upon the neck of the net's handle, in an effort to keep Nola pinned where she was until he could pull off his coat. Once this was done, he replaced his foot with a hand and knelt to begin the precarious business of flipping the cat and the net upward and clamping his jacket over them.

As if able to read his mind, the familiar emitted a furious yowl; and, the instant he lifted the right side of the net's frame from the ground, she squeezed free of the confinement, like a flattened-out field mouse. She then flew up at her would-be kidnapper in what seemed a rabid rage—her claws tearing at the right side of his neck.

Stafford couldn't help yelping at the fiery pain she inflicted. Before he could catch hold of her thin, sleek body, however, she leapt up over his shoulder and took off for the adjacent woods with blurring speed.

"Damn it," he growled, clenching his jaw. "Damn it to Hell, you deuced beast!"

Grabbing his net, he scrambled back up to his feet and was about to pursue the cat, when he heard a voice which shot through him as keenly as if it were that of the cruel headmaster at the boys' school he'd attended in his youth.

"Stafford? What on earth are ya doin'?"

He turned back and saw Selena coming around the left side of the cottage. She was headed straight for him with a deeply puzzled expression.

Without thinking, he hid his net behind him, both hands clamping its long handle to his spine in such a way that its meshwork could barely be seen hanging below his breeches.

"Oh, um, nothing," he blurted. "Only a bit of butterfly catching again, I'm afraid."

She scowled. "But ya know I disapprove of it."

"Oh, yes, my dear. I am quite clear on that point. And it was never my intention to engage in it so near your thatch, you see. 'Tis just that I was on the trail of a particularly rare one and, before I knew it, this is where I found myself."

She looked about him blankly. "You were endeavorin' to snatch it out of the air with your bare hands?"

Feeling his cheeks grow hot, he sheepishly brought his net forward. "Um, no. With this, of course."

"Well, where is it then?"

"Where is what?"

"The rare butterfly you were after."

"Er—it got away from me. Just before you came out here."

"Good for it, poor thing . . . Oh, dear, but ya do look a mess," she went on with a laugh. "Out here swipin' about at God knows what all. Why, it appears you've even cut yourself somehow." She drew up closer and extended her right hand to him, the long fringe of her woolen shawl draping over her forearm. "Come inside for a moment and let me see to that neck of yours. Honestly, the pains you men will go to in the name of huntin'! What children you are sometimes."

"No. I—I shouldn't," he answered, glancing nervously backward in an effort to determine whether Brownwell might have spotted Selena yet. There was still some chance of the investigator intercepting the cat out there in the woods, Pearce supposed, provided he could keep Nola's owner amply distracted. "Go in with you, I mean. That is to say, I believe Mr. Flaherty is having a late luncheon served for me in just a few minutes."

Selena reached out and took hold of one of his wrists with an imperious cluck. "Oh, whisht with ya. If you've time enough for chasin' insects about my back green, you've a bit of time to spare for me!"

She looked, for all the world, the schoolmarm she had seemed in coming out to question him, Stafford thought, as she ushered him briskly around to her front door. She wore a pristine sky blue gown, adorned along its front placket with flower-shaped white ribbons. And her ivory shawl and satin slippers only served to make her appear all the more prim and proper.

This, coupled with her touching concern over his scratched

neck, made it almost impossible for him to believe now that she could have had anything to do with that cataclysmic storm of the previous night. Her touch was just so gentle, her smile and voice so sweet, that her magic as a healer seemed the only kind of which she could be capable.

Her cottage offered a pleasantly cool and shadowy contrast to the hot sunny afternoon, as they entered it.

"Come sit," she invited, going in ahead of him and pulling out one of her dining-table chairs. After patting its seat to encourage him in this act, she walked over to the washbasin, which she kept situated on a stand before her kitchen window. Then, taking up the pitcher, which stood at the basin's side, she poured some water into it.

Though still feeling ruffled by his foiled attempt to capture Nola and almost equally unnerved at finding himself alone with her owner once more, Pearce shut the thatch's door after him as he stepped farther inside. Then he headed for the indicated chair.

"Down with your collar," Selena ordered, as she crossed to him seconds later with a wet washcloth.

She winced slightly as she drew up to him and he pulled his shirt away to reveal the long, bloody scratches.

She pressed the soothingly cold cloth to them. "Sweet Mother Mary, what did ya do to yourself?"

"I—I um chased that rare butterfly through some thorn bushes," he fibbed, thinking it as believable a story as any.

"Faith, you should take more care, love. That dreadful sport of yours will prove the blessed end of ya. Tell me, would ya be mindin' it terribly if I put a bit of whiskey on this?"

He knit his brows. "Whiskey? Whatever for?"

" 'Tis my way, is all. I've always done it with the wounds I treat. Though I must confess that, knowin' how it can sting, there are those who prefer to have some of it poured *into* them before on 'em."

Despite his general uneasiness with the situation, Stafford

couldn't help chuckling at this. "Yes, well, count me as one of those, if you please."

"That I will." She went off to fetch the liquor from one of her kitchen cupboards.

"Still wearin' the amethysts for your friend, I see," she remarked, as she returned to the table and set the bottle upon it with a thud. She uncorked the whiskey and pushed it well into his reach.

Not stopping to respond, he raised the bottle to his lips and took a swig from it with what he knew were tellingly shaky hands. She'd spotted the necklace still on him when he'd lowered his collar for her, he realized.

"Yes," he answered simply, hoping she would make no further comment upon it.

"I thought ya agreed with me last evenin', though, that they would be most secure in the manor's repository."

"Yes . . . But, once that storm blew in," he went on pointedly, the bracing taste of the liquor seeming to give him some newfound courage to counter her, "I thought it best to keep them on my person. We were, none of us, certain that the great house would still be standing by morning. I trust, however, that you were safe down here all the while."

"Aye," she replied in an unreadable tone.

He set the bottle down on the table "Ah, good. I prayed that you were. And I would have come to check on you, had I not had to tend to a lightning strike upon the servants' lodge."

Her voice rose with a note of innocent inquiry. "Oh? I do hope no one was hurt," she added a wishful gleam in her eyes.

"No. Thank Heavens."

Stafford noticed that this answer made her expression sink slightly. Though Brownwell and Madam Kerry had claimed that all witches were clairvoyant, it was as if Selena had somehow been unable to determine the extent of the damage she had caused.

"Oh, well," she began again with a throat-clearing cough,

"I did assume you'd send for me, if my help was needed in treatin' anyone."

He stared at her purposefully. "Yes. Of course."

As though bothered by his probing regard, she lowered her gaze and began to busy herself with pouring some of the whiskey onto her washrag. Then, mumbling something of an apology for the liquor's inevitable sting, she applied it to his scratched neck.

Pearce felt his eyes tear up slightly at the pain, but he didn't make a sound.

Selena cocked her head at him. "So, tell me, have ya bathed lately?"

"Oh, I—I'm afraid I haven't the time for a trip to your hot spring this afternoon, my dear. Perhaps another day."

She gave forth a whisper of a laugh. "In truth, I wasn't askin' it so that you would agree to go with me there. I was simply inquirin' because I was not certain whether or not you're aware that ya smell a bit of fish. That is, if you'll forgive my sayin' so."

Replacing her hand with his in the act of holding the cloth to his abrasion, he did his best to feign surprise. "Do I? Hmm . . . Perhaps one or two of them were blown up to my wardrobe from the sea last night. It would have been no wonder, given the force of that wind and rain," he replied with an accusatory edge to his voice.

A silence ensued, and, after a moment, Selena pushed away from the table and went to sit in one of her hearth chairs. "You know, Stafford, havin' spoken to ya last evenin' about how little ya've come down to visit me of late, I cannot help but wonder now just what part of you ya believe you're losin' in allowin' yourself to love me fully. Can ya honestly imagine that you've any more at stake, than I in all of this?" She turned her chair to face him squarely, then looked him dead in the eye. "Because I swear to ya that ya don't. Your power has been no more diminished than mine since you've taken me as your lover. And that I would vow to ya with my dyin' breath."

Pearce was so surprised by this bone-cutting candor from her, after the verbal cat-and-mouse game they'd played since she'd discovered him in her yard, that he simply let his jaw drop.

"But what could *I* have possibly done to diminish you?" he asked after a moment.

"You've shaken my confidence, to start," she answered without hesitation. " 'Tis true, what ya might have heard about healers. Some of us *do* lose a measure of our abilities when we choose to give away our hearts. Before becomin' smitten with ya, for instance, I would have been much better able, than I am at present, to surmise why ya wandered down here this afternoon."

"But I told you. I was chasing a butterfly."

"Aye. So ya said."

"What? You don't believe me? But, what else could I have been doing out there with a bug net?"

She squinted at him astutely and sat back in her chair. "I don't know. 'Tis likely, though, that there is somethin' more afoot here than there appears to be. And, even one day before becomin' your lover, I would have been able to guess right off what it is. So there are ya the victor in all of this, *Lord* Stafford Pearce. With your velvety talk and princely visage, managin' to strip away what extra wits Nature saw fit to grant me," she concluded, obviously doing her best to suppress the tearful waver in her voice.

"Well, if I have done any such thing," he returned defensively, "you've my word that 'twas never my intent."

"Aye, but I know ya think me somehow guilty of havin' bewitched ya—"

"No," he interjected, for civility's sake.

She thrust a silencing palm at him. "Yes, ya do. So there's no point in denyin' it. We owe each other the truth from here on, if nothin' more. And, bearin' that in mind, I do think you should know that my efforts to enamor ya never did seem to take for some reason. I should have won ya straight off, yet more than a fortnight passed before ya showed me any real affection. And now I realize, with you still capable of schemin' behind my back as ya are, that I never truly succeeded in claimin' ya. As with so many of your fellow Englishmen, you proved far too in love with money and land and power for there to be much room left in your heart for aught else."

Though Stafford was stunned by this indirect confession to the practice of sorcery on her part, the only emotion he let show in response was anger at her last remark. "Now, see here! I feel I have been more than willing to meet the requests you've made regarding my crofters and such."

"Only on pain of my estrangement. Never out of any sense of charity on your part. So, now," she went on woefully, " 'tis not simply you fightin' to maintain your prowess as master of this manor, but I stricken to my very center with fear of newfound impotence in my station as Wexford's healer."

In spite of himself, Stafford felt the core of him begin to sink at the unmistakable sincerity in this claim from her. "Oh, Selena, my sweet, surely you exaggerate my effect upon you."

"Not one whit," she replied, giving each word equal stress; and Pearce became convinced in that instant that she was telling him the absolute truth.

What was more, he was now filled with great remorse at having attempted to steal her pet from her.

"Well, is your neck feelin' better?" she inquired, when, after several seconds, he failed to respond.

He offered her a smile which he hoped brimmed with apology. "Yes. Thank you."

"Good," she said, pushing up out of her chair.

To his surprise, she walked straight to the door and opened it widely, as though wishing to see him out.

"Then, you'll be off for the late luncheon which Mr. Flaherty has waitin' for ya, no doubt."

"Oh, I can tarry a few minutes more, I imagine."

"Aye, but I'd rather ya didn't, my lord. I am feelin' suddenly exhausted and wish to be alone."

My lord, his mind echoed. She had relapsed into addressing him by his title, rather than his name. He couldn't help looking dismayed. She actually wanted him to leave, he acknowledged.

He hesitantly set her whiskey-soaked cloth down upon the table and rose from his seat. "Very—very well."

She was simply going to let him go, he realized once more, as he bent to retrieve his butterfly net, then made a crestfallen walk to the door. He was to take his leave without any fawning on her part. Nor suggestion from her as to when they might meet again . . . Without, quite probably, even an attempt to give his cheek a parting peck.

During the time that had passed since her rather distressing visit to him on the previous evening, the feelings between them had shifted somehow. The neediness suffered by all lovers, each for the other, had mysteriously tilted towards him.

As he made his reluctant return to the great house seconds later, he told himself that it was simply the fact that he was still wearing the repellent amethysts that had made her decide to forgo showing him any sort of affection. In truth, however, he knew that the seeming indifference she had just displayed would tear at him for the rest of his days.

But this was what he'd wanted, wasn't it? What he had been seeking in allowing Brownwell to send for a rival sorceress?

Wasn't being governed solely by his own free will of more importance to him, than anything else he could name?

Perhaps not. Not if it meant that he would never again be more to Selena Ross than just another of the many patients she served as a healer. In spite of everything that Horatio and Madam Kerry had told him about his having fallen victim to her spellcraft, Stafford truly didn't believe he could bear coming to mean so very little to her.

Twenty-three

Pearce entered his suite several minutes later to find his bedchamber cluttered with all manner of necromantic paraphernalia. There were pairs of black candles blazing on every flat surface: the hearth ledge, the windowsills, the top of his armoire, and on each of his nightstands. Madam Kerry stood before a trestle table, which she'd moved to the foot of his bed. Upon this altarlike structure rested a cauldron, which was flanked by yet another set of lit ebony tapers. In front of these were half a dozen tiny bottles which appeared to contain dried herbs and oils.

Katrina had donned what looked to be full witch's attire. Her long black gown and shawl dripped with the fringe which Stafford had read in Brownwell's books was meant to ward off evil spirits. Also in keeping with the Celtic tradition, her brow was adorned with a silver crescent moon. The ornament was affixed to a dark band which encircled her head like the rim of a crown.

As Pearce made his way into the room, he spotted Horatio sitting heedfully in one of the wing chairs near the east window. Stafford's attention was instantly jerked back to Madam Kerry, however, as she spoke a few foreign-sounding words and a loud snap came from the depths of her cauldron. A pillar of gray smoke rose up on the heels of the sound, and it was evident that she'd sprinkled some explosive substance into the kettle.

"Lord preserve us," Pearce exclaimed under his breath.

The sorceress turned to face him with a start, as though only just having noticed his presence. "What was that?" she demanded, frowning.

"Oh, nothing. I simply did not expect such volatility."

She planted her hands on her hips and turned more fully towards him. "You're in my consecrated circle I hope ya realize!"

Feeling as though he had just unwittingly trod upon a steward's freshly scrubbed floor in a pair of muddy boots, Stafford stared dumbly down at his feet. "Oh. I'm frightfully sorry." He did the only thing he could think to do which might set the matter straight. He turned on his heel and made a prompt retreat.

"Nay, nay, ya dolt," Madame Kerry sputtered. "You don't walk out of a witch's circle, ya *back* out of it! By the Saints, you foreigners are past hope! Do ya know no better than to turn your back upon an altar?"

Pearce shrugged, as lost for words as he obviously was for ceremonial etiquette in this case. "What?" he ventured after a few seconds, "Do you want me to step back in, then take my leave of it the proper way?"

"Nay. Never mind," she snarled, pointing her magic wand down at the violated area and moving it slowly from left to right, as though soldering it shut with an invisible spray of flame. "Just keep out of it until I've finished here, if that isn't too much for me to ask of ya!"

" 'Twas not as though it was a boundary I could have seen," he offered in his defense. "And, well, the truth of the matter is that I have changed my mind about having you remove her love spells."

Katrina gasped, and her dark eyes grew large with disbelief. "Oh, but ya can't have."

"Nevertheless, 'tis how I feel now. So, do pack your things, madam, and Mr. Brownwell will see you compensated for the services that you have rendered."

Continuing to glower at him, she threw down her wand with a frustrated cluck. "But don't ya understand? 'Tis already done!

I've been recitin' incantations for the removal of her influence upon ya since you and Brownwell went off to abduct her cat nearly an hour ago. And, what with it bein' the time of the wanin' moon—the ideal phase for bindin' a troublement such as this witch of yours—I hold out little hope of undoin' any of it at this point."

"Oh, quite right, sir," the ghost hunter chimed in, sitting forward in his chair. "The tables have been turned entirely. For, when I saw you thwarted in your attempt to seize the young lady's cat, I took it upon myself to finish the task for you."

"You mean you caught Nola?"

"Yes. And I am happy to report that I caged her and hid her away in the loft of one of your stables."

"Well, go back down and get her, man! I want her returned to her owner at once."

Donning a perplexed expression, Horatio slowly got to his feet. "Lord Pearce, what on earth has happened to you? I thought you wished to be rid of this spellcraft. Please don't tell me that the lady has again won you over!"

"On the contrary. Indeed, she actually asked me to leave her just now. Can you imagine it? 'Tis *my* manor and, in the eyes of the law, hers is still my thatch. Yet she had the gall to ask me to vacate it!"

"The two of you argued then?"

"No. Not exactly. She—she simply made it plain that she no longer feels anything for me," he explained, doing his best not to betray any of the deep hurt he was experiencing over it.

"But that's precisely what we wanted to have happen," Katrina interjected. "Is that not what ya were seekin' from the first?"

"No. I said I didn't want her to have any further influence upon me. Not the opposite, you fool!"

The sorceress drew her head back and hissed at him, like a snake about to strike. "Ah, fool yourself, ya scoundrel! If ya possessed half the wits that you do gold, you'd have realized by now that love spells, by their very nature, run both ways.

In order for a witch to truly claim a man's love, she must be willin' to give hers in return. So, while she likely did grant ya her heart for a time, she must have grown cold on ya. That is, now that I've practiced all this magic of removal against her."

Stafford could feel his fists clenching at this disclosure. "Well, damn it all to Hell! That is *not* what I wanted done in this case!" He shifted his glare back to the investigator. "Now, see matters returned to the way they were, Brownwell, or I shall disengage your services as well!"

"But I—I cannot, sir," he stammered. "If Madam Kerry says it can't be remedied, than who am I to argue? Why, I know little more of sorcery than you do . . . Really, my lord," he continued beseechingly after a moment, "are you quite certain that the young lady did not succeed in beguiling you anew while you were in her company just now?"

"That I am. In fact, she did not show the slightest bit of interest in doing anything, save tending to the bleeding scratch marks which her cat left upon my neck. Then she simply sent me away."

"But surely, sir, you can't want her following you about as if she were a lovesick whelp, when you yourself have no such feelings for her."

"No. But neither do I want the opposite occurring, and I'm telling you, for good and all, man, that she doesn't love me anymore. She does not even seem to *like* me. And I am finding it—well, rather unbearable. For want of a better word."

"You're daft is what," Katrina accused. "Mad as May-butter to be thinkin' that this is some sort of whim-wham I've engagin' in on your behalf, Lord Pearce! Now, the only stipulation I recall ya puttin' on my work for ya was that this beguiler of yours not be harmed in any way." She crossed her arms over her chest and thrust out her pointed chin. "And I've certainly taken all reasonable precautions, while still seein' the deed itself done. So I won't have ya comin' round to me now, like some love-struck schoolboy, claimin' to have suffered a change of heart! What's done is done, and not only will ya have to live with it, but you had bloody better pay me my full fee, lest I see the whole of County Wexford informed of what you two rapscallions have been up to out here!"

"Now, now, madam," Horatio said, rising and crossing to her with an allaying expression, "his lordship is a man of his word, so I can assure you that you will be paid, no matter what the outcome of your conjuring."

"The outcome, as you call it, Mr. Brownwell, is precisely what the pair of ya requested. He wanted to be un-squeeged and *so he is,*" she spat, gathering up handfuls of her bottled herbs and setting them into her cauldron with an angry clatter.

"Then why am I yet in love with her?" Stafford demanded.

"How should I know, ya great bletherin' miser?" she exclaimed. "I myself find it impossible to believe ya capable of lovin' *anyone.* But maybe what ya feel for her has been genuine from the first, and her spells had no part in it. Squeegin' I can remove, but the real thing is another matter entirely. No witch has much power over that. If ya want my opinion, though," she continued, huffing off to his suite's door with the heavy kettle in her arms, "you and this she-cat deserve one another. She, with her murderous lightnin' strikes, and you, with your equally self-servin' ways! So now, gentlemen, please see to payin' my fee and arrangin' my livery back to Londonderry. I've had quite enough of all of this, and do not wish to remain here a moment longer than necessary!"

"Well, damn it, Brownwell," Pearce snapped, as she exited and slammed the door behind her, "go after her, before Mr. Flaherty has the chance to drive her into a corner and question her. Then keep her in your room until you've readied her carriage. In the meantime, I shall go down to the stables and fetch Selena's pet for her. God Almighty, I don't know how you and that woman could have made such a botch of it all. But I can tell you that I shall be unspeakably thankful to have you both gone, so we might see peace restored about this place!"

* * *

Selena was roused from her dazed state several minutes later by frantic pounding upon her cottage's door. There had been a time, less than twenty-four hours earlier, when she would have prayed that this visitor was Stafford returning to try to set matters right between them. However, her jumbled emotions on the subject now made her realize that there was something terribly wrong with her. On the one hand, she knew in her heart that she still loved him deeply. Yet, on the other, she felt so inexplicably numb, so distanced from this sentiment, that she could only conclude that Crafty Katrina was somehow clouding her affection for Pearce.

Selena had done nothing since he'd left her some twenty minutes before, but sit staring at the dying flames on her hearth; and now she found that she scarcely had the vigor to rise and see who was coming to call.

"Eddie," she greeted questioningly as she finally made her way to the door.

The stable boy was clearly out of breath, his cheeks flushed with what looked to be distress. "Mistress Selena, I fear he's stolen your cat," he croaked.

Feeling almost overcome with faintness, Selena clamped a bracing palm to the right side of the door frame. "Who has?"

"That Englishman who the new lord has visitin'. I saw him carryin' Nola to the stables in a cage! Why would he be doin' such a thing?"

Selena scowled, her confused mind barely able to comprehend this dreadful news. "Ah, God, lad, I'm not sure. Are ya certain that 'twas Nola he had with him?"

"Oh, aye. 'Cause I snuck after him, ya see. I followed him up into the stable loft where he left the cage, and then I hid myself behind some bales of hay, as he made his way back down the ladder. What does it mean, mistress? You don't think he will harm her, do ya?"

She shook her head blankly. "I should certainly hope not!"

"Well, I thought about carryin' her back down to ya, but then it seemed best that I come speak to ya about it first. See if maybe you asked to have her taken, for some reason." He ran two fingers under his runny nose and gasped for breath again, and it became apparent to Selena that he felt almost tearful over the incident.

"Faith, no. Of course I did not ask for such a thing! We must go get her," she declared, doing her best to fight the continuing dizziness she was experiencing.

No wonder, she realized in those horrendous seconds. No wonder she was falling into such a debilitated state. There wasn't a sorceress alive who could be expected to remain standing against a monster like Katrina Kerry, without aid of her familiar. And, of a sudden, the Northern witch's sinister plot coalesced in Selena's mind. Stafford had not come down to her thatch earlier in pursuit of a rare butterfly, as he'd claimed. That had simply been some sort of ruse on his part. His true purpose had been to distract her, to keep her attention sufficiently focused upon him, while that beastly henchman, Brownwell, made off with her cat!

She swallowed dryly, sickened at the possibility that the man she so loved could have taken part in such a scheme. "Oh, Eddie," she gasped, "lead me to my dear Nola." Before she could take even one step out the door after the boy, however, she felt herself sinking to the floor and she was engulfed by sudden darkness.

Twenty-four

As Stafford carried the cage containing Nola back to Selena's cottage a short time later, he saw what looked to be one of the stable boys running straight for him from the direction of the thatch.

"Lord Pearce, she's dead! She's *dead,"* he cried out, his voice cracking with desperation.

Stafford kept walking briskly towards him, the name "Edward O'Malley" popping into his mind as the lad's fair features came into closer view. "Who is?"

"Mistress Selena," the child shouted.

His tone was so definite that Stafford's heart began sinking to his feet. "Oh, that simply cannot be, Eddie," he called back. "You can't have gotten it right."

The youngster's voice was half sob, half hysteria, and tears were streaming from his eyes as he finally reached Pearce. "I fear I have, though. We—we were just comin' up to the stable to fetch Nola and, next I knew, Mistress Selena was lyin' behind me in the doorway. Crumpled down in her gown as if she were a melted candle! I've tried wakin' her, but she won't open her eyes!"

Stafford's gaze traveled to the threshold of Selena's dwelling and locked upon the blue-clad figure which was sprawled there. Without an instant of hesitation, he set the wooden cage down in the grass beside him and took off for the cottage at a dead run. "Go and tell Mr. Flaherty to send for the doctor at once, Eddie," he called back over his shoulder. "And see that my friend Mr. Brownwell comes down to the thatch as well!" With that, his feet carried him the rest of the way to his beloved's door, their frantic pounding upon the still-wet ground matching that of his racing heart.

"Oh, Selena, *no,*" he gasped as he reached her. "This simply can't be!"

She was crumpled, just as Eddie had said, into the skirts of her gown, and, though Stafford felt devastated at seeing her in such a state, he wasted no time in bending down and scooping her limp form up into his arms. He then carried her inside and deposited her upon the hearth rug on which they had first made love.

He knelt at her side and lightly slapped each of her cheeks with the back of his hand in an effort to rouse her. "Selena? *Selena,* my darling . . . Dear God, this cannot be," he said again in an imploring voice.

She did not stir, however. As lifeless as Edward had claimed, she was utterly unresponsive to Stafford's zealous attempts to bring her out of her insentient condition. She seemed completely unaware of the desperate kisses he was pressing to her forehead, the fervent pleas he was making that she come back to him and remain his for the rest of her days.

He was so clear on it all finally, so sure that their love for one another was and always had been real, that he couldn't imagine the Heavens proving cruel enough to take her from him now—now that he'd at last come to realize that she was all he would ever need to make him happy.

He no longer required anything else. Not riches, nor title, nor power, he confessed in a hot tearful stream near her right temple. The unendurable emptiness he'd known, since she'd withdrawn her affections from him the evening before, had taught him that nothing else was worth having, if he could not have her.

In a fit of anger, he sat up from her and tore open the front of his shirt. Then he reached beneath it and ripped the amethyst necklace, which Katrina Kerry had given him, from around his neck, sending the purple gems flying in all directions.

Though he was still half crazed with grief by the time Flaherty and Brownwell got down to the cottage minutes later, he did his best to compose himself. Blotting his welling eyes with one of his shirt cuffs, he wrenched his attentions from Selena's still body. Then he took one of her cool hands in his.

"Well, has she a pulse, sir?" Brownwell asked with a skeptical sniff, as he entered ahead of the steward and crossed to Pearce.

Stafford relinquished his hold on her right hand and let his fingers slip down to her wrist. "Not that I can feel."

"I sent for the doctor, just as Eddie requested, my lord," Flaherty announced, his usually rosy complexion looking pale with shock as he reached the hearth rug.

"Good," Pearce replied, directing his gaze at the Irishman just long enough to give him a thankful nod. *Selena would have wanted it that way,* he thought, his throat aching anew with the urge to weep over her deathlike state. She had always had such benevolent feelings towards the servantry; and, somehow, doing things in the way that she would have wished was all that mattered to him now.

"Help me carry her up to her bed," he began again in a growl, returning his attention to Brownwell.

Still looking as though he half believed that this unconsciousness was some sort of ruse on Selena's part, Horatio reluctantly bent down and obliged. He took hold of her ankles, as Pearce moved up to her head and slipped his arms in under each of hers.

They slowly lifted her and proceeded over to the loft stairs. The steward followed fretfully after them, wincing and tsking as they made their precarious ascent with the true mistress of Brenna Manor.

"God damn it, man," Stafford exclaimed under his breath, when they finally reached Selena's bed and laid her down upon it, "if I should learn that 'twas *you* and that impudent hag you hired who caused this to befall her, I shall see you hung!"

Brownwell straightened from the task of setting her upon the mattress and glared over at him with an equally scornful expression. "Ah, to the blazes with both her and you, Pearce," he replied, not returning the courtesy of keeping his voice down so Flaherty couldn't hear. "I've done nothing which would make me to blame for this. Nothing, save try to free you from this power she seems to have over you. But now I see that Katrina was right about the two of you. You *do* deserve each other. So, far be it for me to go on attempting to rescue you from her!"

" 'Rescue' me you say? From *what,* might I ask? From the only woman who could ever make me truly happy?"

"Just see me paid at once, for I wish to be out of this place, even as Madame Kerry was," Horatio shot back, returning to the top of the loft's stairs as though to storm down them.

"Oh, I'll pay you well enough. But not for saving me from Selena, mind. On the contrary, 'twill be for keeping me from her just long enough to make me realize that she and she alone is all I've wanted from the first. Indeed, my dear ghost hunter, I thank you with all my heart for having come between us as much as you have!"

Brownwell turned back before leaving the loft to shake a condemnatory finger at him. "Well, do see that you leash her, should she come around, your lordship, for Horatio Brownwell, Esquire, will most certainly no longer be here to help keep her reined in!"

There was something about this underling's sneer in that instant that made Stafford lose all restraint. Without thinking, he lunged over to where Horatio stood and grabbed him by the throat. "Christ in Heaven, you take that back, you sharper. I will not have the woman I love spoken of in such a manner! As if she were some sort of *animal* one must keep caged!"

The two men scuffled near the edge of the loft for several seconds to the music of Flaherty's horrified gasps below. As

Pearce's large fingers closed ever more tightly upon the ghost-hunter's neck, the latter kicked and clawed to defend himself.

Then, before the steward could seem to summon the nerve to rush up the stairs and pull his employer off of the Londoner, Stafford himself relinquished his near-murderous hold upon him. "By thunder, that's it," he declared in a suddenly elated voice.

"What—what is?" the Irishman asked guardedly, having, by this time, ventured halfway up the ladder.

" 'An animal one must keep caged.' Selena's cat is still where I left her, out in the yard, Mr. Flaherty. Please go and get her at once!"

Looking as though he was even more bewildered by this request than he had been by the inexplicable scuffle he'd been seeking to break up, the steward shrugged. Then he began slowly lowering his portly form back down the stairs.

Having thusly stumbled upon renewed hope that his beloved might yet be revived by being reunited with her familiar, Pearce abandoned any further interaction with Brownwell. Rather, he hurried back over to Selena's bed and again took one of her chilly hands in his. He sank down at her side on the mattress and stared prayerfully into her slumberous face.

He was so lost in this silent supplication that he could not accurately gauge how much time passed before he felt someone tapping him on the shoulder; but when he did so, he was surprised to see that it was neither Horatio nor Flaherty who was seeking his attention, but Dr. Mahony.

"Get up from there," the physician ordered with a scowl. "How am I to examine her with you sittin' in the way?"

Stafford got numbly to his feet and stepped aside to accommodate the man. "Is she alive?" he asked in a trepid whisper, as Mahony took his place on the bed and lowered his right ear to her chest.

"Just barely. But perhaps I can help her recover."

At this Pearce shut his eyes and directed his face towards

the ceiling with the most grateful of sighs. "Oh, thank God! We thought her dead for certain."

The doctor lifted his head from her and began rummaging urgently through the contents of his medical bag. "By the Saints, Pearce," he snarled, "she shows all the signs of havin' been poisoned! I had better not learn that you are behind this, what with her bein' your uncle's only other possible heir! You and that daft business of perpetual tumidity," he went on, giving his head a disgusted shake. "You've been dabblin' in the realm of herbal brews, haven't ya," he accused.

"Good gracious, *no,*" Stafford countered. "On the contrary, I find I am quite in love with this woman, Doctor, and I no longer care who knows it. Indeed, far from causing her to fall ill, I shall pay you any price to see her made well again!"

"Hmm. Well, all right," the Irishman replied, still frowning as though not altogether swayed by him yet. "Get yourself back downstairs then and quit blockin' my light, and I shall see what can be done for her."

"Oh, thank you," Stafford exclaimed, but, before he could hug Mahony to him and show him his unending gratitude for this, he felt someone take hold of one of his shirtsleeves and begin tugging him towards the loft's ladder. He turned to see that it was his trusty steward who was urging him away.

"I need a word with ya," Flaherty mumbled. "Down below, if ya please . . . 'Tis about Nola, my lord," he explained sotto voce, once they reached the first floor.

"Yes. Well, where is she? Pray don't tell me she has come to some harm!"

"Oh, nay, sir. 'Tis just that . . ."

"Yes, Flaherty? 'Tis just that *what?*" Pearce pressed, as the steward seemed to bite his tongue.

"She's been taken up onto the roof of the storm-struck servants' lodge by our little Eddie, I'm afraid."

"Oh, for Christ's sake, man! Why on earth would he do that?"

Flaherty's voice lowered to an almost inaudible whisper.

"Because he believes, for some reason, that you or your friend Mr. Brownwell mean to hurt the animal."

"Oh, God's teeth, what rubbish! Doesn't he realize that we need Nola returned to this thatch in order to help save Selena's life?"

"Apparently not, sir."

"Then let me set him right in the matter," Stafford declared, striding angrily towards the door. "I'll just climb up there and speak with him."

"But ya can't, I'm afraid, my lord. For, as I've just mentioned, 'tis the very same roof that was struck by lightnin' last evenin', and its beams look too shattered and scorched to be holdin' the weight of the lad and the cat, much less that of an adult."

This revelation stopped Pearce in his tracks and he turned back to the steward with clenched teeth. "Bloody Hell, Flaherty! The little devil must have chosen it on purpose."

"Very likely, sir. He's quite bright, as stable boys go. So I certainly would counsel ya against lettin' him see how cross this is makin' ya."

"Well, where is his father, for Heaven's sake? Can't he talk the boy down?"

"Oh, I've every faith that he would, my lord, were he here. Unfortunately, though, he's off at a turf race in County Cork. So I'm afraid 'tis left to us."

Though Stafford felt a nervous lump forming in his throat at the prospect of having to contend with it, he squared his shoulders and gave the front of his waistcoat a determined tug downward. He hadn't had many dealings with children, and he was finding it almost incomprehensible now that he could actually find himself at the mercy of one. "Well, how difficult can it be?" he asked rhetorically. "He's only a boy, after all."

The Irishman furrowed his brow in response. It was, sorrily, an expression which instantly informed Pearce that Edward O'Malley, even at so callow an age, could be most uncompromising when he chose to be.

"Oh, this is ridiculous," Stafford blared. "I alone am the master of this manor, and I simply will not be used for the ends of a snotty-nosed stable hand!" With that he turned on his heel and stormed out of the cottage, leaving his steward to follow apprehensively behind him.

Even as Pearce stepped out of the thatch a second later, Eddie's form was clear to him where it was now perched, with the black cat in his lap, upon the damaged roof of the lodge. He waited to address the lad, however, until he had crossed the wide back green and was standing squarely below his dangling, scabby-kneed legs.

By this time, several of Brenna's other residents had gathered about the building to stare upward as well; but they willingly cleared the way for the manor's lord as he came to personally deal with the situation.

To Stafford's amazement, the boy looked completely at ease as he continued to sit upon the roof's ridgeboard, clutching Nola to his thighs.

"Hello again, Edward," Pearce called up to him.

The youngster's mouth flashed white with a surprisingly amiable smile. "Hello, my lord."

"And what have you there?" Stafford pursued, in the most artless tone he could muster.

"Where, sir?"

Pearce gave forth a dry laugh, amazed at the child's sense of gamesmanship. Nevertheless, he thought it best to take Flaherty's advice and appear to be playing along. "Why, on your lap, of course, silly. What is it you are holding?"

"A cat, my lord," he answered summarily.

"Ah, yes. So it is. And Mistress Selena's cat, too, it would appear."

"Aye. It very well could be, sir," he replied, his tone infuriatingly noncommittal.

Stafford spoke again, this time in the most disarming voice he could produce. He loathed having to cajole a mere youngster, especially in the presence of so many of his servants, but he sensed that he would have hell to pay if he did not at least give it a try. "Well, why don't you bring the creature down here and let Mr. Flaherty and me have a closer look, so we can help you tell for sure?"

To Pearce's dismay, the boy responded to this by closing his arms more tightly about the cat.

"Ya didn't free her from her cage as ya said ya would," he answered scoldingly.

"But that was only because I had to run down and tend to Selena. Don't you remember, lad? Don't you recall how she fainted in the thatch's doorway? And I could hardly be in two places at once, now could I?"

"Nay. I suppose not," Eddie answered grudgingly.

"Then do come down from there now, before one of you falls."

"We won't fall," he declared, sounding as though he was now fully prepared to end their conversation.

"Oh, Edward, you can't be certain of that. That roof was damaged very badly last night in the storm. So I am asking you now, *please,* to find your way back down to us by the same path you took up."

"I can't."

Stafford drew in a deep breath, summoning what remained of his patience. "Why not?"

" 'Cause Mistress Selena would want me to protect her cat."

Pearce couldn't seem to suppress the desperation in his voice as he spoke again. Flaherty had been sadly right about this lad. Save for Selena, he was, indeed, the most headstrong individual that Stafford had come across in a good long time. "Protect her from what?"

"From you, sir. Though I am sorry to have to say it."

Pearce's words rose with incredulity. "From *me?* But that's foolishness. Would I have been carrying Nola back down to Selena's thatch from the stable, if I hadn't meant to return her to her master?"

The eight-year-old cocked his head and gave this a few seconds' thought. His hesitation felt to Stafford like that preceding the downward turn of an emperor's thumb in a Roman arena.

"No . . . I suppose not," Eddie answered finally.

"Of course not, my good little man," Pearce encouraged. "So come on down now and I promise to see both you and Nola returned safely to your homes."

The stable boy remained nevertheless unmoving. "But what about your friend?"

Stafford did his best to offer him an innocent grin. "Which friend is that?"

"Your Mr. Brownwell from London."

"Oh, but he's leaving here at once, Eddie," Flaherty chimed in. "He and Lord Pearce had a bit of a quarrel, I'm afraid, and he's up in the great house packin' his belongin's at this very moment."

"Is he?" Stafford queried out of the corner of his mouth, so the child wouldn't hear.

"Indeed, sir," the steward whispered back, drawing up even with where he stood. "When you were still up sittin' with Mistress Selena, it was. Did ya not hear him slam the thatch door shut behind himself as he left?"

Pearce shook his head.

"Aye. Well, he did, nonetheless."

Slanting Flaherty a grateful smile, Stafford returned his attention to Edward. "So, there you have it, lad. Neither you nor the cat have a soul to fear down here. Do they, all?" he asked, directing a meaningful look about at the crowd that had continued to grow around where he and the steward stood.

A unified "nay" rose up from the gathering.

"What is more," Pearce continued, "we believe that Selena needs Nola with her now in order to recover from whatever has overtaken her." He squeezed his eyes shut for an instant, upon issuing this last utterance. It was all he had left to say, his final and most powerful appeal, and he knew that, if Eddie was not moved by it, Selena might have no more time left to her.

After several harrowing seconds, to Stafford's tremendous relief, the child began getting slowly to his feet.

"There's a grand boy," Pearce praised loudly. But, before he could speak another word, the eight-year-old's right leg slipped from view, as the storm-damaged boards gave way beneath him.

For an instant or two, it appeared that he would go plummeting through the resultant hole; and Stafford and Flaherty reflexively rushed forward with their arms open, as though meaning to somehow catch him. Fortunately, however, this impossible task proved unnecessary as the now-shaken Eddie again gained his balance, withdrew his leg from the opening, and sat back down upon the ridgepole with Nola hugged firmly to his torso.

"Christ in Heaven, Flaherty," Pearce exclaimed, keeping his voice low so as not to scare the youngster further, "we must find some way to go up after him!"

Continuing to stare upward, the steward pivoted slowly, as though in an effort to survey the site from all angles. Then he gave his head a discouraged shake. "I can think of none, sir, save climbin' one of these nearby trees and tryin' to lower a rope to his reach."

Stafford nodded. "Yes That seems as good a plan as any. Get down to the stables, please, and fetch the length we shall need," he concluded, giving the servant a light push in that direction.

"Hold a moment," Eddie called down, before Flaherty could take his leave.

The two men froze in response and stared up at him once more. "What is it, lad?" Pearce asked.

"I can fly," he announced, his voice brimming with triumph.

The steward gasped. "You can what?"

"I can fly down. Mistress Selena and I have done it many times."

Flaherty threw his palms up in horror. "Oh, nay, nay, Eddie. 'Twill not be the same for you as it is when you're with her. You know that she has special—" He paused, clearly searching for a word which would not incriminate her in front of Stafford. "Special *gifts,*" he finished finally.

"That she has *magical* powers," Pearce hastened to add, finding himself half insulted by his steward's continued efforts to cover for her and half amused by them. "Why don't we simply come forth with it, my good Mr. Flaherty? Our resident healer is a witch. And the very best sort, to boot. The kind who can will away fevers and soften the heart of a stony Englishman such as me. She's a witch, Eddie," he shouted upward. "And not only have I known it for quite some time, but I wish to take her to wife in spite of it. Or perhaps because of it. In any case, lad, you stay right where you are until we can get a rope up to you. Selena will be most angry with you, you see, should she wake to learn that you cannot serve as the ring-bearer at our wedding because you've fallen from there and broken your neck!"

"But I won't," the child maintained; and, before Stafford and the rest could say or do another thing to prevent it, his gaze locked upon Selena's thatch and he rose once more and began *floating* away from the rooftop like a whisper-light butterfly.

When he was four or five feet in the air, his slow and wondrous descent began, causing him to drift lower and lower still, until he and his golden-eyed passenger touched down safely on the ground just before where Pearce stood.

"Eddie, by God, you did it! What a splendid clever lad you are," Stafford exclaimed, rushing forward to hug him and Nola as though they were his own flesh.

But, in a very real sense they were, as was every living creature and blade of grass at Brenna. Pearce had finally come to realize that he no longer so much owned them as they him. He was accountable to Heaven for each one of them—as well as to the blue-clad, raven-haired beauty he now spotted standing in the doorway of *her* cottage.

And, from that day forward, in exchange for his sweet Selena's return to health, he silently vowed to believe wholeheartedly in fairies and pucas, in the rights of his crofters and servants, and the protection of butterflies and birds. But, most of all, he would always believe in the simple, everyday magic that comes with falling genuinely in love.

Author's Note

I hope you enjoyed this tale of love and sorcery and that you will look for my next Zebra historical romance, scheduled to be in bookstores in mid-January 1998. In the meantime, you will find my work in a romance anthology to be published by St. Martin's Press in mid-June of 1997. My deepest thanks for all of the wonderful reader mail I've received from you in the past few years, and I hope you will continue to write to me at the following address:

Ashland Price
c/o Kensington Publishing
850 Third Ave.
New York, N.Y. 10022

About the Author

An award-winning author, ASHLAND PRICE holds a Bachelor of Science degree in theater arts/English and communications secondary education and teaches novel writing in adult-education classes in her home state of Minnesota. Formerly an advertising copywriter, she has sold thirteen novels and two novellas to New York publishers to date, including a saga, two suspense novels, and ten historical romances. Her previous Zebra titles include: *Captive Conquest, Autumn Angel, Cajun Caress, Wild Irish Heather, Viking Rose, Viking Flame, Viking Tempest, In From the Storm,* and "Spirit of the Manor," a novella in Zebra's first Halloween historical romance anthology, *Spellbound Kisses. Viking Tempest* was nominated for *two* readers' choice awards for "Best time-travel romance" of 1994, and Ashland is currently negotiating the sale of her first screenplay, a romantic suspense story.

YOU WON'T WANT TO READ JUST ONE—KATHERINE STONE

ROOMMATES (0-8217-5206-5, $6.99/$7.99)
No one could have prepared Carrie for the monumental changes she would face when she met her new circle of friends at Stanford University. Once their lives intertwined and became woven into the tapestry of the times, they would never be the same.

TWINS (0-8217-5207-3, $6.99/$7.99)
Brook and Melanie Chandler were so different, it was hard to believe they were sisters. One was a dark, serious, ambitious New York attorney; the other, a golden, glamourous, sophisticated supermodel. But they were more than sisters—they were twins and more alike than even they knew . . .

THE CARLTON CLUB (0-8217-5204-9, $6.99/$7.99)
It was the place to see and be seen, the only place to be. And for those who frequented the playground of the very rich, it was a way of life. Mark, Kathleen, Leslie and Janet—they worked together, played together, and loved together, all behind exclusive gates of the *Carlton Club*.